DAISY'S RUN

THE CLOCKWORK CHIMERA BOOK 1

SCOTT BARON

ISBN 978-1-945996-18-4 (Print Edition)

Life would be tragic if it weren't funny.
- Stephen Hawking

CHAPTER ONE

"Should we wake them? I mean, the ship is on fire, after all."

Barry didn't seem stressed. In fact, his voice rarely showed any extremes of emotion at all, though that was to be expected of a cyborg.

"It is a bit early, but yes, given the problems I am experiencing with my internal sensors and fire suppression systems, I think that would be prudent," the disembodied voice of Malorie, the ship's artificial intelligence system, replied. "Though I would like you on hand, just in case there are any issues cycling the crew out of cryo-sleep so early, and on such short notice."

"Of course, Mal. Understood."

The handsome flesh-and-metal man with sandy-blond hair rose from his seat in the control room and stepped into the double airlock leading to the central passageway network. Starboard Peripheral Corridor One would have been the faster route, but after the impact, with the possibility of undetected depressurization in any of the damaged and offline pod sections or one of the unmonitored inter-compartmental conduit routing spaces, he'd just have to take the long way. The inconvenience, he reasoned, was certainly preferable to being unceremoniously blasted into space.

The *Váli* was a sturdy ship, and she had only been nudged slightly off course by the collision. There was time to set things right, but sooner was far better than later. At the speed and distance they were traveling, "slightly" could easily become "a lot" quickly.

Normally Mal would simply right the course herself, diverting a fraction of her attention toward adjusting the maneuvering thrusters to gently ease them back on target. In the event of a fire of any significance, however, protocol required her to wake the crew of the *Váli*.

The ship's unusual name had been taken from old Norse mythology, given to it by a cybernetically-enhanced engineer with a fondness for ancient texts. *Váli*, the son of Odin, brother of Thor. A god prophesied to survive Ragnarok, the end of times.

She was a fast ship, no doubt, and extremely nimble, when not laden with additional research, living, and lab pods locked to her support frame for such a long voyage. That bulk-saving performance, however, came at a price. The multiple layers of outer shielding found on larger, sturdier vessels—the kind that would have prevented such a minor impact from damaging them in the first place—were sorely lacking, and so it passed that the ship had succumbed quite spectacularly to what would have been an otherwise minor incident.

Barry reached midship quickly, his flesh-covered mechanical legs pistoning rapidly as he rushed down the corridor. It would have made sense in almost any other situation to have Mal simply deactivate the artificial gravity and propel himself down the passageway between airlocks, but with a potential fire inside a ship, well, you didn't want something like that floating into unexpected places once gravity was gone. It was one of the only things keeping it reasonably contained.

"Mal, I am in the central passageway halfway to the cryo

pods. However, I detect a pressure variance coming from the lower passageway. Are you reading damage?"

"No, but with the impact, it is possible my readings are off."

"I shall divert my route down a level to assess what I can while en route to cryo."

"Understood. My sensors are experiencing faults in that sector, but are picking up some variances that seem to correspond to your observations. Until all systems are brought back online I cannot be certain. I am concerned that one of the pods down there may be breached. If there is severe damage, we may have to disconnect and jettison it. Do be careful."

"Affirmative. Heading to cryo via the lower passageway instead."

Barry stepped onto the ladder leading down the long shaft to the lower deck. Again, he thought how much simpler it would be without the gravity engaged.

We must work with the situation we are presented, he always reasoned. This was no different.

The lower corridor he touched down in looked identical to the one above, as did the topmost level. The *Váli* was quite symmetrical in design, with a core framework of passageways, central, starboard, and port, running in parallel from stem to stern. Three identical passageways on three levels. If the ship jettisoned the myriad pods of various length and purpose that formed its living and work spaces, all of them interlocked and connected by airlocks, it would still remain a fully-functioning vessel, though a rather cramped and uncomfortable one for any organic passengers.

The mission-critical pods were located between the central and peripheral passageways and housed crew quarters, the galley, engineering, and, of course, the cryo-pod chamber. Those pods only connected to the central passageway and the port or starboard one, depending on which side of center they lay.

While every pod locked into the framework of the ship could

be moved and rearranged depending on mission parameters, the basic configuration was typically the same. Some pods were longer than others, but the height and width never varied, allowing for a seemingly fixed size and unibody ship that was actually highly customizable to fit mission requirements.

The outer pods were designed for greater accessibility and had three connections instead of two. The airlock leading to the common passageway was located in the middle of each pod, regardless of length, while the airlocks connecting each external pod to the adjacent one were all mounted off-center, only a meter from the central wall.

While the outer wall had slightly thicker shielding protecting it from the harsh environment of space, should the unlikely event of an exterior layer breach occur, the off-center placement of the airlocks at each end was determined to provide a far greater likelihood of helping connected units survive intact.

Tedious as it would be cycling through each set of double airlock doors, if one truly wanted to, they could pass the entire length of the ship from pod to pod, avoiding the corridors entirely.

"I have located the problem," Barry said matter-of-factly. "Debris has torn through Port Storage Pod Twelve." He looked at the monitor flush in the wall beside the double airlock doors. "Extensive damage, but not catastrophic. The outer wall, however, is breached. Recommend Level One Isolation."

"As I feared. My scans are still non-functional in that section. Is nothing salvageable?" Mal asked.

"I cannot say for certain, but it would seem unlikely, at least not until we reach Dark Side base for parts. It does appear, however, that the pod itself can be salvaged."

"Very well. Lower Port Twelve, isolating."

No sound was heard through the thick doors as the airlock space between them was instantly flooded with flash foam. In under a second the pod was sealed off from the rest of the ship.

Mal could have jettisoned it, blowing the external bolts holding it to the ship's framework, but not now. Not if it could be salvaged at some point, and certainly not with the crew still in cryo.

"Proceeding to cryo pods," the cyborg said as he made his way down the passageway to the next ladder and quickly ascended back up to the central corridor.

"Do hurry, Barry. On top of possible damage to an unknown number of pods and part of my sensor array, it seems the short-range navigation system is also damaged. I'm flying a bit impaired at the moment. Additionally, one or two stubborn little fires appear to be off sensors and evading the automatic suppression system."

"Understood. I will make haste."

Barry knew all the way to his base code that, while not too big a deal in planetary atmosphere, out in the vacuum of space, a fire on board a ship could pose a huge problem, and quickly at that.

"I'm here," he said as he entered the cryo pod chamber. "Beginning cryogenic stasis awakening protocols. Spooling down neural stimulators." He glanced at the readouts over the crew's pods. "Mal, several are still in a deep neuro-stim cycle."

"There's little we can do. They must be woken."

"Proceeding." Barry's hands flew over the control panels as the pods began cycling up. "Physio-stim systems increasing to eighty-five percent," he noted as the crew's muscles were gently triggered in a steady rhythm as they slowly emerged from cryogenic stasis.

The pulsing action not only maintained muscle tone while asleep, but helped keep their bodies ready for situations such as these. Just enough stimulation as they slept to keep them fit and stave off atrophy.

In a few experimental cases, the system had been used to build increased muscle mass in transit, but there were potential drawbacks, such as delayed-onset muscle soreness of epic proportions, often greatly hindering efficient performance of duties upon awakening. As such, the practice was largely avoided.

"Calorics have increased to eighty-five percent." He stepped back and looked at the crew of nine as the systems slowly shifted states, rousing them from their long sleep as the pods unsealed with a soft hiss.

Daisy Swarthmore, the lean, twenty-five-year-old redheaded communications and electronics expert, was the first to wake, snapping to consciousness with a start.

"What? Who the hell—?" she croaked as her pod opened with a cold hiss.

"Daisy, it's Barry. Don't speak. You are waking from a deep cryogenic sleep. You need fluids. Drink this electrolyte pack, but slowly."

She gratefully accepted the plastic pouch, cracking the top with a twist before eagerly sipping the contents. The feeling of soothing fluid in her throat was utter bliss.

"The crew is being woken from stasis early," Barry informed her. His face was emotionless. Calm. "There was an impact. Some of the systems that have been compromised have also had their monitoring and control feeds damaged. Mal can't see them on her scans, and I do not currently possess programming to affect repairs. This is one of your areas of expertise."

Barry paused, assessing the groggy woman. Around the chamber, others were starting to rouse.

"Can you speak now? You've been in cryo for a long time. Your throat may still need time to adjust."

"Yeah, I can talk," she managed in a croaking voice. "Wait, where am I?" She looked around at the composite walls and artificial lights. A confused haze clung to her consciousness as she tried to clear her head.

This doesn't look right, she mused, taking in the cryo lab around her. *No, wait. I was walking down a beach. I was going home.*

"Is everything all right?" Barry asked her, pausing his scan of her cryo pod's vitals readout to survey the groggy woman.

"I was having a dream," she said, rubbing the sleep from her eyes.

"A dream? No one dreams in cryo," Barry replied, eyeing her with an odd expression. "Perhaps it is merely data ghosting. I had to pull you from the neuro-stim cycle prematurely. That might be what you experienced. You have had many years of information fed into your mind as we traveled, after all. Do you know the crew roster? Your duties? All the relevant data for the voyage should have been trickle-fed through your neuro-stim unit during transit."

Daisy looked at him, confused.

"You're aboard the *Váli*. We're still six months from the moon's Dark Side base, orbiting Earth. I understand you may be feeling groggy or disoriented, but I really do need to tend to the other crewmembers. The cycle was not complete, and you are all still coming out of your stasis-sleep. The neural stimulators were—"

"What in the hell is going on with my ship?" Captain Harkaway bellowed as he lurched from his cryo-pod, yanking the physio-stim electrodes from his skin as he hopped to his feet. His metal leg impacted the floor with a jarring clang. From hip to tip, Daisy noted, his left leg was entirely mechanical. He rubbed a hand through his gray crew cut.

"Dammit, Mal, what's the sitrep?" he growled to the ever-monitoring computer.

"We have experienced an unexpected impact, Captain," the AI calmly informed him. "Short-range nav is down, multiple communications systems and sensor arrays are compromised throughout the ship, and there is unknown external damage.

Port Storage twelve has been sealed, and we have been knocked slightly off course from the impact."

"You're designed to handle these things, why did you wake us up? Hell, you could have sent Barry out for that. The whole point of having a cyborg with us is he doesn't have to go into cryo-sleep and can do—"

"There are also several small fires on board, and my sensors have been unable to detect them all."

"Oh. Shit," he said as a burst of adrenaline flooded his system. "Get the others up!"

"On it already, Captain, as per protocol," Barry replied.

"I'm heading to the bridge." He cast a curious look at the groggy tech. "Swarthmore, you all right?"

"What?"

"Daisy, are you with me?"

"Yeah. Just feeling a little weird."

"It's to be expected. Try to pull yourself together and get your head on straight. This is what you do. You're the tech guru. I've got a feeling I'm going to be needing your expertise once we get this whole burning-to-death-in-the-void-of-space thing under control."

"Yes, sir."

Daisy slowly slid to her feet, steadying herself on awkward-feeling legs.

"Mal, send a full report to my station in the command pod. Barry, get the others up and moving. If we've got a fire, I'm going to need every damn hand on deck, ASAP," Harkaway barked.

A shining metal fist smashed through the hardened shell of the stasis-pod nearest the cyborg.

"Barry, handle it," the captain grumbled, then stormed out of the chamber's airlock doors.

The fist belonged to Tamara Burke, a sturdily muscled brunette with wisps of gray hair streaking her temples. Her entire right arm from the shoulder down was metal, thin seams and indentations crisscrossing the surface at the wrist, elbow, and shoulder joints. Where the metal met her flesh, the foreign material seemed to meld to her body, a faint scar the only sign she wasn't born with it.

Her metal hand began tearing free of the pod as if it were paper, not heavily-reinforced polymer.

"Tamara, calm down," Barry soothed her from a safe distance.

She paused, the stasis fog clearing from her head. A slight blush colored her cheeks.

"Oh hell. Sorry, Barry. Training. What the hell happened? I was mid-upgrade when you snapped me out. You know what can happen when you interrupt a neuro-stim cycle."

"I am aware. However Mal and I concurred it was best to have the entire crew awakened at once. We suffered an impact, and there appear to be one or more unlocated fires on board."

She rapidly scanned the chamber until her eyes fell on Daisy, standing unsteadily beside pod and looking groggy, while the rest of the crew slowly clambered from theirs.

"Shit, you really did mean everyone. Hey, new kid. Good morning." She nodded a greeting to Daisy.

"Hey."

The occupants of two more pods sat up. One was a middle-aged olive-skinned man with thick black hair. *Gustavo,* Daisy found herself knowing instinctively. *The navigator and third-in-command.* The other man was in his early thirties and sported a short haircut and muscular physique. *Vincent, the mechanic.* The name came to her as he swung out of his pod and onto unsteady legs. He stumbled a few steps, clumsily stepping on Daisy's foot as he nearly fell over.

"Ow!"

"Oops," he said, regaining his balance and stepping back.

"You nearly break my foot and all you can say is *oops*?"

"Seemed appropriate."

"How about, 'Sorry'?" Daisy groused.

"Well, if you'd given me a chance, that would have come next," he replied with more than a little snark.

"Oh, for chrissake, shut it, you two. We've got a situation, here," Tamara said as she jumped out of her pod, landing solidly on steady feet and heading for the chamber's heavy airlock doors.

"Barry, you have the waking process under control?"

"Yes, Tamara," he replied.

"Okay, get the others moving. We don't have time to waste. I'm going to get to my station and make sure the botany pods are secure, engage the emergency air filters, and look for signs of fire in those sections. Mal, if you can hear me, I'll check in when I'm there."

"Thank you, Tamara. Do be careful. It is disconcerting having a problem of this nature off my sensors."

As she hustled out of the chamber, another young woman Daisy's age dry-heaved over the side of her pod. Daisy threw one last annoyed look at the rubber-legged engineer, then turned to scope out her newly-awakened crewmate.

"Hello, Sarah." Barry leapt into action, electrolytes in hand. "You are waking from cryo early. You need fluids. Drink this electrolyte pack, but slowly."

CHAPTER TWO

Within minutes the crew was charging through the ship to their duty stations. Reggie, the stocky co-pilot, passed through the thick airlock doors of command and dropped into his seat beside Captain Harkaway.

"Captain, what happened? Mal woke up *everyone.*"

"I know. Impact on the port side. Sensors are down, and there's fire on board."

"Are the engines all right? I can head down there—"

"Barry's already on it. They seem to be untouched, but we've had a few artificial gravity fluctuations, so he's going to examine the pulse feeds. Once he's done there, I'm having him do an EVA outside to check the collection panels for damage."

The *Váli*, unlike most ships, possessed an unusual secondary propulsion system, one that allowed for extremely long-range travel without draining power. While the standard fusion engines would provide basic propulsion and maneuverability, the collection panels would gather cosmic energy and solar radiation when deployed, gradually filling a series of reserve power stores, while also directly feeding a supplementary pulse drive.

Without the resistance of an atmosphere, this system allowed the ship to progressively ramp up its speed over time. It also allowed, should an emergency occur, for several short, but intense, bursts of speed. The only drawback being such an act would drain the entire system and require quite some time to recharge.

"Captain, what about the shuttle?" Reggie asked.

"Impact was up top, so it was protected by the body of the ship. Good thing it's mounted upside-down to the bottom. Unfortunately, that means our comms and navigation array are what took a beating. How are the others coming?"

"I saw Vincent and Finn gearing up. Do we know where the fire is?"

"Negative. We have to do a full-ship check, starting with compartments in proximity of the damaged area. Where the hell is Gustavo? We're flying blind here."

"Here, Captain," Gus called from the airlock door. The command center's lights reflected off the exposed metal patch of his skull near his cybernetic eye. The metal, like Tamara's arm, smoothly blended into his skin. Whatever had happened to him, they'd done extensive repairs, including not just his skull and eye, but part of his ear as well. The navigator slid into his seat.

"Plug in," Captain Harkaway barked. "No wireless, it's glitching. Go hard-line and tell me what you can see."

Gustavo pulled a high-capacity data cable from his station and plugged it into the slot at the base of his skull.

"I see where Mal's problem is, sir. Several relays near Starboard Seven have been damaged. Possible fire, though I can't be sure."

"Starboard as well? Get Swarthmore and Moore in there. Those two are going to have their work cut out for them."

"Affirmative, sir," he said, switching on his mic. "Daisy, Sarah, do you copy?" Gus asked over the wireless comms.

"Copy," Daisy replied through her headset. "Sarah's still suiting up, but she copies too."

"Okay, listen up. Captain wants you to hit the Narrows. One of you in the exterior layer, port side near Pod Twelve, the other starboard near Pod Seven."

"We're on it," she replied, clicking off the comms.

"The crawlspaces. Why does it have to be the crawlspaces?" Sarah lamented.

"Because of our slender builds," Daisy quipped grimly. "That, and we're the only ones who know how to re-wire this thing by hand if need be," she added, strapping a slim tool kit to each thigh and one to her left forearm.

Captain Harkaway's voice crackled over the comms.

"Swarthmore, Moore, make sure you each bring a respirator and extinguisher. Mal says we may have a small fire somewhere, but her scans are inconclusive. It could be in the Narrows for all we know."

Wonderful. Just how I wanted to wake up. A crew full of strangers and a squeeze through a crawlspace... oh, and it might be on fire. Ugh. Kill me now.

"Copy that," Daisy said in her outside voice. "We're on it."

The two women looked at one another. Sarah was twenty-five years old, just like Daisy, something she knew from the crew roster trickle-fed into her mind as they journeyed toward Earth. They had largely similar skill sets, but given the nature of the vessel they were flying in, that redundancy made perfect sense. There was a lot of work for a tech on a ship like the *Váli.*

"All right," Daisy said. "Let's get crackin'. I'll hit starboard."

The women bumped fists as if they'd been friends for years, then split up. Daisy felt a comfortable confidence in her partner, though logic told her she'd only just met her.

Freaky thing, those neuro-stims, she thought.

An entire crew of strangers, uploaded into her head as she slept. They were strangers, but not. Years upon years traveling through space, a drip-drip-drip of information slowly feeding into each of them, keeping their minds active and sharp. The system even uploaded new skills and training updates given enough time, though that was all very carefully controlled.

It was said the early neuro-stims drove people insane, pumping far too much data into their minds at once. Only after the inhibitor safeties had been invented and fine-tuned did the system finally gain widespread use. Twelve safeties, in all. It was a lot of redundancies, but then, when it's your mind at risk, better safe than spiraling into paranoid insanity.

"Entering the Narrows," Daisy transmitted.

"Copy that. Plug in and update when you're set."

"Will do."

The crawlspaces, while part of the vessel, were the one place standard wireless comms didn't work. The necessity of protecting vital wiring and processing equipment in those tight areas resulted in the little spaces also being the thickest parts of the ship, shielded from just about anything they could think of. Even so, she and Sarah wore Faraday suits. The thin material wouldn't protect them from the elements, but the fine mesh would shield them from any unexpected bursts across a wide spectrum of waves and radiation levels.

It was eerily silent, having no comms chatter during a crisis situation. Until she plugged into a hard-line terminal, Daisy was on her own.

She crawled ahead, as one is wont to do in a crawlspace, slowly inching her way toward the area of suspected damage.

Just lovely, she thought as she scooted forward. Up ahead she could see a data hub that had overloaded. It was smoldering, but there was no fire. Her sense of unease was a constant. The weight, or rather the *lack* of weight directly on the other side of the wall pressing against her side was unnerving. She knew the bulkhead was solid, but having the void of space so close, and while stuck in an area too small for an EVA suit, let alone a hard-hat helmet, left her uneasy.

"I found the source of smoke," she said, plugging in to the nearest comms port. "I'm swapping out the parts now. Should only take a few minutes. There's a fair amount of scorching, but only a few relays were damaged, and there's no fire."

"Copy that, Daisy," Gus replied from the command pod.

Daisy carefully pulled the tools she needed from the pouch on her left thigh and stuck them to the Velcro on her forearm. The dim light surrounding her flickered briefly. While the Narrows had illumination, they were almost never accessed, so it was the flashlight collar's steady glow that provided most of her light.

One by one, she removed the melted pieces. The smell of smoke was still thick in the air.

That can't be good to breathe, she noted, putting the respirator over her nose and mouth.

Ah, better. The smell of smoke filtered out, she pulled the last relay, stuffed it in her rear hip pouch, and set to work locking in the replacement parts.

"Venting Port Four," Vincent said as he typed the command into the small panel of the passageway's airlock door. Inside the chamber, a warning claxon sounded. Moments later the outer airlock door opened to space, extinguishing the fire inside.

"Re-sealing Port Four," he informed Command.

The door cycled shut. Moments later a green light appeared on the panel. Vincent keyed open the interior access and stepped into the in-between space in the threshold. The door sealed behind him, then the inner door to the pod opened.

It was a mess. Fire had destroyed most of the equipment in the room. Tool fabrication machinery was melted, as were several racks of raw materials. Fortunately, the metal storage bins seemed to have withstood the blaze. It would have smelled awful, but the thick helmet protected him from any toxic fumes.

"Looks like we can salvage a lot, sir," he transmitted. "Finn, how's it looking in your neck of the woods?"

The jovial ginger opened his comms. "If you don't mind tea for a while, I think we'll be fine. Some damn piece of who-knows-what blew through the external storage in Starboard Eleven. Looks like we lost a lot of our coffee supply before the auto-foam sealed the leak. Gonna have to reconfigure the food replicators to stock us up with another batch once I get this mess cleaned up. Can't be drinking sealant foam with breakfast, now can we?"

"Glad you have priorities, Finn," Vincent said with a laugh.

"Hey, food *is* my priority. If we're stuck awake a full six months longer than anticipated, shit's gonna get old real quick if we don't have all our culinary options available."

"You're the man, Finn."

"So I've been told. Now go clean the rest of that crap up so we can call it a day."

"Cut the chatter, you two," Captain Harkaway interrupted. "Keep the comms clear. We've still got crew in the Narrows, and a possible fire."

"Sorry, Captain," the pair replied.

"All right, all right. Get back to work, and be careful," he said, then turned to his pilot. "Let's just hope it was only bad sensors. I do not need an uncontrolled fire aboard my ship on top of all that's happened today."

CHAPTER THREE

"Come on you bastard, get in there!" Daisy struggled in the cramped space, angrily wiggling the last, stubborn relay circuit that simply did not want to click into place. She'd spent several minutes longer than expected cleaning melted plastic from the contacts.

A lot of that got in there. Too much, actually.

She brushed a few hairs from her eyes as a pressure change sent a waft of air across her face.

Great. Somewhere, there's yet one more thing for me to fix. After this current pain-in-the-ass task, that is. Come on—fit, you bastard!

Click.

The piece slid home at last, surprising her with its sudden obedience, and Daisy wound up whacking her elbow from the unexpected lack of resistance.

"Son of a bitch!"

She looked at the soot that smeared across her throbbing arm. *There really shouldn't be so much.*

"Everything all right, Daisy?" Gustavo asked.

"Yeah, I guess I leaned on my transmit button. Sorry. Just hit my elbow, is all."

"So how's it coming in there? Sarah's done, and it looks like the rest of the ship is under control."

"Just locked in the last relay. Hang on, I'll power it back up." She reached out and reactivated the unit. "Okay, it's on. You reading the corresponding points?"

"Affirmative. That's the last of it."

"Great, it's about time."

"Yeah, tell me about it. Now hop on out of there."

"You don't have to tell me twice."

Daisy felt herself unexpectedly floating.

"Hey, did you kill gravity down here?"

"Negative. Must be another glitch. I'll have Mal run a diagnostic."

"Copy that," Daisy replied. "I'm gonna get out of here. It looks like—"

She froze. A flickering, drifting light was approaching.

Rapidly.

Fire.

"Oh, shit, there's a—" Her comms cut out as she forcefully pushed back from the panel, yanking the cord from the connector.

Shit, shit, shit! No wonder there was too much soot. Fucking busted antigrav let the fire float away.

The ball of strangely pulsing flames drifted near, closing the gap rapidly as another pressure shift caused a slight breeze, pushing it toward her even faster. Daisy passed from one section to the next, scrambling backwards as she went. Her legs abruptly slammed down into the hard metal as she crossed the transition into the segment behind her.

Goddamn antigrav, make up your mind!

"There's a fire! I repeat, there's a fire!" she shouted into her comms.

No reply.

"Fuck!" Daisy crawled backwards as fast as she could,

banging her knees as she went, the floating fireball becoming hotter and hotter against her skin as it neared. She whipped the fire extinguisher from her hip and fired it. The stream of foam arced then fell short, the gravity of the section she was in taking hold before it could reach the zero-gravity section and continue to its target.

"You've gotta be kidding me!"

The gravity beneath her suddenly went out, and she felt herself floating again, the fireball moving closer at a dangerous speed.

The access hatch has to be only twenty meters behind me. Straight shot. I can do this in zero-g.

Daisy pushed, hard, rocketing backwards toward the open access.

Yes! I'm going to—

Artificial gravity slammed her knees into the metal again. She didn't stop to think. She didn't even stop to swear. A fiery death was speeding toward her. All Daisy could do was scramble backward as fast as she was able. One foot cleared the lip of the access hatch. She gave a final shove, sending her body out the narrow hole, but was yanked abruptly to a stop, pain shooting from her arm to her shoulder.

Her forearm tool kit had become snagged on something.

Panic flowed over her as the flames raced closer. Gravity fluctuated on and off, but she could not break free. Her gaze drifted across old scribblings decorating the tight space around her. She hadn't noticed them before, and now it looked like she would never get a chance to look closer in the future.

Because she didn't have one anymore.

Of all the ways to—

Daisy felt powerful arms wrap around her waist, yanking her from the Narrows, her tool kit tearing free with a painful wrench. She tumbled to the deck in a heap and looked up to see Vincent aiming a fire extinguisher into the shaft.

"Come on, you bastard." He eyed the space intently. "Gotcha!"

The gravity shifted again as he fired. The stream of thick foam blasted forward, propelled the full length of the gravity-free crawlspace, its force enhanced by his solidly anchored body. Vince had leaned into the zero-g space to take the shot, but had the presence of mind to keep his feet firmly out. The foam utilized that extra force and slammed into the speeding fireball, blasting much of it into oblivion, coating the entire crawlspace. Despite the apparent mess, the specially-designed foam would evaporate to vapor in a few minutes, leaving no trace.

Unfortunately, a sizable ball of fiery death had escaped and was hurtling toward the opening. Vince pulled himself free and dove to the side, just as the flames leapt from the open access panel into the pod.

While gravity was now taking hold, making the fire more traditional in form, that, combined with the speed with which the flames exited the zero-g Narrows, made it spray out like a mini flamethrower. In a split-second, the condensed ball had grown into a wall of flame spreading across the pod floor and walls.

"Look out!" Daisy yelled, shoving Vince out of the way of a rapidly advancing tendril of fire. "Come on! We've got to get out of here!" She tugged fiercely on Vince's arm as he scrambled to his feet.

"Wait! The Narrows!"

She realized what he was saying. If they didn't seal the access, the blaze would just make its way back to the zero-g space in the walls, bigger and stronger than before. They'd be even worse off than before.

"Clear a path to the door! I'll seal the panel!" she shouted over the now-roaring flames.

Vince nodded and took off in a hunched-over run, staying

below the smoke as best he could. Daisy dove low and slid on her belly, snatching up the access panel from the deck.

"Please let it be here," she said, digging in her rear pocket. "Gotcha!" she cried triumphantly, pulling a spare power ratchet from its depths.

She slammed the panel in place and quickly torqued the first two bolts into place. Her eyes were already burning from the smoke, and her lungs ached from holding her breath, but she knew there was no other choice. The panel had to be sealed, and she was the one to do it.

Her lungs burned, desperate for air, as the power ratchet whirred, the remaining six bolts driving home, sealing off the Narrows from smoke and fire alike. Daisy felt her legs wobble as she dropped to her knees, pressing her face to the floor, desperately searching for a breathable gulp of air in the blazing pod.

Gotta get up, she told herself, but her oxygen-starved body wouldn't respond. She felt light, almost like she was floating in the air. It took a good several seconds before she realized she actually *was* floating. Well, to be fair, she was being carried, but whatever her means of transit, she was off the floor and rapidly heading for the airlock doors.

Vince cycled open the inner door and jumped into the narrow space, then sealed it and opened the outer one to the corridor. With no time to lose, he slid Daisy to the deck as the door slid shut, his fingers rapidly typing in a series of commands on the wall-mounted panel.

"Mal, I can't activate the suppression system! Purge the pod, quick!"

"Are all humans clear, Vince?"

"Yes! Just do it!"

The airlock door to the void of space cracked open, the vacuum sucking the air from the pod in an instant, extinguishing the flames entirely before sealing shut again.

Vince reached down and helped Daisy to her feet.

"How did you—" She broke into a coughing fit.

"I heard your comms cut out. Sounded like you were in trouble."

"I..." She stared into his concerned eyes as the crazed adrenaline surge began to slowly clear from her system. "I'm sorry I was rough on you earlier. Thank you," she managed. "I'm Daisy, by the way."

"Yeah, I know. I'm Vincent. Vincent Cooper, but you can call me Vince."

The sooty pair shared a smile, and Daisy found herself vaguely remembering learning something about attraction being heightened in dangerous situations.

"Swarthmore, Cooper, is everything all right down there?" Harkaway called over the comms.

"Yes, Captain," Vince answered. "The fire is out, and everything is okay now."

The captain sighed audibly over the open comms.

"Good work, all of you. I want you to clean up, eat something, then get some rack time. Being pulled out of your cryo and neuro-stim cycles and thrown into a situation like this is going to feel far worse than a hangover tomorrow. We all need to get some rest. Mal and Barry will keep watch."

As Daisy showered off the sweat and soot from her ordeal, she couldn't help but think about the turn her day had taken.

Still six months from home. That's a helluva long time, she mused as the warm water flowed over her body, easing the stress of the abrupt wake up.

She rinsed her hair, dried off, slipped into the clean sweats she had brought to the shower pod, and stepped out into the hallway, running smack into the likewise freshly-showered man passing by, his hair still damp and mussed.

"Oh, sorry," she blurted.

Vincent laughed.

"This is how you repay me? Attacking me in the corridors and stepping on *my* foot, now? Such a violent woman," he said with a grin. "Well, I suppose we're even, now. And for the record, I *am* sorry I stepped on your foot earlier."

The pause left a crackling in the air as they stared at one another.

This is crazy. You just met the guy.

Daisy's heart beat loud in her ears, and she could feel the heat in her belly spreading lower. She studied Vince. Tall, fit, and damn good-looking.

I almost died, she rationalized. *What the hell. Just a meaningless fling. I deserve it.*

She grabbed him by the hand and pulled him down the passageway.

"Um, where are we going?" he asked, a little surprised.

"My place," she replied, matter-of-factly.

The quickening pulse suddenly thundering in his neck revealed his thoughts on the idea.

"Um, okay."

Daisy cycled open the first door and pushed him inside, shutting it behind her. By the time the inner airlock door opened, they were both in an advanced state of undress.

"Come here, you," she growled, pulling him to her. Her hands traced the musculature of his body as he pressed his mouth firmly to hers. He trailed off to the sweet spot below her ear, gently latching on as Daisy shuddered and groaned reaching out and grabbing a shelf to steady herself against the bulkhead as her knees suddenly went weak.

Not a bad way to wake up from cryo-sleep. She smiled to herself. *Not bad at all.*

CHAPTER FOUR

The cold bite of hard metal ringing off your forehead is one hell of a way to wake up, and Daisy was none too amused by it.

She had jerked abruptly to consciousness in her bunk, as she had so many times in the six months since her rude cryo-awakening, but this time Daisy had actually bolted upright and somehow managed to slam her head into the titanium rack above her bunk in the cramped space.

"Fuck! Sonofa—" she blurted, her fingers gingerly feeling the rapidly growing bump on her head as she checked for signs of blood.

Clean fingers. Be happy for small victories. It would be oh-so funny if the crewmember whose job relied on her sharp analytical skills suddenly rendered herself comatose, she grimly mused.

She had been having that strange dream again. Beautiful green trees, fresh air, and blue skies.

And silence. Total silence.

Lingering on the fringe of the vision, there had been something else, but she couldn't quite put her finger on it, and the nascent ache in her head put a quick end to any hopes of remembering further details, at least for the time being. Pretty much everything was momentarily on the back burner as the rapidly increasing pain demanded her full attention.

It was going to be a double-dose of pain meds kind of morning.

Gingerly, careful not to add insult to painful injury, she removed the slender neuro-stim band wrapped around her head and sat up in her bed. While she had a visceral unease with the mechanical parts stuck on human bodies, she found herself able to rationalize using the neuro-stim far easier, though self-loathing would sometimes seep through in spite of herself.

It wasn't an *actual* replacement part, after all. She wasn't physically changing her body. It was just a simple tool, and one she could give up anytime if she wanted to. For now, however, it was keeping her sharp and letting her do her job a little bit better. Kind of like taking a stim pack when working a double shift.

She'd used more than a few of those when weariness threatened the quality of her work in those first frantic days, but she soon decided she couldn't risk the residual effects. Even with the chemicals fully metabolized out of her system, Daisy hadn't really had a single good night's slumber since she'd woken six months prior. To be fair, however, many of those sleepless nights were also due to a certain well-muscled engineer.

So much for a one-night stand. Daisy smiled at the thought, cozy and reluctant to leave the warmth of her covers. Of course, she knew if she dilly-dallied too much Sarah would just come and lean on her door chime until she had no choice but to rouse herself for their daily pre-breakfast Qi Gong routine.

Why did I ever agree to join her?

"It'll help you center yourself," Sarah had said. "Find your balance, focus your energy. Maybe you'll even sleep better."

Daisy had picked up the simple movements quickly. Her muscle tone and fitness were exceptional. The muscle-stim surface electrodes had done their job admirably, keeping her body in top-notch physical condition as she slumbered through the lengthy voyage. Now she met with Sarah every morning, and though her friend was far more advanced than she was, Daisy was pleased to find she had little trouble keeping up.

A few months into their routine, Sarah suggested they add Tai Chi. It would be a little bit more strain on the body at first, adding all those unusual movements, but physically, Daisy had no problems with it. Mentally, well, that was another story.

The neural stimulator was the issue. Daisy and the rest of the crew had all been hooked up to one during their lengthy stasis, and once awakened, had continued utilizing the smaller versions Mal had wired into their quarters.

The massively complicated devices were supposed to not only regulate brain activity in cryo-sleep, keeping the wearer in a restful state, but would also gently impart useful information and training updates to the unconscious mind in a slow trickle.

The theory behind it was that mission-specific knowledge could be drip-fed and learned en route, allowing individuals to jump headfirst into whatever tasks awaited them as soon as they woke upon arriving at their destination, rather than spending days, or even weeks, training after being roused from their slumber.

For everyone else on the crew, the system seemed to work perfectly. For Daisy, not so much. It frustrated her to no end that despite her technical know-how, she simply couldn't figure out why.

Apparently, the early prototypes of the machine had tried to simply upload massive amounts of information to the wearers at once. It seemed logical, the storage capacity was certainly there, but the AI who had designed the system hadn't fully taken into account the remarkably delicate nature of human gray matter. In the first series of tests, those who didn't die outright, invariably went mad.

Eventually it was determined, through much trial and error,

that only the slowest drip of information could be safely absorbed. A steady but small trickle rather than a flood, and closely regulated and monitored at all times. There wasn't all that much you could learn in a short trip, but on a longer one such as this, during those months and years of cryo-time, a traveler could effectively update their technical skill set and incorporate any new revisions to operations protocols.

Unfortunately, while the rest of the crew slept well and were fully able to wear their neuro-stims out of cryo stasis with no issues, Daisy found early on that she could only use the neural stimulator if she flooded her brain with copious amounts of sleep drugs. That simply wasn't an option for someone whose job depended on a clear and logical mind. So it passed that she resolved to see if she could find a fix.

That's when she began tinkering with the device.

After her first week of unrestful sleep, she decided to try a new work-around, tweaking a few lines of the device's base code and disabling a pair of inhibitors from the machine, altering the rate and intensity of data flow during her sleep sessions. It took a little trial-and-error, but fairly quickly, she found a mix that worked well enough most of the time.

As she tinkered with the neuro-stim, Daisy had been pleasantly surprised to find herself innately aware of the ins and outs of the complex system, though at the same time, she also felt that a full understanding was always just out of her reach. She was a tech, and a damn good one, but the neuro-stims were simply far beyond her training, and much of the time she was working on instinct alone. It was hit-and-miss, and, unfortunately, that occasionally meant bad dreams.

And bumps to the head when she woke from them.

Given the option, she'd have simply chosen to go back into cryo, but after the accident there had been so many repairs to make, and so many lingering glitches in the ship's systems, that the captain had felt it best if they all stayed awake the remainder of the trip.

At least she had Vince to help pass the time. Him and the massive entertainment collection Captain Harkaway had seen fit to load onto the ship before departing.

Currently, she and Vince were spending their evenings together working through the science fiction and horror classics of the twentieth and twenty-first centuries. As crew of an actual spacecraft, they found themselves regularly amused at things that weren't supposed to be funny. If only the filmmakers had known how far off their predictions of the future would be.

Daisy sighed and finally resolved to get up, sliding her feet to the warm metal floor. She cautiously rose onto her slightly off-balance legs, hoping she hadn't hit her head harder than she thought. Of course she was fine. The artificial gravity just always felt a bit off near her bunk at the far end of the sleeping pod. An annoyance, but one she'd finally grown more or less accustomed to.

"Okay, that's not so bad," she muttered, then slipped into her workout sweats. Ready to start the day, she cycled open the pair of airlock doors and headed into the belly of the ship.

No compartment in the entire vessel was sealed by a single door. The redundant airlocks not only provided an extra layer of security against catastrophic air-loss, but were also an essential element of the ship's re-configurable pod system.

They varied in size, the largest ones nearly twenty meters long, while crew quarters and storage were far more compact. The design allowed pods to be moved, reconfigured, and aligned with one another according to mission needs, and should a true emergency need arise, they could even be sealed off and jettisoned into space.

Daisy began a slow jog to warm her muscles. The workout facility was located in an outer section pod, portside, and was large enough for the whole crew to exercise at once if they so desired. Fortunately, at this hour, it was most often just Daisy and Sarah.

"Good morning, Daisy," Mal greeted her warmly as she made her way down the corridor. "The time is 08:23."

"Thanks, Mal."

At least the crew pods were off the AI's non-stop monitoring grid. That privacy, she was grateful for. It was a little thing, sure, and Daisy knew there was a good reason for the design, but it still felt weird having the AI keeping constant tabs on not only the ship's systems, but its crew as well.

Finnegan Hay was prepping vegetables for the evening's meal at his work station in the galley as Daisy passed through to grab an electrolyte pouch en route to the gym pod.

Finn's right arm was speedily dicing, far faster than a regular human-grown limb could. It was a replacement part of shining metal from just above the elbow, and like Tamara's, it blended perfectly into his flesh, though his was a less bulky design. Part of that was due to the nature of Tamara's work needs as the ship's botanist. With her much sturdier arm, she could swap her hand out for a wide variety of gardening equipment attachments, all of which were most useful as she tended the ship's garden pods.

Tamara the farmer. With her gruff manner and sturdy build, Daisy was shocked when she learned the muscular woman was a vegetarian.

"You all can eat whatever disgusting clone meat you want," she had said when asked about it. "I'll stick with things that I know where they came from."

"But, Tamara," Daisy teased, "it's just ship-grown cow and chicken muscle fiber. No animal was hurt putting these steaks on our tables."

Tamara flashed her a look.

"They *tell you* it's cow. When your meat just shows up in perfect little trays like that, how can you *really* know? You might be eating people steaks for all you know."

"Gross, Tamara."

"Just saying," she had replied, only half-joking.

In any case, they had all benefited from Tamara's gardening prowess.

Fresh produce in space. Daisy never stopped marveling at how lucky they were, and Finn possessed a near-magical ability to make almost anything taste delicious without resorting to heavy sauces. He liked to call it, "Seasoning food with food," and had spent a few months working with Tamara on some hybrid herbs and spices. Once they were mature enough for harvest, his recipes had become consistently exceptional.

"Hey, Daze. Off to see Sarah?" Finn asked, not looking up from his cutting board.

"Yep. She's teaching me Tai Chi now."

"Ooh, Tai Chi. Cool. Stop by after. I'll whip you up something nice and healthy for breakfast."

"Savory or sweet?"

"Hmm... I don't see why not a bit of both," he replied with a knowing grin.

"Ya see, Finn, *this* is why we get along so well."

"That and the fact that you're happy to be my culinary guinea pig. Tell Sarah the offer stands for her, too."

"Seriously, Finn, just tell her."

"Tell her what?" he said, blushing faintly.

Daisy groaned. "Fine, but one of these days she may take a liking to Barry and leave you kicking yourself. Remember, it's better to regret something you have done than something you haven't."

"Well, fortunately for me, Barry's a cyborg, so he's not exactly her type."

"I don't know," Daisy laughed. "I hear he may have a multi-speed—"

"Lalalalala! I can't hear you!" Finn cried out. "Go on, you. Shoo! Stop procrastinating and go work out already."

Daisy laughed and opened the airlock's inner door.

"All right. See ya in a bit," she said, then flashed Finn a wicked grin as she made motorized vibrating sounds.

"Oh, come on!" he lamented, her laughter cutting off as she cycled the airlock door closed behind her.

"You're late. I was about to start without you," Sarah said, looking up from her splits on the floor.

"Damn, girl, that flexible and still single?"

"Well, you're the one who jumped Mr. Sexypants only a few hours after we thawed out. I never stood a chance!"

"There are other options, you know."

"Yeah, yeah. There'll be plenty of men to choose from once we get home. Now come on, let's get started."

For the next forty minutes, Sarah led her friend through the one hundred twelve complex movements at painfully slow speed. Daisy's thighs burned from the effort, just as her mind ached trying to memorize all the new moves while simultaneously problem-solving the day's pending repairs in her head.

"So, I was thinking," Daisy said mid-move. "If I take Faraday suit number three and add a reverse-polarity buffer, then route it all back through a miniature pulse feed, splitting all the frequencies into segregated positive and negative channels, it might create a solid base for my retrofit idea."

"Which is?"

"Well, if it's then looped into a micro-mesh layer on top of the existing dampers, it should effectively block out not only the standard stuff we're worried about, but pretty much every EM blast imaginable as well. I figure it's the spare suit, so why not give it a try?"

"Interesting idea. So if you could make it work, we would be able to spend more time in the open portside pods near the damaged bits, even when stronger pulses are coming in?" Sarah looked impressed as she flowed into the next motion. "Huh, that's really clever. I mean it's *far* beyond the suit specs, and something even Mal never thought of, but in theory, it should work. You want help wiring it up?"

"Well, I kinda already did. Just thought I'd run it by you before taking it for a spin."

"Of course you did. Never stops churning, that brain of yours. I'm amazed you ever sleep."

"Good old gray matter," Daisy said, tapping her head with a chuckle. "The one thing we have over the AIs. Thinking outside the box is second nature."

"Always with the tweaks and modifications. You're such a tinkerer, Daze."

"Just call me MacGyver."

"Who?"

"It's an old entertainment program from the captain's videos. Vince and I binge-watched it a few months ago. I can lend it to you, if you want."

"Cool. I'm happy that you two are still going strong."

"Yeah, it's crazy, right? I mean, who knew a quick adrenaline-fueled fling would actually turn into something substantial?"

"Substantial? You don't mean—"

"Maybe," Daisy replied, distracted enough to mix up the next sequence of Tai Chi moves.

"Concentrate. Arm like this, then the leg like so." Sarah showed her the move again. "Anyway, you were saying?"

"I was saying that we talked about maybe getting a place together when we get to Earth."

"Wow, that *is* pretty serious. Hang on. It's the left arm over, right arm under." Sarah broke her pose and put her hands on Daisy's wrists, guiding them to the correct position.

"I'm sucking at multi-tasking today. Sorry, Sarah."

"No worries, it sounds like you have a *lot* on your mind."

"If you'd stop being such a prude, maybe you'd have a lot on your mind too. There are still a few eligible men on board. If you don't mind replacement parts, that is."

"Yeah, count on you to get the only guy without any metal bits. Although, now that you mention it, maybe I'll just settle for Barry. I hear he might have a multi-speed..." She flashed a wicked little grin.

"Oh my God, I was just saying that!" Daisy chortled. Both women lost their composure for a moment, and the Zen of Tai Chi went out the window in favor of a robust belly laugh between good friends.

CHAPTER FIVE

"Daisy! I've been wanting to speak with you."

Doctor Leah McClain, the woman pulling double duty as both ship's physician and psychologist, hurried her pace to meet her patient.

Oh hell. All Daisy wanted was to be left alone as she headed to quiet the steady rumble in her belly.

No such luck.

"How is your energy these days, Daisy? Are you sleeping any better? You know you're a bit overdue for our next session," the doctor said, intently watching Daisy's face in that disquieting way some shrinks have made into an art form.

"Yeah, I know, Doc, I've just been busy. I promise, I'll come see you soon, okay?"

Doctor McClain stared quietly a moment longer, then relented.

"All right, but don't wait too long."

Daisy quietly breathed a sigh of relief as she watched the older woman walk away with the slightest of limps in her step. She was most definitely not a fan of people digging in her head, even if it was only with words.

Daisy strode up to the galley doors and punched the open command on the keypad.

Captain Harkaway nodded a greeting as she cycled through the dual airlocks and entered the large crew mess hall. He was seated at the galley table, holding a mug of brass-cleaner strong coffee you could smell from across the room. When the grizzled, gray-haired man brewed a pot himself, it was a safe bet no one else on the crew would touch it.

Tamara sat with him, sipping a mug of herbal tea, made from plants she had grown in one of her garden pods. A far cry from the captain's mug of bitter hot death. Behind the counter, the ever-festive madman chef was whipping up breakfast for the pair.

"Hey, Daisy," he said, waving a cheerful hello.

"Hey, Finn."

"Got that grub for ya. Made something special."

"Thanks," she said, reaching for the offered bowl. It was a yin/yang swirled oatmeal of some sort.

"I know it'll be delicious, Finn, but what exactly is this?"

"Well, since you were practicing your Tai Chi, I thought I'd go with a dichotomy of life theme for breakfast. Dark and light. Male and female. Hard and soft." He smiled and pointed with his spatula. "The lighter side of the *taijitu* is a spiced apple flavor with a tiny hint of vanilla and almond essences. Very delicate and sweet. The savory half is a bit stronger. A relatively mild mélange of slightly spicy grilled jicama, diced and mixed with smoky black sesame and minced soy protein."

Daisy was impressed, both with the quality of the food, as well as the thought the deceptively flippant chef put into the dish. More than once she'd thought there was more to him than met the eye.

"You never cease to surprise me, Finn."

"Then my mission is a success," he laughed as she took her bowl and crossed the long room to join her crewmates.

"Swarthmore, what the hell did you do to your head?" Harkaway asked as he got a better look at the lump growing above her eyebrow.

"Just whacked it, Captain. No biggie."

"Don't go concussing yourself. I need you clear-headed, unlike this nutcase." He gestured to the man in the kitchen.

Finn chuckled and continued his meal prep. Daisy watched his hands fly as he mechanically diced the fresh vegetables. His metal arm and hand moved in a blur, as if they had minds of their own, which, given the electronics embedded in them, linked to his neural inputs and providing a reflex-relay, technically, they sort of did. From time to time, though, she noticed, his arm would jerk a little from the speed. Just a tiny bit, and almost unnoticeable if you weren't looking for it, but it seemed to her almost as if his own meat and the metal limb couldn't quite mesh.

Replacement parts. She held back a shudder.

Daisy never could get used to seeing them stuck to real live people. The cyborg, well she expected it from him, but ironically, despite being entirely artificial, his metal skeleton was hidden, completely covered with flesh and blood. Only the humans sported their shiny bits exposed for all to see.

Some, like the captain, you'd never notice if you weren't paying attention. His hip-down replacement was always covered by the same pressed trousers. Only on exiting the cryo pods had Daisy ever even caught a glimpse of it. She had no idea what had happened to him all those years ago, but his leg was of a much older design than the rest of the crew.

Unfortunately, in the early days of replacement parts, the more severe cases resulted in a permanent implant-to-flesh bond that could not ever be removed and replaced. What you got was what you kept. The captain walked with a little hitch in his giddy-up, and though he took great care of his aging limb, nevertheless it was showing signs of wear. It was durable, but only to a point.

Tamara was using her more slender lower arm and hand attachment at the table. Of all her assorted options, this was the one that most closely resembled a regular human forearm and hand. It allowed for fine motor skill uses, while also permitting the user to wear long sleeves and a glove to go unnoticed if they so desired. Mind you, Tamara's sturdy build and scowling gaze meant she'd probably *never* go unnoticed, but being able to cover the arm at least helped somewhat.

Reggie was a skilled co-pilot whose lone visible replacement was his left hand. The metal was perfectly fused to his arm just above the wrist. What she knew of him beyond that was that he had several artificial organs as well as five replacement ribs, a metal femur in his left leg, and a handful of composite vertebrae. Some disease had ravished his body, and only the most aggressive of treatments had saved his life. All it cost him was fifteen percent of his humanity, more or less.

"Gus, how's the pulse drive refill coming?" Captain Harkaway inquired over the comms. "There was a pretty strong solar wind. We need to capture as much of that charge as we can."

"I'm adjusting the flow as we speak, Captain," Gustavo replied. "We hit a bit of an unexpected lull, so the next pulse will be delayed by"— he ran a quick calculation—"five hours."

Gus. Now, *his* replacements actually spooked Daisy.

Massive head trauma had resulted in a partial jaw, cranium, and full left eye replacement. The new eye was able to see multiple spectrums, including radio and radiation waves, but it just looked creepy. Worse, at least in Daisy's mind, were the several access ports on the back of the metal portion of his skull. A partial AI had been installed in his head, helping him jack in and communicate with the ship's systems directly. He was human, but Daisy couldn't help but wonder at what point in receiving replacements and upgrades someone would cease being one.

"All right," the captain said. "Keep on it. I want to make sure we have a maxed-out charge by the time we reach Earth's orbit and Dark Side base. Gotta be primed for full maneuverability should we need it." He glanced at Tamara, who shared a knowing look.

What's that all about? Daisy wondered. Dark Side base should be a relatively simple approach, and any drastic maneuvering shouldn't be required.

From what she knew of it, the facility located on what was known as the dark side of Earth's moon, though that was a misnomer as it actually received plenty of sunlight, held a repair station as well as much-needed parts. Despite Daisy and Sarah's diligent efforts, the *Váli* was in dire need of work they simply couldn't do with their somewhat limited resources.

"Hey, guys!" Sarah chirped as she cycled in through the airlock door. "Captain," she added respectfully when she noticed he was joining them this morning.

"Ooh, what's that, Daze?"

"Finn whipped up some Tai Chi-themed oatmeal."

"Finn, sweetie, can I pleeeeease have some too?" She flashed him a warm smile.

"No," he replied.

"Um, what? Why not?"

Daisy glared at him, mouthing, "*Dude, what the fuck?*" from across the room. He ignored her as best he could.

"Because," he began, "I have a far more interesting meal in mind for you. Allow me to tempt you, if I may, with a multi-plate offering of sweet and savory. Protein and clean carbs, the way you like." He slipped a quick glance at Daisy. "And yes, it will stick to the morning's theme."

A smile replaced her frown. "Okay. I trust ya, Finn."

"And that was your first mistake," Tamara grumbled with a little grin.

"How's the re-routing of the long-range nav-transponder coming?" Captain Harkaway asked as she pulled up a seat. "Whatever bit of space crap we ran into left us flying a bit more blind than I'm comfortable with. I'd hoped that would be fully operational by now. You two have had nearly six months."

"Still working on it Captain," Daisy replied. "Sarah's been fine-tuning the life-support arrays and tracking down all the burned-out relays inside the Narrows while I've been re-re-reconfiguring the replacement module. It's getting closer, but I'll still need to do another few EVAs before my jury-rigged gizmo will be ready to test."

"I can fabricate any additional parts you require, Daisy," Mal chimed in. "My facilities are repaired and in excellent working order now and are well-equipped for a wide array of production needs. Please let me know if my resources can be of assistance."

Always listening. God, that bugs me.

"I don't even know what I need yet, Mal, but thanks," she replied. "The problem is, no standard piece will work, given the amount of damage we sustained. Everything is custom-built to not only fit the need, but also handle the unreliability factors from the faults we haven't been able to pinpoint yet."

"You know, I'm happy to send Barry out to help," the captain said. "You've been spending a lot of time outside working on this. I know how exhausting it can be, and he doesn't get tired. Plus, he won't run out of oxygen."

Barry.

Why the cyborg had chosen that name upon achieving consciousness she had wondered countless times. All the names in the known galaxy, and he chose Barry. It was only after flipping through old animated Earth television programs with Vincent one lazy evening, that she thought she may have stumbled upon his reasoning. Unlikely, but perhaps he had a sense of humor hidden in there after all. Then she reminded herself, he's just a machine. Machines don't have a sense of humor. Not really, do they?

His AI seemed benign enough, always happy and ready to lend a helping hand, but something about the artificial human always put her the tiniest bit on edge. She knew it was irrational, but she just couldn't help it. Something in her gut felt it was wrong.

"You know me, Captain," she finally answered. "I design on the fly as the situation reveals its surprises, and I work faster by myself. An extra set of hands getting in the way would just slow me down."

"Okay, but you know Barry has valuable skills at your disposal should you need them."

"I'm sure he does, Captain," she replied, briefly flashing back to her conversations about the cyborg's *special* features with both Sarah and Finn only that very morning.

Daisy felt a slight flush trying to work its way to her cheeks. She knew better than to look at Sarah. She could *feel* her friend struggling to contain herself as well. Just one glance and they'd both lose it.

Keep it together; you can do this. Daisy breathed deeply, using one of Sarah's meditation techniques to desperately try to pull back from the edge. Slowly, the urge started to pass. *Just don't look at her.*

"So, Sarah," the captain said, breaking the tension.

Whew, that was close.

"Daisy seems to be well taken care of. Is there anything I could have Barry help *you* with?"

The women's eyes met, and no amount of willpower could stop it.

"Bwahahaha!" Daisy and Sarah burst into peals of laughter, tears streaming down their faces as their confused captain and shipmates looked on. A very perplexed Finnegan caught Daisy's eye, and that just made it all the worse.

"Um, okay, then," Captain Harkaway said. "When you two are done with your sorority party, I want you to get Starboard's wiring upgraded to match Mal's new configurations for that array. The gravity and half the sensors are still shot in that pod. It looks like we won't be able to fix it until we reach Dark Side, but we can at least make sure the surrounding systems are tip-top. Is that clear?"

"Yes, sir," the two women managed.

"I swear, the two of you..." He trailed off as he stepped out through the airlock door.

Tamara rose and collected her breakfast from the galley. "Box it, Finn, I'll take it to my garden."

He slid her frittata into the box and handed her the container as she beelined for the exit. Tamara paused a moment, looking at the two younger women.

"Idiots." She sighed, shaking her head as she walked out.

The two women had eventually reined in their mirth, though laughter bubbled just beneath the surface for the remainder of their breakfast. Eventually they'd have to get back to work, and of that there was plenty.

The crew being woken from their cryo-sleep early was an annoyance in itself, but the never-ending maintenance was wearing on everyone. The ridiculous part was that whatever had hit them was tiny. So small it didn't even show on Mal's scans, but at the speed they were traveling, with the modified pulse drive pushing them just a little bit beyond the capabilities of a normal ship, just about any impact could cause serious damage.

Of course, that was why they had such a specialized shielding system, but somehow this one thing had hit at just the right point in their pulse-shields, avoiding the deflective force and slipping in just as they phase-shifted to a different frequency.

It was like winning the galaxy's shittiest lottery, where that a one-in-a-million chance was bound to happen eventually. Unfortunately for the crew, eventually happened to be on their watch. They were just lucky the shuttle mounted upside down on the ship's belly was unscathed or they'd be stuck using their cramped hopper ship when they reached Earth. That would not be fun. The tiny vessel was not designed for comfort, and would require multiple uncomfortable trips to ferry down the crew a few at a time.

Despite that one bit of good luck, the rest of the ship was in desperate need of repairs, something that had filled every day of the near six months they'd been awake.

Under normal circumstances they would have woken from their cryogenic stasis a full two weeks prior to arrival at Earth to run diagnostics and whatnot. The big brains back home had determined that to be the optimum length of time for the crew to regain full muscle reflexes and restore digestive strength with normal food from the ship's garden pods before stepping back into the planet's full gravity. Homecoming with weak limbs and weaker bowels was something no one wanted to experience.

As it stood, they now were winding down from close to six months of awake-time, but at long last, Earth was a mere seven days' journey away. Sure, they'd have to stop at Dark Side for a few critical repairs first, but the staff there could handle those while the crew of the *Váli* took the shuttle home to that gorgeous blue-green orb.

For Daisy, home couldn't come soon enough, though truth be told, aside from the grueling work schedule, she really wasn't minding her extra up-time.

In more ways than one.

"Hey," she called out to Sarah as they walked to their next

tedious repair job. "I'm gonna wash up from our morning workout. I'll meet you there, okay?"

"Sure thing. Enjoy your shower," she said with a knowing laugh.

Daisy certainly intended to.

CHAPTER SIX

"Mmm. Oh yeah, that's perfect."

A pair of strong hands traced the curves of Daisy's body under the hot water. While a good scrub was an enjoyable side effect of the attention, that was most certainly not their primary objective.

Vince had received her impromptu message, and after giving her a little good-natured grief about only using him for his body, he joined her in the shower for a break in his morning engineering shift. His coveralls lay tossed in a pile on the floor with Daisy's discarded sweats, the clothing blending together, entwined, just like its owners, as they moved in unison in the steaming water.

One of the great things Sarah had pointed out early on, was that the efficiency ratings of the *Váli*'s moisture recapture systems were exceptional. It even drew humidity from the air as they exhaled. That, combined with its wastewater recycling and hydrogen collection arrays pulling in molecules as the ship passed celestial bodies, all meant that lengthy, steaming showers —heated by the drive engines with no added energy expenditure—wouldn't cost the ship one drop of water.

For lovers of shower sex, this was a wonderful bit of news. Lucky for the rest of the crew each of the ship's two bathing compartments not only had sturdy airlocks, but were also quite soundproof.

"I can't feel my feet." Daisy said, stumbling from the shower a short while later.

"Don't worry, I've got you," Vince murmured, arms tight around her as he held her close. "Damn, woman, that was intense."

"You're telling me?" She chuckled, sensation slowly returning to her trembling extremities. "And lesson learned. Shower head sounds great in theory, but the reality is much more like waterboarding, only with more dick."

He snorted a laugh. "Noted."

Daisy watched appreciatively as he pulled his uniform back on. *Damn, how did I get so lucky?*

"Hey, you wanna watch some more old anime tonight, or do you feel more like one of Harkaway's old sci-fi movies?" Vince asked as he opened the inner airlock door.

"Either works for me," she replied.

"Okay, I'll just surprise you. Until this evening, then."

"See you, space cowboy," she called after him as the door cycled shut.

There were no hydraulics in Daisy's shoes, but she had a noticeable spring in her step as she walked down the central passageway.

"Hey, Sarah, you ready to get crackin' on Starboard Nine?"

No reply.

"Sarah, come on already."

"I'm sorry, Daisy," Mal chimed in on open comms. "I am not reading Sarah's signal anywhere on board."

"Aw, hell. All right, Mal, thanks. I think I know where she is."

Daisy veered left and grabbed a hold of the cool smoothness of the inter-deck ladder, gently sliding the whole length to the lower deck. It was down there that Sarah had been working on the sticking airlock mechanism that controlled the long shaft that plunged through the entire ship all the way down to the shuttle mounted on its belly.

It was possible to climb down to it in a straight shot through the floor-mounted access airlock from the main deck, but the lower airlock door had been experiencing a lag in its opening sequence. Nothing major, just a few seconds of inconvenience, but Sarah always loved an interesting side project. Plus, the mysterious scribblings in the Narrows were much more interesting down there.

A tool bag Velcroed to the wall next to the open access panel on lower deck central passageway Pod Six confirmed Daisy's guess.

"Hey, Sarah!" Daisy shouted into the dimly lit, claustrophobic crawlspace. "Saaaaraaaaah!" Still no reply. "Damn. So much for an easy shift."

Daisy leaned forward and hauled herself into the Narrows and began crawling. If Sarah couldn't hear her, that meant she was most likely off on one of the side branches rather than the main crawlspace.

Left or right? Daisy mused as she reached the first junction a good fifteen meters in. *Eeny, meany, miny... ah, fuck it, I'm going left.* With an uncomfortable twist, Daisy rounded the bend and began the long crawl. Twenty meters later, she saw a brighter light shining from one of the even smaller side junctions containing the ship's dense crew cabin sensor arrays.

"Sarah!" she called out.

A muffled clang.

"Shit, you startled me, Daze," Sarah's voice drifted from the shaft. "Why didn't you just call me on comms?"

"I did, but one, you're not jacked in, and two, Mal lost you on her scans before you even climbed into the—Hey, are you wearing suit three?"

"Yeah, why?"

Daisy stared at her, amused eyebrow cocked.

"Oh, right. Suit three. I forgot about your mods. No wonder Mal lost track of me. I guess it shields from more than EM pulses. But I did plug my comms in at the junction."

Daisy looked, and indeed, the hard-line was plugged in, but there was no signal. One more thing to repair.

"We can fix that some other time. No one ever comes down here but you anyway. I don't know what you find so fascinating."

"It's all these notes and drawings," Sarah said. "I mean, have you ever really read them? Some of the things they wrote don't sound like the graffiti you'd expect from the construction crew. Like this one over here." She crawled forward a few more feet. "Hang on, where is it?"

Daisy scanned the smooth walls of the crawlspace, noting the occasional jottings of those who'd traveled its lengths before her.

"Dark in here, isn't it?" She laughed.

"What do you mean, Daze? There's plenty of light."

"No, on the bulkhead. Someone wrote that. '*Dark in here, isn't it?*' I wouldn't want to be stuck in here if the power went out. That'd be a very dark and very uncomfortable crawl back out."

"Don't creep me out, it's claustrophobic enough as it is," Sarah grumbled. "Ah, here we go. Check this one out. It says, '*Real stupidity beats artificial intelligence every time.*' Sounds to me like someone wasn't too thrilled with Mal sending them off to do repairs our resident supercomputer couldn't do herself."

"Well, we've seen what can happen when relays go wonky. Mal still isn't fully in control of all parts of the ship."

"It's nothing major," Sarah replied.

"Yeah, sure. At least that's what you keep telling me, Ms. Life Support Expert, but little things still keep glitching. I mean, you've crawled as much of this ship as I have, and the damage and wear seems far worse than you'd expect from our short little hop back to Earth."

"Freakin' space debris nearly killed us, Daisy."

"Yeah, sure, we took a big hit, and probably a few smaller ones that auto-repaired, but sometimes it feels like the *Vâli* was ready to fall apart before we even woke up. Why didn't Mal keep things in perfect running condition?"

Sarah pulled her legs tight and wriggled around to face her friend.

"How brilliant can a super-genius computer really be when she's small enough to fit in a box?" She paused and looked closely at her friend.

"What? Is something on my face?" Daisy asked.

Sarah smiled. "You're glowing. And not the radioactive kind. Someone got some action!"

Daisy blushed. "Shut up."

"No, really, good for you. But one thing, does he have multiple speeds?"

Daisy felt the laughter welling inside.

"Stop, I don't want to hyperventilate in here."

"Okay, but you can't blame a spinster for asking."

"I am so setting you up with Barry," Daisy chuckled.

The duo turned in the confined space and began the slow crawl back to the main passageway access.

"So, did you at least get the sticking door working while you were here, or were you too busy reading the words of wisdom of sweaty construction workers?"

"Seems to be working now. I just don't know why we use a shuttle that's such an outdated model. No AI whatsoever, and the components are an absolute pain in the ass to maintain."

"Yeah, not having an AI on it *is* kinda strange," Daisy agreed. "I mean, they're designed to be swappable from ship to ship, after all. Sure, they probably lose a little something by being so portable, but once they're plugged into a new command cradle, everything should work perfectly. Not like they don't have specs and control configurations of every ship ever made tucked away in those massive brains of theirs."

"So why a 'dumb' shuttle?"

"I don't know," Daisy admitted. "Maybe Mal didn't want to have a competing intelligence on board. Not like they could disconnect her and offline the entire ship while they carried her to the shuttle anyway. Though gravity would be off, so I suppose moving her would be easier."

"Life support would be off too, Daze, so there goes that idea."

"Well, speaking of zero-g, we have to get up to Starboard Nine and knock out the captain's busy work," Daisy said with a groan.

"I still don't know why you hate that pod so much," Sarah said. "It's fun."

"Zero-g is not fun. Maybe outside the ship during an EVA, but then at least you have a horizon line from the ship's hull. There's an up and a down, even if you can't feel it. Now that Starboard Nine is totally empty, it's just too easy to get disoriented in there."

"Nah, it's fun, you just have to be open minded and embrace it. Me, I love floating in zero-g without needing to wear an EVA suit. It's liberating."

"It makes *me* feel sick."

"You just have to let go of the notion of up and down. There is no up or down, just the direction you're going."

Daisy laughed grimly. "Sure, that's all well and good until gravity kicks in unexpectedly and you find yourself upside down on the ceiling. *Then* it would really help being right-side-up. And I mean *proper* right-side-up."

"You're such a downer," Sarah said.

"No, just a realist. You want to talk about a downer? Did you see the note on the bulkhead up in the upper deck Port Thirteen Narrows?"

"I must have missed that one. What did it say?"

"Lots of doom and gloom stuff in that one," Daisy replied. "Like someone was really not having a good day. Hang on, I copied a few of them." She wriggled to her side and pulled a small pad from her pocket. Even in space, pens and paper—a plasitcene/paper matrix, to be precise—were invaluable. Tablets break, batteries drain, but paper lasts.

"Okay, listen to this one. They wrote, '*Light thinks it travels faster than anything but it is wrong. No matter how fast light travels, it finds the darkness has already got there first, and is waiting for it.*'"

Sarah was silent a moment. "That's kind of messed up, Daisy."

"Yeah, but that doesn't mean it's not true."

She stopped crawling.

"Hey!"

"Hang on a minute," Daisy said, then pulled a fresh pen from her pocket and scratched out a message of her own, then started crawling again.

"'*Without a little darkness from time to time, man would forget that he dwells in the light,*'" Sarah read. "Who said that one, Daze?"

Daisy continued her crawl for the exit.

"I did."

As expected, Daisy felt her stomach flip after only a few minutes in Starboard Nine, but work was work, so she forced down the bile and focused on the panel in front of her.

"It still smells in here," she grumbled.

"Oh, come on, Daisy. Even after Mal purged all that nastiness into space, this pod was cleaned and scrubbed top to bottom. It's all in your head."

The zero-g pod had been one of Tamara's fertilizer experimentation lab spaces before the mishap. It was a smaller chamber, only ten meters long, but the tubs of decomposing plant matter and racks of condensed nutrient fluids had been more than enough to create a disgusting cloud of rotting nastiness when the pod's gravity had abruptly ceased functioning several months prior.

Barry had helped, able to ignore smells as easily as turning off a switch, as had Vince, and even Finn, when they weren't busy with engineering tasks, but the bulk of the cleanup had fallen to Sarah and Daisy. Compressed air was used to blast every seam and riveted joint where debris might have lodged itself, an attached vacuum system sucking the bits of waste into a disposal bag before they could contaminate anything further. The process had taken weeks, but Sarah was correct, the empty pod was as clean as any compartment in the ship. Maybe cleaner, even.

"I can't wait till we reach Dark Side. Let the maintenance crews do all this dirty work while we head home and sip margaritas on a beach." Sarah smiled at the thought as she changed out a temperature regulator. "Okay, that was the last one. You wanna join me for a night session of Tai Chi? Maybe we could practice in zero-g. You seem to have acclimated."

"I'm actually training with Vince tonight."

"Oh, that's what you call it." Sarah flashed a mischievous grin.

"Ha-ha. He's been showing me some fighting stuff. I guess with all the wrestling around it was only natural, eventually. Anyway, I'm gonna get a quick scrub, then go track him down. I'll see you at dinner, though."

"Sounds good. Don't let him beat you up too badly. I would hate to have to kick his ass for you."

. . .

Standing in the galley kitchen, Vince smiled down on his handiwork. Not bad. Not bad at all.

"I still don't get why you won't just let me do it for you," Finn said as he slid a tiny tray into the modified heating unit he'd jury-rigged in his workspace.

"I told you, man, I know the replicator can do it, but it just means more if I make them myself." Vince measured a teaspoon of vanilla and poured it into the ceramisteel bowl in front of him, folding it into the thickening mixture.

The eggs were in a pourable container, with no hens on board to lay shell-covered ones, but the other ingredients lay strewn about the counter much as bakers had done for millennia. Flour, butter, sugar, white and brown, baking soda, baking powder, chocolate chips. Even some pressed, rolled oats the food replicator had managed to produce despite Finn's proclivity for having the machine provide the steel-cut variety.

"She's gonna flip. I mean, coming from you, it would be expected, but me baking cookies for her? And by hand, no less? That's gonna to sweep her off her feet."

Finnegan laughed as he wiped down the counter.

"Seriously, Vince, you're gonna get some anyway, cookies or not."

"Well, duh. But it's not about that. We're stuck way out here, a bazillion miles out in space, so that kind of limits the nice things I can do for my girlfriend, ya know? But this? This is something I can do."

"With my help."

"With your help, obviously. I mean, I'm a pretty terrible cook, normally."

"I know. We all know."

"Zip it," Vince said with a laugh. "Anyway, I really do appreciate you helping me out. Even just a little bit of romance goes a hell of a long way in making a woman feel loved and appreciated."

Finn's smile faltered ever so slightly.

"Oh, dude. Why don't you just tell her?" Vince urged.

"You've been talking to Daisy, I see."

"No. Well, yes. But no, that's not how I know. It's obvious you like Sarah, so why not make a move?"

Finn popped a few chocolate chips in his mouth, slowly chewing as he sought the right answer.

"The time isn't right," he finally replied. "Not yet. But soon."

"Okay, man, it's your life. I just wouldn't want you to wait too long."

Finnegan just smiled, then pulled the first of the small trays from the food reheating unit he had modified to help his friend on his quest for cookies.

"Oh, those smell amazing," he said. "Even if it was you who made them."

"Ha-ha. Thanks a lot," Vince joked.

"Don't mention it. Though once we're on Dark Side base I'll have a proper oven at my disposal. *Then* I'll show you how it's *really* done."

"I look forward to it. For now, just find me a box to put these in. I've got a hot date."

CHAPTER SEVEN

A few months prior, Vincent had introduced Daisy to an unusual sport he'd discovered on a media chip containing athletics documentation spanning several centuries. It was an obscure practice, but one that caught his eye.

Chessboxing.

The rules were simple enough. Alternating rounds of five minutes with the winner decided by either checkmate or knockout. Its origins seemed to have been either Germany or Russia, and really, either would have made sense given the nature of the contest.

He had shown the videos to Daisy one afternoon on a whim, and, surprisingly, she was hooked. Thus, their new couple's pastime began. Mind you, they didn't compete in actual boxing. Vince was much larger and far too proficient at that, but they did play a lot of chess.

After months of no-holds-barred brutality, where pawns and knights alike were savaged by ravaging bishops and queens, Daisy was finally holding her own in their matches. What she didn't tell him was she had removed a few filters from her neuro-stim, allowing her to increase the trickle flow of chess strategies and game theory she downloaded as she slept. At long last, the mild headaches had finally paid off.

"Checkmate!" she cried out triumphantly.

About goddamn time too! she mused.

"Impressive," Vince said as he studied the board. "Wow. Totally did not see that coming."

"Silent Death. Like a ninja, only sexier." She smiled coyly. "Now come on and get sweaty with your woman."

"Don't have to tell me twice."

Vincent moved the chess set back to its drawer, retracted the table deep into the hidden recesses of the wall, and began to limber up.

"So, you think you can handle me, eh?"

"I'm looking forward to trying," she said with a little smile.

"Okay, then. How about working on your stand-up game today? Or would you rather we get horizontal for a while?"

"Why not both?"

Vince smiled. "I'll get the pads, then."

A few minutes later a thin sheen of sweat glistened from his arms as he parried and dodged Daisy's attacks. Vince was far stronger than she was, and keeping that in mind, he had taught her early on to not try to out-power him, but rather, to use her speed and agility to her advantage, though her strength was increasing at a healthy pace as they upped the intensity of their training.

"That all you got?" she teased, dodging a slow roundhouse kick.

Vince snapped a quick jab, lightly tapping her forehead.

"Don't get too cocky, now," he chuckled through his mouth guard.

Daisy threw a combination at him, a flurry of rapid punches followed by a faked leg kick that transitioned into a knee to the ribs. With her somewhat questionable style, the move took him by surprise. An amused grin spread on his face as he launched a counterattack, launching quick punches as he advanced.

Her footwork shifted as she adopted a stance he hadn't taught her.

Vince paused, but only a moment as he wondered what she was doing. Then he pressed the attack.

Daisy's chin tucked further as her elbows dropped tight to her body, almost to her center-line. With squared hips, she began quickly parrying his jabs, speeding her hands as she redirected his attacks, following with a series of quick counter punches.

Faster and faster they went, hands a flurry of speed as Vince found himself unable to land a single blow. Her hands were simply too quick.

Without warning, as it should be in combat, Vince threw a looping roundhouse punch. It was an easy-to-read fake, but rather than the spinning back-fist follow-up that Daisy expected, he dropped low, sweeping her legs out from under her.

Daisy hit the mat hard, but was quickly scrambling to bounce back to her feet when Vince rolled on top of her.

"You had enough?" he asked, sweat dripping from his forehead.

"I was about to ask you the same thing," she replied with a smile. "You think you're '*up*' for a different challenge?" she asked with sparkling eyes.

They both spat out their mouthguards and locked lips in a deep kiss, tongues engaged in a far different type of combat.

"Damn, woman!" Vince gasped when they finally broke their embrace. "You're insatiable."

"That didn't sound like a no to me."

"That's because it wasn't," he answered with a hungry smile. "But not here. These mats? Nasty! How about something different? Maybe, Starboard Nine?"

"Stop asking, Vince. I'm not doing it in zero-g. Besides, I'm the one who'd have to clean the place up afterwards."

"But think of the fun," he said.

"But think of the nausea, and bruises, and mess," Daisy replied.

The heavy airlock door quietly cycled open across the room.

"Hey, guys," Reggie said to the sweaty pair on the ground. "Am I getting a show with my workout today?"

"Eww, Reggie," Daisy chuckled.

"Yeah, gross, dude," Vince added.

"Hey, with you two, I never know." He laughed jovially as he hefted a massive kettlebell from its secure rack with his non-metal hand.

Come lunchtime, Daisy and Vince joined Sarah, Tamara, and the others in the galley to see what Finn had dreamed up this time.

Tamara's crop of zucchini and crooknecks had been prolific, as squash tend to be, and Finn, presented with a wealth of produce to work with, had endeavored to transform ordinary vegetables into a masterpiece of seasoning and texture.

"Mouth feel," he'd often say, "is as important as flavor."

The yellow squash were roasted, then carefully diced, while the deep green zucchini had been spun in Finn's mechanical hand while his human one held a knife to it. The result was a massive bowl of thin pasta-looking zucchini strands that he seasoned with fresh garlic and a flavorful olive oil of his own design. Trees couldn't be grown on the ship. There simply wasn't enough room, so for things like olives and tree fruits, he relied on Mal's food replicators. Luckily, there were several high-quality genetic templates from which to fabricate his desired supplies.

For those who wanted it, a tasty Bolognese sauce was offered in both vegetarian and meat varieties. Tamara stuck with her herbivore option, while the others dug into the hearty meat sauce.

"Hey, Finn, what's the meat in this? It's got a stronger flavor," Gustavo noted.

"Buffalo. Thought I'd try something different. You like it?"

"Yeah, it's really tasty. Good one, man," Gus said through his full mouth.

"So, how was your workout, you two?" Sarah asked, flashing Daisy a sideways grin.

Vince thankfully missed it, or at least he pretended to. "Daisy finally beat me at chess today," he said. "Plus, she is getting really good at sparring. It's like her body knows what to do even before I show her."

Sarah's jaw clenched, and her lips twitched, but she managed to keep a straight face.

Barely.

Daisy blushed. "Yeah, about that. I should come clean. I kind of cheated a little."

"Daisy, you can't cheat at sparring. You either got it or you don't."

"Yeah, but I got it because I added some kung fu to my neuro a few weeks ago."

"A few weeks? That's not nearly enough time to make any sort of a difference. That skill? It's all you, babe."

Daisy hesitated a moment, her face transitioning to a deeper red.

"Yeah, about those few weeks of neuro time..."

"What did you do, Daze?" Sarah prodded.

"I kinda pulled a few inhibitors as well. Nothing major, just enough to speed things up a bit."

Tamara dropped her fork and flashed an angry look.

"For fuck's sake, Daisy, you'll fry your goddamn brain tampering with that thing."

"I've got it under control, Tamara. I am the ship's resident tech guru, after all."

"Hey!" her friend interjected.

"Sorry," she apologized to Sarah. "*One* of the ship's tech gurus."

"I don't care how clever you are, that's dangerous stuff you're fiddling with. There's a good reason those things have a dozen inhibitors on them. You think they'd have built in that much redundancy into the safeties if they didn't have to? Jesus, you're like a fucking child!"

"Oh, come on, Tamara. You're a goddamn botanist. What do you know about tech, and neuros and combat training? Just take your Swiss Army arm and stick with playing in the dirt."

"Hey, not cool!" Finn called from the galley.

"Yeah, Daze, that's fucked up," Gus added. "I suppose I should take my Swiss Army head and stick to navigating the ship. At high speeds. While not getting us killed, I might add."

Daisy shrank in her seat.

"Guys, I'm sorry, I didn't mean it like that."

"You're a bigot," Tamara said, slamming her seat back as she rose. "Finn, box this up for me. I'm going to eat with my plants. They have better manners."

"I'm right behind you," Gus said.

Daisy, for once, didn't know what to say. Instead, she sat quietly as Tamara and Gus stormed out the airlock door.

She had tried to calm her mind after dinner. A centering meditation trick she'd learned from Sarah. Sitting quietly on the floor, Daisy focused on her breathing, trying to isolate each muscle in her body, becoming aware of every fiber of her being. Only her being was simply too wound-up.

"Dammit," she grumbled as she got to her feet.

Okay, let's try something a little more dynamic.

The breathing was the same. Focusing energy as she concentrated on her body, but this time she was in motion. Ever so slowly, but in motion nonetheless. The first dozen movements in the lengthy Tai Chi routine flowed easily, and with them, she felt her stress dissipate. It was effortless, and for a moment, she actually understood what Sarah had been trying to teach her about the technique.

Ten more movements into the series, Daisy began forgetting what was next, and what had started as a relaxing endeavor quickly became another source of stress.

Frustrated, she gave up.

I've got to make this right.

Daisy cycled open her pod's double doors and walked to Gustavo's quarters, then paused. After a long minute, she took a deep breath and keyed his comms pad.

"*Yeah, what is it?*"

"Gus, it's Daisy, can I talk to you a minute?"

There was a lengthy pause before he answered.

"*Okay, hang on.*"

She felt, more than heard, the heavy inner door slide open and closed. Moments later the door to the corridor quietly opened.

"Look, Gus, I don't know how better to say it than I'm sorry. Sometimes when I get heated I just say shit I shouldn't. I know it's not your fault you were in an accident, and I didn't mean to be so insensitive. I wasn't thinking." She tried to sound as convincing as she could, pushing back the sense of unease his artificial eye always brought her. At least the patch of gleaming metal skull had some hair flopped over it.

She heard a tiny servo as his eye shifted focus on her.

"Well, I guess I forgive you, then," he relented. "I knew you didn't really mean it, but it was a shit thing to say, Daisy."

"I know, and I'm really, really sorry."

"Well, don't worry about me. We're okay. Tamara? She's a bit more sensitive about her enhancements."

"Yeah, I'm going to see her next."

"Good luck with that."

He paused before closing the door. Daisy focused on his human eye.

"So we're good?" she asked.

"Yeah, we're good. But we'd be better if you brought brownies."

"I'll ask Finn to whip up a batch in the morning."

"Cool. G'night, Daisy."

"Night, Gus."

His door closed, leaving Daisy to her next stop. Unlike Gustavo, however, Tamara was one to hold a grudge.

"*Who is it?*" her voice asked through the comms box.

"Tamara, it's Daisy. Look, I was wondering if we could talk a minute. I wanted to—"

"*Fuck off.*" The comms went silent.

Okay, then. Looks like I need to give her a bit more time to cool off, Daisy grumbled to herself. *Guess I'll try again tomorrow.*

She turned from the angry woman's door and padded off to the comfort of Vince's shoulder and an old movie.

2001: A Space Odyssey. It was old, it was weird, and it was really, really slow. Maybe on any other day she'd have enjoyed the film, but this wasn't the day. That and the creepy computer with its unblinking red eye creeped her out. HAL was the villain and he was a prick, but what was most frightening was how, despite his actions, she could see how he *believed* what he was doing was right.

It was so very much not the kind of entertainment she'd been hoping for that evening. Nonetheless, it was comforting there, curled up against Vince on his bed, and he had actually made her cookies. Like, real, homemade cookies. It was one of the sweetest things she could imagine, both figuratively and literally, so she watched the whole movie with him, all the way through, even if this particular choice wasn't to her liking. Fortunately, the steady supply of sweets took the edge off in a most delicious manner.

Why he kept opting for old space movies, she never could figure, though she had to admit the Alien series had been rather fun, if wholly inaccurate about space travel.

As the creepy computer on the screen started singing her name, Daisy decided that *she* was picking the next movie they watched together.

A comedy, most likely.

A few hours later, Daisy walked back to her quarters, still ruminating over her careless insult. She liked Tamara, at least when she wasn't being gruff, which honestly wasn't all that often. *Bigoted? Prejudiced?* Was she really those things? *It's just that those replacement parts aren't natural,* she rationalized. *It's perfectly normal to be creeped out a little, right?* Even if true, she needed to keep her tongue in check and smooth things over with the *multiple* people she'd managed to insult.

She entered her pod and sealed the heavy double doors behind her and took a seat on her bed.

I hate this! I need to be able to turn off my brain. To find something to occupy my mind to help me unwind.

She looked at the neuro-stim unit a moment, a brief flush of self-loathing rising like bile. For all her dislike of technologically altered people, she still relied on the neuro. She bent her own logic to justify its use, she knew, but it had proven far too useful to just put aside.

It's not the same as metal limbs, she rationalized, then began scanning its data stores for the one thing she thought might actually help.

Gotcha.

Daisy loaded the Tai Chi program into her already-overflowing feed queue, then began typing a rapid series of commands into the device. Several flashing lights and warning tones later, the neuro-stim was ready for her night's sleep.

It was only a couple more inhibitors, she rationalized. *Still plenty of them left.*

Daisy placed the thin band on her head and activated the machine, then lay back onto her bed, looking forward to the new information she'd wake up with.

Tai Chi, she mused as she drifted off to sleep. *I'm going to know Tai Chi.*

CHAPTER EIGHT

"What's cookin', Finn?" Gus called out as he strode through the airlock door. Despite Finnegan's other duties, like maintaining the hydroponic systems, the mess hall was most certainly his culinary domain.

"Come on, amigo, I'm starving!" Gustavo groused before swiping a piece of toast from the counter.

"Hold your horses, I'm working on it," the mad chef replied. "And, by the way, don't you have a ship to be flying?"

"Not my job," Gus replied. "I'm the navigator, remember?"

"Fine. A course to be plotting, then?"

"Only my job if the AI goes on the fritz or needs extra manpower. Mal's fine on her own at the moment."

"You're killing me, man." Finn laughed. "I'll have something for ya in a couple of minutes. You want spicy?" His knife was a blur as it slapped out a staccato rhythm against the cutting board, Tamara's bounty of vegetables quickly cut into tiny pieces. Taking big things and cutting them into smaller things seemed to be a task that most chefs had quite a proclivity for.

"Spice is nice, my man, so yeah, kick it up a notch if you want. Hey, you got red peppers over there?" Gustavo asked as the quiet servos adjusted the focal ring on his cybernetic eye to get a better look across the room.

"Yeah, Tamara just picked 'em today."

"Pretty handy, having all those gardening tool attachments she can swap out. She's hands down got the most kickass upgrade on the ship. Beats the hell out of your weak-ass arm. Maybe you could talk to Mal and see if she'll hook you up with a built-in knife, or a blender attachment or something."

"Ha-ha, funny guy. Now shut up and let me work."

The rhythmic sound of chopping started again, and the pile of sliced and diced vegetables quickly grew into a small mountain.

The doors quietly slid open again.

"Hey, Finn, what's cooking?"

"Jeez, Reggie, is everyone going to keep asking me that?"

"Yup. Until we're chowing down anyway," he answered.

"Go fly the ship, Reg."

"Captain's shift," the co-pilot said with a chuckle.

"So you decided to come harass me."

"Yup." He reached out and snatched a piece of chopped pepper from the cutting board. Finn took exception to the invasion of his work space and flicked his wrist, sending the knife darting toward Reggie's polished-silver hand in a blur.

Clang.

"Dude, not cool! Just because it's metal doesn't mean you can just go beating on my hand, man."

"Fingers off my cutting board, then."

"Quit bickering, you two," Vince called out as he and Daisy stepped in through the airlock door. "I swear, y'all are like caffeinated toddlers around here."

"Look who's talking, Mr. Half-hour Showers."

"At least I'm clean."

"In body if not mind," Gustavo chimed in.

"Oh, that's most assuredly not clean," Daisy added with a smirk.

The co-pilot flashed them a look and shuddered.

"Great. We drink that recycled water. Thanks, guys. Thanks a lot. There goes my appetite."

"Reggie, *nothing* kills your appetite."

"Funny you should say that, because today I'm making a special—"

Finn's piercing shriek startled them all, but not nearly as much as the blood spurting from his lone human hand, while his mechanical arm kept chopping, flailing dangerously, the knife held tight in its grip.

"Shut it off!" Finn cried out, angling his body away from the runaway appendage.

"Reggie, grab his wrist while I get to the access from behind!" Vince called out.

"Dude's waving a knife around, Vince! You grab it."

"Reggie, your hand's metal, for fuck's sake!" Gus shouted. "Hurry up and grab him!"

"Dammit," Reg grumbled as he cautiously closed in on the flailing arm. "Turn toward me, Finn, and if you have any control, don't stab me!" His arm moved at human speed, but his mechanical hand flew true, metal fingers deftly wrapping around the injured chef's wrist and pinning the arm to the cutting board.

"Quick, get a towel!" Vince shouted as he darted behind Finn and started unbolting the access on the back of his arm. Daisy rushed to the rack and yanked the first clean towel she could find, tossing it to Gustavo, who tightly wrapped Finn's hand.

The material quickly blossomed crimson.

"He's still spurting!" Gus shouted.

"I know! Just hang on a second longer, I've almost got it." A metallic clang rang out as the access panel on Finn's arm fell to the deck. "Daisy, your hands are smaller, reach in there and pull the connection."

She scurried to Vincent's side and slid her fingers into the small opening in Finn's arm. "Hang on... Got it!"

Finnegan's arm flopped limp, the knife dropped from its lifeless hand.

"I received notification of an emergency situation. What is the status?" Barry stood just inside the doorway. In all the commotion, he had somehow arrived with no one even noticing. "An injury! Please, allow me to assist."

The cyborg picked up the injured man as easily as if he were a child and quickly rushed him through the double doors and down the passageway to the medical pod.

"Mal, get Doc McClain to medical, and notify the captain that Finn has been injured," Vince shouted.

"I have notified them both, Vincent. I have also prepared an auto-sedation unit in medical should it be required."

"Wait!" Daisy called out. "His fingers!"

Vince, never the squeamish one, didn't hesitate. "I've got 'em," he said as he snatched up the three bloody digits from the cutting board and took off to the med pod.

The unexpected burst of adrenaline was a shock to her system, and Daisy found herself a little queasy as she looked at the pool of blood coating Finn's work area.

"Hey, you don't look so hot. Go sit down and take a few deep breaths. We'll clean this up," Gustavo offered. Her legs a bit wobbly, Daisy decided that was a fantastic bit of advice.

"What the hell was that?" Reggie asked. "I mean, did you see his arm, man? It was going nuts, like it had a mind of its own."

Gustavo retrieved some gloves and cleaning supplies from the sanitation compartment flush-mounted next to the refuse disposal and compost repurposing unit.

"Well, technically his arm *does* have a mind of its own, just not a very sophisticated one," he answered. "My guess is they'll have to do an AI wipe and reinstall once they run diagnostics."

Daisy's ears perked up at that.

"Wait, his arm is an actual AI?" she asked, stunned. "I thought it was just a mechanical enhancement."

"Well, not a full AI like Mal or Barry. What the more complex replacement limbs have is more like a basic task awareness unit to help the mechanical interface respond to the electric impulses sent from the host's nervous system. There's no *real* consciousness there. No complex thought. I suppose you could even call it a 'dumb' AI, if you wanted an apt descriptor for it. Basically, it just helps interpret what the wearer wants it to do."

Daisy looked at Reggie's hand a little uncomfortably.

"Hang on, so does that mean his hand could go haywire at any time?"

"Nah. Reggie's hand is far less complicated than a whole arm replacement. I'd wager it only has the tiniest of boosters right about at the seam where they joined the reinforced flesh to the metal, but nothing like what Finn has, and certainly nowhere near Tamara's."

"I guess with all those different attachments she can swap out, her arm would have to be a bit more... what should I call it? Robust?" Reggie pondered.

"Seems like a bit of overkill for a gardener," Daisy said.

"Ooh, don't let her hear you call her that. Best to stick with *botanist* if you know what's good for you."

"Oh, I'm already on her shit list," Daisy lamented. "Doubt I could do much to make it any worse. And now Finn's out of action for a while."

"Yeah, did you see that? I wonder what the hell happened," Gus said.

"I don't know. Maybe he was watching some contraband

porn and got a virus," Daisy said with a dark, gallows humor chuckle.

A look of concern flashed across Gustavo and Reggie's faces.

"Not a virus!" Gus blurted. "What are you talking about? The ship is totally firewalled, and besides, out here in the middle of nowhere, there's nowhere for a virus to even come from!" A hint of red colored his cheeks.

"Okay, okay, take it easy. It was just a joke. Don't worry, you guys aren't going to suddenly go haywire. I get it," she conceded. "Anyway, thanks for cleaning up, I'm going to head to my work pod. I think I need a little quiet time."

Deep down in the belly of the ship, Daisy sat silently amongst her beloved tools, surrounded by a daunting mountain of assorted gadgets that needed repairing. She had thought giving her hands something to do would help take her mind off Finn's screaming and all that blood, but, unfortunately, the devices strewn around her were providing more frustration than relief.

This stuff isn't even part of my normal duty assignment, she lamented. *I don't see why we don't just wait until we reach Dark Side and let the techs there handle it. I know the captain wants them fixed, but I can't for the life of me figure out what's wrong with these. And why do we have so many old environmental probes and med scanners?*

While Daisy and Sarah were the two tech experts on board, neither had been trained in portable electronics repair, with all their miniaturized parts. They'd been prepped to handle only the larger systems that kept the *Váli* up and running. She had added some additional repair protocols to her neuro feed when Mal asked her if she wouldn't mind seeing about working on them, but at the rate she was learning the new information, it was a bust so far.

It takes years to properly absorb that stuff. I'd be just as well-off wearing a blindfold and going by instinct, she thought.

Her body still felt on-edge. Abuzz. The adrenaline surge from Finn's accident had left her discombobulated, a state of being she was entirely unfond of. *Okay, work isn't going to cut it. What the hell, I'm going to take a few minutes of 'me' time.*

Daisy pushed the medical scanner and mountain of components crowding her worktable back a bit to give herself a little more room and took a seat in her chair. Then she focused on something she did every moment of her life but never really paid much attention to.

She focused on breathing.

Slow and steady, deep but not over-oxygenating herself to the point of hyperventilation, that was the ticket, and gradually, she felt her body start to settle down and her mind release its panic-grip on the bloody scene she'd witnessed. Everything was becoming less intense as the harshness slowly trickled away, but still, she couldn't make it over that final hump.

Whatever the block was, it didn't seem to want to go anywhere no matter what she did, so rather than focus on it and get all wound-up and frustrated again, Daisy decided to give her brain something to do. She chose to run through her newly-upgraded Tai Chi lessons, but given the clutter of her workspace, she did so in her mind.

The first forty movements came to her easily, as they typically would when she wasn't distracted. The motions that came after, however, were where she always had problems.

Today was different.

Perhaps it was because she had "primed the pump" by meditating before beginning, maybe it was the adrenaline still in her system, or perhaps it was the simple act of taking out the physical body-awareness aspect. Whatever the cause, Daisy whipped through the entire series in her mind with perfect ease.

When she repeated the feat a second time just as easily, a little smile grew on her face.

The combination of breathing and focus also made her feel something new. She felt a ball of warmth in her belly, flowing through her body in a cycle from crown to tailbone. It was Qi Gong breathing and energy work, one of the first things Sarah had taught her, and suddenly, it all made sense.

Meditation, Qi Gong, and Tai Chi were an open book, she realized. Whether it was entirely due to the inhibitor-lessened neuro feed, or just her own nascent understanding, Daisy felt the beginning of a new awareness tugging at the edges of her consciousness. Everything she'd been drip feeding was beginning to color the storage regions of her mind, awakening areas of knowledge she hadn't thought she was absorbing at all.

I get it, she thought. *The inhibitors weren't just in the neuro stim. I had blocks hindering me in my brain too.*

Daisy opened her eyes but maintained a soft gaze, taking in the space around her with a calm, heightened perception. Breathing steadily, basking in the feeling of positive progress and healthy energy in her body, Daisy didn't even notice her hands instinctively moving in front of her as her mind began to unlock its tightly held secrets.

An hour later, she gently pulled herself out of the near-trance state, relaxed and calm, but also knowing she really should get back to work.

Then she noticed the medical scanner in front of her. That and the entirely new device sitting beside it.

What the hell?

While not plugged in to a power source, the scanner was back together in one piece, a small pile of ruined components off to one side, where she had apparently placed them as she effected the repairs without even realizing she was doing it.

Somehow she *knew* the machine would work now. All those

repair protocol drip-loads were there, she had just never known how to access them.

Until now.

The other device was something entirely different, she realized. It was a manifestation of one of the crazy ideas she'd had but never thought to actually even try to build. A plasma modulator that would internally merge a series of cascading energy fields until they build up a greater level of energy potential than their individual parts.

It was a tiny unit, easily able to fit in both hands, but if her theory was correct, the deceptively small device could amplify power fields far more than anyone would expect. Looking at her creation with curious eyes, she wondered if she could actually make it functional.

Tuning out and letting her mind flow free from the tangle of her conscious thoughts was apparently the key, she realized. And not just the key to Tai Chi, it seemed.

Huh, so that's how it works, she mused, excited by the discovery. *I wonder what other things I can do.*

CHAPTER NINE

"I told you, Doc, I'm fine. I just got a little light headed is all. It was a lot of adrenaline, that's it. I mean, it's not every day someone chops off their fingers in front of you."

Doctor McClain studied Daisy with a practiced gaze. As not only the ship's doctor, but also psychologist, her raison d'être was to ensure the crew didn't go mad (or worse) during their voyage. The austere woman tapped her pen against her leg unconsciously as she assessed her patient. Little did she know, the faint metallic clinking sound put Daisy even more on edge.

Replacement parts.

It seemed everyone on board had them, everyone but Daisy, Vince, and Sarah. The flesh-and-blood musketeers.

"Daisy, are you listening?"

"Sorry, what? I spaced out for a minute."

"I was saying I want you to take it easy today."

"Doc, I already had a really productive bit of downtime. I'm good, my spirits are high, and my batteries are charged. Figuratively, that is."

"Even so, I know you haven't been sleeping well these last few months, and it concerns me. You know, Daisy, proper REM sleep is how the brain deals with events and problems you've encountered during the day. If you are unable to get good, deep sleep, your mind will remain exhausted."

"My sleep has actually been a bit better lately. Sarah showed me some meditation techniques, and I've finally got my neuro-stim dialed in just right."

"Mal and I have both warned you about tinkering with that, Daisy. The technology is far beyond your training."

"I know, but it just seemed so, I don't know, *intuitive*, ya know? Like I had this idea how to make it better and it actually worked. Who knows, when we get back to Earth, maybe I'll even transition into a new job. 'Enter the exciting field of neuro stimulation devices! Sign up now!'"

"So, you're excited to see Earth? How long has it been, Daisy? How long since you first headed out into space?"

"Wow, I haven't even thought about that in forever. I mean, I don't remember how old I was when I left. I was just a little girl, but I've been dreaming of it a lot."

"Oh?" McClain seemed intrigued. "And what are your dreams about?"

"Mostly the fresh air, the trees, seeing the ocean and smelling the salty breeze."

"And what of the people?"

"People? Uh, I almost never actually have any in my dreams. Is that normal?"

McClain jotted a note on her tablet.

"Perfectly. You're just focused on the Earth you know, and your mind has fixated on it. Once we stop at Dark Side, we'll delve deeper into your Earth dreams and memories, but for the time being, so long as you are getting rest, I see no issues. Now, speaking of rest, I really do want you to take the afternoon off."

"Can't, Doc. I've got an EVA in an hour. Captain needs that comms array fixed, and I don't think the concept of taking a break due to stress is something that exists in his world."

"Perhaps you could send Barry in your place. I'm sure he'd be happy to help out."

Daisy gritted her teeth and forced a normal expression onto her face.

A cyborg doing my job? Messing up my hard work? Not on my watch.

"Thanks, Doc, but I'll be fine. It was just the shock of all that blood is all. Anyway, I really should be getting to it. Nothing like a little work to take your mind off unpleasantness, right?"

"Very well, but do take it easy, and contact me the instant you feel unwell. Agreed?"

"Will do. Thanks again."

The inner airlock door quietly whooshed open, and Daisy stepped into the space between them.

"See ya later, Doc," she said as the door shut behind her.

Then nothing.

"Oh, come on. Seriously?" She pushed the flickering button to the second door. "Open, you stupid thing."

Still no-go.

She keyed the comms panel. "Hey, Mal, could you take a look at the relay on Doc McClain's door system? I'm stuck in here between her office and the central passageway."

"I'm not showing a fault, Daisy," Mal replied. "What seems to be the issue?"

"The issue is I'm stuck in here, and while I'm not claustrophobic, and I know there's plenty of air, I'd still rather not spend my entire afternoon in here. Can you try an override from Command?"

"Stand by, please. I will attempt a pod-level reboot. This may take a moment, I need to inform Doctor McClain she will experience a brief loss of power and artificial gravity. Once she has secured all items of concern, I will begin the process."

"Great."

Three minutes went by before the lights flickered, then went out, along with the artificial gravity, leaving Daisy floating in the dark.

"Oh, yeah, that's *much* better," she groused.

Slowly, the lights and gravity cycled back on. Feet solidly on the ground again, Daisy tried the exit sequence once more, and once more, the door would not open.

"No love, Mal. I'm gonna pop the panel and see if I can't hotwire this one relay. If it's just that part of the mechanism itself, I can swap it out with a replacement after my EVA."

"Very well, Daisy," Mal replied. "I believe the Narrows in that section were scheduled to be given a once-over by you and Sarah. Has that occurred?"

"What are you trying to say, Mal? Me and Sarah screwed up? We already went through this part of the network, and everything checked out fine. I'm beginning to think we may be suffering from some contact faults in the pod interlock mechanisms themselves. Might explain some of the signal lags and glitches."

"That is a definite possibility; however, at our current speed, it would be not only impractical to attempt to dislodge and reconfigure the pods, but would also be very unsafe. Far beyond mission parameters, in fact."

"Well, that settles it, then. We just have to wait until we hit Dark Side base to let the techs there deal with the underlying issue. For now, let's just jury-rig this thing to work for the next few days until we get there."

She popped the cover to the control panel open and began testing the dozens of wires with the pocket-sized voltage meter she carried at pretty much all times.

"Found what seems to be the problem," she said a few minutes later. "Looks like the drive coupling has power but somehow jiggled loose. Must've been improperly seated, and the vibrations shook it out over time. That's an easy fix. I'll just push it back in and—"

The door hissed open far faster than its safeties should have allowed.

"Whoa, easy there," she said, jumping back. "Hey, Mal, it's working, but I want you to keep an eye on this door until Sarah and I can give it a proper once-over. Something still seems wonky about it."

"Very well, Daisy. Thank you for your assistance."

"Hey, it's what I do."

She stepped out into the passageway and nearly toppled over Barry, where he stood just outside the doorway.

"Daisy, my apologies. I did not know you would be there."

"Uh, no problem, Barry."

"Finn is doing fine."

"What?"

"I thought you would want to know his status. Finnegan is doing fine."

"Oh, thanks." She softened a bit. "You did good, Barry, getting him to medical so quickly. I don't know how you got to him so fast after the accident, but good work."

"I aim to help any way I can. I'm sure Finn will soon be back to work, and better than before."

Something about the way he said the word *better* made Daisy ever so slightly uncomfortable.

"Wait, you did what now?" Sarah looked at Daisy with a questioning gaze.

"I said I hacked into his file. Look, I was curious, okay? Besides, it was the absolute lowest level of encryption, so it couldn't have been that big a deal, right?"

Her friend did not relent with her disapproving gaze.

"He's your boyfriend, Daze. Why didn't you simply *ask him* when his birthday is?"

"Well, yeah, obviously that's an option, but that's the *boring* option. Besides, a surprise isn't a surprise when the surprisee isn't surprised by their surprise."

"You practiced saying that, didn't you?"

"Maybe once or twice," Daisy replied with a grin.

"Okay, so let's just say I'm okay with you hacking into the crew's files to find out Vince's birthday—which I'm totally not, by the way—then what do you plan on doing with that information? And hey, you're a wire-pulling tech monkey, not a code geek. How did you even know how to do that?"

Daisy blushed and looked away.

"Jesus, Daze! Another mod to your neuro stim? You've gotta stop switching off those inhibitors before you fry your brain."

"Hey, I've still got nearly all of them left," she said.

Technically only four, if you want to be specific, but that's only a slight exaggeration, Daisy mused to herself.

"Plenty of redundancies to protect me," she continued. "And besides, I only added a few relatively simple coding protocols I thought might come in handy, which they have, by the way. It's really cool, actually. I think I've finally figured out how to get all those little neuro-stim upgrades to work." She paused, a slight look of unease on her face.

"What? What aren't you telling me?" Sarah asked.

"Well, the weird bit is sometimes it feels like there are things in there that I shouldn't even have in my feed."

"Like what?"

"I don't know, I only get flashes of them. But crazy stuff. Advanced AI design, ship specs, even the medical equipment. Did I mention I think I got that portable scanner working?"

"But that's been busted for nearly five months."

"I know, and I didn't even add any new repair protocols to my feed this time. It just happened. Like I said, crazy."

"I wonder..." Sarah mused.

"What?"

"I was just thinkin', all of our neuro-stims are routed through dedicated servers in our quarters before tying in to the ship's primary storage banks, but during cryo we all shared that one main hub. I wonder if maybe something glitched and started trickling other people's feeds into yours. Like medical info. That's Doctor McClain's area. Or ship specs. You'd expect the captain or Reggie or even Gus to be downloading that data, not you."

"You think that's a possibility?"

"Hell if I know. Your guess is as good as mine, but so far as I can tell, you're the only one it happened to. I just hope you don't lobotomize yourself fiddling around with the thing. That's some dangerous tech if used improperly."

"Would I ever do that?"

Sarah didn't dignify that with a response.

"So, what's this surprise you want to do for Vince's birthday?"

A huge smile broke free on Daisy's face. "I'm going to bake him a cake!"

"Seriously? With what?"

"Well, Vince baked me cookies. Actual handmade cookies, can you believe it? Anyway, I wanted to one-up him, and Finn said he'd hook me up with some substitutions that should work. It won't be a totally traditional birthday cake, but it should do the trick."

"And would that trick be getting you laid?"

"Oh, honey, I don't need a cake for that."

Sarah laughed.

"All right, I'll help you with the festivities. What else do you need? And don't say candles. You know how the captain is about fire on board."

"I was thinking balloons."

"Balloons?"

"Yeah. Think you can wrangle something up? We have helium in the labs, so..."

Gears turned in Sarah's mind.

"I think I can manage that. All that Mylar we used for long-term packaging. If I tape the seams, I bet I could make a pretty darn nice bunch of balloons."

"Sweet! See? I knew I could count on your brain-box to come up with something. I owe ya one!"

"I'll hold you to it when we finally get back to Earth."

"Less than a week and we'll be sipping margaritas on the beach. First round is on me. Just you wait and see, it'll be excellent."

CHAPTER TEN

Daisy had arrived at the galley a little earlier than usual the following morning, and was surprised to see Finn at his usual spot, playing with his knives, as always. He held up his hand for her to see.

"Yeah, they're awesome. Better than new!" he said. "And now I don't have to worry about chopping them off again!" Finn was obviously over the trauma of the prior day.

"As a bonus from the whole ordeal, Mal was able to upgrade my arm's AI linkage, so there should be absolutely no more glitches like there were before. I'm bomb-proof!"

Finn was showing the others his shiny new fingers. His state-of-the-art, top-of-the-line, bright metal fingers. Daisy's stomach did a little flip-flop.

"But why didn't the medbot re-attach your old ones?" Daisy asked. "Vince brought them to the med pod, and the cuts were clean."

"Who cares? Look at how cool these are!" He flexed the metal digits as easily as if they were his real fingers.

Replacement parts.

Daisy felt sick.

Finn was right, though. His fingers were the most modern replacement parts of any crewmember. Mal never stopped designing and re-imagining new attachments. This latest improvement also included an even stronger bond between the bio-engineered flesh and the metal mesh that trailed into the new appendages. It was human flesh, grown from the patient's own stem cells, but it was improved in the lab. Stronger. More resilient. Extremely fast healing, and possessing incredible tensile strength. Of course, given the forces a mechanical limb could exert, it was only natural the connecting tissues would have to be ridiculously durable.

Computers modifying human tissue, Daisy thought, disturbed by the image. *Replacement parts are bad enough. Some things should be left to nature.* She found herself feeling more than a little uneasy.

"Hey, are you okay? Tell you what, I'll whip up some waffles with a strawberry balsamic reduction. Tamara just gave me the first ones picked from the new crop. Sound good?"

"No, I'm fine. Thanks, Finn, but I'm not really hungry."

"Turning down food? You? You're not getting sick, are you? 'Cause we're in a sealed ship a bazillion miles from the nearest pathogen."

"Ha, tell me about it. No, I'm just tired is all."

In truth, she wasn't fine, but that was entirely beside the point. She was disturbed. Why had Mal opted to give Finn yet another set of replacement parts rather than simply reattaching his own fingers? The medical technology was there, and would have been quite simple compared to the process of adding artificial appendages.

People seemed to be having bits of themselves replaced with metal more and more often, but was it all so necessary? At what point, she wondered, would people made of boring-old flesh cease to exist entirely? If Mal had her way, it might be sooner than she was comfortable with.

Six days. Just tough it out for six more days.

That was all that stood between her and margaritas on a sandy beach. Not even a week to go until they reached Earth. A mere six days until fresh air, warm sun, and normal people made of simple stuff, like flesh and bone. Daisy found herself smiling at the thought of lazy Sunday afternoons in bed with Vince, no more ship's duties, just the two of them with all the time in the world.

It's less than a week. All I have to do is make it six measly days and I'll be home. Finally back on Earth after all these years. Easy-peasy. What could possibly go wrong at this point? she mused.

The cynic in her should have known better than to tempt fate like that.

"Daisy, get on the environmentals with Sarah on the lower deck. She needs extra hands." Captain Harkaway's voice barked at her over the comms.

The captain sounded calm and in control, as he always did. Hell, the ship could be on fire and decompressing into space and he'd still maintain that tone, but there was a little edge of concern in his voice. Something that hinted at the potential seriousness of the situation.

Why didn't I just keep my big mouth shut?

"Copy that, Captain. Heading there now. Sarah, I'm on my way to you," she said, switching to direct comms. "What's your location?"

"Just exiting the Narrows under Lower Port Ten. Something's really weird and glitchy with a whole bunch of pods over here."

"I'll be there in two minutes."

Daisy stopped at one of her conveniently placed caches of gear stowed on every level and strapped a pair of additional tool pouches to her thighs as she hustled toward the ladder to the lower deck. The unexpected spike in her heart rate left her with a minor headache as she went from zero to sixty in a matter of seconds, and running with tools was never fun.

Daisy mounted the ladder, opting to let gravity, artificial though it was, do the work. She grabbed the vertical poles and jumped on, pressing her feet to the outsides of the rails. The descent was quick, and she landed with a solid thud on the slightly-cushioned base panel at the bottom of the ladder.

Something caught her eye. The lights on the lower level seemed a little bit *wrong* down there. Nothing big, just ever so slightly different. Like they were running on a fractionally different current. Her headache was getting worse.

Just seeing things, Daze. Get on with it, she told herself.

She moved toward the peripheral corridor on the port side and saw Sarah hunched over an open control panel. She didn't look up from the wire she was soldering into place as Daisy approached.

"Hey, Daze," she greeted her friend.

"What's up, Sarah?"

"I pulled and re-connected the junction relays in the Narrows and have been swapping out some buggy switches in the control panels. When I get this last one dialed in, I'll need you to pop the doors between Port Twelve and Eleven, then seal Port Ten and Thirteen. I'm going to equalize the pressure between the two, then re-seal to see if one of them is our culprit. Something isn't seating properly, and we're losing air."

Daisy became very serious very quickly.

"Oh, shit. How bad? How much time do we have? Maybe we should grab EVA suits and seal the level."

"Sorry, I should have been clearer. It's a tiny leak. It wasn't reading on the ship's main systems, but my portable scanner caught the variance. I'd almost call it inconsequential, but every breath counts in a pressurized can like this one."

Sarah had spent the better part of the morning doing everything she could think of to track down and stop the slow leak of air from their ship, but it seemed to be somehow circumventing the airlock system designed to prevent exactly this type of emergency.

"I had some door-sealing problems when I was leaving Doc McClain's yesterday. Had to completely power down and reboot the whole pod."

"But those doors don't connect to space, so they wouldn't affect our O2 levels."

"I know, but that problem was up on the main level, and we're on the lower one now. You think maybe there's more to this? It could be a ship-wide issue."

"What did Mal have to say?"

The AI, hearing her name, chimed in.

"Did you need my assistance, Sarah?"

"No, Mal, we were just discussing possible anomalies with the pods. Have you noticed anything unusual with connectors or pressurization?"

"Only what you and Daisy are currently working on."

"No variances in oxygen levels? I was manually running some numbers, and they weren't matching your readouts."

Mal was silent a moment. "There's no need for that, Sarah. I can assure you, consumption levels are exactly within parameters."

The women looked at one another, sharing an unspoken thought. *That was weird.*

"Okay, thanks, Mal. We'll keep plugging away at this."

There was the slightest of clicks as Mal exited the comm channel.

"So, could it be a leak through one of the conduit gaps between pods in the Narrows?" Daisy pondered.

"No, those should all be triple-sealed." Sarah pulled one of the emergency oxygen rigs from the wall and looped it over her shoulder. "Just in case," she said, noticing Daisy's look. "I'm seeing a sort of pattern emerging here, but I can't quite figure it out. The readings from a pair of Main Level Starboard pods near Tamara's botanical units were also off."

"Wouldn't want to interrupt her gardening—there'd be hell to pay."

"Tell me about it. Thing is, there's an oxygen deficit in the starboard pods, and if anything, her plants would cause a slight bump in O2, not a drop. It just doesn't make sense." A worried look flashed across Sarah's face. "Unless we somehow missed a slow leak."

"But it's been months since the impact. We evaluated the ship and ran full damage control. It was the first thing we did. Unless it was a weakened spot that took until now."

"Yeah, who knows what it is. For now, how about you use that big brain of yours and run a quick airlock seal cycle between the pods down here. I think, I *hope*, I found the issue, but it'd be good to have another set of eyes confirm it."

"Ah, yes, the rare instance where your life-support specialist skills and my grease-monkey training overlap."

"There's no grease on wiring, Daze."

"You know what I mean. Get moving. I'll meet you up starboard side as soon as I run the diagnostic cycle. Should only take a few minutes."

"Sounds good. I'm going to run a basic integrity check through the starboard pods, then, while you're cycling these."

"Meet you up there when I'm done."

Sarah headed off at a quick trot, leaving Daisy to her task.

"Mal, I'm going to power down and reboot the doors in sequence between numbers ten through thirteen, then cycle them individually through their locking phases. Please monitor the air pressure in those pods for any changes."

"Very well, Daisy. I shall monitor as you requested."

"Okay, starting now." Daisy began manually powering down and rebooting the door systems. A few minutes later, all of them had flawlessly cycled through their sequences.

"Any pressure variances?"

"Negative, Daisy. I believe you have addressed the problem. Perhaps it was just a minor connection seating issue between the pods, resulting in a bad seal and pressure shifting from one pod to another."

"Maybe. As long as we're not losing air, that's all I care about for now. I'll let Sarah crunch the numbers later when we're done. Thanks, Mal. I'm heading up to the main level to give her a hand."

Daisy saw the emergency oxygen tube resting against the wall in the corridor when she arrived, but no sign of her friend.

"Sarah?"

"Hang on a minute," a muffled voice called from a tiny open panel. Moments later a pair of feet slid into view. Inch by inch, Sarah backed out of the tight crawlspace between Starboard Six and Seven.

"Everything good down there?" she asked when she had finally crawled free of the particularly claustrophobic section of Narrows.

"Taken care of," Daisy replied. "I cycled the doors, and Mal says there are no leaks. She thinks it may be the sealing boots between the pods that had somehow slipped a bit, making pressure shift from one to the other."

"But between four pods? Even if things shook loose at these speeds, that still shouldn't happen."

"Hey, I'm just the messenger."

"Do you think you can re-run that door cycle on the lower port pods again from up here while we're working on these? Something just doesn't seem right to me."

"Yeah, I should be able to tap in to that level from here with no problem. I'll just open a parallel terminal so it doesn't interfere with what we're doing on this one. What's the deal up here, anyway? More of the same thing as down on the lower deck?"

"Yeah, air pressure levels aren't matching up. I'm wondering if Starboard Pod Eight might have developed a leak in its outer door. It would be a shame to have to seal it off."

"I just did an EVA out of that pod yesterday to fit the new linkage to the comms array, and there didn't seem to be anything wrong with it."

Sarah shrugged. "Just a thought. Anyway, I'm going to go through each one of the pods in this block and give the internal seals a good once-over while I'm checking pressure and oxygen levels for any sign of the culprit behind this pressure drop. Once we figure which one the leak is coming from, we can focus on plugging it."

"Look at you, all efficient with your plans."

"Yeah, yeah," Sarah laughed. "Okay, I'm gonna get started. While I'm at it, how about you pull the panels in the starboard passageway and double-check all the regulators and power supplies?"

"No problem. I'll get on it, and then run the cycle down on the lower port pods again."

"Cool. I'm gonna head in."

"Be careful, Sarah."

"Hey, we're perfectly safe in here, it's not a big thing. We just need to get this leak sorted before it actually becomes one."

For the next hour, the duo moved from pod to pod, Sarah slowly inspecting each one from the inside, while Daisy shifted from access panel to access panel out in the passageway, checking each bundle of circuits and relays one by one.

Okay, I've leapfrogged far enough ahead, Daisy thought as she paused to tap into an unused terminal. She double-checked her readouts, then began the process of overriding the pod-to-pod airlock doors on the lower port level again. While she was at it, she also remotely adjusted the sensors without Mal's assistance, to restrict their reading for just the specific areas she was testing.

"Hey!" Sarah gleefully called out over the comms. "Winner, winner! I found a big stash of Mylar. Looks like Vince is going to get a bunch of balloons to go with that birthday cake after all!"

"My sister from another mister, saving the day again!"

"Damn straight!" Sarah giggled. "And as an extra special bonus, I've just cleared the first two pods. Making good time now that I'm not stuck crawling around in the Narrows. All the data so far is coming back clear on the internal pod instruments, but my portable reader is still acting kind of odd. Could you verify the readouts on your end?"

"Sure thing, send them over."

"Coming your way."

Moments later a flurry of data arrived on the wall-mounted terminal beside Daisy. Code flashed brightly as both ship-run and portable readouts flew by on the screen.

"Can I be of assistance?" Mal asked abruptly.

"Jesus, Mal, you startled me," Daisy said. "Thanks for the offer, but we're fine on our own. Your redundant systems somehow didn't pick this up the first time through, so now we're doing it the old-fashioned way."

There was a brief silence. Daisy almost felt bad, hurting the ship's feelings. Then she remembered, it was just a machine. Sure, a self-aware machine, but a machine all the same. Its calm voice spoke again.

"I am most sorry I did not detect any leak. I fear some of my sensors may have functionality issues. I have tasked Barry to help resolve the issue."

"Fine, whatever you need to do. Just stay out of our way for a bit while we track this down."

"As you wish, Daisy," the AI intoned. She could have sworn it sounded a little upset, but the mood-stabilizing software hardwired into her base code was there to ensure against such emotions.

Moments later, a confused voice crackled over her comms.

"Hey, what are you doing?" Sarah asked with a concerned tone. "Not funny, Daze."

"What do you mean? I'm just cycling the pods like you asked."

"You're supposed to do Lower Deck Port Ten through Thirteen *only*. Main Deck Starboard Pod Eight just locked me in."

"The EVA and supply transfer pod? That's not me. I've got the code working on a completely different part of the ship, just like you asked me to."

"Well, the freakin' doors to pods seven and nine keep cycling between locked and unlocked."

"That's not right," Daisy said. "Maybe it's the fail-safe?"

"But there are no leaks in here. The alarms wired to the external airlock would have—"

A shrill alarm sounded, resonating through the passageway.

"Sarah, what's happening?"

"Shut it down! Shut down all power to Starboard Eight!"

"But the doors will seal you in!"

"Just do it! Hurry!"

Daisy's fingers flew over the keyboard, executing commands as fast as she was able.

"Come on, Daisy!"

"Almost there!"

Sarah looked in horror as the green light to the external airlock flickered ever so slightly.

"Hurry up!"

The inner of the two doors cycled open. Only one separated her from the cold vacuum of space.

"Daisy! Hurry!"

Daisy entered the last sequence. "Got it! Power is down,

doors locked," she called to her friend over the comms. "Now would you mind telling me what the hell is going on? You scared the shit out of me."

"You and me both," Sarah said, a hitch in her voice. "The external airlock," she continued. "It started to cycle open."

"But that shouldn't be possible. There are safety protocols. *Multiple* safeties."

"Yeah, well, so much for those. The inner door is still open, Daze, so I'm not sure how much I trust those safeties at this point."

"Sarah, get to the lockers and grab an EVA suit. I don't want to take any chances, okay? There's no way I'm going to power that pod back up until you're safe and sound in a suit."

"You don't have to tell me twice."

"What the hell is going on down there?" the captain barked over the comms. "I'm reading a power outage in starboard pods seven through nine."

"There was some sort of malfunction in starboard pod eight, Captain. I had to shut down the linked pods in order to isolate it in time."

"In time for what?" he growled.

"It's me, Captain," Sarah chimed in. "I had her do it. I'm stuck here in Starboard Eight. I was checking some fluctuations in air levels in this block of pods when the connecting doors failed."

"Tell him the other bit."

"What other bit?" the captain asked. "And what's that rustling noise?"

"Sorry, Captain, I'm putting on an EVA suit while we're talking. The external airlock door was malfunctioning. Shutting down power was the only way to stop it—"

The lights flickered.

"What was that?" Sarah asked. "Don't power back on yet! I'm not ready!"

"It wasn't me, Sarah," Daisy said, trying to understand the blips on the readout screen in front of her. "Just hurry up and get into that suit." Daisy had a bad feeling building in her gut.

"One step ahead of you. I'll be suited up before you can—"

The ship lurched slightly as the airlock door blew open, jettisoning Sarah into the void in a rush of air and debris.

Alarms sounded as the ship's AI hurried to compensate.

"Decompression in starboard pod eight. Environmental danger on Main Deck. All crew, don emergency oxygen masks."

Even in an emergency, Mal sounded calm and collected.

"Starboard Eight airlock door now re-sealing," the computer's voice informed the crew a minute later.

"It is now safe to remove emergency oxygen apparatus."

"Crew, report to your stations for damage assessment. I want a full systems check. All non-essential compartments are to remain sealed until I say so. Stay sharp, and note *anything* out of parameters. You will each be called individually for a debrief once this situation is under control," the captain called over the intercom.

Daisy felt disconnected from her body as it somehow ran through the emergency protocols that had been drilled into her on autopilot.

Deep inside herself, Daisy's mind was in shock. Overcome by a state of disbelief as she envisioned her friend's smiling face. But that wasn't her anymore. The reality was undeniable. Her best friend was frozen and drifting away deeper into space. Alone in the vacuum.

Sarah was gone.

CHAPTER ELEVEN

"We should get her body." It was Reggie who floated the idea. "It's not right to just leave her out there."

"If we could, I'd agree with you, but that's just not possible," Captain Harkaway replied. "You know I don't want to leave any crewmember behind, but we just lost a lot of air, sustained unknown damage, and the hopper can't reach her given our trajectory. Our shuttle is the only thing with enough speed to catch her now, and even then it would burn through all of its fuel chasing her the opposite direction the ship is moving in. At these speeds, it just can't be done." He paused, casting a gaze across the assembled crew.

"We have to move forward, assess the damage, and figure out what our status is. Sarah is gone, and she wouldn't want her crewmates jeopardizing their lives over her corpse. We took a hit, and lost a friend, but we all still have jobs to do." He paused and looked over his dejected crew. "One more thing, and this goes for all of you. Doctor McClain is here to offer counseling and support to anyone who needs it. We just suffered a great loss, and there's no shame in needing to talk about it. I encourage all of you to utilize her services. That is all. Now get to work, people."

The captain lurched through the galley's double doors and headed back to Command, while the crew slowly rose to return to their tasks. Daisy, eyes and nose a fierce red, pulled herself together as best she could. She kept turning Sarah's environmental scanner over in her hands. Clipped to the rack as she'd tried to don her space suit, it was the one thing that hadn't been blasted into space.

'Don't be a pussy, Daze,' Sarah's voice teased her. *'You're tougher than this. If I knew dying would slow you down so much, I never would have done it.'*

"Very funny, dumbass," she muttered.

"What was that?" Vince asked, studying her as she rose to her feet.

"Nothing."

"You need me, you know where I'll be, okay?" He rested his hand on her shoulder and pulled her closer. "Come see me tonight. We can talk, or just sit. Whatever you need."

"Thanks. I think I just need to get moving and put my mind back on a project, ya know?"

"Yeah."

"Look, I've got to go. I'll see you later."

Vince let his fingertips slide from her shoulder as she left. Sarah's loss was a blow, but for now, they had jobs to do.

"Captain." Daisy caught up to the limping man as he made his way down the passageway. "I'm not the life-support expert, but from what I can tell by the data Sarah was collecting, it looks like the secondary air scrubbers had possibly shorted out. My guess is that's a new problem, though, and not what she was originally tracking down. It was most likely the force of the vacuum hitting the unprotected systems without a proper compartmental seal prior to decompression that caused a shear to a supply line. At least, I hope that's all it is."

Harkaway looked at her, waiting for Daisy to get to the point.

"Anyway," she continued, "until we figure out what exactly needs to be done to repair them, we're going to need to be running on a low oxygen protocol, just in case. It could be nothing, but we can't risk it. I recommend we do what we can to reduce excessive physical activity as much as possible while we work through this problem."

"And what does Mal think about this?" the captain asked.

"I haven't discussed it with her yet, Captain. Some of the anomalies weren't showing up on her readings, and Sarah noted several discrepancies in the oxygen consumption data, and—"

"My environmental systems are functioning at near-optimal levels, Daisy," Mal interrupted.

Always listening, aren't you?

"Maybe so, Mal, but you still have some sensor outages, and now we have lord knows what kind of damage to track down in the Narrows."

The computer thought a moment. "This is a correct assessment. However even after the loss of oxygen, I can assure you, the crew is in no danger."

"Tell that to Sarah," she muttered.

"What was that?" Captain Harkaway asked.

"I said we need Sarah," Daisy said. "We're down to just one Narrows worker, and on top of that, she was the environmental and life support expert."

"Just do what you can. I don't expect you to fill her shoes, Swarthmore, but knowing how stubborn you can be, I won't be surprised if you try."

"Thank you, Captain. I think."

"All right, then. Mal, I want you to figure out how much air we have currently, and if our consumption can be sustained."

"I will verify the figures and have them for you immediately, Captain."

"Gustavo," he said into the comms.

"Yes, Captain?"

"Plug into the ship and double-check our course. Given the glitches of today, I'm not entirely confident Mal has plotted the most efficient trajectory. It's probably nothing, but I want a second set of eyes on it."

"Copy, Captain."

"I can assure you," Mal chimed in, "the trajectory is ideal for mission parameters, Captain."

"Nothing personal, but I want it double-checked anyway. And Daisy, that goes for environmentals too. Figure out what Sarah was working on and check our oxygen consumption. We need true readings, and if there really is possible damage to the scrubbers, we need the most accurate data possible."

"I'll get right on it, sir."

"One more thing. Your replacement communications array, how powerful is it?"

"I tried to replicate what we had before the impact as best as I could with the parts on hand. It should be close to the original unit's power ratings."

"Good, though despite all the work as you've put into it, I would really rather not have to rely on that jury-rigged long-range communication setup. Nevertheless, we may need to try to reach out to Dark Side base to see if they can meet us halfway with replacement O2 scrubbers if we can't get ours back online. Can your gizmo handle a tier-three encrypted transmission?"

"Captain?" Daisy asked, confused.

"Tier-three, Swarthmore. Can it handle it?"

"Um, I don't know. It should be able to, in theory anyway. But that's high-level military encryption on a pulsed phase-shifted frequency. Why would a repair base use that?"

Harkaway looked at her but said nothing.

"Oh shit," she gasped. "Dark Side has a secret military facility as well?"

"Like you said, it's secret," he answered.

"Then why are you telling me, if you don't mind me asking, sir?"

"Because our fan is covered in shit, Daisy, and what I just told you is need-to-know information."

"But I'm just a tech. I don't need to know that."

"You do now," he said grimly. "Barry!" he barked into the comms.

"Yes, Captain?" The cyborg had somehow approached them while they were talking without being noticed.

"Jesus, Barry, I hate it when you do that," Daisy said, nearly jumping out of her skin at his stealthy appearance.

"Sorry, Daisy."

The captain turned to the mechanical man.

"Barry, I want you to suit up and do an EVA to the exterior area of Lower Port Ten through Thirteen. See if there's any damage we may have missed from the inside. Mal says we're ship-shape down there, but I'd like to confirm it."

"I'll get right on it, Captain," Barry said, turning and heading for the ladder to the lower deck. Daisy watched him disappear down to the bottom level.

"Trust but verify," she said.

"What's that?"

"Just something I read in an old book," she replied. "But, Captain, there's something that's been bothering me. The *Váli* isn't that old, but a lot of her systems seem to be in fairly advanced states of failure. It's not readily apparent, but in some spaces, like the Narrows especially, well, it just looks like some of the components are outdated."

"The Narrows, huh? Well, that would make sense, I suppose. The one place the ship's auto-maintenance doesn't cover."

"Captain, there's something else."

"What is it?"

"There are things written in the Narrows. Drawings and gibberish, mostly, but also messages scratched out on the walls in nooks and crannies." Daisy pulled her notepad from her hip pocket and flipped through the pages. "I wrote a bunch of them down. Like this one. It was particularly dark. 'We can never go home. This is our home of glass and steel. Yet still we hope for green pastures.' - Lt. Burke, *Icarus*."

Captain Harkaway swallowed hard as he silently stared at the bulkhead. "Some of these pods," he finally began, "were originally from other ships, like the *Icarus*. When the *Váli*'s framework was commissioned, it was configured to best serve the mission's needs, and pods from ships that fit the bill were installed as needed. That's all it is, Daisy. Just a few pods that are a bit older than the others. Now, get going. I want you to get as much done this shift as possible, then get yourself a good night's sleep. I know we all need it."

Daisy would have liked to do as the captain ordered, but a good night's sleep was something that hadn't been in the cards for her for quite some time. Sure, she'd sometimes wake truly rested, though more often than not, those were the mornings after Vincent had kept her up well past her normal bedtime.

As she lay in her bunk, running the day over and over in her mind, Daisy could find no fault in her actions. Nevertheless, she still felt like somehow, someway, Sarah's death was partially her fault.

Never should have run those diagnostics from up there. What if that little tweak to the command structure started the whole thing?

She knew that hadn't been what happened, just like she knew none of the other dozen scenarios playing out over and over in her head would have changed things. Still, her friend was gone, and no amount of replaying the events would change that.

"Let it go, Daisy. It wasn't your fault."

"Stay out of my head, dead girl," she muttered. "That shit's not helping."

"It's your psyche, hon, not mine."

"Touché," she said to the air, then turned out the lights, hesitating as her fingers touched the neuro stim beside her bed. *Not tonight*, she decided, and settled into her bed, leaving the device where it sat as she gradually drifted off to sleep.

Daisy found herself in a busy metropolitan area. The skies were a clear blue, and happy clouds dotted the horizon. In the distance she could see the mountains, covered with lush trees, their peaks capped with pure white snow.

It was a dream she'd been having since they first emerged from cryo. Memories of home, but now something felt different. Wrong.

Daisy turned her gaze from the mountains and looked to the sea. Logically, she knew the sea and mountains were much farther apart than that, but in the construct of her slumbering mind, distance held no sway over her environs. The water was a deep blue, a salty breeze blowing the fresh smell of clean ocean air across her face, leaving the faintest deposit of salt on her skin. Seagulls circled above as she strode onto the beach, the warm sand squishing between her toes.

All I need now is a margarita, she thought. A feeling of cool moisture tingled in her fingers, and looking down, she noticed a chilled glass was already in her hand. *That's more like it.*

Sarah was there, wearing a scandalously small bikini as she lay out on a beach chair. A vacant seat waited beside her, inviting Daisy to get comfortable.

"This is the life," she happily murmured, sinking into the soft material.

"It is for one of us," Sarah replied.

The two women sat quietly for a while, sipping margaritas

and watching glistening-bodied surfers jog through the waves. One of them exited the surf and spread a towel on the sand nearby. Rather than laying out for some sun, the rippling-muscled man started doing some yoga stretches.

"Oh, thank you for that." Sarah smiled.

"For what?"

"You know what. Always looking out for your little sis, aren't you? But I still have to wonder if it has different speeds."

Daisy sat up in her chair.

"What are you talking about, Sarah?" Then her gaze fell on the man as he pushed up into a cobra pose.

Shit. That's—

"Hi, Daisy," Barry said. "You know, I always wanted to see a real beach!"

Daisy lurched awake, sitting up in her bed.

Jesus, Barry was in my dreams? What's the world coming to?

She took a long drink from her water bottle, then lay back down to sleep.

No more cyborgs visiting my dreams, please, she thought as sleep took hold once more.

She found herself in the middle of the city, just as before. Once more the mountains rose, majestic yet surprisingly close, while the sea was likewise both near and far. In her dream, she was in the city, the mountains, and the beach all at once.

Daisy wished for a margarita, but when she looked down, she found a portable environmental scanner in her hand rather than a refreshing beverage. What's more, Sarah was nowhere to be seen.

The machine in her hand began to beep, a faint rhythm invading the tranquil world surrounding her. None of the scores of people seemed to notice. In fact, now that she thought about it, none of the people paid her any heed at all. They all seemed to be in a rush to get somewhere, but she had no idea where that might be.

"Excuse me," she called out to a well-dressed man walking past. He ignored her and continued on his way.

"Well, that was rude," she grumbled. "Hey, you," she directed toward a woman walking a small dog. "Where is everyone going?" The woman didn't seem to hear her, instead, turning from her and walking away.

Didn't even pick up her dog's poop, Daisy noted.

Somewhere in the back of her mind, she couldn't help but feel like she was being watched, but when she spun around, scanning the crowd for observant eyes, she came up empty.

Okay, this is getting silly, she thought, just as the device in her hand began beeping louder. A steady noise that only she seemed to hear. She looked down at it and noted a steady stream of letters she couldn't read scrolling across the display. When she looked up, she was no longer in the city, but now stood in a crowded transit port surrounded by hundreds of men and women. Determined, she strode across the terminal to a ticketing counter.

"Hey, where's everyone going?" she asked the woman typing away at a computer terminal. "Hello? Earth to ticketing lady, come in, ticketing lady." As with the others, there was no reply. "All right, this is ridiculous." She reached out to grab the woman's wrist. "Hey, I was asking you—"

As soon as her fingers wrapped around the woman's wrist, she shrieked. It wasn't just the one woman who screamed. Every single person, both in the transit port and outside—in fact, the whole population of her impossible dream world—all cried out at once as their bodies turned to dust before her eyes.

Daisy looked at the handful of human powder and screamed.

She snapped awake in her bed, heart racing as sweat beaded on her brow. Her hands felt for the device she'd become so accustomed to wearing, but the thin band was still resting beside her bed.

Holy shit, what the hell was that? she wondered. *That's never happened before.*

Gathering her wits, Daisy took several deep breaths and focused her mind on slowing her racing heart. In a few moments she felt her panic subside. The dream had felt so much more real than a regular one. Almost tangible. As if she was really there. On top of that, it had the multi-layered reality feel of a neuro stim dream, all those dozens and dozens of drip feed streams trickling into a single reality, but she hadn't even been wearing it.

No, it was just a strange dream, that's all. Nothing to it, just my mind processing things, like Doc McClain said.

The beeping jolted her out of her calm.

Sitting across the pod among her pile of work gear was Sarah's portable environmental scanner. And just like in her dream, it was trying to tell her something.

CHAPTER TWELVE

Sleep simply wasn't an option. Not after those terrible dreams. On top of that, the flashing light on Sarah's scanner kept blinking at her, an accusing eye gazing in disapproval, nudging her into action.

"All right, I'm getting to it!" she grumbled to the inanimate piece of machinery. "It's not like I'm a super-genius environmental engineer like Sarah is." She caught herself.

Was.

The innocuous device didn't care about her protests, nor were her rationalizations holding any sway over it. Rather, it just continued being true to its nature. Persistent. Continuous. Incorruptible.

Hang on a minute. It's a dumb machine. No AI at all, which means if it wasn't networked in with Mal's systems, it would be true to its own readings regardless of what the other scans said.

It was an interesting theory, but one that still didn't help much, given her lack of understanding how the cursed thing functioned.

Daisy glanced at the clock mounted to her wall. Nearly midnight. So much for a full night's sleep. She threw on her sweats and headed for the door. If she couldn't sleep, at least Vince might be able to take her mind off of things. Even if they just wound up sleeping and nothing more, his warmth would help put her at ease.

Daisy reached out for the door controls, then glanced back across her quarters. Sarah's scanner steadily flashed its light, staring at her like a lonely puppy being abandoned for the night.

Oh, all right, Daisy thought as she picked it up. *Might as well take it along. Maybe Vince will have some ideas.*

"Babe, I have no idea," he said as he showed her into his quarters. "I mean, I know what basic type of device it is on a basic engineering level, but this was totally Sarah's ballpark."

"Well, it was worth asking." Daisy sighed.

"Sorry I couldn't be of more help." Vince took the scanner from her hands and rested it on his desk, then wrapped her gently in his arms. "You know, I *can* think of one thing I can do for you. If that's what you want, that is. Or we can just talk. Or sleep. Whatever you need."

"I just want to turn my damn brain off for a while. If only it were so easy."

"Maybe I can help."

He gently laid her down on his bed, softly kissing a trail from her collarbone, slowly moving lower and lower.

"That's really nice," she said with a shudder, "but now that I'm here, I don't know if I'm in the right headspace for it."

"Sorry, babe. I just thought it might distract you," he said, resting his head on the pillow beside her, then wrapping his in his arms and holding her close. Like I said, whatever you need."

"You sure? I don't want to leave you with blue balls."

"Daisy, that's not even remotely a concern. It's been a really tough couple of days, and besides, we'll have plenty of time once the captain removes that 'don't exert yourself' restriction for the crew. It's not like we're going to actually run out of oxygen before we reach Dark Side anyway, right?"

Daisy glanced at the portable scanner sitting on his desk.

"Not likely, no, but I really do need to figure that thing out. Captain's counting on me. I've got some ideas, and I've seen Sarah run the inputs in the past, but it's not really my thing, so I didn't pay much attention."

"You're a smart cookie. I'm sure you'll work it out."

Daisy shook the sleep from her mind, slid off his bed, and slipped out of his bunk.

"Look, I'm gonna grab a snack and work on this some more. You get some sleep." She kissed him deeply. "And thank you for listening. That was just what the doctor ordered."

The galley was empty at that late hour, as one would expect. It was a little unsettling not having Finnegan in his usual spot, chattering away non-stop while he whipped up some new dish, but the silence would be good. Daisy needed to brain, and distractions would not help things any.

With Sarah gone now, Daisy really had her work cut out for her. She knew it would be a lot to cover, and the more she thought about it, the more daunting the task seemed. Her specialty was comms, with electronics and environmentals being a tack-on skill set that conveniently allowed her to help when Sarah needed it. Their parallel and overlapping talents provided a taken-for-granted redundancy that the crew would have been very glad to have, now that they found themselves in a low-oxygen crisis.

Okay, we're down one, so that's nine crew remaining, sucking up our precious air. Daisy pulled a cocoa packet from the storage pantry and inserted it into the hot beverage dispenser. "Cocoa, full-fat milk," she said to the machine. A whirring buzz sounded behind the metal panel, and moments later, it swung open, a perfect cup of cocoa waiting for her.

So, nine crew, she continued her machinations. *Of course, Barry doesn't consume more than a minute amount of oxygen to keep his flesh covering alive, so really, we're looking at oxygen needs of eight. I have everyone's weight, muscle ratio, and cardio fitness from the basic med logs, so it should just come down to doing the math.*

She plunked Sarah's scanner on the dining table and pulled up a seat. The data was mumbo-jumbo, and became even more unreadable the longer she stared at the screen. She took out one of the small flexible data tablets that Sarah liked to use and tried to reconcile figures between that and the frustrating machine resting in front of her.

A solid hour and three cups of cocoa had gone by, but Daisy, stubborn and bleary-eyed, re-entered the figures again for the umpteenth time. It was a losing battle. Without Sarah's ready-knowledge to interpret all that complex data, it was taking far too long to assess the results.

At long last, something she keyed in seemed to have finally worked as the little machine sputtered out a line of data on the screen.

"About fucking time," she muttered.

"I'm sorry, did you need something?" a disembodied voice asked in the dimly-lit room.

Shit. She'd forgotten she was working in a public space and not her private quarters. Of course the ship's AI was listening. She was always listening.

"No, it's nothing, Mal. Just talking to myself."

"Very well. Please inform me if you need my assistance. I'd be ever so glad to help."

"Thanks, I'll let you know."

Daisy picked up her tablet and the portable device. *Better if I continue this in my pod,* she thought. She gathered her things, grabbing a couple of protein bars from a drawer and sliding them into her pocket, then turned to head back to her personal space. *At least there will be no intrusions there,* she mused. *And what was with Mal's speech pattern? 'Ever so glad'? Where the hell did it pick up that one?*

She paused a moment longer, slipping a few electrolyte pouches into another pocket, then cycled the doors and stepped out into the hallway.

"Oh, pardon me," Barry said, nearly bumping into her. "Can I be of assistance, Daisy?"

Daisy jumped, nearly dropping the scanner.

"Barry, what are you doing here?"

"I do not understand the question," he said, puzzled. "I thought you were in your quarters." He looked her up and down curiously. "Are you all right, Daisy? May I be of assistance?" he asked, eyeing the scanner in her hands. "I can help interpret the data from that device if you wish."

"Um, no, thanks. I'm good. Just doing a little work and having a snack."

"I see. Unable to sleep? Perhaps I could make you a nice cup of herbal tea. I understand that often helps with a restless mind. And really, I do not mind running through the data for you."

"No, really, I'm fine. Thanks, though."

It really is creepy when he just stares at you, she noticed as Barry paused, formulating a reply to her statement.

"My pleasure, Daisy. Please do not hesitate to ask if you need me," he finally said.

She nodded and turned away from the odd cyborg, making her way down the passageway toward her quarters.

What does he actually do when we're all sleeping? she wondered.

Back in her quarters Daisy did some quick math and made a decision.

There are still four inhibitors left, so I should be fine if I only pull a couple. One way or another, I need to process Sarah's data, especially if Barry and Mal are sniffing around it. Something about this just doesn't feel right.

The lid to the neuro-stim device slid off easier than usual as she gave it a now-practiced twist. The tiny inhibitor control switch stared at her, its solid red light daring her, tempting her to throw caution to the wind.

Okay, I'll only disconnect two of them. That'll leave two still running, which should be plenty.

She took a fine probe and depressed the left-hand inhibitor deactivation button for ten seconds until the light pulsed five times.

That's one.

She repeated the process until the light slowly pulsed five times again, though this time it followed with a sixth, flickering pulse.

Huh, that's new. Probably a warning light. Well, I've got two left, and even I am not foolish enough to remove those.

With the device ready, Daisy plugged in a new series of protocols that would help her understand Sarah's work. It was a huge amount of information on top of the other things she had been trickle feeding herself, but it was critical she understand those readings. Nevertheless, she hesitated. It was a lot of data, but her only other options were letting Mal and Barry handle it —which would put the accuracy of the results in question in her mind—or learning the codes and processes the old-fashioned way, and that would take weeks, if not months. They simply didn't have that much time.

She looked at the clock—2:17 am.

I'll just put all of the feed's focus on this new stuff and turn the others to their lowest settings. I just hope that gives me at least a little understanding of what she was talking about.

Daisy slipped the delicate neuro band around her head and sat on her bed.

Two for Tai Chi, two to learn chess, two for kung fu, two more for those hacking skills for Vince's birthday surprise, and now two more so I can understand Sarah's work. Ten inhibitors down, two remaining. Piece of cake, Daisy. Okay, time to do this.

She pushed the activation button on the device and swung her feet up onto the bed. It would take the neuro-stim a minute or so to begin gently nudging her mind, and then, if all went according to plan, she'd wake up several hours later, well-rested and able to understand Sarah's notes enough to be of some real use to the ship.

Tai, Chi. Chess. Kung Fu. Hacking. Sarah's work. All in all, not bad for an untrained tech. She'd been good about fiddling with the machine, despite what her friend had said about her recklessness.

Besides, tweaking the stupid thing was what let me finally sleep decently in the first place. Her eyes went wide. *Shit! Two more for sleeping! That's all twelve of them!*

Daisy tried to snatch the deceivingly delicate-looking band from her head, but the now-inhibitor-free device had already taken hold. Her arms wouldn't obey her commands, and a millisecond later, she was yanked under by the powerful machine.

She didn't dream. At least not like she was used to. Huge amounts of information flooded her mind, her head feeling like a giant water balloon that kept filling closer to the bursting point while somehow remaining intact. Data flashed to the forefront of her awareness. In an instant, all of Sarah's calculations make perfect sense. As if she'd been a fool for not seeing how simple they were sooner. But then that was washed away by the flash flood of other things. Things that shouldn't even be in her mind. There was kung fu and Tai Chi, but they were only a fraction of the martial styles swirling in her head. The entire specification log of the *Váli* pulsed over her awareness, and she realized she knew the ship down to every last wire. But there was more. Ships she had never seen. Ships that didn't even exist. Fighters and destroyers, tankers and transports. Experimental recon ships, and devious war machines, all tumbled in her brain.

I... what is—

Bursts of foreign tongues were clear as the spoken word. Machine language made sense deep in her bones. She felt as if her mind would explode from the strain, and she didn't know if she could take much more of it. Daisy's mind had been a slow-filling vessel her entire life, absorbing more and more data every second of her existence, but now she saw the past, and strained to see the future, and at that moment, she felt her sanity on the edge.

No more!

Somehow, she forced her mind to stop, and miraculously, the information deluge ceased.

Daisy rolled to the side of her bed and threw up a thin stream of half-digested cocoa.

At least I missed my shoes, she thought grimly, amused that she had not only avoided going mad, but had also retained her sense of humor.

Slowly, her body aching as if she'd gone ten rounds with a heavyweight champion, she sat up and pulled the band from her sweaty brow. Her head throbbed, but the endless expanse of unrelenting data was gone. She looked at the clock on the wall.

2:30 a.m.

She had been under for just thirteen minutes.

Daisy swung to her feet and stood, wobbling unsteadily in her quarters. The pounding in her head was growing. Intense. Like she'd had her skull pried open by a number four cranial lavage kit, though how she even knew what that was remained a mystery.

A wave of pain sent her to her knees.

Shit, shit, shit. What did I do to myself? I need Vince.

Ignoring her shoes, Daisy staggered to her double door and managed to key the mechanism despite her mildly doubled vision. In the passageway, she kept one hand on the wall for balance as she slowly stumbled toward Vince's quarters.

He's probably still up watching a movie. God, he's going to be so pissed.

Voices rumbled through the ship, distracting her from her path.

What? Who's that chattering?

She followed the sound until she was standing outside a thick set of doors.

How did I wind up at Command? she wondered, then cycled the doors open. Gustavo sat alone in his chair, a pair of dense data cables protruding from the back of his head as he monitored the ship and the space around it.

"Oh shit, I didn't hear you come in!" He said, jolting at the sight of Daisy.

He popped the cables from his head, the static-filled noise filling the pod.

"Sorry, my bad," he said, reaching for the volume controls.

"No, wait a second," Daisy said. "What are they saying?" The words were strange, but almost made sense. She noticed Gus looking at her strangely.

"What?"

"That's solar radio chatter, Daisy. It's not people. Just noise blasting past us as we get closer to Earth. It's kind of soothing, so I sometimes listen to it when the captain's not around."

"Oh. I guess I must've been hearing things."

"You okay?" he asked, concern showing in his lone human eye.

"Yeah, just slept really poorly and wanted to get some air. Thought a walk might help. Anyway, I'll leave you to it. Night, Gus."

"Good night, Daisy. Hope you sleep better."

She exited Command and started back toward her quarters.

Oh man, what did I do? Am I having a schizoid embolism or something?

As she walked, her body slowly began to feel more and more her own, and the persistent fogginess began to lift, but as it faded, it was replaced with something just as upsetting.

A creeping paranoia.

Great, now I'm freaking out over, over what? I don't even know. Come on Daisy, pull it together. You're okay. Everything is fine. At least I think it is, so long as I don't suddenly start telling myself to get my ass to Mars.

She neared Vincent's door, but a strange thing happened, though given the events of the past hour, it was probably one of the least strange things of the evening. As Daisy put her mind to it, she felt a surge of excitement as she realized she had retained an understanding of Sarah's work.

She passed right by Vince's pod and hurried down the passageway back to her quarters, clinging to the nascent clarity, afraid the flash of understanding might abandon her at any moment.

A few minutes later she was comfortably propped up on her bunk, scrolling through the reams of data stored in both Sarah's tablet and portable scanner. The information made sense, and it corroborated between both devices. Validation from two separate non-AI units. Daisy began jotting down notes as fast as she was able. Sleep was no longer a concern, only finishing her analysis before the knowledge she had acquired so recently could slip from her grasp.

Data confirms it. Given the parts per million of oxygen, nitrogen, and carbon dioxide, taking into consideration the pressure fluctuations between individual pods, levels, and even the Narrows, we most definitely have a slow leak somewhere on board. Likely the main deck by the look of things.

She sat up and cracked her neck. Hours had passed hunched over the readouts and notes, but she had finally put it all together. A smile spread across her face.

Okay, then. So, based on the amount of oxygen still in the ship, and compensating for off-gassing from Tamara's plant life, taking those factors combined with the slow leak we still haven't found and the remaining eight crewmembers consuming oxygen given their individual biological mass, minus that of their inorganic components, it looks like we should have enough to make it to Earth orbit without significant issues.

She paused, mid-thought, and stared in shock at the numbers on her screen. A realization hit her solidly in the gut.

"This can't be right," she gasped in disbelief. "No way. No fucking way."

She checked and re-checked her data, re-ran her calculations, then did it again, but the results were the same. Based on the physiological profiles of the men and women on board and the percentages of their bodies that were mechanical, a very specific rate of oxygen consumption was a known fact. The calculations she stared at were correct, only something was wrong.

"There's too much oxygen for this crew," she realized with horror. "Someone's not using enough oxygen. Someone besides Barry is a cyborg."

CHAPTER THIRTEEN

Daisy walked down the passageway toward the galley in a daze, which was really saying something, given she had a full load of adrenaline coursing through her veins. She hadn't slept a wink that night, and after her revelation, she wondered if she ever would again.

Another cyborg.

There was no way Mal wasn't aware. Something that big couldn't slip by her, and prior to the accident knocking systems offline, the powerful AI continuously monitored vital signs of the entire crew. And Barry? It seemed only logical that he would recognize one of his own kind.

That meant the two AIs were hiding the existence of another artificial person from the rest of the crew, and that put Daisy dangerously on edge.

"Are you all right, Daisy? I sense an elevated blood pressure," Mal commented, as if reading her thoughts. Daisy jumped in surprise but quickly composed herself.

"I'm fine, Mal, just still stressed out with what happened to Sarah," Daisy replied to the disembodied voice.

And if you knew Sarah was on to you, was that really an

accident? The possibilities whipping around in her mind were horrifying.

"Perhaps you should talk to Doctor McClain, Daisy. She is a skilled psychologist and is very good at her job."

"I'll keep that in mind."

"I can schedule a session for you, if you wish."

"No, thanks. I'll handle that myself if I feel I need it, but thank you, Mal."

That's right. Act normal, and keep on her good side until you know what's up.

Daisy reached her destination and cycled open the galley's double doors, only to be greeted by the unexpected, yet welcome, smell of fresh brownies wafting in the air.

Oh yeah, I promised Gus I'd wrangle him up some brownies. Good old Finn. At least I've got one more definite human on my side.

"Hey, Daze," Finn called across the galley. "So, about those brownies. I was saving my secret stash of chocolate chips for a final homecoming treat. You know how Mal can be about repurposing the organics replicator for non-staple food items and all, but when you mentioned baking, well, I thought given the last few days, we could all use a treat right about now, so I kind of made a bigger batch," he said, offering her a warm brownie from the tray.

Finn's obviously human. I saw his fingers come off. Down to the bone. I saw him bleed.

"Thanks, Finn," she replied, her expression carefully neutral-pleasant as she slowly chewed, savoring the chocolate as it melted on her tongue.

Okay, let's work this through. It's obviously not me or Vince, and it's not Finn. But if not him, then who?

She pulled up a seat to think. Think and observe as the others slowly filtered through the galley.

The airlock door cycled a few minutes later as Captain Harkaway stepped into the compartment, his heavy, metal leg impacting slightly harder than his flesh one as he walked.

"Engines at eighty-seven percent optimization, Captain," the ship's AI informed him.

"Thank you, Mal. Let me know when they've cycled back to the mid-nineties."

"My pleasure, Captain."

'My pleasure' again? What's with this computer? She's been acting weird lately. Using more personal sentence structure. Like she's trying to be, well, a person. Damn thing is creeping me out.

She watched the captain as he walked toward her. He may have had an older replacement leg, but Daisy had seen his records and had noticed him wiping a bloody nose on several occasions when the ship's air humidifier had problems a few weeks prior. The dry air gave him nosebleeds for days before they got it back operating at full-efficiency.

Cyborgs don't get nosebleeds.

Obviously not the captain, she noted. *Though I don't know how much I can trust him yet.*

"Thought you'd be here," he said, approaching her table.

Or maybe Mal told you. She kept the thought to herself.

"How are you holding up, Daisy?" he asked.

"As well as can be expected, Captain."

"I know it's tough on you, and if your work weren't so necessary, I'd just tell you to take a few days to get your head clear. Unfortunately, we don't have that luxury, and I want you to know I appreciate the effort you're making." He paused and sized her up, apparently pleased with what he saw. "So what about the air supply issue and those problematic systems? Any progress?"

"Some, Captain, but I'm concerned. It may be nothing, but as I scan back in the logs, it seems a great many of the ship's systems have been acting glitchy since we woke up."

"I've noticed that as well, and it worries me that there may be issues unrelated to our initial impact."

Daisy nodded in agreement.

"Captain, I have to ask you. Have you come across anything *unusual* in our systems?"

"What do you mean?"

"I don't know. I guess, anything out of the ordinary, no matter how small. Something that might help explain why things are buggy?"

"You're the chief electronics expert now, Daisy. I leave that to you. But since you mention it, the ship does seem to be having more out-of-parameter power fluctuations as we get closer to Earth. Gustavo noticed it as well the other night when he was double-checking our course. You have a theory?"

"I'm not sure. Let me dig a little more, and I'll be sure to let you know if I find anything."

"Do. We can't afford any more problems with the *Váli* before we reach the moon. We're too damn close for Murphy to start messing things up for us with his stupid law."

Harkaway walked over to the kitchen counter and surveyed the still-warm treats.

"Thanks, Finn," the captain said, grabbing a brownie off the plate and heading back to Command.

Daisy repositioned herself at a table facing the main doors and settled in. She had food, and she had notes and busy-work in front of her, and to anyone observing, that was what was occupying her time. In reality, she was far more interested in the men and women of the crew than the work on the table or the food on her plate.

Shortly after the captain departed, Gustavo and Reggie both made their way to the galley.

"I hear there are brownies in here!"

Gus and Reg swarmed Finn's workspace.

"Hey, don't crowd, guys. I made enough for everyone." Finn

slid another steaming batch onto the half-full plate on the counter.

"Oh my God, these are amazing. You're the man, Finn!" Reggie said through a mouthful of melting chocolate joy.

Metal hand and some artificial organs from what I hear, but with an appetite like that, he's got to be human. Even a cyborg would have a hard time processing the amount of food that guy puts away.

Daisy tentatively checked Reggie off her mental list and put him in the 'unlikely' column. Gustavo, well, she wasn't so sure about him. The extensive work he'd had done, both internally and externally, made her uneasy. The fact that he had access jacks built into his head, well, that also seemed obviously more machine than human. Still, he was her friend. At least as much as a half-machine man could be, she supposed. It was that damn mechanical eye. It always put her on edge and made her wonder just how much of the real Gustavo was inside that metal-enhanced skull.

Mark Gus as a 'maybe,' then.

"Hey, babe!" Vince called out when he walked in twenty minutes later. He grabbed a mug of piping-hot coffee and a few brownies, then sidled over to join her. "How's my girl?" he asked, leaning in to give her a kiss.

"Doing all right, I suppose," was her reply. "Still a little foggy-headed, ya know? Trying to get back to firing on all cylinders before we park this heap at Dark Side and hop the shuttle down to Earth."

"Well, I don't have to start my shift for another hour. You up for a quick game? Might get the brain going."

"Sure," she said, not wanting to leave her table with a view.

"Excellent, I'll grab the board."

Twenty minutes later, Doctor McClain finally came for her usual, boring breakfast, eschewing Finn's baked treats for a bowl of plain oatmeal and a cup of tea.

Way to live up to the stereotype, Doc, Daisy mused as she

casually watched the stuffy woman's actions between her turns on the chessboard. She seemed human, but who was to say? And Tamara? She hadn't shown up for breakfast at all, and Daisy found herself no closer to knowing who the cyborg was than when she started.

"What are you up to, Daisy?" Vince asked.

"Huh?"

"You heard me. I know you're plotting something."

"Wait, I'm not plotting anything, I—"

"Oh, come on! You're totally sandbagging. Sacrificing your bishop like that? I know you better than that. You've got something up your sleeve."

"Maybe I do." She forced a laugh. "Tell you what, how about you swing by my quarters in a half hour."

He flashed a mischievous smile.

"Twist my arm, why don't ya," he said.

He was in for a surprise, all right. Daisy just wondered how he'd take the news.

~

"Are you serious?" Vince asked incredulously as they sat on Daisy's bed.

"I triple-checked the numbers, Vince. With all variables accounted for, and factoring in oxygen consumption compared to remaining crewmembers and their metabolic needs based on percentage of non-organic parts, I'm sure of it. Even when going back and including the data for the past several months, it all adds up the same. The oxygen usage is just too low. Someone besides Barry isn't human."

Lying in his arms, head on his chest, Daisy felt strangely calm given the nature of their conversation. Listening to the slow, rhythmic thumping of his heart always helped soothe her frazzled nerves.

"Have you told the captain?"

"No, Mal was active in the room. She's always listening, Vince. Only our quarters and the Narrows are off her monitoring grid. Until I know what's going on, I want to keep this on the down-low."

"But he's the captain."

"And he's also the highest-ranking person on board. It's still possible he's in on it."

"You're getting paranoid. The captain's a good man. And we know he's a man, right? I mean, those ridiculous nosebleeds—"

"I remember. Nope, Captain's off that list. So is Finn. That leaves Gus, Reggie, maybe, Tamara, and Doctor McClain."

"What about me?" he asked, kissing her forehead.

"You and me are the only ones I'm entirely sure about. And Sarah, of course." Daisy fell silent.

"Just be careful. If there's something going on, you want to know all the facts before you do anything rash. There might be a reasonable explanation."

"I wish you were right."

Her door chime sounded.

"Shit, hang on!" She stumbled to her feet and cycled the doors open.

"Hello, Daisy. I wanted to discuss the airlock issue that caused Sarah's demise. Do you have a moment?" Barry inquired. The cyborg was always so damn polite. It was unnerving.

"Hey, Barry!" Vince called out, reclining on the tiny bunk.

"Ah, Vincent. I did not realize you two were occupied. Daisy, we can discuss this at your earliest convenience. Apologies for the intrusion."

He turned, the door sealing behind him.

"That thing creeps me out."

"Hey, don't be so harsh on Barry. He's a person, Daze, just not the kind you're used to."

"He doesn't breathe, Vince. He doesn't eat. He's just a

machine covered in flesh. I mean, the others, at least they have their inorganic parts clear for all to see. It's more honest, I guess. You know what you're getting. With Barry, it's an entirely artificial creation. He wasn't born, he was built, and then, rather than let him simply be a metal-skinned robot, they had to go and slap a layer of flesh and blood over him. Seriously, Vince, they went to such great lengths to make him appear human when, in truth, he's the least human of all of us."

"I see where you're coming from, but, technically, he does breathe; it's just a minimal amount, is all. All cyborgs have to keep their flesh oxygenated and alive, and that means intake of oxygen through respiration, and yes, even some food."

"Maybe," she relented, "but it's still creepy as fuck."

"He's not so bad. You just need to give him a chance."

"Unless he's going to tell me who the other cyborg is, I'll pass, thanks."

CHAPTER FOURTEEN

Three days to Earth, and Daisy was no closer to figuring out who among the others was not human. She couldn't very well go around probing and groping the crew—with the exception of Vince, of course—while trying to feel for a pulse, or lack thereof. Worse yet, having conspicuously exposed artificial parts did not preclude anyone from suspicion.

She had sat for hours upon hours, ensconced in the privacy of her quarters, scanning through the minimally secured crew files she'd been able to access. It seemed the coding tricks she'd learned for Vince's birthday surprise were having real-world applications she hadn't expected. Unfortunately, the files were all normal.

Too normal. As if someone had crafted them to read just the way they would be expected to if someone were to gain unauthorized access and dig through them.

With few leads to go on, Daisy found herself antsy, resigned to wandering the ship in her off-time, thinking as she moved. Running scenarios through her head. Trying to get a grasp on the bigger picture.

It comes back to Mal, most likely, she thought. *And Sarah's accident.* She shuddered at the thought. *What if it wasn't an accident? What if she was getting too close to something? I mean, this could potentially put the entire Dark Side base at risk.*

Daisy felt her mind spin. The implications were incredible. *Are the AI trying to take over?* she found herself wondering.

"This is ridiculous," she muttered to herself. "But what if—"

"Do you need any assistance, Daisy?" Mal asked. "Your blood pressure seems rather high."

"She's always keeping tabs on you, ya know. You need to go somewhere she can't scan," Sarah's voice whispered in her head. Somehow, Daisy's internal manifestation of her dead friend seemed to have gained strength since she nearly fried her brain.

"Yeah, I know," she said out loud.

"You know *what*, Daisy?" Mal asked.

Shit.

"Nothing. I was just talking to myself. Thanks for checking in, Mal, but I'm fine." Daisy forced herself to walk normally, but she also focused on the lesson Sarah had taught her.

One, two, three... She tried to sense her heartbeat.

"That's it, Daze, just like we practiced," Sarah's voice encouraged.

Four, five... Slowly, she began to feel her pulse and breathing fall under her control. *Six, seven, eight...*

It was one of Sarah's little centering tricks. A simple thing, really, but one that Daisy had found she was actually pretty good at, even before she decided to embrace a handful of neuro-stim-implanted techniques. Once those additions had taken hold, her control had only improved.

"I must have suffered a scanning error, Daisy. Your blood pressure appears to be perfectly normal. Perhaps even a little on the low side. Might I suggest adding more salt to your next meal?"

"Thanks, Mal," she replied, not losing count in her head. "I'll remember that at dinner."

"A good idea. I will also ask Barry to bring some sodium tablets by your quarters later. Proper electrolyte balance is of the utmost importance."

Daisy kept walking, quietly counting in her head.

"I know where you're going," Sarah's disembodied voice mused. *"I thought you hated that place."*

"I do, but you loved it," she replied, keeping the discourse *internal* this time, away from Mal's ever-listening ears.

"So sentimental. What have you done with that sarcastic girl I know and love? Are you sure you're the real Daisy?"

"Very funny coming from my imaginary friend," she replied silently. "But there's another reason. The scanners in there are still offline."

Daisy felt the nausea rise in her throat.

Maybe this wasn't such a good idea.

Floating weightless in the empty space of Starboard Nine was making her stomach flip-flop, as usual, but Daisy redoubled her efforts, focusing her breathing, concentrating on the tasks at hand—namely, keeping her body calm, figuring out how to weed out the hidden cyborg in their crew, and, of course, not barfing in zero-g.

She used a tether line to help anchor her in the gravity-free room, then let herself unwind, closing her eyes in the dimly-lit compartment. As she focused on breathing, relaxing her body as she did, a surprising thing happened. The nausea that plagued her whenever she visited that pod was a little different in her mind. It became something tangible. Something she had control over. Gently, she wrapped her mind around the discomfort and squeezed it down, compressing the ill-feeling into a tiny sliver of itself until it subsided completely.

Cool!

Daisy opened her eyes slowly. Direction was no longer an issue. Up and down, forward and back, nothing mattered but where she intended to be. The notion finally clicked, and just like that, she was as comfortable as an otter swimming in the sea, with every direction at her disposal. She tugged the tether, sending herself toward the bulkhead. Just as she was about to make contact, she flipped her body around, landing feet-first and pushing off at an angle.

She used a little too much force, which sent her flying to the opposite wall a bit too fast, but with another mid-flight twist, she shifted her impact and again pushed off in a different direction. This time the rebound was better.

This is awesome!

"Told you so," her dead friend approved.

Daisy spent the better part of a half hour experimenting with zero-g flight without the burden of an EVA suit. It was everything Sarah had said it could be.

I finally see what you meant, Sarah. I wish I'd listened when you were still alive.

The voice in her head remained silent.

Eventually Daisy drifted to the center of the pod again and allowed herself to become still. There was a problem to work through, and after unwinding with a little relaxing fun, she felt refreshed and ready for the challenge.

Interestingly, she found that while she'd been playing in the weightless environment, her subconscious had been busily working away at the dual problems of tracking down that problematic air leak, as well as the more troubling issue of there being an additional cyborg hidden among the crew.

Much like the medical scanner she'd reassembled on auto pilot without consciously thinking about it, or the odd little plasma cascade device she'd created while 'in the zone,' which she'd been tinkering with ever since, this solution to her new problem came to her without her even realizing it. And interestingly, it involved that very same piece of medical equipment.

It seemed that, like those hidden-image pictures, things were coming to her much easier now that she'd learned that all she needed was to shift her perspective in order to see them. Unfocus and the big picture becomes clear.

If I strip it out of the massive housing, the key bits will easily fit, she thought. *And it aligns with what I was already doing so perfectly.*

A cheerful smile blossomed alongside the idea.

She finally had a plan.

Daisy had been putting together a sensor array in the airlocks between pods to gauge pressure changes from one section to the next, hoping to pinpoint the culprit. It was tedious work, and her installations occasionally irritated crewmembers, as they were forced to go around through a different set of airlock doors while she ratcheted all of the pieces into place, but everyone accepted it as part of her daily routine. More importantly, it was a routine that the captain had ordered her to do.

The installations were a part of her duties as the ship's technical expert, and a huge thing working in her favor was that no one else really knew what exactly her sensors were doing. Barry might spot something obviously not aimed at gauging the air volume, but adding a stripped-down body scan array from the parts at her disposal shouldn't be too difficult, and she could easily hide them in the existing design. No one would know the difference.

The only potential issue she could envision was that she needed the crew to stay in one place for her scan to run. It would take several seconds, but that was the beauty of her plan. While they stood in the airlock space between the doors as they waited for them to cycle, that would provide the machine plenty of time to do a quick scan and gather the data she needed.

Unfortunately, she couldn't leave a readout tablet attached to the unit, lest people see what she was up to, so she modified one of the partially damaged units on her workbench to act as a pure receiver only. It took a bit of re-wiring to alter its inputs, but in the end, she managed to configure it to communicate directly with the scanner, but without any connectivity to Mal. The information from the scanner could be directly sent back to that unit alone, and would be totally partitioned from the mysterious AI's prying eyes.

It was somewhat rudimentary—she only had so many pieces she could cannibalize for the device, after all—but after several hours hunched over circuit boards with a soldering gun in her workspace, she had a fully-functioning, and fully-camouflaged body scanner. The problem was, she only had enough parts to make one.

Now, where to put it?

The galley's main entryway, she eventually decided.

It was the most logical place to install the device, as most of the time the crew used the entrance from the common passageway. Rarely did they enter via the connecting pod doors adjacent at either end. With only three doors, she had a thirty-three percent chance of getting the crew as they gathered for their meals, if you went by pure math. Taking into consideration the habits the crew had formed when coming to chow, she gave herself a solid seventy percent.

Daisy hauled the contraption to the galley and cycled the passageway door open, then heaved the curved, composite housing into the space and began removing the mounting bolts lining the walls. She'd replace them soon enough, and with them, the scanner would be in place, running from just below knee level, hugging the wall as it passed across the top of the small chamber.

"Shit, sorry, Daisy, didn't know you'd be putting that in here," Reggie said as he stepped into the somewhat cramped space.

"Yeah, sorry about that. Captain's on me to find that pressure leak, so I'm setting up down here next. Sorry about the inconvenience. It'll be mounted in ten minutes."

"No worries. I just wanted to grab a little snack before lunch. I'll circle around to botanical and pop in through from there. I should probably say hi to Tamara anyway and thank her. She took a special request and grew me some purple carrots."

"What's so special about that?"

"Nothing. I just like them, is all. Anyway, she humored me and grew a few bunches. She's really not so bad once you get past that gruff botanist façade."

"Well, save me a carrot, then. I'll be in, in a few minutes."

"Will do."

Reggie stepped back out into the passageway and made his way around the long way. Less than ten minutes later, Daisy completed the installation, powered on the device, and waited for it to charge.

A design constraint had been the unit's power consumption. Scanning a body took huge amounts of energy, but Mal would immediately notice a power draw of that magnitude. Daisy had finally worked around the issue when an inspiration hit her. It had to do with the neuro-stim, the way the device itself worked.

Simple, she thought. *By drips.*

Like the neuro-stim filled a mind with data, she structured her scanner to charge the same way. Rather than one big cable feeding the unit, the housing now contained scores of portable batteries, daisy-chained together and tied to a trickle charger. To Mal, it would just look like a constant low-level pressure-measuring device pulling power, but in reality, the machine would slowly build enough stored energy for a self-powered, and totally covert, scan.

She figured the machine was likely operational when the

captain passed through the device a few hours later. He had been followed a few minutes later by Tamara, who paused to examine the strange contraption mounted between the heavy airlock doors, but, unfortunately, remained unscanned as the machine needed over an hour before it could capture another image.

One is better than none, she thought.

A short while later, Daisy casually strolled back to her quarters, munching on a purple carrot Reggie had saved for her. As soon as her door closed behind her, she excitedly powered on the readout tablet. She had been correct, only one scan had been sent to the device, and the captain, as expected, was human. His entire left leg from the hip down was cybernetic, and while she couldn't achieve the resolution to pinpoint what had been his exact injury, she could, however, see where the junction between bone and metal was slowly breaking down. It wasn't an alloy or a servo issue, but a flesh & bone one.

Wow, sorry, Captain. That's got to be getting painful.

Daisy noticed several other anomalies in his scan. Internal scar tissue everywhere, and lots of it. At some point, it seemed, Captain Harkaway had undergone some incredibly invasive procedures throughout much of his body. It was a miracle he wasn't perpetually crotchety, given what he must have gone through.

By the end of the afternoon, Gustavo and Reggie were added to her growing database, though it had taken a bit of wrangling to keep Finn from messing things up and walking through the doorway, draining the charge on a useless scan while she waited for Gus to head back to Command after dinner. Daisy had been forced to use the only trick she had at her disposal, and it really wasn't much in the way of tricks when you got right down to it. More like a dare, if you could dare yourself, that is. In any case, it was right up Finn's alley, and that was all that mattered.

Finnegan had one weakness aside from food, and Daisy intended to use it to her full advantage.

"Hey, Finn," she called out when he headed toward the door that she'd just spent the better part of the hour watching recharge. "Come here for a minute."

Gus was finishing his meal, and provided he didn't go back for seconds, or heaven help her, dessert, he'd be exiting soon. Likely less than five minutes, if her estimate was correct.

"Yeah, Daisy, what's up?" the metal-fingered chef asked.

"I wanna show you something. A game I learned the other day."

"Daisy, I really should go clean up. How about tomorrow?"

He turned and started for the door.

"It's got *knives*."

Finn stopped in his tracks, slowly turning with an impish grin on his face.

"Oh, *reeeeally?* Well, why didn't you say so?"

"I just did. Bring me your cutting board. And a knife."

Finnegan was intrigued, and despite having so recently had a run-in with the wrong end of a very sharp bit of cutlery, his love of all things bladed hadn't diminished in the least.

He placed the cutting board and a medium-sized chef's knife in front of her on the table.

"Okay, so color me intrigued, Daisy. What sort of game needs a cutting board and a knife?"

"You a fan of *Aliens*?" she asked.

"What, like little green men in UFOs? Is this going to be some stupid joke, Daisy?"

She slapped her hand down on the board, fingers spread wide.

"Not a joke at all, Finn," she said, looking him in the eye.

Something in the way she smiled made him ever so slightly uncomfortable.

Daisy picked up the knife in a stabbing grip and rested the point on the cutting board, between her thumb and index finger.

"Uh, what are you doing, Daisy?"

"I told you, it's a game." Her eyes darted to Gus as he began gathering his dishes.

"I don't think I want to play this game," Finn said. "Maybe we should just put that back in the kitchen, okay?"

Daisy took a deep breath and focused. It was getting easier every time she did it, she found. The focusing was becoming second nature, and the pattern formed by her spread fingers made geometric figures flicker behind her eyes. It was just simple mathematics.

She started stabbing the board. Slowly at first, the knife traveling from left to right between her fingers as she went. Horrified but fascinated, Finn couldn't take his eyes off it.

Faster and faster, the knife thunked into the spaces between her fingers, coming so close, but leaving her flesh unharmed. Soon her knife-wielding hand was a blur of speed. She was in the groove and in total control. She couldn't miss, and Finn was enthralled.

Daisy broke her concentration for a split second and allowed herself a little smile as she saw Gus finally head for the door from the corner of her eye.

"Ouch!"

A small blossom of red dotted the cutting board beneath her nicked thumb.

"Shit, Daisy, now I've got to wash that again," Finn whined, but behind the words, she could see he thought that was ridiculously cool. As her metal-fingered friend gathered up the knife and board, Gus stepped into the double door and sealed it behind him.

Finally!

"You know something? You're nuts, Daisy. But you're my kind of nuts," Finn said with a laugh. "I mean, I already have metal fingers. Is this just your way of saying you're jealous and want some too?"

"Not on your life. I like my bits just like they are. One hundred percent human. Catch ya later, Finn."

"Yeah, yeah. See ya, crazy girl."

Daisy made her way back to her pod thinking about what she'd said to Finn.

One hundred percent human.

She looked at her bandaged finger and had a flash of doubt.

It didn't cut deep enough to hit bone, she reluctantly admitted to herself. *And there've been rumors of AIs who don't even know they're artificial. But, no, there's no way I could be one. I bled more than a skin-job would, didn't I? And besides,* she placed her fingers on her neck. Thump-thump, thump-thump. Daisy smiled and relaxed. *Cyborgs don't have a pulse.*

She put those thoughts aside upon arrival at her quarters, cycling the doors open as fast as they'd allow, then anxiously snatching up the readout tablet. Two more scans out of the way, and it wasn't even dinner yet. Not bad.

She pulled up the readouts for Reggie and Gus. While they were both alive and human, the results surprised her.

Reggie's hand, the scan confirmed, wasn't his only replacement part. He was also sporting one partially metal leg, though Daisy had never noticed any physical tells on Reggie's part. Of course, how could she? The femur had been replaced with a stronger metal replacement, but that didn't really matter. It wouldn't affect his oxygen consumption by much at all.

In Gustavo's case, while she knew the basic extent of his modifications, it seemed his eye was part of a larger network, one which intermingled with his nervous system, running directly into his brain and spine. The tendrils of fine wires fed into servo assists in his arms and wrists. Multiple organs were also synthetic, as she already knew, but seeing them on the readout made her wonder what exactly had happened to him to require such drastic measures. It was unusual, and somewhat unsettling, but he was still a man.

Getting scans of Tamara and Doctor McClain had been proving more difficult. The botanist spent most of her time in her series of interconnected garden pods, and the doctor, well, she liked her routines. Unfortunately, that meant Doctor McClain made a habit of using the opposite airlock door than the one fitted with the scanner, while Tamara, likewise, often decided to enter by another route.

Daisy had to find a way to lure them through the right one.

CHAPTER FIFTEEN

"Are you all right?" Barry sounded genuinely concerned, which for a machine was a rather unsettling thing in Daisy's opinion, given what she now knew about her fellow crewmembers.

She wiped the tears from her eyes. "It's just getting to me, you know?" The frustration and sadness in her voice was palpable, her face flushed as her pulse raced. "Sarah, I mean... she was snatched away in a split second, gone so quickly. I don't know who to talk to."

The cyborg momentarily cocked his head like a confused pup, or a dog hearing a whistle only audible to its ears. His head straightened, then without further hesitation announced, "I'll get Doctor McClain. Please, remain here."

"Thank you, Barry." She sniffled. "I'll be in the galley."

Daisy concentrated on keeping her heart rate elevated. With her newfound meditative control, she found it was becoming easier to do.

Gotta keep up appearances. She dabbed her eyes once more. The burning was immediate, tears flowing freely. *Okay, that's more than enough*, she thought as she sealed the tiny piece of onion stolen from Finn's kitchen back into the small plastic pouch in her pocket. She took the long way to the galley, using the adjacent pod's access rather than the main one, and took a seat. Now all she had to do was wait.

It didn't take long. The airlocks were soundproofed, but she saw the lights change as someone keyed into the controls and stepped in from the other side.

Gotcha!

Barry emerged first.

Shit!

Doctor McClain stepped out right behind him. Apparently, they'd come through the airlock together. She hadn't expected the cyborg to personally escort Doctor McClain all the way to her, but whatever. She already knew what his scan would show. What really interested her was the woman who stepped out behind him.

"Daisy, dear, what's troubling you? Are you okay?"

"I don't know, Doc. I was doing fine. As good as I could expect, that is. I mean, I *thought* I was doing fine, but then I made some headway on my work and was all excited, so I went to tell Sarah about my progress isolating the leak, and then I realized—" She sniffled loudly for effect.

"It's all right to cry, Daisy. You experienced a terribly traumatic loss and still haven't fully processed it. Working through grief takes time, and you simply haven't been afforded the opportunity to deal with these emotions. I'll tell you what, I'll talk to the captain and see if we can have Barry take over testing pressure variances. I'm sure he wouldn't mind, would you, Barry?"

"Of course not, Doctor McClain. I'd be glad to help in any way that I can."

"Excellent. Come, Daisy. Why don't we go to my office pod? We can discuss it in private as long as you like."

"Thanks Doc," she said, wiping the tears from her eyes. "I appreciate it, really, but I've got to finish this. Occupying myself completing Sarah's work actually helps me get through the day. Like I'm honoring her memory by making sure it gets done, if that makes sense. Is it all right if I take you up on that offer a little later? If I focus on the task at hand, I can keep the dark thoughts out of my head, at least for the time being."

"Of course. I don't want to push you in any direction that makes you uncomfortable. If work helps, then by all means, keep at it, but if you need a break, you can count on me to talk to the captain for you." Doctor McClain turned to leave. "My door is always open for you, Daisy, whenever you need me. I want you to know that."

"I appreciate it, really." She turned to the artificial man observing quietly. "And Barry, thank you too. It's nice knowing you're looking out for my best interests."

My ass, she added silently.

"It is my pleasure, Daisy. Anything I can help with, please feel free to ask."

"I will." She wiped the tears from her face. "For now, I had better get back to it. These tests aren't going to run themselves."

"We'll leave you to it, then," Doctor McClain said, exiting the galley. Barry hovered a moment longer, watching Daisy gather her things.

"You coming, Barry?" McClain asked from the open door. The cyborg paused, then moved to the airlock.

"Right behind you, Doctor McClain."

"Thanks, guys. And, hey, if you see Tamara, could you ask her if she could spare a few carrots or a pepper? I think a little fresh produce might help settle my stomach. If she can spare a few, of course. I'll be right here, working on this for a while."

"I'll mention it to her," the cyborg replied, then stepped in and cycled the inner door closed.

Daisy just hoped the scanner would be able to recharge before Tamara made her way to the galley. *If* she wasn't still too pissed, that is.

She shouldn't have worried. Tamara eventually came to see her, all right, but she entered the galley via the airlock at the far end of the room. The one connecting to the equipment storage section of one of her botanical pods.

What was she doing in there? Daisy wondered as the sturdy woman walked toward her.

"Heard you wanted some produce," she said, carefully placing a small bunch of washed carrots and a small red bell pepper on the steel table in front of her. "Look," she said uncomfortably, "I'm really sorry about Sarah. I know how close you two were."

Daisy accepted the gift, and despite being on a mission to ferret out the truth, she still felt like an ass. She'd been putting this off, but now was as good a time as any. Maybe better, even.

"Thanks, Tamara," she said. "It really means a lot to me." She paused, uncomfortable. "I wanted to apologize for what I said the other day. About your replacement parts. I was upset, and I was speaking impulsively, and I didn't think before I went and blurted out something stupid. I hope you can forgive me and my fool mouth."

A faint grin formed on Tamara's face. Or maybe it was a trick of the light. Whatever the cause, her hard eyes softened ever so slightly.

"You do have a temper on you," she agreed. "Though it's not like I'm one to talk, I suppose. Apology accepted. Shake on it?"

She reached out and offered her metal hand. The gesture was not unintentional. Very little she did ever was. Daisy didn't hesitate, taking the cool metal hand in hers.

"Thanks, Tamara."

The older woman smiled at her and headed back to work. For just a moment it looked like she was going to pass through the central doors, which were almost certainly recharged, but she paused, as if in thought. Moments later she shifted course and exited the way she came.

"Damn," Daisy muttered. "So close."

Something had to be done. Dinner would be in a few hours, and once the crew started to filter in, there'd be no way to control when the auto-charging scanner would use its limited power. Tamara was the one she needed, but how could she—

I'm a goddamn genius!

Daisy cycled the door open and set the scanner to standby. It had a full charge and was primed, but with a two-hour timer locked on to the release mechanism, she could be certain it would be ready for one specific scan window beginning in exactly two hours.

Yeah, this should totally work, she hoped, not nearly as confident as she pretended to herself.

She tightened the locking screw on the panel, then stepped out of the galley, leaving her notes and tablet on the table as she jogged down the passageway. When she reached Tamara's main work pod, she stopped and keyed the door's intercom system.

"Yeah, what is it?" Tamara finally asked.

"Hey, Tamara, it's Daisy. I was wondering if I could borrow your portable chemical analyzer. The DMZ-2200. Mine's been acting up, and I really need to verify some of the trace gas readings I collected before the accident. Would you mind?"

A silence hung in the air as Tamara mulled over the request.

"Well… yeah, I guess. Hang on, I'll grab it for you." A minute later the door cycled open, and Tamara handed her the bulky device. "Take good care of it, all right?"

"Promise. Thanks a lot!"

"Uh-huh."

Tamara closed the door and returned to her work, while Daisy hurried back to the galley, lugging the heavy piece of equipment, which she tucked under her metal table as she focused her attentions back on her calculations.

One hour and forty-two minutes. Where's Finn?

She needn't have worried as Finn entered the galley minutes later to begin his meal preparations. Since Tamara was the lone vegetarian on the crew, her meal was always a pretty easy one to prepare. That's not to say it was uninspired or lacking in any way. Far from it, in fact. Finn took great care to ensure her food was every bit as flavorful and interesting as the rest of the crew's. What it did mean, though, was that Tamara would more often than not be served and done before everyone else. That was something Daisy was counting on.

Vince came in not too long after and sat down across from his girlfriend.

"Hey, what's this?" he asked, tapping the large device with his foot.

"Be careful with that, it's Tamara's," she replied. "She lent it to me so I could run a few scans. Mine's been acting up for some reason."

"You two make peace?"

"Yeah, I think we're on good terms now."

"Cool. Not trying to be a dick or anything, but you *did* sound a bit prejudiced. I can see why she was offended."

"I wasn't trying to be. It just came out that way."

"Well, someday you'll accept that the mechanically enhanced and AIs are people too, just like everyone else. Anyway, I finished my ridiculous to-do list a bit early today. You wanna join me for a little movie time later?"

"I know what that means," she replied with a knowing smile. "But I really need to finish this stuff first. Rain check?"

He leaned in and gave her a kiss. "Sure thing."

"I'm sorry."

"Not a problem, babe, seriously."

"Okay, as long as you're not just saying that."

"You know me. Subterfuge is not my forté." He flashed that grin she found so irresistible and took another bite of his dinner.

Gradually, the rest of the crew filtered in, and not long after, everyone was happily eating, a full fifteen minutes before the scanner would power back on, no less.

Excellent, it's all timing out just right.

With five minutes to go, Tamara got to her feet and scraped her tray into the compost bin before turning for the secondary doors.

Shit! Too soon!

"Hey, Tamara!" Finn called out. "Don't you want any dessert?"

"You know I don't eat most of that stuff, Finn."

"Correct-o-mundo. That's why I decided to make my world-famous vegan saffron crème brûlée."

"Vegan crème brûlée? You pulling my leg, Finn? You know I could snap you like a twig," she joked.

"Cross my heart. You can even run it through a scanner, if you want. I see Daisy has one under her table there, which I'm not sure if I should be offended at, come to think of it."

"Just running tests, Finn," she answered. "And not on your food."

Tamara turned back and accepted the ramekin.

"What the hell. I can't remember the last time I had one of these."

She sat back down and cracked the caramelized sugar top of her dessert, lifting a spoonful to her mouth.

"Oh damn, that's really good, Finn."

The chef beamed with delight, as Daisy looked on with silent gratitude.

Saved my ass there, Finn. Thanks for that.

By the time Tamara had scraped the ramekin clean, the scanner had powered back on, right on schedule.

Now time for part two.

"Hey, Tamara, could you give me a hand with this? I think I'm going to finish the rest of my work back in my quarters, but with all these notes and things in my arms, I wouldn't want to risk dropping your scanner on accident."

"I can get that if you like," Vince volunteered.

"Thanks, but it's her scanner, and I know she's as particular about her gear as I am." Daisy gave Tamara a conspiratorial wink.

"Okay, Daisy, I'll give you a hand."

Daisy loaded her arms with her notes and portable tablet, then headed for the doors. The *main* doors. Tamara hefted the machine easily with her robotic arm and followed. The inner door cycled open, but Daisy paused.

"Crap, I forgot my tool pouch. Go on ahead, I'll be right behind you."

"I swear, you'd forget your head if it weren't bolted on," Tamara teased as she stepped into the airlock. The door cycled as Daisy retrieved her tools, sitting on the floor, exactly where she intended them to be.

Gotcha.

CHAPTER SIXTEEN

The ship was quiet as it flew through the cold vacuum of space on its path to Earth, and the men and women safe within the protective walls of the *Váli* were sound asleep.

Well, almost all of them.

It was many hours past dinner, and the crew had long since retired for the night, but Daisy's mind was racing as she lay wide awake in her bunk. She looked at the clock on her wall.

1:27 am.

She needed something to take her mind off the horrible paranoia threatening to swallow her whole, but she didn't dare fire up the neuro-stim. Not now. Not even with all twelve inhibitors fully engaged. A line had been crossed, she could feel it, and she really didn't know what would happen if she disturbed the sleeping beast inside her, even slightly. No, she would just have to deal with the insomnia and troubling thoughts running through her brain like a storm-panicked herd of wild horses running blindly toward a cliff.

None of them, she thought, over and over. *Not a single one of them is a cyborg.*

The revelation was a kick in the stomach.

After dinner, once Tamara had carefully dropped off the chemical analyzer at her quarters, Daisy had pulled her tablet from under her pillow, her pulse racing. She took a moment to breathe, lowering the staccato beat. She needed a clear head to plan her next moves. She powered up the display and opened the images.

This was it. She'd managed to get both women through that door, and the results were waiting for her. Doctor McClain and Tamara's secrets would finally be revealed.

Human.

Both of them.

But that can't be right. I've quadruple-checked my numbers. Oxygen consumption, as a percentage of total air volume, is decisive. Even with that leak, the overall volume of air is slowly lessening, but the ratios are the important part.

Daisy scrolled through all of the scans she'd managed to capture of the crew, and although they had an unusually high percentage of artificial parts installed after trauma or illness, they were all undeniably human. Sure, Tamara was a bit more reinforced with sturdy replacement parts than most, and Doc McClain's metal leg included a fully replaced pelvis, which surprised Daisy, but no, they'd all been merely patched up by that machinery, not constructed of it. Looking at their repairs, she realized the process had probably saved their lives, no less.

"Well, you're well and proper fucked now."

Shut up, Sarah.

"Maybe I was a cyborg. Have you thought of that?"

You weren't a cyborg. I would have known.

"You so sure about that?"

Daisy picked up a bracelet from her desk. A slender thing, made of a few braided wires from a scrapped sanitation unit. A silly little gift from Sarah one day after they'd been forced to crawl through a particularly foul-smelling bit of the Narrows they both hoped to never revisit.

With a heavy heart, she slid it over her hand. Despite the almost non-weight of the thing, feeling it gently touching her skin was comforting.

Would I have cared if she were a cyborg?

The thought was disturbing one.

Would she have cared if I was?

"You know I'm not prejudiced," Sarah's voice answered. *"You, on the other hand, I'm not so sure about."*

A dark, creeping thought kept forcing its way into her mind. Something she was horrified to even consider. It was all rumor, really, but what if?

There were stories of experimental AIs. Machines who were unaware of their true nature. Cyborgs who thought they were human, programmed to perceive themselves as such. She had always passed the idea off as impossible. After all, how could a machine not know it was one? But if the programming was good enough, and its perception filtered by coding, could it be possible?

Daisy swallowed hard, the knot in her stomach tightening as an unwelcome thought floated back to the surface of her worrying mind. She knew about the others, she had their scans right in front of her, but she had neglected to test the one person she took for granted as human.

Herself.

This is nuts. There's no way... but deep down inside, the seed of doubt had been planted. If she didn't deal with it now, that seed would quickly sprout roots and grow into a tree.

Only one way to be sure.

Daisy got up and pulled on her sweatpants and a T-shirt, then opened her doors and stepped into the hallway.

Just go. It's better to know than not.

She clenched her jaw and started walking with a deliberate stride. As she made her way down the corridor, a flash of doubt crossed her mind. A need for comfort. She found herself pausing in front of Vince's door, wanting desperately to talk to someone about the dilemma racing through her thoughts. She placed her hand on his door chime touchpad, then hesitated.

I'm being ridiculous. Get moving, Daisy. This is something you have to do. Stop procrastinating.

"Hello?" Vince's voice called out through the tiny speaker. "Reggie, are you messing with me again? Helloooo?"

Shit.

Daisy stayed tight-lipped and lifted her hand from the touchpad, then quickly turned, making a beeline for the galley doors. A minute later she found herself standing outside of them, hesitant.

Go time, she thought. *Just do it already.*

Steeling herself, she keyed the pad beside the double doors and opened the galley's airlock. Her sensor array was quietly waiting for her, right where she'd put it. After a moment's further pause, she moved forward.

Daisy had only just stepped inside when she was roughly grabbed from behind, a pair of powerful arms wrapping around her.

"What the hell!"

Vince pulled her close and silenced her with a kiss as the door closed behind them.

"Vince, what are you—"

His hand slid deftly between her legs, her knees going momentarily weak at his expert touch. With his free hand, he paused the airlock cycle.

"A little privacy," he said in a husky voice. She looked down at the bulge in his sweatpants visibly straining the material.

"Seriously, we can't," she said, only half believing her own words.

"Uh-huh," he said, spinning her to face the wall as he pulled down her pants and freed himself from his own. Daisy felt her pulse spike as his hand snaked up inside her shirt, letting out a hot breath on her neck as he slid inside her from behind.

They both quivered with pleasure, then began frantically grinding against one another, the taboo, public nature of the deed arousing them even further and quickly bringing them both to a rapid climax.

"Holy hell," Daisy managed, fine beads of sweat clinging to her brow and chest.

"You said it," Vince replied with a happy sigh.

"What got into you? That was *so* hot."

"I told you I'd make up for the other day when we had time," he said with a wicked grin. "*Someone* hit my door comms. At such a late hour, I figured it was either Reggie being a dick, or you wanting one."

Daisy rolled her eyes. *Seriously, Vince?*

"When I saw you way down the corridor, I figured, hey, it's been a couple of days, so I'll just come to you. I heard you were upset earlier today, and I thought maybe you could use a little, um, *distraction* with all that's been going on."

"You thought right."

"So, what, you swung by my place, then thought better of it and decided to come down here? I'd like to believe I'm a better option than a midnight snack? You know I can always think of things to do with your nighttime hours."

"Well, I was feeling a little hungry," she lied. "But now I'm feeling pretty exhausted, thanks to you, though a snack actually sounds really good right about now. I hope you don't take it personally, but after that, I think I need to get a little food in me and then catch some shut-eye."

He studied her a moment.

"Of course, whatever you need. Grab a snack and get some sleep, babe. I'll catch up with you in the morning."

"You not coming?"

"I'm sorry, Dave, I can't do that," he said in his best robotic voice.

"Dork, you know I didn't like that movie." She chuckled, then whacked him playfully. "Okay, go to bed, then. I mean if you're just going to use me and toss me aside..."

"Oh, I'll be back for more."

"Right answer," she said with a smile. "Okay, get moving, sexy boy. Sleep tight." She gave him a tender kiss, then he turned to leave.

"Hey, Vince," she said as he stepped back into the passageway. "Who told you I was upset?"

"Barry did. It was the weirdest thing. I was taking a quick catnap in engineering, and when I opened my eyes, he was just standing there, staring at me. Said he didn't want to wake me but thought I should know something."

"That's pretty creepy."

"I know, right? Anyway, you know you can always come to me if you need to talk. Or more than talk," he said, flashing a wicked little grin.

"That's abundantly clear. And thank you, babe. I guess I really did need the release."

Vince gave her a final kiss, then slowly walked back to his quarters. Daisy stepped into the galley and pocketed a power bar and electrolyte pouch to take back with her. She paused and looked at the refrigeration unit. Come to think of it, she *was* a little hungry, thanks in no small part to her boyfriend's efforts.

She took a few fresh strawberries from their cold bin and placed them on the counter. She then retrieved a small pot and some oatmeal from the storage compartment beside the convection heating unit. Twenty minutes later, she sat in deep contemplation, slowly eating her midnight snack straight from the pot.

"You know you should be using a bowl for that, right?"

Daisy jumped.

Where did he come from?

"I mean, I know you'll wash it, that's not the thing. It's just that food tastes better when you properly plate it." Finn gathered up the open oat container and replaced it in the storage shelf.

"I didn't hear you come in."

"Yeah, you were totally zoned out over there. Everything okay? I know a bowl of oatmeal, even *my* special oatmeal, isn't good enough to make a woman glaze over like that. Though a fella can wish, can't he?"

"Couldn't sleep, is all," she replied. "I figured I'd come down here and get a snack. I guess I wound up kinda absorbed in my own thoughts a bit."

"Well, at least I'm not the only one who can't sleep," he said. "Been having weird dreams since the accident." He tapped his metal arm with a spoon, then began placing ingredients on the counter. "I mean, I know we wiped it and did a clean reinstall, but in my dreams, it's like the arm has a mind of its own. It wants what it wants, and the two of us are bickering over who's going to get their way." He tossed some thick-sliced bread on the counter, along with a container of ship-grown eggs, ship-grown milk, and ship-grown ham and cheese. He then dug up powdered sugar and oil from a storage bin.

"Finn, is it you, or is it your rogue arm that's gotten totally confused with ingredients over there?"

"Sometimes the most unlikely of combinations make the most wonderful of meals," he answered. "Monte Cristo sandwich. It's a ham, turkey, and Swiss cheese sandwich, battered and fried, then sprinkled with powdered sugar. Some folks use jam or syrup, but I prefer honey and a little mustard."

"That sounds... interesting."

"I'll let you try a bite. Trust me, it sounds off-putting, but it's really quite nice."

He began preparing his snack, but Daisy noticed something unusual. His arm was moving at normal speed. Human-slow.

"Finn, what's up with your arm? You're usually much faster."

He looked at his appendage with a questioning expression.

"I've been trying to control it," he began. "Make it act more like a human arm."

"But I thought you enjoyed having a super-speedy robot arm."

"Daisy, I'm a chef. By my very nature, I love chopping things up into little pieces at high speed. It's something we all do regardless of whether our arms are metal or not. But the thing is, sometimes I just want to feel like a normal human, ya know?"

"Yeah, I suppose."

"We weren't supposed to be awake this long before arriving. It makes things a bit weird sometimes. Lonely, even. You're lucky —you've got a real connection on board. That in itself will ground you. The rest of us, well, we're all a bunch of roommates and friends, but without any benefits." He fell silent, staring at the wall.

Finn quietly went back to preparing his meal, and didn't speak another word until he was done.

"So what do you think?" he asked as Daisy chewed a slice of the unusual sandwich.

"Actually, quite tasty."

"Told ya." He had begun warming up again once he got into his cooking rhythm. They both loved Sarah in their own ways, and her loss was a common source of grief that brought them closer.

"Finn, how do you feel about all these replacement parts?"

"What do you mean?"

"In the context of humanity. Like, we have the technology to grow and repair living tissue, yet whenever someone is injured or ill, the AIs automatically go to the replacement part option.

It's like they don't even want to try to make you normal." She blushed. "No offense."

"None taken."

"Like, what's the next step in our evolution? In theirs? Are they trying to bastardize mankind until we are as much machinery as they are? And why do humans have exposed metal, while full-on robots are covered with flesh?"

"They're probably just trying to make us feel comfortable around them, is all. Familiar faces and all that."

"But why cyborgs? I mean, take Barry for instance. He's basically a sentient toaster covered in steak—"

"I think he might take issue with that description."

"You know what I'm saying. Why not let robots be robots and people be people? Or is it that they strive to be human? Are they jealous of us?"

"I don't know, Daisy, but I do know the AIs have humanity's best interests at heart. You'll just have to trust me on that."

"I wish I could be so sure."

A short while later, after their impromptu discussion on artificial intelligence and its role in human society, Finn finally downed the last bite of his sandwich and rinsed off his plate.

"All right, gonna go try to get a few hours of shut-eye before the breakfast rush."

"Finn, it's eight people."

"Fine. The breakfast *meander.*"

He walked out the main doors and left Daisy alone with her thoughts, which turned back to her task at hand. The chat had been a nice distraction, and that, along with her little quickie with Vince, had really helped loosen that ball of stress that had been weighing her down. Finn was right, she was lucky to have a real connection on board.

The warm feelings quickly melted away as her real task pressed back to the forefront. Daisy may have been more than momentarily distracted, but she had done what she came to do, albeit in a rather unintentional manner.

Got laid and got scanned. Not bad, Daisy. Helluva night.

She cleaned her dishes and headed back to her quarters, the anxiety that had temporarily left her once again building as she worried about who she was and what the readout would reveal. Though she felt sure she was human, all the way down to her bones, a little splinter of lingering doubt nagged her nonetheless as she walked.

It was time to find out what she really was.

CHAPTER SEVENTEEN

The flashing light on the tablet pulsed in a steady rhythm. Daisy eyed it warily, torn, hoping for the best yet fearing the worst.

Naturally, it was the first thing her eyes fell on upon entering her quarters. She hesitantly picked the device up, then sat on her bunk, staring at the dark screen. It would be so easy to turn on, just a few quick taps and the answer would be there, plain to see.

Come on, she chided herself. *You have to know. Whatever it says, you're still you.*

She steadied herself, then keyed in her password, the screen illuminating with new data.

Oh, it had actually powered up enough, she noted as the unexpected images flashed on the screen. Finn had inadvertently provided her with a scan of himself after their little chat. The device showed her nothing unexpected, however. She had already known he was human. At least, she had been almost certain. Now there wasn't a doubt. One arm, and three fingers, and that was it. Finn was one of the least modified of the entire crew.

Daisy swiped his information off the screen and scrolled to

the second most recent scan. The moment of truth. She only paused for a second, then forced herself to reluctantly tap the screen. What she saw both thrilled and horrified her.

Her scan showed a perfectly normal human female, not a single metal bit or replacement part on her. She was the picture of perfect *human* health, confirmed in glowing color on the screen in her hands.

The other scan was not so straightforward.

Vince looked normal on the outside, as you'd expect of a flesh-and-blood man with a beating heart. Unfortunately, only part of that was the case.

Daisy nearly vomited at the sight of his cybernetic skeleton, the advanced composite matrix of metal and bone grown together into a sturdy framework, hidden beneath his muscles and organs.

Metal in the bones means built. Metal doesn't grow.

She flipped the image and looked closer at an unusual spot on the back of the skull. From what she could tell, a small AI unit was lodged in his cranium, a mix of human brain and computer controlling his every move. The rest of him seemed relatively normal, though rather augmented. He was made of real muscle, but it was denser and stronger than average.

Jesus. I was fucking a machine. Tears flooded her eyes in shock as she stifled a grim laugh that threatened to send her over the edge of sanity.

No wonder he had so much stamina, she thought with a morbid chuckle, remembering her many late-night girl-talk conversations with Sarah.

"And here we'd been joking about Barry's junk," her dead friend grimly mused in her head.

"Not now, Sarah," she told her imaginary companion.

"Sorry."

Daisy forced herself to look at the pictures in detail. This was not the time to freak out. She needed to understand exactly what it was she was dealing with. Ignoring her own scan, she dragged the image of her lover to the center of the screen and zoomed in.

Not a full-cyborg. Some kind of weird hybrid, maybe? I don't understand why, though. A real heart, real muscles. She looked closer. Some of his organs seemed enhanced as well. Not artificial, just different. Designed for efficiency. Everything added up to less oxygen consumption.

Daisy snatched up her notepad and began running calculations. She took into account his size and the newfound data on exactly how much of his mass was metal, and how much was merely different. The numbers matched.

Vince wasn't using enough air for a man his size. At least not for a fully human one. He was the anomaly she had been looking for, and he was right under her nose. Literally, at times.

But they built him with a heart, she kept thinking, horrified. *Every single person on this ship is modified to some degree. They've all got replacement parts in them, and some even have minor AI helping operate them, but who is in on this? For sure, the captain has detailed crew files, and so does Doc McClain, but what about the rest? My God, does the whole crew know*?

Across the pod, her door began to cycle. Only one other person on the ship had access to her quarters.

The inner door slid open.

"Hey, you! I couldn't sleep, and I figured maybe you'd still be hungry, so I made you a sandwich," Vince said merrily as he offered her the plastic-wrapped snack.

Daisy wiped her eyes quickly and took his offering, shying from his touch, unsure and freaked out.

"Hey, are you okay? You don't look so hot." He laughed, flashing her a bright smile. "No, wait, that sounded wrong. You *always* look hot—I mean, just look at you. But seriously, are you feeling all right?"

"My boyfriend is a computer," she muttered.

Vince laughed it off. "Yet you still beat me at chess. Pretty shitty computer, if you ask me. Must be a programming glitch, but at least I have a beautiful singing voice."

"Don't, okay? Just don—"

"Daisy, Daisy, give me your answer, do. I'm half-crazy, all for the love of you—"

"Jesus, shut the fuck up!" she blurted, cutting off his song. "That's not funny."

"I thought it was. Jeez, you really *are* upset. What's up?"

Daisy flipped the tablet to face him.

"You're a fucking machine, Vince! What in the actual fuck? Are you some kind of sick AI who gets off on torturing me?"

"Hang on, what is that?" he asked, studying the screen. His face paled as he realized what she was holding. "Where did you get this?"

"I built a scanner into the galley airlock, Vince. Someone wasn't using enough oxygen on this ship, and I was trying to figure out who it was. I just never thought it would be you."

He bristled at her words.

"That's a serious invasion of privacy, Daisy. That's some seriously unethical shit you just pulled," he said defensively, anger creeping into his voice.

"Ethics? You're talking to *me* about ethics? You're a goddamn machine, Vince! You don't get to lecture me on ethics."

"I'm not a machine. I'm a real person, flesh and blood. You should know that better than anyone."

She shuddered at the thought.

"You're meat on a metal composite endoskeleton, that's all."

"I'm alive, Daisy. My bones aren't what make me a man. I feel, I think. What we have between us is real. It's all so obvious, why can't you accept that?"

"Because you were built. You've never been a child, you never grew up. There may be parts of you that are human, but you were never born. You were grown, and you're still a machine on the inside."

"If I'm just a machine, how can I love you?"

Oh, for fuck's sake. After all this time, he finally says the L-word, and it has to be like this?

"No, this is some serious conspiracy-level shit, Vince. You and Mal are plotting something, I know it, and Barry's probably in on it too."

"Whoa, babe, hang on, you're getting seriously carried away. There's things you should know. I can explain."

"No! Just get out!"

She shoved him hard, driving him back into the open airlock door.

"Daisy, hang on."

Her hand flew to the console, slapping the close button. The sturdy door started cycling shut, but abruptly stopped.

Vince's arm reached through the opening, triggering the automated safety protocol, the door stuck partially ajar.

"Daisy, let me explain. This isn't what you think," he said through the small gap.

"Move your arm, Vince."

"Not until you talk to me, Daisy."

"Get the hell away from me!" she shrieked.

"You're being unreasonable. Let me back in. I can explain all of this. Don't be so difficult."

Vince waved his arm as he awkwardly tried to reach the control panel, but Daisy was faster. Quickly, and without consciously knowing how she did it, she entered what she somehow knew was an override command into the keypad, disabling the safety.

There was no siren, no warning announcement. Nothing at all, before the door slammed shut with a wet crunch.

Vince's bloody arm flapped around on the ground a moment, jerking as severed nerve endings fired, uncontrolled.

Then it was still. The door had taken it off cleanly, right at the shoulder.

That thing is probably screaming its head off right now, she thought grimly, a madwoman's laugh threatening to escape her lips as her mind reeled.

A shell-shocked grin flashed on her face, replaced by one of disbelief as her mind tried to cope with what just happened. She looked at the smear of blood trickling down to the severed arm on the deck.

Nice for me the door is soundproof. She chuckled morbidly as she fought off the creeping fit of hysteria.

Then she sat down hard on the deck and sobbed.

CHAPTER EIGHTEEN

"Daisy? Where are you?" Captain Harkaway stood angrily in her quarters, surveying the bloody scene. "Dammit, Swarthmore, I know you can hear me. Where the hell are you?"

Doctor McClain chimed in. "Daisy, I know you must be scared and upset, but please talk to me. We don't know how this horrible accident happened, but it looks like Vincent will pull through. Please, talk to us. He lost a lot of blood on the way to medical before losing consciousness in the passageway. Daisy, please. Vince is with the med bot now, and is in serious condition. I'm sure hearing your voice would do him a world of good."

No reply.

"Daisy?"

"I do not believe she wishes to speak with us at this moment," Barry opined, stepping over the drying blood to survey her quarters.

From the hallway, where her scans could reach, Mal concurred. "Agreed. She is not registering on any of my bio-readings for common areas. It is possible she has merely entered another off-scan crew quarters. I recommend checking Vincent's pod next. Of course, as our chief electronics expert, it is entirely possible she has altered my sensors in an attempt to mask her whereabouts."

"Can she even do that?"

"Her skills appear to have far exceeded her anticipated parameters." Mal sounded a little concerned, but also curiously puzzled.

"What do you mean, Mal? She's a quick learner, but I hadn't noticed anything that out of the ordinary in my evaluations."

"I understand, Doctor McClain, but she appears to be accessing far more implanted skill set data than she should be able to at this point. Additionally, it would appear that she executed a base command override of the safety mechanisms on her compartment door. I'm afraid what happened to Vincent was no accident."

"Impossible. Those two are nuts about each other."

"Maybe so, Captain, but the readings are correct. Barry, I cannot scan inside the personal quarters of crew. Please verify my findings, then do a survey for any relevant information."

"Glad to oblige, Mal," the cyborg replied, then began riffling through her quarters while his portable terminal interfaced with Daisy's internal door control panel.

"Hang on a minute," Captain Harkaway said. "Before we start going through her personal possessions, we should at least verify that—"

The terminal emitted a small ping as it finished its scan.

"Mechanism history for the door unit corresponds with Mal's assessment, Captain. I will now execute a full search."

"Well, shit." Captain Harkaway didn't know what else to say.

"Mal," Doctor McClain said, "what is the likelihood that Daisy would act in a violent manner against a member of the crew?"

The computer ran the numbers.

"Previously, twenty-three percent, though slightly higher for Barry, given her dislike of artificial life-forms."

"And now? Given what we've seen?"

"Now I would reassess and adjust that figure to forty-eight percent. She and Vincent had an emotional connection, and humans are far more likely to achieve extremes at either end of the emotional spectrum when those feelings come into play."

"Mal," Barry interjected, "I am examining Daisy's neuro-stim unit. It appears she has added a multitude of additional protocols to her trickle-feed queue, including Sarah's technical skill set. I am also seeing indications she accessed detailed ship's schematics far beyond those required for her duties."

"Most disconcerting. She was not supposed to have that information available to her. Unless there was some cross-leakage during cryo while all neuro-stims were interlinked, but even so, this should not be possible. They are genetically tied to the individual."

"Agreed, it *shouldn't* have happened; however, she does seem to have that skill set in her possession. Judging by the looks of her neuro-stim unit, she has been reconfiguring it since the first days after the crew was awoken. I see she has also accessed files for environmental engineering and life support systems, computer subroutine systems design and troubleshooting, including improvised hacking, combat training, advanced military tactics and strategy—"

"Hang on," Captain Harkaway interrupted. "That's not what that says. It says chess."

"Indeed, Captain. However, nearly every protocol has multiple layers of additional skill sets embedded in them, depending on the settings," Barry explained. "Normally, it takes months if not years for a proper assimilation of a skills update or training module, however, these have all been loaded with none of the standard parameter guides on them."

"Oh dear," Mal said from the passageway. "Even at a

trickle, she may have accessed some very dangerous information and abilities. I must now alter my earlier assessment to sixty-four percent likelihood of violence toward crewmembers."

"Shit," Barry said matter-of-factly.

"Did Barry just swear?" Doc McClain asked in disbelief. The captain, too, was utterly surprised.

"That he did. I heard it."

"Barry?" Mal inquired. "What is the matter?"

The cyborg raised his gaze to look at the humans in the room.

"Daisy fully removed *all* inhibitors from her neuro-stim device. She appears to have performed a subroutine bypass as well. It is unclear to what degree her downloads have been affected, but logs show she had more than ten minutes of wide-open access."

"Shit," Mal said in an exasperated tone.

"Is it me, or did both our AIs just swear?"

"Not just you, Doc. Mal, what the hell is going on?" the captain demanded. "Is she dangerous?"

"Daisy has always been dangerous, Captain, now, incredibly more so. Re-assessing." She paused a moment as new calculations were confirmed. "New likelihood of violence against crew stands at ninety-two percent."

Captain Harkaway's face drained of color.

"Shit."

The two humans and their cyborg companion quickly walked back to Command. The captain barked out orders over his comms as they went.

"Command, switch access to Authority Code Seven. Swarthmore is to be considered dangerous. She attacked Vincent and may be unstable."

"Why would she do that?" Gustavo keyed over the comms. "I thought what happened to Vince was an accident."

"We thought so too, but now we aren't so sure. In any case, whatever happened, I can't have an unstable crewmember missing somewhere on my ship." The captain pushed the override for full-ship intercom. "This is Captain Harkaway. As you know, Vincent has been seriously injured. At this time, Daisy Swarthmore is missing and considered a potential threat. All crew, secure your workstations and stay put. Mal will be running a ship-wide scan in two minutes. Once that is complete, you are to report to Command to initiate a ship-wide search. We begin in twenty minutes."

"She undoubtedly heard that, Captain."

"I know, Barry. That's the point. Mal, you can begin."

"Scanning now, Captain."

The lights on every level dimmed to ten percent as the massively powerful AI directed the whole of her attention to the living spaces within her walls. Deck by deck, pod by pod, every life sign was registered and logged, while any anomalies were cataloged for further follow up. Barry would be the one handling that job, as his metal endoskeleton and overall design made him the least likely of the crew to be critically damaged should their rogue shipmate do something rash.

Again.

Safe in her main botanical chamber, Tamara scanned her retina and spoke her keyword to a seemingly innocuous section of the bulkhead.

"Tamara Burke. Access: Thunderhead."

Seams appeared in the smooth wall with a faint hiss, then a long storage rack slid out. On it were a variety of arms and attachments that went far beyond simple farming tools. Tamara keyed in a code to the textured metal behind her elbow and detached her arm from that point down. She had been tilling soil and harvesting snap peas with one of her more delicate attachments. Smiling, she picked up a much sturdier one. An arm with thick, strong fingers and a small pulse beam weapon built into the wrist.

"Not going to cut this baby off in a doorway."

She closed the panel and resumed her work while she waited for Mal to complete her scans. At long last, when the appointed time came and the lights returned to normal, she exited the pod at a jog, rushing to meet her crewmates and join in the search.

Outside the ship, the captain's transmission had indeed been received loud and clear in Daisy's EVA suit. She had plenty of oxygen, enough for several more hours of space-time, but there was work to do. She had overridden the airlock sensors, so Mal shouldn't have noticed her slipping out the external airlock on Lower Port Twelve, but, eventually the slight variance in air pressure would clue the AI in to her trick. Daisy needed to come up with a plan, and quickly.

She was riding in a ship full of dangerous AIs and their sympathizers, possibly even collaborators, and they were speeding toward Earth. The possibilities worried her.

What would happen if they made it to Dark Side base with the AIs in control of the ship? What if the moon base's systems became compromised? Was there an even bigger picture? Ultimately, it didn't matter. Daisy had to warn Dark Side, and then Earth itself.

Earthfall was only two days away, and she had a plan. At least, the beginnings of one. She just hoped the search team would pass by Starboard Pod Eight without too much scrutiny. It was a long walk to the other side of the ship, and she certainly did not wish to redirect to a different airlock if she could avoid it.

As she carefully made her way across the outside of the ship near her modified communications array, making certain not to touch anything that might alert Mal of her position, Daisy once again assessed the damage dotting the ship's skin. She was always amazed at the char marks on a few sections of the ship's hull when she did an EVA. They almost looked like blast patterns, though she knew that to be impossible.

She vaguely remembered their launch not so long ago. The *Váli* was only a few years old, built just before they departed the distant space station to head back to Earth. But why, then, did the exterior look like a ship that had been through a whole lot more than a milk-run home? Daisy wondered what they could have possibly flown through while in cryo-sleep that would have battered the ship to that extent.

No time to worry about that, she thought, grimly. *I've got much bigger problems on my plate.*

"Mal, I'd like you to clarify a few things for me if you can," Doctor McClain said as she went over Daisy's files in her office. "I'm looking over Daisy's neuro-stim logs from the duration of the voyage, and there do seem to be anomalies. Have you seen them?"

"Yes, Doctor, I noted them as well."

"Why didn't you address them at the time? It was a lengthy voyage. I'm sure there was ample time to fine-tune the neuro-stim system."

"It started as such a minor variance that it went unnoticed in the grander scheme of things. You see, we now have the benefit of reviewing the entire timeline at once. Naturally, these things will stand out in a most obvious manner when viewed in such fashion. However, in the incredibly slow pace of daily and hourly data streaming, it was easy to miss."

"That makes sense," she agreed, but was still not happy with what she was seeing. "But what about this crossover? It looks as though entire data stores were being redirected at her command. While unconscious in cryo. It shouldn't be possible."

"No, it should not."

Mal flashed several screens of data onto the illuminated wall.

"Due to the nature of Daisy's mental makeup, it would seem that she has far greater capacity than the mission planners had anticipated. Further, it is my belief that she may have been acting well outside of parameters without even knowing she was doing so. Cryo sleep does not allow for conscious thought."

"Yes, but there's something else. A note in her record from the first few minutes after we were woken after the impact. She said she was dreaming of Earth."

"Impossible. As I stated, cryo sleep does not allow for conscious thought."

"Yes, you said. But what about subconscious thought? Could she have been processing things, learning and adapting all that time?"

"But humans cannot dream in cryo."

"Daisy did."

Mal was silent.

"I'll take that as you not knowing, then," Doctor McClain noted. She flipped through several more files detailing all the massive amounts of information Daisy had flooded into her mind.

"Mal, this was a firehose of data. Untempered information pouring into her mind with no inhibitors whatsoever. Whatever she had been gifted with before then, is it possible she irreversibly damaged herself during her last neuro session?"

"It is possible, yes. While I would like to assess her first-hand, I place a seventy-nine percent likelihood of serious mental break occurring as a result."

"And a potential symptom would be extreme paranoia, yes?"

"That is correct."

"And she has not only full access to the ship, but also knowledge of its systems, scanners, and internal security networks?"

"Also correct."

"Tracking her down is not going to be easy if she doesn't want to be found. This is a total clusterfuck."

"Yes, Doctor. That is correct," the ship replied. Little did she know just how accurate she was.

CHAPTER NINETEEN

The search had been thorough, at least as thorough as could be expected with a small crew covering such a large space. Conducted in leapfrogging teams, they worked for hours until they had finally covered every pod and corridor in the vessel. They even searched the tiny two-person emergency hopper shuttle riding in the cargo hold, but it was no matter. Every attempt on every level came up empty.

"Captain, perhaps she is not inside the ship at all," Barry opined.

"Reasonable assumption, Barry. Mal, has the shuttle been activated?"

"No, Captain. As the access hatch is located in the central floor of the main passageway, I have been able to maintain constant surveillance. If she had made an attempt for the shuttle I would have detected her."

"Very well. Thanks, Mal."

"Captain, as it appears Daisy is nowhere to be found inside the *Váli*, I request permission to perform an EVA and examine the exterior of the craft," Barry said.

"Granted. Just find her. And be careful. We don't know if that damn neuro overload caused her to go schizoid on us."

Barry nodded once, then strode off to suit up. He might not need much oxygen to function, but the vacuum of space would make quick work of his flesh covering if he exited unprotected.

"The rest of you, get back to your duties, but keep your eyes open. If you see anything, call the others. You all know what she did to Vince, and we don't know how much more she's capable of."

Daisy heard the entire exchange from her hiding place in the Narrows, safely wedged between pods.

They think I'm still outside. Good. Let 'em run on that goose chase while I do what I have to.

Coming back inside through Starboard Eight had been a risk. She knew that, but the search pattern was executed as her tactical know-how had anticipated, and it had left her the tiniest of opportunities to sneak back into the *Váli*. She'd made it in, safe behind the search teams in the now-checked-off sections. They wouldn't look for her there. Not for the time being, at least.

From there, it was easy enough to deactivate a few sensors temporarily so she could grab her tool pouches and Faraday suit three from its rack, then make her way undetected into the Narrows. Between the enhanced shielding of the suit and the nature of the Narrows, she felt confident no one had a clue where she was. In addition to the crawlspaces being totally off-scan, their interconnectivity circumvented choke-points in the search grid within the ship's corridors, and were, by far, her best way to navigate through the ship undetected.

It was a different type of crawl, this time. A long slog, more about covering distance than merely reaching a nearby terminal in need of repairs. The farther she dragged herself, the more she realized just how extensive the interconnected network really was. Sure, she and Sarah had been in over eighty percent of the tiny crawlspaces over the prior six months, but always in small increments, and always close to a convenient, and open, exit panel.

Now Daisy was sealed in, crawling farther and farther into the ship. She had her tools, and could open a panel from the inside, but the added sense of mild claustrophobia hit her just the same.

Another inconvenience was the delay moving from one section to another. She'd always just walked the corridors to her destination in the past, but that was simply not an option any longer.

Cycling the narrow double airlocks between pods while crawling on her belly took a lot of additional time, since she was now forced to manually re-route the keypads and sensors to stay clear of the ship's prying eyes. If Mal's readouts showed a keypad accessed, Daisy's goose would be cooked. Fortunately, even before the neuro-stim did whatever that thing was to her head, she had more than enough knowledge to run a simple bypass. It was time-consuming, and frustrating, but soon enough she had made her way halfway through the vessel on her way to the communications array hub inside the ship.

Why the hell couldn't it have just worked from outside while I was there?

"Because you're a dumbass and designed it for the highest level of efficiency. Unfortunately, that meant a fat-pipe data input from the ship, not that dinky little wireless from your space suit."

You know I love you, Sarah, and God knows I miss the hell out of you right about now, but if you're not going to be a more helpful imaginary friend, would you please shut the fuck up for a bit?

The voice in her head went silent.

"Thanks," she grunted as she crawled around a tight bend.

The plan was relatively simple. First, get to the bundle of comms fibers running to her jury-rigged communications array. That would be a fair bit more crawling through the Narrows, but so be it. Once she arrived at her destination, Daisy would run a parallel misdirect circuit to a different part of the ship. It wouldn't fool Mal for very long, but hopefully long enough to afford her time to tap in and achieve step three.

That was the crucial bit.

If she was successful sending a message out to Dark Side, or even to Earth, depending on their line-of-sight past the moon, maybe, just maybe, the people back home could come rescue her from this ship full of not-quite humans. Even if not, at the very least, she could warn them about what was heading their way.

Nearly an hour later, with bruised hips and scraped forearms, Daisy was quietly sliding through the walls of the medical bay when she heard the faint sounds of conversation as she passed a poorly-sealed switch array panel leading into the room.

Sounds like Barry's back from his EVA, she noted.

She tried not to listen—she had a job to do. Being distracted was not an option.

Keep moving, Daisy. Curiosity killed the cat.

She continued to crawl forward, but stopped dead when she heard one voice in particular, clear as a bell.

Vince.

"I told you, I don't know where she went," he said. "The trauma sent me into some kind of stasis mode. I didn't even know I could do that. I mean, I lost a shitload of blood."

Dammit, I have to know.

Ever so carefully, she backtracked until she found a suitably large switch bracket. Quietly, she loosened it from the inside and slid it aside, giving her a narrow, quarter-inch viewing window of the medical bay. Hopefully no one would get close enough to the switches to notice an eye staring out from where a toggle switch was supposed to be.

She scanned the room. Barry was there, *naturally,* as was Finn.

Finn? But he's human. Why is he with them?

Barry turned and spoke to Vince.

"Obviously, her discovery of your true nature was an unfortunate turn of events, especially this close to our arrival at Dark Side. Her reaction was extreme, and she is potentially unstable. The brutal attack on you only further demonstrates how vital it is we find her." Barry actually sounded concerned. Worried about what she might be capable of doing. For some reason, Daisy felt proud of that.

"Look, guys," Finn chimed in, "she just had one hell of a shock. She just found out her boyfriend isn't exactly what she thought he was. I mean, it's actually pretty natural that she'd be freaked out."

Thanks, Finn, she thought. *I knew I could count on you.*

"That said," he continued, "you fuckers better catch her quick. We need to get her before we're anywhere near landing. Far too much is riding on this for her to run free."

Son of a bitch!

"Agreed. Let's get back to it." Vincent swung his feet to the deck.

"You sure you're good to go, man?"

"Yeah. I'm not a hundred percent, and it still hurts like a bitch, but I'll be fine."

As he stood and reached for a shirt, Daisy saw the thin red scar on his shoulder where his arm had been re-attached.

He didn't get a metal replacement arm, she realized. *I wonder why that is?*

Despite the lack of a computerized appendage, she looked one last time at the re-attached limb and shuddered.

The two men and the cyborg gathered their things and headed back into the central passageway, ostensibly to continue searching for their missing nuisance.

Catch me before Dark Side? Fat chance.

Daisy quietly slid the switch back into place and tightened

the bracket from the inside. Once that was done, she resumed her long crawl toward the communications array cable-feed goal. A few short minutes later, she wiggled through yet another airlock and into the long crawlspace leading to the airlock to the adjoining pod.

Hang on. Something feels different.

Daisy paused, then started moving again.

Yep, something's off.

It took her a good minute before she finally realized what it was. As she crawled, every so often, her ears would pop.

A pressure change? But this is dead space in the ship's basic structural framework between pods. There shouldn't be anything here but bulkhead and data cables.

Daisy looked around the narrow space, searching for anything out of the ordinary. Once more, cryptic words were scrawled on the bulkhead.

"*And the great difference between man and monkey is in the larynx.*" - *Wells*, said one.

"*A human being is the toy of God, so we must live playing,*" read another.

Not necessarily ominous, per se, but the words certainly captured Daisy's attention enough to make her stop crawling for a moment, which turned out to be fortuitous.

There before her was an almost seamless access plate tucked into the smooth metal. To her, something about it looked ever so slightly different from the others she'd seen all throughout the ship, though she couldn't quite put her finger on it. At least not until she *actually* put her finger on it.

To the touch, it seemed *almost* normal, but upon closer examination, as she began slowly turning the hex bolts holding it in place, she noticed something quite unusual indeed.

The screws were threaded in reverse.

Now that's interesting, she noted, ever so slowly reversing direction with her screwdriver. It wasn't until she'd managed to loosen each of the eight bolts an eighth of an inch that she could insert her slender fiber optic camera and accompanying light. What she saw was an elaborately designed sensor array, wired to the panel on four sides. It wouldn't take her long to clip them off and run a bypass, but it was the *other* unusual feature that really caught her eye.

Thick glass vials were mounted directly beside each bolt, with just enough space that they'd remain unbroken so long as the panel remained flush. The reverse-threaded screws, however, would catch a less attentive person unawares, and before they realized they were tightening and not loosening the panel, the glass would be crushed, releasing whatever toxic chemical they contained.

It was a particularly nasty booby trap, and one she felt confident was likely designed to kill, not disable. Any normal person who happened to make it this far without killing themselves would recognize the imminent danger and back away.

Daisy was anything but a normal person.

Nothing piqued her curiosity quite like a "Stay Out" sign, which the booby-trapped panel and array of alarms most certainly were.

"Okay, I've got the tools for this," she muttered as she dug in the larger of her pouches. "Damn, I'm still lugging this thing around," she said, pulling her little plasma cascade device free. She was tempted to just leave it there, one less thing to haul as she crawled through the Narrows, but the project had become sort of a meditative pastime for her, so she tucked it safely back in her pouch, then lay out the necessary tools.

With her adrenaline flowing and her senses firing on all cylinders because of it, disarming the devices was nothing more than a temporary inconvenience. In short order, she had bypassed them all and fully removed the bolts with her power-ratchet. A faint whoosh of air sucked past her into the dark space. A slight vacuum. *Interesting.*

I know I'm good, Daisy thought, *but even for me, that seemed a little too easy.*

"Maybe you fried your brain," her friend chimed in. "Made yourself a super-genius or something. Or maybe this is all a dream and you're actually still strapped to your neuro, drooling on yourself while you have a schizoid embolism."

Shut up. You never even watched that movie, so what do you know?

"I'm in your head. I know what you know."

Then you know this schtick is going to get old really quick.

"Hey, I'm not the one conjuring me up. You obviously need me for something beside my witty conversational skills, so what is it?"

I wish I knew.

"Well, come on, then. We might as well drop on down there. Nothing ventured, nothing gained!"

Easy for you to say, you're already dead.

She heard Sarah's goofy laugh, a jolly voice whispering in her head.

"Morbid, Daze. Just morbid."

Daisy cracked a little grin.

Well, who knows. I may be joining you sooner than expected, she thought as she lowered herself into the dark space below.

CHAPTER TWENTY

Daisy felt her ears pop slightly as they equalized once more as her feet softly touched down in the unlit compartment. The hiss she heard as she opened the access panel made sense; there was a noticeable atmospheric differential between the unmarked space and the Narrows. Looking around, she realized something else that felt wrong about it. The room was not only dark and narrow, it was somewhere a room shouldn't be.

Sonofa... Hidden right under my nose all this time?

Carefully, Daisy eased her way forward into the pod, bumping something at hip level as she did. She'd already run a rudimentary bypass of the pod's alarms and scanners, but froze in place regardless.

No sirens sounded. It appeared she was successful in her security re-routing efforts, and so long as she was in that pod, she would effectively be a ghost.

A faint bubbling sound and the smell of ozone wafted to her nose, causing a faint discomfort to her eyes. On top of that, an overall musty odor permeated the space despite the dry air. Almost as if an animal or something had once lived in the darkened chamber.

"Okay, let's get some lights on in here," she said quietly, motivating herself to get moving. She fired up her flashlight, casting a beam about the walls, the light dancing briefly over storage lockers, medical equipment, and scientific tools, until she finally spotted the light switch.

Daisy hesitated a moment, then flicked it on. The overhead lights fired up immediately and illuminated the clean-scrubbed chamber from end to end.

She suddenly wished she'd left them off.

Surrounding her on both sides were thick-walled glass vats, and in them floated body parts.

What the fuck?

Appendages of different sizes, shapes, and genders bobbed in the primordial soup, suspended by a thin matrix of nutrient lines connected to the main blood vessels. She couldn't believe what was looking at. An arm, a leg, a hand, an eye. There were even a few fingers floating in the bubbling translucent-pink soup.

Shit, she thought, momentarily frozen in her tracks. *Finn—my God, does that mean...?*

She had never seen Tamara's arm or Reggie's hand, but the limbs bobbing gently in the thick liquid were all roughly the same size as the artificial limbs on her crew.

Whoever was behind all this was storing bits of people.

Could Mal actually be that far gone? And if she is, does that mean the captain is part of this too? I mean, it's his ship. How could he not know?

Smaller limbs floating in translucent containers toward the back of the space caught her eye. Limbs too small for any of the crew.

My God, are those from children? But where did they get them? Could they have been harvesting from kids before we even launched?

Farther back, she noted the much larger tanks. Big enough for far more than just parts.

They can't be—

Daisy snapped out of her shock as the touch of the slightest of drafts wafted across the sensitive skin of her cheek.

A draft. In a sealed ship. Where one shouldn't exist.

Daisy put her revulsion aside and turned her mind to a new task. One that she'd actually been working on for some time now. Oh, how the universe could throw you curveballs.

In any case, gift horse. Mouth.

She dug in her kit for a pair of sharp wire snips, then deftly unscrewed a panel on the wall. It contained nothing of critical importance, and crucially, none of the wires were leading to anything Mal would notice a fluctuation in. Daisy clipped a hot wire, holding the ends apart from one another with her insulated clippers.

While fire can be deadly on board a space ship, and thus, open flames are strictly prohibited, other things can relatively safely give off smoke, if you know what you're doing. Daisy quickly stripped the two ends of the wire from inside the panel, then touched them together, arcing the electricity, causing a brief flash.

The small puff of smoke given off drifted toward the near wall, as if pulled by an invisible magnet.

Gotcha!

It was tiny. Just a pinhole, really, but in the vacuum of space, it was more than enough to cause a deadly loss of air, given enough time. From the looks of it, a heavy piece of equipment had hit the wall at just the right angle and weakened the metal, though as she studied the small, damaged area, she noted it almost looked more like someone had been slowly scraping away at the wall over a very long period of time, rubbing that heavy corner back and forth for many, many years. Of course, that was impossible. The ship hadn't even been traveling very long at all, but still, it gave her pause.

Daisy pulled her thinnest fiber optic camera from the pouch

on her thigh and slid it gently through the minuscule hole. It barely fit, but barely would have to suffice.

There you are.

Though blocked by a bundle of tightly bound cables, Daisy could see a tiny tear in the bulkhead in the formerly airtight compartment housing them.

No way I can get to that without Mal noticing, she realized.

The small puncture was probably from a piece of debris that had impacted the ship at some point. It was just dumb luck that the internal wall became compromised. The fail-safes were designed to prevent such an occurrence from causing serious harm. Areas were compartmentalized, and a breach would activate the countermeasures. Only this one was too small and too delayed from the initial impact to trigger the automatic sealant foam. It was a one-in-a-million chain of events that led to the continuous leak, but that sort of thing seemed to be happening far too often for comfort on this mission.

Daisy dug in her kit and produced a small tube of vacuum-active dry adhesive and a metal patch. The stuff was stronger than underwater concrete, and it could work in sub-freezing temperatures and didn't need any air to function. She carefully withdrew her camera and stored it back in her thigh pouch, then applied the tiniest dollop of sealant to the hole, being extremely careful not to get any on herself, lest she become an unwilling addition to the *Váli*'s superstructure. Less than a second after she applied the small patch, the hiss of escaping air ceased as she successfully sealed the gap.

"Way to go, Daze. Nice one!" her invisible friend cheered.

"Thanks, Sarah. At least that's one less thing to worry about. Now back to the plan. As twisted as this shit is, my number one priority at this point is still to contact Earth and the moon base."

"Makes sense. Get safe, then figure the rest of this mess out."

"Exactly."

Daisy looked again at the body parts floating around her.

Hell, if anything, making contact is even more of a priority now. Who knows what they'll do if I allow them to dock at Dark Side.

Daisy cast a curious gaze around the space, this time looking beyond the horrors floating in the sealed tanks and taking greater care to note anything non-body part related that might be of importance.

The compartment was well-hidden, and its width was significantly less than other pods. A secret lab, nestled in the *Váli*'s main structure rather than a removable pod.

You could walk from pod to pod right past this and never even know it was hiding only a few feet away.

"You see that, Daze? Over there, on the far wall," Sarah pointed out.

Daisy looked and saw there was a solitary double air lock door. One way in, one way out. From the inside it looked just like every other set of pod doors on the ship, but Daisy suspected this one led somewhere unexpected.

What the hell, let's see how far this rabbit hole goes, she thought as she opened the first of the matched doors and stepped inside.

She reached for the second door's activation panel as the first door sealed behind her. Hesitating just a second, she touched the control, and the second door slid open with a whisper.

"Jesus, Daisy, you startled me!"

Tamara jumped up from the red peppers she was tending, accidentally crushing her watering spout with her cybernetic hand. The unit automatically self-sealed, preventing any loss of water.

Behind her, Daisy heard the airlock door slide shut, blending seamlessly with the chamber's wall.

"Tamara? It was you? But you're human. How could you do something like this?"

"Wait, what?" Tamara said, a confused look momentarily flashing across her face. It was quickly replaced with one of realization. "Oh, you mean the parts in the bio lab. No, I don't deal with that stuff. It's not my department. I just grow the food."

"This is insane. You're working with the cyborgs! How many of you are in league with them? Does the captain know? And what about Gus and Reggie?" Daisy's mind was spinning. "My God, Sarah wasn't an accident at all, was she? She knew something was wrong, and you killed her!"

"Whoa, hang on a minute, Daisy, it's not what it looks like! This is all just a big misunderstanding. Come on, calm down. Let's go talk to the others, and we can clear this all up."

"Clear it up? You people are sick."

"Trust me, it will all make sense if you just talk with us."

Daisy's eyes trailed down. Something wasn't right.

Her hand, she realized. Tamara had been pressing the intercom button since she entered the room.

Further, the arm Tamara was sporting wasn't her usual gardening variety. Sure, it looked benign enough, but it was actually a highly-advanced cybernetic combat arm, complete with a full complement of anti-personnel and defensive measures hidden under its sleek exterior.

How do I know that?

"Better question is, what are you going to do about it?"

Daisy took off in a sprint, twisting as she darted past Tamara.

Just need to make it to the adjacent pod, then I—

A flash of bright metal shot out, a hot pain radiating up her arm as the powerful mechanical hand gripped her by the wrist.

Damn, she's fast.

"I've got Swarthmore. She's in the botany facility in Starboard Six. She found the parts lab," Tamara shouted into the open comms. "Hold still. I don't want to hurt you."

The slow cracking sensation in her arm told Daisy otherwise.

Daisy focused, forcing the crushing pain from her mind as

best she could as she flailed her free arm and grabbed the nearest thing to her.

A small plant in a metal pot. It would have to do.

She swung it hard, a dull gong ringing out from the container as it connected solidly with Tamara's head. The botanist stumbled, and though she didn't release Daisy, her grip did lessen slightly. It was enough, barely, to give Daisy the leverage to twist around and grab the sturdy metal hand with her far-weaker flesh one.

The elbow.

As if on auto-pilot, her free hand instinctively darted to the small uneven spot that she somehow knew was there. Code flashed in her mind, a series of commands and override options presenting themselves in an instant. Without hesitation, Daisy quickly punched a pattern into the nearly invisible access pad on the cybernetic arm. It was supposed to be keyed only to Tamara's DNA, but little did she know, like just about every program in existence, its designers had built in a back door.

This had better work!

With a pop and a click as Daisy's fingers flew, typing in the sequence by touch, Tamara's arm loosened its grip, then powered down entirely. A moment later, the hand abruptly disconnected from below the elbow. Then the hefty mechanism finally released Daisy's arm as it cycled off.

Daisy didn't hesitate.

She pulled free and was already running the second the disembodied hand let go, hitting the deck with a clang as she bolted through the far door.

"Shit, she disarmed me and is heading out of Starboard Six into Starboard Seven!" she heard Tamara shout into the comms before the airlock shut behind her.

Faster, dammit! She pounded on the airlock door impatiently. Finally, the first door locked shut and the second one slid open.

Pod Seven was empty—no one was waiting for her. At least not yet.

Not stopping to thank her luck and tempt fate in the process, Daisy sprinted to the next door and started cycling it just as she heard the one behind her open.

"Daisy, wait!" she heard behind her. Tamara was lurching through the airlock while clumsily attempting to re-attach her hand as she chased her.

Daisy ignored her and was already into the next airlock, keying in bypass codes, temporarily blocking all comms to the area and overriding the door's safety mechanism as it slid shut behind her. When the inner door opened, she grabbed an EVA tether and jammed it in the open door. She then grabbed a power driver from her tool pouch and popped the door's control panel.

The wires were easy enough to splice, and she felt confident the workaround *should* hold. So long as something was in the doorway, the safety wouldn't allow the other airlock door to open. Daisy had simply created a safety loop for the entire pod that tied the jammed door's protocol to the main door as well.

I only have a few minutes before they work around my bypass and figure out how to trap me in this cluster of pods, she realized as she stepped into Starboard Eight.

"Oh, I remember this pod," Sarah said.

Daisy ground her teeth.

"I died here."

"Shut up, Sarah, just shut up! I don't need this right now," she barked at the voice in her head.

"It's so cold out there, Daisy. And no air."

"Not helping," she huffed as she ran to the far side doors leading to Pod Nine.

"It's okay, Daisy. I don't blame you. It was the others' fault."

Listen, this is really not the time for this, okay? I'm begging you, please leave me alone!

The voice went silent.

Sarah?

Nothing.

Daisy set back to work, grabbing a spare tether line and running to the far door at the end of the pod. Secretly, she found herself almost hoping to hear her friend's voice once more.

No time for moping, she thought as she re-routed her bypass on the pod, allowing the unblocked door to Starboard Nine to slide open.

Starboard Nine. The zero-g pod.

A gravity-free place she had once despised with a passion, but now something that she could use to her advantage. Clipping the tether to her belt, Daisy pushed off into the room, aiming for the D-ring mounted on the ceiling. Only it wasn't a ceiling. Or a wall. Or even a floor. It was simply the direction Daisy wanted to go.

Forcing her body to relax as she floated, she snapped the tether in place as she flew by, giving a gentle tug and redirecting herself with ease to the door leading to Starboard Ten. If she could make it to Starboard Twelve, she'd be able to cut through the central passageway to the port side without them noticing. That should buy her at least a little more time as she made her way to the comms array while they tried to get to her in a pod she was no longer in.

Daisy gently landed next to the keypad, firmly grasping the handle next to the door before reaching for the control panel.

It lit up, ready to cycle open, and she had not yet touched it.

Shit!

Her fingers flew across the keypad, but the inner door began to open before she could enter her bypass codes. For a moment it hummed with the strain of conflicting commands, then finally stalled in place.

Just a few more seconds and I'll have it, she thought as she keyed in the commands to override the inner panel and close the door.

"Daisy, talk to us. This can all be explained," Gustavo called to her through the narrow opening.

"Bullshit, you're in league with the fucking robots!" she yelled back.

A dark metal tube jutted through the gap, blocking the mechanism and engaging the no-close safety just as she overrode the door commands.

Dammit!

A blast of compressed air brushed her cheek as the tube sent a projectile flying into the opposite wall, where it sparked brightly upon impact.

"A stun rifle? You motherfucker!"

Daisy released the door, positioned her body out of the line of fire, locked a foot under the handle, and grabbed the barrel, tugging hard, but Gustavo was too strong to be so easily disarmed. Using both his hands to yank the stun rifle back from her, he pulled as hard as he could.

Of course, that was her plan, though she didn't know how she knew so clearly what to do when facing an attacker in an unusual tactical situation like this. Regardless, Gus fell backward when she unexpectedly released the weapon, Daisy's body barely kept from flying the other way in the zero-g chamber by her anchored foot.

With the opening now clear of the obstruction, she quickly executed the override command, sealing the door, but once again, it stayed ajar.

"His leg, Daze!"

Sarah was right. Gustavo's boot had jutted into the gap when he fell.

Sonofa—

The door slid open, and Gus dove at her headfirst. Daisy had just the slightest of moments to yank the tether she was still tied to, sending her gliding out of his reach.

She bent her legs just before she reached the wall, then pushed off hard as soon as her feet made contact, twisting in mid-air so she was traveling feet-first.

Gus took both of her boots to his face, the impact sending him crashing into the nearest wall, then rebounding into the ceiling. Daisy, on the other hand, was used to the quirks of the zero-g pod, an edge she was damn sure to use to her fullest advantage while he was still stunned.

"You don't understand—" was all Gus managed to get out before he found himself whipped into a spin, flying toward the far wall. Daisy had braced herself with her tether, then yanked Gustavo's nearest leg, resulting in a nausea-inducing ride, smack into unforgiving steel.

Daisy unclipped the tether and pushed off again, deftly attaching the loose end to Gustavo's belt, then kicking him into a tight spin, wrapping him in the tether as he flailed.

It won't take him long to get out of that.

Gus made a horking sound as he vomited in the zero-g pod.

Okay, maybe it'll take him a little longer than I thought.

"No dicking around, Daze. Get the hell out of here," Sarah urged.

"You don't have to tell me twice," she silently agreed, then made her way back into Starboard Eight, jamming the door behind her.

She was locked in, with pursuers desperately trying to catch her at each end. And with Gus going so far as to start shooting at her, she now knew just how serious they were, and to what lengths they would go to capture her. She had only one option.

She knew what she had to do, and knew she had no other choice. Nevertheless, the thought of the EVA doors that had taken her friend sent a small shudder running up her spine.

CHAPTER TWENTY-ONE

"Override disengaged," Mal announced, having finally regained control of both the doors and comms for the small conglomerate of pods Daisy had somehow managed to take control of. The normally calm AI found the ease with which she had been blocked out more than a little disconcerting and was pleased when the code blocks unexpectedly fell to her access attempts.

Starboard Seven and Nine both cycled open their doors into Pod Eight at the same moment, Tamara and Gustavo visually ensuring the other was not about to be ambushed, silently nodding to one another as they stepped in and sealed the doors behind them.

"She didn't come out my way."

"Mine either," Tamara replied, looking at the weapon in Gustavo's hands. "Jesus, Gus, a stun rifle? Really?"

"Hey, Captain said whatever it takes, and this was the least lethal thing in the armory. You know how important she is."

Tamara gave him an unhappy look as she reached for the comms panel.

"Is that puke?"

"Shut up."

"Jesus, Gus, you trained for zero-gs. And what happened to your face?"

"She ambushed me."

"Ambushed, huh?"

Tamara's raised eyebrow told him just how much she believed him.

"Captain," she said into the comms. "Daisy ran to Starboard Eight, but she's not here. She must have made an EVA outside the ship. She could be anywhere out there."

"I read you, Tamara," Captain Harkaway replied from Command. "Daisy disabled a lot of our equipment in that section, but I'm going to have Mal scan the ship's surface as best she can. Standby."

Gustavo looked around the pod. All of the strapped-down containers were too small to hide in, so it really did seem their shipmate had opted for a space walk.

"She actually did it. I mean, why an EVA? She has to know we'll find her out there. Was she hoping to keep us locked out long enough to pop back in on the other side of the ship?"

"Probably," Tamara replied. "She couldn't have guessed we'd get past her overrides so quickly. But now that we're in and know what she's doing, she's kind of screwed. There are a limited number of external airlocks on the *Váli*, and now that we know what she's up to, all we have to do is grab her when she finally comes back in."

"Why didn't Mal notice what she was up to, though?" Gustavo asked.

"She's the electronics expert, Gus. Plus, with all that extra stuff Mal had the neuro-stim pumping into her head for all those years, I'm sure she has more than a few tricks up her sleeve none of us could have foreseen."

The captain's voice came back over the intercom. "All right, you two, get out of there. She's still not reading on external scans. I'm going to send Barry to suit up for an EVA to go find her."

"I can do it, Captain," Gustavo offered.

"I know you can, Gus, but I need you up here backing us up on navigation in case she tries to fiddle with those systems. And besides, Barry doesn't get tired."

Reluctantly, Gustavo accepted the order. "Copy that, sir," he said dejectedly as he opened the door back to pod nine and stepped through, cycling it closed behind him. Tamara's door wouldn't budge, however, leaving her inconveniently stuck in Starboard Eight.

"Hey, the access back to Seven won't open." Tamara grunted as she tugged on the sealed door. "Gus, what's up on your end?"

"I made it part way. I'm stuck in between Pod Eight and Nine," he grumbled. "So yours is jammed too? Wonderful. It looks like neither door will open now. We're stuck."

"Freakin' Daisy. Leaving us yet another little surprise. Hey, Mal, can you get this damn thing open for me?" Tamara asked.

Silence.

"Mal? Aw, shit. Gus, it looks like she must have left some kind of worm behind in the comms. Mal's been locked out again. What can you see from your end?"

"Hang on, I've got to access everything through this shitty little terminal in here."

Gustavo bent over and eyed the device, then began tapping out a few minor systems check codes.

"Looks like she embedded a secondary override," he said, entering a longer string of commands into the tiny console on the wall between pods. "Give me a minute. I think I can find us a workaround. I should be able to have us both out in no ti—"

The blast would have been deafening, if there was sound in space, but when Starboard Eight blew its explosive bolts, the entire external airlock assembly broke free in a blink of an eye and silently emptied the pod of oxygen and crew alike. Tamara held on as long as she could, but the force was too strong, and finally, she too was jettisoned out, with neither a bang, nor a whimper.

"Sarah sends her regards," Daisy muttered with grim satisfaction.

Safe in the sealed, pressurized crawlspace of the Narrows above pod eight, she began the long crawl toward her salvation.

"Daisy, Daisy, give me your answer, do..." she quietly sang to herself. "Dammit Vince, you got that stupid song stuck in my head. Just my freakin' luck. First my boyfriend turns out to be a cyborg, then he lays that stupid earworm on me. We should never have watched that movie." She was most certainly *not* amused.

Daisy's elbows, knees, and hips were rapidly becoming unbearably sore from all the crawling through the ship's wiring and conduit system. Normally she'd have simply switched off the artificial gravity in the area to take the pressure off. It would have made life much easier, but there was no way Mal wouldn't pick up on that particular trick, no matter how much she tried to mask it.

"Looks like I'm just going to have to be black and blue for a while," she muttered, crawling farther along in the cramped Narrows. "Probably a few shades of purple and green in there too."

A half hour of discomfort later, she finally arrived at the closest communications nexus. It wasn't the main uplink, and it would require a bit of creative wiring, but seeing as how she designed the repaired comms array currently perched atop the ship, Daisy felt confident of her odds of success.

Of course, patching in would have been much more of a breeze if she weren't forced to do it with minimal equipment, lying on her belly, and with jury-rigged gear accessing things from the wrong side of the console. Nevertheless, once she got started, the path to success seemed clearer and clearer.

Daisy knew she could make it work. How long it would take, well, that was another question.

Nearly an hour later her task finally neared completion. Beyond merely accessing the system from the inside, she had found it necessary to connect several other terminals to create a hard-wired misdirect to prevent Mal from tracking her access point. That meant a lot of crawling, and a lot of rewiring. It helped that Daisy knew which wires she could safely disconnect to use in the endeavor, but even so, the level of safeguards against unauthorized transmission she encountered were quite astounding.

What were you up to with all that extra security? she wondered.

"Daisy?"

Vince's voice quietly reached out to her through her comms.

Bastard's on the override frequency.

"Daisy, I need you to listen to me."

Fat chance.

"I understand why you did what you did to me, and I want you to know that I don't hold it against you. I just wish I could have told you sooner. Maybe this all could have been avoided. Won't you please talk to me?"

Daisy silently continued her work.

"Okay, if you won't talk, then at least listen. The thing is, well, I know I haven't been exactly forthcoming with you. None of us have, really, and there's something you need to know—"

The microphone blared feedback in her ear as he was pushed aside.

"Daisy, this is Captain Harkaway. You have no idea what you are doing. This is a far more complicated situation than you are aware of, and you are jeopardizing everything. I want you to stop whatever it is you are doing and turn yourself over to us immediately. You'll be safe and treated well. We mean you no harm. You have my word on that. You just need to talk to us."

Silence.

"Are you sure this thing is transmitting?"

"Well, she's the comms expert, but yeah, it should be." It was Reggie she heard in the background.

So, that's it, then. Every single one of them is in on it.

She was nearly done re-routing the array. Her best bet would be to first attempt to send a message to Dark Side. If that didn't work, she'd try reaching out to Earth. But listening to the crew's voices gave her an idea. The uplink could wait a few minutes longer. There was one more thing she wanted to try.

She pulled one of the comms connectors and clipped its fiber optic data cluster to a neighboring one. The loop was physical, not a coded one, and ideally, it should create a two-tiered result. One, while useful in delaying her adversaries from coordinating their search, was really just a diversion. The second, however, would provide some much-needed intel as she crawled blind in the Narrows.

Daisy double-checked her connections, then keyed in a quick command sequence to her portable terminal.

The comms throughout the entire ship spat out a burst of shrill static, then they all went silent. All except the one in Daisy's ear. Though no one could tell, all other comms were locked open to transmit.

"What the hell did she just do?" Harkaway barked.

"I don't know, Captain. It looks like she just shorted out ship-wide comms. I can't see a coding solution just yet. Whatever she did, it was certainly creative," Gus replied.

"Wonderful. We should have known all that crap in her head would come back and bite us on the ass. Mal, are you able to locate the problem? Mal?"

"Hang on, Captain," Gustavo said. "I need to locally re-route her outbound comms to this terminal. Mal can hear us, but she can't answer just yet."

"This is ridiculous. We've got to get this under control. We're only forty-one hours from the moon. If we don't find her before we reach Dark Side, things could get ugly. Reggie, I want you to hand out the other stun rifles, then I want you to spread out and work in teams. Stay within voice range at all times. Don't lose contact with one another. I want the smaller of each pair to crawl into the conduit system, while the other paces them in the pod network below."

"But, Captain, we're all kind of big to fit in the Narrows," Reggie said.

"I don't care about your claustrophobia, dammit. The crawlspaces were designed for humans to fit in them. Just because it's easier for her doesn't mean the rest of us can't go there too. We don't know if she's in the pods, the passageways, or in the Narrows, but Barry found no trace of her on the exterior of the ship. Yes, I know this is doing it the hard way, but we have no choice. Cut her off. Flush her out. Shit just got real, people. Stop her at all costs."

Daisy felt a chill run up her spine. *At all costs?*

The captain hefted a stun rifle and held it out to the cyborg.

"Barry, I want you to take this and cover the shuttle airlock," the captain continued.

"Sir, I am much stronger than her. I will not need a stun—"

"Just take it, Barry. That's an order. We can't risk her trying to physically reach the Earth's surface."

Seriously? They really must be worried if they think I'd resort to spending two days floating in space in that old thing. But why Earth?

"I don't know, Daze. What if Dark Side is already compromised?" Sarah said.

"I hope to hell that's not the case," Daisy silently replied to the dead woman in her head.

The magnitude of the implication shook her. *If they have*

agents on the moon working with them. The possibilities spread out like a choose-your-own adventure book, only all of the options were shit.

"Very well, Captain, I will prevent her accessing the shuttle, should she be foolish enough to attempt it," she heard Barry say through the hot-miked comms.

"The rest of you, get moving."

Daisy turned and crawled back to the communication nexus she'd so diligently rewired. If they were going to start searching the Narrows, there really wasn't much time. If she was going to get a message out, it was now or never.

With the final connections hastily made, she powered on her makeshift jumper box and tapped in to the transmitter to send. For a few moments at least, it would appear to Mal that the transmission was being sent from an entirely different part of the ship.

"Mayday, mayday, does anyone copy?"

Nothing but a silent, static hiss.

"Mayday, mayday, this is Daisy Swarthmore of the *Váli*, can you read me? Dark Side base, do you copy? Does anyone—"

"Daisy, you really mustn't do that," Mal scolded over the open comms. "I know you can hear me, and I also assume you've rerouted your signal to alter your transmission location to a different section of the *Váli*. Very clever. You really have far exceeded my wildest expectations. Your skills are blossoming in ways far outside the mission forecasts. I'm proud of you, Daisy, but I need you to stop what you're doing."

"Mayday, mayday, this is the *Váli* calling any—"

"You might want to save your breath. I anticipated you would attempt to access the transmission relays from inside the ship and have already sequestered the entire external array. Additionally, Barry physically severed the hardwire line directly from the exterior and rerouted it straight to my neural array in Command. You cannot override it. Please, Daisy, it must be awfully cramped in there, and the others are so worried about you. Won't you come out and talk with the captain? He has much to tell you."

Daisy checked the signal feed, setting it to receive the outgoing message. The answer she feared stared her back in the face. Mal was telling the truth. Nothing she transmitted was even reaching the communications array.

"Please, Daisy, we can make this all right. I know Vincent is eager to see you as well. You hurt him, Daisy. Quite badly. But you don't need to worry, I fixed him up, good as new. Well, almost, anyway. I know he loves you, and if you—"

She yanked the comm from her ear. Sure, it was useful to track the others' movements as they combed the ship for her, but a headache was brewing behind her eyes, and she just couldn't take Mal's stupid mind games. Not right now, anyway.

So external comms are blocked. Clever, Mal, I have to hand it to you. She rolled the thought around in her mind, letting her options present themselves. *Transmission is out. Takeover is out. Hiding... even if I managed to avoid them if they somehow squeeze into the Narrows, they could simply put off landing and just keep us in a low orbit until I run out of water packs and have to come out.* Her options were indeed slim.

Well, then, she thought with morbid realization sinking in. *Thanks for the idea, Captain. It looks like the last resort is here.*

CHAPTER TWENTY-TWO

It was an uncomfortable way to move through the ship, that was certain, but Daisy felt strangely at ease in her unease. It was, she posited, much as Houdini likely felt, wrapped in familiar shackles and chains that would make any other man blanch.

She had logged a lot of hours in the Narrows and knew the majority of their twists and turns. At least the main passages, anyway. It was the crawling that was the real problem. Without the option of negating the artificial gravity to take some of the pressure off her body's contact points, Daisy's hips, knees, and elbows were aching something fierce.

Oh yeah, I'm going to be a lovely shade of purple when this is over, she thought as her bruised hips slid across yet another pressure seal between Narrows compartments. She further banged herself up wiggling around to access the panel controlling the airlock, carefully sealing it behind her while executing a minor sensor tweak to ensure its operation would not show on Mal's readouts.

Reluctantly, Daisy turned the comms system back on. While Mal and the captain's attempts to sway her were annoying, if they hadn't found her workaround that hot-miked the entire crew's comms, she might still be able to listen in and glean some useful information from their idle chatter.

"...I agree, Mal, but it's too much of a risk that way," Captain Harkaway's voice crackled through her earpiece.

Still works, I see, she mused with a grin.

"Captain, it is indeed a risk, but so is Daisy's continuing evasion of our crew. Her attempts to send external communications are demonstrable proof that she is a threat to the entire mission. If we do not apprehend her and put a stop to this, years of planning and decades of resources expended will be for naught."

"Decades? How far does this rabbit hole go, Daze?" Sarah wondered in her head.

Hell if I know, but if they're talking tens of years, they could have compromised countless systems, waiting for the moment to—well, to whatever it is they're up to.

The captain's voice interrupted her musings.

"I agree, Mal, but we can't risk it. While depressurizing the Narrows would knock her out, it could also lead to her panicking when she realizes what we're doing. If she senses the air is being sucked out, well, you know as well as I do just how much she's capable of. If even a fraction of that potential has been unlocked, dear Lord, just imagine what mayhem she could cause from the Narrows. She has access to damn near *everything* from in there."

"A valid concern, Captain," Mal replied. "It is most unfortunate that this eventuality, however unlikely, was not foreseen and prepared for."

"Sir, can I suggest something?"

It was Gustavo's voice joining the conversation.

Ah, so they're discussing this in Command. Good. That means less of them out helping with the search.

"Yes? What are your thoughts, Gus?"

"You have a valid point that pulling the air out of the

Narrows would make her panic. Hell, I know I would. But what if we could oxygen-starve her brain without her knowing it? Knock her out in a way that would prevent her from having the time to damage the ship?"

"I'm sorry, Gustavo, but we do not carry any manner of aerosolized anesthetics or sleeping agents on board," Mal replied. "I could likely reconfigure the biological fabricators to process some, but adjusting them for such an out-of-parameters task would take some time."

"No, nothing like that," he said, "but rather, using what we already have at hand."

Not liking the sound of that, Daisy thought as she began crawling faster, ignoring the ache in her hips and knees. *Not liking the sound of that at all.*

"We can't risk damaging the ship, and we want Daisy back intact. A lot of effort went into her. We can't risk permanent damage."

Oh, but temporary damage is okay, then? Thanks a lot, Captain.

"If I'm right, and Mal, please double-check my calculations here," Gus said. "If I'm right, we could utilize the ship's air filtration system to back-feed pure nitrogen into the Narrows. If we seal them off from the rest of the ship, it shouldn't take long at all to raise levels to a high enough percentage to knock her out."

"Mal, is this possible?" the captain asked.

"It is, Captain. While the air filtration system was not designed for such a purpose, it should be relatively easy to re-route the nitrogen bleed-off back into the feed system. It would require a manual adjustment, but we should be able to systematically flood sections of the crawlspaces with nitrogen."

"And this won't cause any permanent harm, correct?"

"It should not, Captain," Mal said.

"Yeah, that was my thinking, Captain. It's the basics of confined-space rescue protocols, but used to our advantage.

Unlike creating a vacuum, which makes you feel like you're suffocating, because, well, you are, nitrogen and helium both react in the human body like breathing air. The thing is, they *aren't* air, so you become oxygen-starved without even feeling it. No panic, no rash acts. Just suddenly passing out."

"So she wouldn't know what was happening? No chance of her causing catastrophic damage to the ship before she loses consciousness?"

"Not a chance, sir. With nitrogen, that is. Helium, well, if we used that and she happened to be talking to herself in the Narrows, she'd hear the change in her voice. With nitrogen, it's totally undetectable until it's too late."

Fuck.

Daisy picked up her pace.

"Captain," Mal chimed in, "I believe Gustavo's plan is a sound one. I can closely monitor the time each section is flooded with the gas to ensure Daisy is not without oxygen long enough to cause permanent damage."

"What if she wakes up before we find her? We'll have to send teams into each section as we go," Captain Harkaway said, hesitant.

"We can simply time the process, push out the nitrogen to allow a short window of fresh air, then flood each area again," Mal replied. "We then repeat the whole thing until we have been able to search each of the sections. It will be time-consuming, but it should work. Further, with each subsequent exposure to the nitrogen, Daisy should be more quick to succumb, as her body will be exhausted and somewhat oxygen-starved. This will result in the requirement of far less gas than prior sessions."

"But she'll notice if we start locking down random sections of crawlspace from here, and we know she has the skills to pretty easily override that from inside the Narrows," Gustavo pointed out.

"A valid concern, but if we were to not try to pinpoint her

exact location, instead locking down multiple connected sections at a time and hoping she is somewhere in the middle, the odds of her noticing would be greatly reduced."

Captain Harkaway scratched his stubbly chin as he mulled over the option.

"I don't like it, but I really don't see a better option on the table. Mal, what do you need done?"

"There are manual valve overrides in the atmospherics that will need to be cycled in order for me to affect this plan."

"I'll do it, Captain. I have a basic idea what needs to be done already."

"No, Gus, I need you in Command monitoring navs and comms. Daisy's loose in the guts of this ship, and if she gets any wild ideas, I'll need you here to help with damage control. Mal, can you send the instructions to Reggie's tablet remotely?"

"I'm sorry, Captain, but I am still trying to work around Daisy's rerouting of our internal wireless communications system."

"Well, shit on a shingle. With those comms still out, I'll have to go track down Reggie on foot. Fine, we'll do it the old hardwired way. Upload the instructions onto this," he said, plugging a tablet into an open port. "I'll get it down to him and have him get to work on it. Do you know what Reggie's last location was?"

"I believe he was attempting to access the upper level Starboard crawlspaces near Pod Two, Captain."

"Sir, why don't we just send Barry? We know where he's at, and it would save a lot of time."

"We need to protect the shuttle, Gus, and Barry's the best qualified of all of us to do it. Mal, once I track down Reggie, how long before we can start the process?"

"It should take less than twenty minutes to implement. I also wish to inform you that I believe comms should be functional by the time you return."

"Great, stand ready. As soon as I get back, we start immediately."

That's my cue, Daisy thought as she paused her crawling to pull components from nearby control panels. *I just hope this works.*

"Still no sign of her, Mal," Barry said into the wall-mounted communications box, a holdover of ancient tech that had never been removed.

The comms crackled, despite being hard-wired, and Mal managed to reply through the fuzzy connection.

"Understood. Continue at your position. We have implemented the beginning of the plan and should have Reggie accessing the Narrows shortly. Stay near the communications box. We will advise you as things progress."

The comms clicked off, leaving Barry standing atop the round hatch in the floor leading to the shuttle, a patient and formidable guardian of flesh-covered cybernetics. With his heightened reflexes, far-above-human processing speed, along with the fact that he never, ever, got tired, he was the logical choice to stand guard. And in the unlikely event someone did manage to get past him, it was still a good forty-foot climb straight down. Plenty of time to catch up with them for the nimble cyborg.

Three-quarters of the way down the ladder there was a large turn-around space, which allowed a descending climber to flip over and change their body orientation to that of the belly-mounted shuttle. That is, if the shuttle's own artificial gravity had already been activated. Again, an easy point at which to capture his quarry should she somehow make it that far.

With no means of communication to Earth, Daisy was well aware this really was her last chance. If she couldn't manage to get past Barry, she was screwed. There was no way she was going to risk doing it half-assed.

In the tight confines of the crawlspace, she worked feverishly as she moved, pulling components from whatever she needed, not worrying about Mal eventually figuring out where she was as scavenged systems began showing glitches. That wouldn't be her concern, at least not for much longer. If she moved quickly enough, she'd be out of there long before they flooded the Narrows with nitrogen and the subsequent search team ever arrived.

Daisy's fingers moved almost independently of her body, expertly assembling the jumble of salvaged components into an apple-sized gizmo of questionable functionality.

"How the hell do you know how to do this?" Sarah wondered as Daisy added another seemingly random component to the spike-covered, battery-powered orb in her hand.

"Beats me. All I know is, if I'm right, this should do the trick."

As she snaked her way through the last set of turns and approached her destination, she clicked the final piece into place and pressed the red power button. The small device let out a faint, yet deadly-feeling hum as it rested in the palm of her hand.

Well, this will go one of three ways. Either this will work, it won't and Barry tackles me, or we'll all be reduced to a pile of ashes when the whole ship blows up. She took a deep breath. *One way to find out.*

Daisy quietly opened the access panel at the far end of the corridor from where Barry was standing guard. She had wisely loosened all the bolts well in advance of this plan becoming a necessity, though, at the time, she thought perhaps it was a bit paranoid of her. Now it was a bit of foresight she was grateful for, as Barry's hearing would undoubtedly have picked up the faint sound of her power-ratchet if she used it in such close proximity.

"Barry, I want to talk." Her voice sounded so small in the corridor. Sad. Defeated.

The cyborg turned to where the voice had originated. He clicked the wall-comm. "Daisy has been located. She is behind the Narrows service hatch aft of the shuttle access."

"Why would you do this to me?" she asked, keying in the remote power-up sequence to the shuttle into her portable link on her forearm tablet, while temporarily cutting Barry off from the comms panel. She knew the quick patch to the localized comms hardware would be overridden in under a minute, but that was all the time she needed.

And it was all the time she had.

"Daisy, we mean you no harm," he said, walking down the corridor toward the Narrows hatch. "This has all been a terrible misunderstanding. Please, come talk with the captain. He can explain it all. It's funny, really, once you understand the truth of things. A comedy of errors, if you will."

Keep talking, you titanium son of a bitch.

"A comedy of errors?" she said in a whisper as she keyed another command into her small forearm tablet, her finger hovering over the *enter* key. "How is Sarah's death comedic, Barry? And don't you care about your friends? I blew one of 'em right out the goddamn airlock."

"Most unfortunate, what you did to Tamara, and quite unnecessary. I wish you had just listened to us."

Silently, Daisy slid her body out of the hatch, her feet softly touching the artificial gravity of the corridor's floor as she simultaneously pressed the flashing *enter* key on her tablet. At her touch, the remote speaker her voice had been coming from that she had previously mounted behind the access panel at the other end of the corridor started yelling a recorded verbal barrage.

"Why, Barry? You're not even human, so why are you doing this? You're a fucking traitorous machine, and you killed my friend, you piece of shit!" The sudden shift in volume temporarily blocked Barry's hearing. Long enough for Daisy to execute the other remote command and get a running start before he noticed her.

The second command she'd entered was the one that opened both top and bottom airlock doors to the long ladder leading to the shuttle. Safety protocols should have prohibited it, but Daisy found herself becoming quite adept at overriding all manner of those. She only hoped she'd given the antiquated ship enough time to power up.

Too late to worry about that.

Barry realized something was amiss and turned. His cybernetic eyes actually looked quite startled to see Daisy sprinting right at him.

"Why are you running toward me, Daisy?" he asked, confused.

Scratch that. She wasn't running at him, she was *sprinting,* and not toward him, but rather toward the hatch now sliding open in the floor. Realization dawned on him, and he instantly sprang into action, his legs pistoning rapidly as he raced to stop her.

Running at full-speed, Daisy depressed the red button on the spiked orb with her thumb, then threw it as hard as she could. She knew it was a one-in-seven chance she'd be remotely on target, and wondered how she knew not only that, but also the exact trajectory and force needed to have it arrive where she intended. Either way, she had only one chance. The second device she'd gathered parts for was still only half-completed.

Fortune was with her, and the orb flew true, striking Barry dead-center in the middle of his chest, but the little ball didn't cause any injury. Barry noted that the metal barbs were embedded in the flesh covering his cybernetic body, but the impact had done no damage at all. He did not feel pain like a human would, and the ball simply hung from his skin, dangling like an evil, shining Christmas ornament.

He ignored it. The useless little spiky thing caused no damage, and—

His sensors detected an unusual energy signature suddenly spike as his processors quickly assessed the makeshift device.

"What is—" he said, pausing as he just began to realize what the device truly was.

If a cyborg could show fear, at that moment he would have. Instead, his eyes went wide with surprise just as the pulse building inside the orb discharged.

The blast was greater than Daisy had anticipated, blowing him clean off his feet with a massive electrical burst, knocking out several lights and readout panels in the corridor as well.

Daisy didn't hesitate. Best case, he was dead, but more likely than not he was merely down and possibly damaged, but most likely rebooting, which might only take him seconds. In any case, she wasn't going to stick around to find out.

She ran closer, the barbecue smell of cooked meat finding its way to her nose just as Barry sat up with a jerk. He was moving slowly, not all of his systems back on line, his eyes barely focusing as he got one last glimpse of Daisy right as she leapt through the air above him and plummeted feet-first into the lengthy shaft, not even attempting to grasp the ladder's rungs.

It was four long stories down, and Daisy fell fast, only narrowly missing the walls. Her tablet took the brunt of her lone contact, glancing off the metal ladder as she plummeted, smashing the reinforced screen.

While it had taken most of the impact and had certainly saved her from a broken arm, the unit had shattered, embedding shards of glass into her flesh. She bit her lip and tried to ignore the pain. There were far bigger things to worry about.

Like falling to her death.

She looked down and saw her feet about to clear the entrance to the shuttle.

At speed.

I didn't give it enough time to power up. I'm going to di—

The artificial gravity in the shuttle grabbed her as she rocketed through the hatch, arresting what had been a downward fall, reversing it and saving her life in the process. With up and down suddenly switched, her downward fall had become an upward trajectory.

Despite slowing dramatically, she nevertheless hit the ceiling hard enough to see stars, then fell back onto the deck, nearly sliding into the open access hatch. Daisy, though stunned, still had her wits about her enough to roll clear and frantically slap at the airlock mechanism.

Luck was with her again, and the outdated hatch sealed shut, the access passage decompressing and locking down tight before the smoldering cyborg managed to regain functionality.

Daisy lay still for a long moment, her head swimming.

"No time to rest, Daze. Get moving."

"I know, I know," she grumbled to her dead friend.

Not wasting another moment, Daisy forced herself to her feet and bolted for the cockpit. It was down to a race between her and Mal. If she didn't initiate the launch protocol before her bypasses were overcome, Mal would know her plan, and lock down the ship from Command, and now that she was in the shuttle, there was no way she could access the *Váli*'s systems again. The game would be up, and she'd be trapped with nowhere to run.

She reached the cockpit and took a long look at the myriad buttons and display panels.

So much to figure out.

She shook the fog from her head and set to work. The impact had nearly knocked her senseless, but now, with the massive flood of adrenaline coursing through her system, she realized she knew exactly what to do.

Was this already inside my head, too? she wondered as she fired up the ship's onboard systems, quickly working to block out Mal from all access. *What else did the neuro-stim stick in there?*

Code flashed in her mind, her fingers executing the commands even as she marveled at her own prowess. She knew she was good, but she never knew she was *this* good. The directional thrusters fired up, the docking clamps released, and the shuttle slowly drifted away from the ship. All hardline ties were broken.

Then, and only then, did Daisy allow herself to breathe easy.

I actually made it.

"Daisy, you have no idea what you're jeopardizing," Mal's voice crackled over the shuttle's open comms.

Of course. Different system. Not tied in to the Váli's regular comms array.

"What we've been trying to tell you is tha—" Daisy switched off the communications system.

Much better, she thought as she sighed with relief at the blessed silence. She then slid into the padded seat nearest the shuttle's navigation station and plotted a course for Earth.

CHAPTER TWENTY-THREE

"Mal, go after her!" Captain Harkaway bellowed.

The massive ship did not change course.

"I'm sorry, Captain, but we seem to be unable to accurately adjust course to track the shuttle at this time."

"Gus?"

"Yeah, something's wrong with the nav system, but not from here."

The grizzled captain's shoulders slumped slightly as he pinched the bridge of his nose and let out a defeated sigh. "What did she do this time, Mal?"

"Uncertain. However, the wireless comms system is back online. I will have the crew immediately begin manual checks of the suspected attack points. I do not detect any fatal overrides, but prudence would be the wisest course of action."

"Agreed. Get on it. Gus, head down and help the others. We've got to track this down, whatever it is she did this time."

"Will do, Captain," Gustavo said, exiting Command.

The captain sat back in his chair, allowing himself a moment to take a deep breath and center himself. With a resolved sigh, he rose to his feet.

"You know what, wire details to my tablet and update me as more results come in. I'm going to join the crew."

"But Captain, protocol requires one human to always be present in Command during a crisis."

"I think we're flying a bit outside of protocol at this point, don't you? We need every hand we can working on this. Now, send me the damn details."

The device on his forearm beeped.

"Thanks. Keep tracking her, and let me know if there's anything crucial you need me for."

The weary veteran lurched to his feet and trudged off to help fix his ship, a sense of impending doom hanging in the air around him.

Thousands of miles from the *Váli*, a distance that was still growing, Daisy had five minutes left in her fifteen-minute power nap. It was a small luxury she allowed herself after spending a solid half hour digging remnants of the shattered tablet from her forearm.

The shuttle, she had discovered, carried only a very old first aid kit, stocked with yellowing bandages and rolls of tape that had long ago lost their usefulness. Fortunately, the hermetically-sealed antiseptic swabs were still intact, so at least no infection would set in.

Really, she was amazed that her arm hadn't broken from the blow, despite the tablet taking the majority of the impact. That she'd hit hard enough to break the supposedly unbreakable device spoke to just how much force had been generated.

She bit down on a tongue depressor as she dug in the wound until she felt certain no more debris was to be recovered. She then applied some antibiotic cream and tightly wrapped the limb. It was only at that point, once the sharp bits of glass and polymer frame were no longer embedded in her flesh, that she allowed herself a few moments of downtime.

She felt she'd earned it, given the hell she had just gone through. More importantly, however, was the knowledge that she had quietly afforded herself a bit of breathing room before disconnecting from the *Váli*.

The idea had been rustling around in her head as she crawled toward the shuttle access, and she was thrilled to find that reality was as good as theory. It was subtle. So subtle that she doubted even Mal would notice the tiny little worm embedded in the diversionary code blast she had thrown at the ship as she overrode its attempts to prevent the shuttle's launch.

She had fired off the one last trick up her sleeve, delivered via the hardwired umbilical to the shuttle. A parting gift, if you will.

It would be hard to even notice unless they knew where to look. A minuscule tweak that would force the *Váli* to steer just *slightly* off course. Sure, their readouts would show them pursuing her, but the reality would be a fraction of a degree off. Not a lot in the short run, but over the vast distance of space, they could be tens of thousands of miles off their intercept course.

They'd see the problem soon enough, of course, but by the time they figured out exactly what Daisy had done, she would already be long gone. Soon she'd be at Dark Side base, in the clear and bringing back the cavalry to deal with the corrupted AI and the tainted crew once and for all.

Without her clever little trick, even with the delays restoring other systems, it would have been little effort for the *Váli* to follow her. Given its drive abilities, it would have easily overtaken the much smaller and much slower shuttle. Fortunately, it was already at-speed when it released from the larger ship, and in space, there was no friction to slow its progress, but they could have accelerated and caught her regardless.

So, a clever little worm was the solution, but not in their navigation system. No, they'd have spotted something like that quickly, between Mal and Gus scanning for traces of her intrusion. Rather, it was just a devious little bit of code inserted in the timing systems that controlled the thrusters and engines.

Hardware, not software, though technically it *was* a minuscule software tweak that affected the hardware. Just a little change, but one that locked them to thrust just a tiny bit off course, leaving her enough room to escape.

Daisy had considered doing more to the ship, even briefly weighing the option of going so far as sabotaging the drive systems, leading to a total engine overload. That urge had changed when she heard Vince was alive, if he could really be called that. Hearing his voice...well, the idea of killing him and all the others was just too distasteful. Up until hours ago they *were* her friends, and despite learning what they really were, the thought of mass murder left a bad taste in her mouth.

"Good call. It's not cool to kill your friends, though you did space Tamara. Of course, you two were never really all that close. I guess we can call that one even."

"I thought you were gone," Daisy groaned.

"Nah, just leaving you on your own for a bit. You seemed stressed out. Figured you wanted some alone time. You forget how well I know you."

"And yet here you are, a chatty ghost in my head. Thanks, Sarah. Not creepy at all."

"It's your head, not mine. Obviously you've got stuff on your mind. So, the doctor is in. What's up?"

"Are we really going to do this?"

"You have anything better to do? It's a long flight."

Daisy sighed.

"Fine. The thing is, it's not just an issue of killing people.

Humans have done that forever. Or even about killing friends, though that part still doesn't sit right. But what's really got me riled up is their being complicit with the whole thing. Humans working with machines *against* humanity. It's fucked up, Sarah."

"Are you sure you didn't knock your head falling down that shaft?"

"Why?"

"Because you really are being obtuse. Hell, Daze, there are so many more shades than just black and white. Why are you so fast to categorize them?"

"This isn't just another variant on politics, sexuality, or identity here, this is about man and machine. Good and evil. Trying to kill me versus trying to help."

"But how can you be so sure? I mean, they did say they wanted to talk with you."

"They also wanted to gas me out of the Narrows."

"Because you attacked Vince, Daisy. Hell, you even cut the dude's arm off. With a freakin' hydraulic door! I mean, the fact that he's still talking to you after that, you've got one hell of a forgiving boyfriend."

"He's not my boyfriend. He's just a machine. Nothing more."

"Uh-huh. You and I both know that's some serious bullshit you're talking there. And he was always trying to help you, since the first day you two met. And he was good to you. I mean, really good to you. And he was pretty secure in his sexuality, if I remember your play-by-play correctly."

"Oh, shut up, Sarah. You're dead—you don't get a say in this," Daisy said with a grumble.

"Like that would stop me from calling you on your shit. Ha! Fat chance. Or maybe I'm really just a secret chip implanted in your head. A conscience given to the prodigal daughter because your machine overlords knew you didn't have one."

"Ha-ha. Very funny. First, you know damn well I have a conscience. I never told Barry about you admiring his multi-speed package—"

"Hey!"

"And second, I saw the scans. I'm clean, no chips in my head. Just one hundred percent organic human gray matter up there."

"Well then, that must mean I'm all in your mind. Damn, girl, you've got a pretty messed up imagination."

"Oh my God, will you shut up? I swear, I wish you were still alive so I could kill you!"

The voice in her head remained silent.

"Shit. I'm sorry. I miss you, Sarah," Daisy whispered, a quiet confession drifting in the cold, dry air.

Daisy slept poorly, her stomach upset from her unexpected meal of extremely outdated dehydrated food rations. She had found herself wondering if everything else about the shuttle was antique as well. She had spent the majority of her first day aboard reconfiguring the faulty navigation system. All of her time spent in the Narrows still hadn't prepared her for the arduous task of rewiring such an old vessel. It was time-consuming, tedious, and unfortunately, was absolutely necessary if she hoped to reach Dark Side base. The ship simply wasn't designed for such a long flight.

The navigation readouts were easy enough. She had those up and running and displaying a true heading—despite multiple other systems malfunctions—within mere hours. It was the rest that was taking so much time.

Connecting the guidance to the engines and maneuvering thrusters was far more complex than she felt it needed to be. By the end of the day, however, she thought she finally had everything in order. At least it held together and flew true to course, though the myriad warning lights that still lit up the old-time display console like a foreboding Christmas tree were troubling, to say the least.

"I really need to figure out a way to reduce the pressure on fuel line two before it becomes a problem," Daisy griped to herself.

Ever listening, Murphy would soon rear his ugly head and address her concern.

Less than twenty minutes later, the ship rocked to the side as the fuel line ruptured, spewing precious compressed liquid fuel into space. Fortunately, the vacuum froze the combustible fluid into a solid block and prevented ignition as the metal housing sheared free from the sudden pressure, but the vacuum was also unforgiving in its effect on bodies in motion. Sure enough, the shuttle quickly veered off course.

"You've got to be kidding me!" Daisy scrambled for the emergency shutoff valve. "If the frozen fuel hits the engine wake—"

The silent explosion triggered as the burning exhaust touched off the frozen fuel sent the shuttle spinning. Even with artificial gravity, the unexpected gyrations threw Daisy into a dizzying tumble. Her stomach, already uneasy from less-than-wonderful rations, emptied itself in a painful heave, its contents impacting the bulkhead with an unpleasant wet smack.

Daisy ignored her stomach and lunged for the shutoff. The knob, naturally (courtesy of Murphy, once more), was stuck open. Daisy's knuckles turned white with strain as she tried her best to turn it.

"Go, you sonofabitch!" she yelled, directing all her energy into that one hand. "Come on, you bastard!"

With a screech, the shutoff began to turn.

"That's right! Turn!"

Using all her might, she managed to turn it the rest of the way, cutting off the flow of fuel from the ruptured line. The engines sputtered and fell silent, their steady vibrating hum suddenly noticeable in its absence.

With no time to rest, Daisy quickly set to the task of damage control. While the engines were now cut off from fuel, only one of them was damaged. Murphy's law seemed not to apply to the ship's living compartments, however, as they escaped unscathed and were still holding pressure. Unfortunately, the same couldn't be said of the work bay on the shuttle's back.

The explosion had bent open one of the access hatches. Daisy was sure of it. The angry little red light flashing in her face told her so. So, too, did the video display showing the ever-so-slightly buckled metal, now open to space, right at the seam. While her living area was secure, Daisy found herself unexpectedly with no access to the tools housed in the work bay.

Or the protective space suits stored there.

Without a suit, there's no way to do an EVA to fix the fuel line. Daisy forced down her panic, took a deep breath, and cleared her mind as best she could. Then she focused on the problems facing her and pondered them as objectively as she could.

Okay, nothing to be done about the fuel for now, so deal with that later. First things first, get the ship flying level and back on course.

The engines were completely offline, and that meant the directional vector panels would be useless. Likewise, the maneuvering thrusters seemed to be malfunctioning.

"I bet the air-feeds to the thrusters purged when the fire hit as a safety precaution," her friend suggested.

"Great minds think alike, Sarah. But I can't get to the access panel to reset the system from here. The bay is in a total vacuum now, and I don't have any way to fix it."

"Well, there is one thing you could do, but it will make the rest of the trip rather unpleasant."

Daisy knew what she meant. It was not an option she was at all fond of.

"But I *need* that air. I'm breathing it."

"Won't do you much good if you shoot right past the moon, now, would it?"

"I hate it when you're right."

"So, pretty much always, then?"

"Zip it. I've got work to do."

"Okay, but remember, breathe shallow."

After far too much exertion to open the small access panel, despite lack of proper tools, Daisy finally managed to gain entry to the correct cluster of pipes, tubes, and wires. The old-school technology was ridiculous to her high-tech-accustomed eyes, but she would have to make it work. Somehow.

Teeth clenched, Daisy got down on all fours and carefully wiggled forward until she wedged herself up to her waist in the tiny routing conduit behind the bulkhead. Unlike the *Váli*, the shuttle was not designed for ease of access, and even accustomed as she was to tight spaces, Daisy found herself feeling rather claustrophobic in the restricting environment.

Her elbows and shoulders ached from repeated impacts with pipes and beams as she set to work using only cobbled-together hand tools for a job that demanded power ones. The process would work, but it would also take hours. Gritting her teeth, she set to her task.

"That should do it," she said triumphantly some time later as she tightened the last compression fitting. "Am I awesome or what?" she joked to herself. "Victory is mine!" she said with a laugh, then promptly banged her head on a pipe as she slid back out of the narrow space.

"Ow! Sonofabitch." She ran her fingers through her hair and checked her hand. No blood, but she'd probably have a nice bump on her head, knowing her luck.

With exhausted hands, she gradually eased open the pair of valves jury-rigged to feed into the thruster system. It was ugly, it was far from ideal, but she knew it would almost certainly work. Sure enough, small puffs of compressed air vented out the thruster nozzles, slowing the spin. *There we go. A few more like that and I'll be flying level. Then I just have to nudge this bucket back on course.*

It was very slow work, the venting of air to steer the ship, but it had to be. Anything faster, and it could be the end of her. Sarah was right, she'd need to take shallow breaths, but at least she would be back on course. All it had cost her was roughly half the air in the living spaces, cleverly re-routed into the pressure feeds to the directional navigational thrust system.

She was still moving at a high speed, even without the engines firing, thanks to the friction-free physics of space travel, and within a few more minutes she had finally succeeded in nudging the vessel back on target to Dark Side Base.

Daisy figured she would be okay. So long as nothing got in her way, that is.

Any drastic avoidance maneuvering would likely overload what little integrity the overtaxed electronics still maintained, not to mention dropping her oxygen stores to zero.

Zero air would not be good.

Daisy was desperate for a break. She had been running on pure adrenaline for over a day, but she knew she had to power through the exhaustion and aches. There was still one more very important job to do. She had to reconfigure the engines.

The plan was to allow the one functional engine to fire for emergency purposes, while keeping the damaged engine completely offline. Combined with the compressed air to the thrusters on the damaged side, she was pretty sure she could compensate for the off-centered thrust and keep the ship flying straight.

It was a good plan, and a vital one if she wanted to survive any unlikely obstacles or debris floating in her trajectory. Unfortunately, it had one far-from-small flaw. She would have to open the emergency shut-off valve to prime the engines.

Fuel was already extremely low, but if she ever wanted to use the lone engine, it would require a sacrifice. Not one of blood, tears, or virgins, but of precious fuel. She figured she had one, maybe two decent bursts at her disposal before the ruptured line drained the reserve tanks dry. It wasn't a win-win situation by any stretch. More like a win-lose one, but it would have to do.

The work took the better part of three hours, but when it was finally complete, Daisy felt a weight lifted from her shoulders. She had done all she could, and the rest was up to fate and fortune.

Better than nothing at all, she mused, then settled into as comfortable a position as she could to try to rest.

If she could.

The routine was repetitious.

Breathing in, briefly holding her breath, then slowly letting it out as she focused on relaxing every muscle in her body from head to toe and back again was getting beyond boring after so many hours. With nothing else to do, Daisy felt it best to follow her own advice and conserve as much air as possible. No sense tempting fate, after all.

For the first few hours, she had found herself beginning to tap into that near-trance state, which previously helped her calm herself. She was surprised to find that the deeper she turned inward, the more the tantalizing fringes of her nascent abilities began to tickle the edges of her awareness.

Exactly how much the neuro-stim had put into her head was a mystery, but the human mind was long-known to only use a fraction of its processing and storage capacity, and she suddenly felt that she only knew a tiny portion of what was in there.

As she relaxed even further, Daisy found herself at increasing ease with the skills she recently discovered in her possession. Coding and machine language at a whole new level suddenly made sense, now that she was looking at it in a non-panicked life-or-death situation. *Of course* it would flow like that. The knowledge was as much a part of her as knowing how to tie her shoes. How had she ever thought otherwise?

Technical weapons engineering adapted from salvaged parts at hand? The knowledge was there. She hadn't really known the full potential of the electromagnetic pulse grenade she had fabricated while crawling through the Narrows on her way to the shuttle, but somewhere in her mind, the survival combat skills and technical prowess to put them to use, were lurking just below the surface.

If the situation wasn't so dire, she'd have reveled in the newfound discoveries and delved even farther into the still-clouded areas of her subconscious as they gradually came into focus. Unfortunately, the low oxygen alarms shrieking from the shuttle's console had eventually disrupted her calm enough to put any further thoughts of true self-discovery on the back burner while she figured out how to mute them.

For the time being, focusing on conserving air would have to suffice. Once she arrived at Dark Side, a proper counterstrike team would be readied, and *Váli* and its traitorous crew would be dealt with before their plans could be realized. Only *then* would she let herself truly relax.

CHAPTER TWENTY-FOUR

"Dark Side Base, this is *Váli* shuttle, do you copy?"

Silence.

"Maybe we're just too far out for them to read our signal. They are on the far side of the moon, after all."

Daisy considered the possibility. A base located in the part of the moon not visible from Earth likely took its security a bit more seriously than your regular space-port. Still, not getting a reply was becoming more than a little disconcerting.

"Dark Side Base, this is the *Váli* shuttle on distant approach, do you copy?"

Still nothing.

The shuttle was moving at a rapid pace, thanks in no small part to the hours upon hours of hard labor Daisy had put in re-working the thrusters and drive system. The ship had stayed on course, and at her present speed, it would reach the moon in less than a half hour.

No sense saving these now, Daisy thought as she rummaged through her flight suit. She'd eaten only the old freeze-dried rations on the long flight to the moon, fearful of exactly how long the flight might take, but now that she was finally almost safe and sound, she felt it was all right to dig into her emergency stash.

The bars had been tucked away safely deep in her pockets and were somewhat worse-for-wear after all that crawling, but they tasted wonderful to her hungry taste buds. She took a quick survey of her hoard as she chewed.

Two nutrient bars, a packet of electrolyte gel, and a handful of candy-coated stim tablets were all she had.

Don't need those, she mused, tucking the stimulants back into their cozy home. The electrolyte gel and one of the bars, however, were fair game, and she made quick work of them, washing the disproportionately satisfying snack down with a sealed water pouch before sliding into the lavatory pod to relieve herself.

And there I go, contributing to the water reclamation system. She couldn't help but laugh.

The lights flickered and dimmed, then brightened back to normal levels.

"You know, we really should have gotten to that, Daze," Sarah chimed in.

"If we'd known the shuttle would become such an urgent priority, I suppose we would have put the upgrades higher up on our action agenda. As it stands, the old bird seems to be holding up all right, all things considered."

"There you go, tempting fate again."

"Yeah, yeah. Such a daring person, I know. Sure, it's a little colder than I'd prefer, but bringing the heating system up to modern standards wasn't really high on anyone's list after we got hit. And what's with this thing anyway? I mean, the creaks and rattles, this shuttle has to be at least seven generations earlier than the *Váli*. Why strap an antiquated thing like this to its belly when they could have used any one of a number of vastly superior designs?"

"Maybe it was all they had on hand."

"Come on, Sarah, we both know there are dozens of variants of configurations that could have been mounted there, any one of which would have sufficed."

"Maybe because this one has actual wings, while the others were designed mostly for space travel."

"And what does that have to do with anything? How do wings help?"

"Think about it, Daze. If, by some odd set of circumstances, the drive system were to go offline, all of the other variants would pretty much drop from the sky if they tried to enter the atmosphere. This old bucket of bolts, however outdated it may be in all other regards, is one of the only designs capable of gliding without thrust."

"So you're saying it's really more of a lifeboat than a shuttle?"

"You have to admit, it makes sense."

Daisy paused a moment, considering the possibility. But if the shuttle was meant for emergency egress only, what was the plan once they arrived in Earth's orbit? Sure, Dark Side was there to conveniently patch up their hurt from the impact that had so rudely woken them from cryo-sleep, but that had never been the actual plan. So why a ship that could glide?

A man's voice crackled out from the comms array speaker.

"*Váli* shuttle, this is Dark Side Base. We have received your transmission. Do you register this message?"

Daisy quickly finished her business, pulling up her flight suit and locking down the waste recycling port before hurrying back to the command chair.

"*Váli* shuttle, this is Dark Side Base. Once again, we have received your transmission. Do you register this message?"

Daisy reached for the comms button, then paused. Something felt wrong. *Off*. Nagging at her brain. It took her a few seconds to put her finger on it.

The way the man spoke. It was something in his cadence. The tone of his voice.

"*Váli* shuttle, this is Dark Side Base. We have received your transmission. Do you register this message?"

The inflection. Exactly the same each time. *Exactly.*

"Goddamn it, Sarah, it's a fucking AI."

"Of course it is. They're standard on all ships, and who do you think runs the docking arrays in the spaceports?"

"I know. You're right. It's just that after Mal, I don't know anymore."

"You disabled Mal's long-range comms, so what's to worry about? They'd have had to physically fly here before us to poison that well. Look at the scans. No sign of the Váli anywhere. So come on, let's go get reinforcements and handle things with that rogue crew before they get even more out of hand."

"You and your damn logic." Daisy turned her attention to the ancient monitors in front of her. "You're right. Scans show no sign of the *Váli*. The base has no vessels at all docked on the exterior—"

An uncomfortable silence filled the cabin.

"What is it, Daisy?"

"Why aren't there *any* ships there?" A look of deep worry flashed across her face. "I'm going to pull up a higher resolution scan."

"*Váli* shuttle, this is Dark Side Base. We have received your transmission. Do you—"

"Yes, I read you, Dark Side. We're experiencing some minor technical issues with our communications systems, please stand by."

"Copy that, *Váli* shuttle. Standing by."

Daisy adjusted the nose-mounted camera array and zoomed in on the barely illuminated base. Hidden among the rocks of the moon––which happened to be in shadow at the moment as Earth made its orbit around the sun––it was almost impossible to make out. Adjusting the resolution, Daisy switched to expanded-spectrum and surveyed the area. What she saw took her breath away.

"Shit," she gasped.

"Oh no. That can't be right."

"No, Sarah, it can't." Daisy quickly flipped on the reserve power cells before lunging across the cabin to the emergency shut-off valve.

"Are you sure, about this?"

"You saw it. The base has been almost entirely destroyed. That was a debris field out there, Sarah. The battle already got here before us, and it's an AI running the show."

Daisy primed the engine and spun the valve wide open, then slammed herself into the command chair and buckled in. The moon's gravity had begun to take hold of the approaching shuttle. This was going to use far more power than she'd anticipated.

"*Váli* shuttle, I detect a fuel leak from your number two engine. Your systems appear to be engaging in rapid power-cycling mode. Do you require assistance?"

"Um, negative, Dark Side. Just adjusting a few things up here. Nothing to worry about." She quickly checked her calculations. The shuttle was coming in way too fast for her liking. "Dark Side, may I please speak with the commander in charge?"

A silence hung in the air.

"There's no need for that, Daisy. We just want to talk to you. Please, your ship is obviously damaged. Come in and dock, and we can explain."

"Daisy? How the hell does that thing know your name? I mean, it couldn't. Not unless Mal was sending messages long before—"

"My thoughts exactly," she said, then slammed the ignition button, firing up the lone functioning engine.

The shuttle rumbled violently with a deeply unsettling

vibration as it abruptly changed course and powered away from the moon. Despite the massive burn, it wasn't enough.

"Daisy, the trajectory is still inadequate to clear gravity!"

With no hesitation, Daisy entered another sequence into the engine and flipped a series of flashing red switches.

"Wait, are you sure it can withstand—"

The engine blasted full-open throttle, the maneuvering thrusters firing to help correct the overpowered drive trajectory. Then, with a horrible, metal-rending shudder, the engine tore itself apart as it sputtered out. It was enough, but only barely, and the crippled shuttle limped its way from the dark side to the light.

"Daisy, please," the voice pleaded. "You don't know what you're doing. Just listen a moment and I'll expla—"

She powered off the comms.

"Bite me, fucking machine," she growled, just as the lights flickered and went out.

Only the most basic core systems still functioned, their console buttons glowing dimly. Heat? Fat chance. That was done for, as was eighty percent of life support. Comms, however, still seemed functional, but for how long was anyone's guess. Unfortunately, while she remained uncaptured, the damage the vessel incurred in her escape left her quickly running out of options.

The shuttle had pulled free of the moon's mass, settling into a weak trajectory, but one that nevertheless, was heading toward Earth, Daisy noted as she read the command display.

Finally, a little luck. It's about time.

She ran navigation calculations while the system still had power, then flipped a series of relays and used her final burst from the compressed air thrusters to steer her on course. It was her last chance, and a limited one at that. If she used any more, she'd have no air left to breathe.

Okay, that should do it. If I plotted our trajectory right, this should set us on course for a re-entry. Daisy sincerely hoped she was right.

"Hey, Sarah, guess what? Looks like you may have had a point about that gliding thing. I just hope those controls still work once we hit atmosphere."

She adjusted the comms array to a wide broadcast and clicked open the transmitter. "Mayday, mayday. This is *Váli* shuttle approaching Earth orbit without power. Does anyone copy?"

Silence greeted her query.

"Well, I suppose that would have been too easy," she said with a grim chuckle, then slowly rolled through the open frequencies, listening for any chatter. All were silent but for static, though a few times the rolling hisses and squelched noise almost seemed to make sense to her.

Nah, just static, she told herself. Hopefully someone would answer before she made landfall. *If* she made it. Her battle with the moon's gravity had scrubbed off a great deal of the shuttle's velocity. So much so that she was now almost drifting at space debris speed toward the bright blue orb hanging in the cold vacuum.

It really is beautiful, she noted as she stared out the window. She just hoped her air would hold out long enough to make it there.

Hours later, bundled up in every piece of protective gear she could find, Daisy sat quietly, conserving oxygen while focusing her energies on keeping her body warm. Without heating systems functional, the shuttle had quickly begun a descent from chilly but moderately comfortable to freezing and potentially deadly. Fortunately, Daisy had a trick up her sleeve.

Sarah's Qi Gong lessons were paying off in spades, now that she was finding herself able to tap into her meditative state with increasing ease. The principle was simple enough: Direct the body's energy in such a way to generate heat in your hands. Energy healing, some had called it, a phenomenon documented over centuries.

Daisy was now modifying that practice to suit her survival needs, focusing her energy not on simply warming her hands, which were quite toasty in their gloves despite the freezing temperatures, but also on heating her entire body.

It was the sort of thing one might expect of a monk sitting atop a frozen mountaintop, not a somewhat-snarky twenty-something spaceship electronics technician, but there she was, sitting silently and nearly breaking a sweat from her focused efforts.

The process also allowed her to reduce her respirations, the oxygen required in a meditative state being far less than were she to be moving about the cabin. If not for her ability to tap into this newfound level of self-control, she might very possibly have run out of air and frozen to death well before she finally breached the Earth's atmosphere.

The heat generated by re-entry would warm the ship nicely, but it wouldn't be until she had descended below twenty thousand feet that the automatic venting system would purge the CO_2-filled air and replace its stale dampness with fresh outside air.

Slowly, she roused herself from her deep meditation and checked the readout on the external collision scanner. She had rigged it to warn of impact as she glided through the increasingly dense debris field lazily drifting around the planet. She couldn't tell exactly what was out there; the machinery was far too damaged to give an accurate read out, but she guessed it was defunct satellites along with assorted space junk that had taken up residence in the planet's orbit.

So far her path remained relatively clear. Small bits

periodically banged off the hull, but there were no impending impacts of any meaningful size.

She refocused her attention and reached for the communications array. She had her internal clock dialed-in, and found she could quite easily slip back into full consciousness every few hours to attempt contact once more.

"Mayday, mayday, this is *Váli* shuttle, does anyone copy?"

Silence yet again.

Everything looks all right, but something must've shorted out. That, or Mal somehow booby-trapped the communications system long before I ever got on board.

"But you were able to talk to Dark Side."

Yeah, but maybe that was the only channel she left functional to transmit. Anyway, it's too late to worry about it now. I've just gotta make it to L.A. Once I touch down at Schwarzenegger International Space Port, we'll set things right. They may have taken over the moon, but we'll get that sorted soon enough.

Daisy switched off the comms and closed her eyes, slipping once more into a meditative state.

Over the past twenty hours, drifting as she was, she found herself becoming increasingly adept at turning her attention inward. She also discovered the faint traces of blocks in her mind.

Artificial ones.

Neuro-stim residue was all over them. What secrets they were hiding, she had no idea, but she was damn sure going to change that.

All right, then. Back to work, she thought as she redoubled her internal efforts.

She once again began chipping away at the edges of a barricaded segment of her mind, eager to find what secrets lay waiting behind the carefully hidden doorways.

As she sat in silence during the long drift toward Earth, her attention focused inward, Daisy came to gradually recognize some semblance of a pattern to the mental blocks. As if they were layer upon layer of data, carefully compressed to best utilize the vast, wet-meat storage space inside her head. She had seen this kind of partitioning and compression before in her work as a technician, but only in machinery.

Her mind had been used as a hard drive, and she was determined to find out what had been put there.

She also noticed that while she may have inadvertently dumped huge quantities of data into her head when she mistakenly removed the final safety on her neuro-stim, this information cache was something far more complex.

Detailed. Massive.

But this makes no sense. This isn't a few days, or even a few months, worth of data. This is huge. There's no way my neuro-stim could have possibly— The realization hit her, spiking her heart rate ever so slightly, even in her meditative state. *Unless they've been lying about how powerful the neuro-stims really are. My God, how much could I have accidentally pumped into my brain?*

"Lucky you didn't have a stroke. No wonder you keep talking to me in your head. You must've really messed yourself up, fiddling with that thing."

"I'm meditating, Sarah. Go away."

"Okay, fine. I just thought it was worth mentioning is all. I mean, what if you lobotomized yourself and this is all just a dream?"

"Not helping."

"Okay, okay. Shutting up."

"Good."

"But one last thing."

"Oh, dear Lord, what?"

"The captain used the words, 'what she's capable of.' That sounds a lot more like they were playing with your mind long before you went and removed the inhibitors."

Daisy quietly mulled over the possibility. Much as she hated to admit it, Sarah was right. While a lot of her newfound knowledge was dumped in by her own actions, it was highly likely that all sorts of things had already been lurking in her mind. Possibly even traps laid within her own psyche. The question now was, if so, what could she do about them?

Don't worry about that now. First get on solid ground. Once you're down, I'll have a medical team run a neural scan to unravel this mess and figure out what they did to me.

She mentally reached for the nearest block of masked knowledge.

It smells like—huh, 'smells' like. Maybe it affects or enhances my sense of smell. Don't see how that would be of any use, but what the hell. Let's keep going.

Daisy once more began chipping away at the mental block, not knowing what exactly she'd find, or whether she'd even make that discovery before landfall. In any case, it was progress. She only hoped the doctors on Earth could put things right in her head.

CHAPTER TWENTY-FIVE

The city of Los Angeles was bustling, its millions of residents scurrying about like so many fleas on the back of a giant beast. It had grown over the centuries, absorbing neighboring municipalities until its mass was enough to engulf a good several dozen smaller burghs. To the west, the clear ocean gleamed in the afternoon sun, while the surrounding mountains blazed their verdant glory for the city-dwellers to see.

Daisy marveled at how smoothly the automated vehicular flow functioned in tandem with the manually-operated units. Both land-bound and airborne, collisions were a thing of the past, and while the city's once-sprawling Red Car transit system had been long-ago purchased and dismantled by automobile and oil conglomerates, the system that had eventually sprung up in its place centuries later was one of the crown jewels of public transit.

A vast system not only consisting of above-ground pods whisking people to their destinations throughout the region, but also a robust subterranean network that not only served the city, but also tied in to the global loop-transit network. With vacuum-sealed lines spanning the planet, supersonic travel in the zero-resistance pipelines had led to a coming-together on a global scale as face-to-face meetings with associates worldwide were as easy as a few hours spent in a loop-tube.

Another benefit had been the near elimination of the closed-minded bigotry that had plagued the world for millennia. Now that even the poorest of denizen could visit far-flung parts of the globe for a tiny fraction of the cost of air or space travel—which, by its nature, was still far more expensive—the exposure to foreign cultures first-hand had nearly eradicated the misguided xenophobia that had previously shaped political strife and mistrust for generations.

As she walked among the multi-ethnic commuters, Daisy couldn't help but stare up at the impressive residential towers that managed to gracefully achieve just the right balance, allowing for greater density of living, while not tarnishing the natural beauty of the region. The city planners had set firm boundaries between urban development and lands reserved for natural habitats. The electric pulse walls separating the two allowed observation of nature without intrusion, and incidents of mountain lions or coyotes wandering into a person's yard and eating their precious Fluffy were a thing of the past.

She stepped into the lobby of the glass-covered tower stretching upward before her and joined the throngs heading for its uppermost reaches. Exiting onto the one-hundredth floor observation deck, she could see why so many had crowded into the elevator.

In the near distance the pristine beaches stretched from Malibu to Palos Verdes, both of which, while retaining their names for nostalgic reasons, were now part of the greater Los Angeles area.

The palm trees look so tiny from up here, she noted. *It's good to be back on solid ground after all those months in artificial gravity. It just feels right. I remember that first step on real terra-firma after I landed...*

Daisy paused, her brow furrowed in confused thought.

After I landed... Wait. How did I wind up here? Wasn't there something I needed to—

The shuttle bucked abruptly as it hit the very edge of the Earth's atmosphere, snapping Daisy awake, firmly strapped into her pilot's seat.

"Aww, sonofabitch," she muttered through clenched teeth as she quickly rubbed the sleep from her eyes and checked the barely-functional navigational array. "My approach is off."

"This angle will drop you smack-dab in the Pacific Ocean."

"Yeah, I see it."

She quickly typed in a series of alternate trajectories, every last one of which told her the same thing: she'd have to adjust her course immediately, or she would be taking a very long swim if she hoped to reach land. Without hesitation—for hesitation would have meant likely demise—she sealed off the command center from the rest of the ship and hit the purge valve, directing the precious gasses into the silent thrust system.

"If you do that, you'll only have whatever air is in this capsule, and it's already dangerously high in carbon dioxide."

"Don't have much of a choice now, do I?" Daisy flipped the switch, sending one controlled burst to the appropriate thrusters. The shuttle lurched as its trajectory against the edges of the atmosphere altered. There wasn't much resistance yet, but even a minute's delay and she would have been too far into the buffeting ionosphere for the thrusters to have made enough of a difference. Only in the vacuum of space could they do what she needed them to.

The rattling increased, and while the rapid spike in temperature was a welcome sensation, it was a bittersweet one. If her trajectory was too steep, the shuttle would not only warm up, but would burn to a crisp, disintegrating into so many pieces of flying debris. It would provide a pretty light show for the people down below, but it would be a truly rotten ending to Daisy's already difficult day.

A small explosion rocked the ship, shorting out a wide swath of the command center's panels.

There went the auxiliary scanning array, she grimly noted, her jaw firmly set as the turbulence increased. *I wonder what other parts are peeling off and burning up?*

All around the ship, bits and pieces were indeed shearing off, leaving the shuttle resembling a meteorite breaking up upon entering the atmosphere. Despite all that, the main power still held.

For a brief moment, a red blip appeared on her navigation system. A blip that was closing distance fast.

What the hell is that? It's moving too fast to be a support ship.

"Mayday, mayday, this is *Váli* shuttle, on emergency descent to Los Angeles Space Port. Incoming object detected. I am not a hostile vessel. Repeat, not a hostile vessel. Does anyone copy?"

She fought the steering column as the ship finally cleared the ionosphere and entered the atmosphere with a final jolt, the violence of which shorted out the entire cockpit.

"Oh. Shit."

The shuttle had lost all power, and while it was still gliding more or less on course, it was completely dead-stick, with not a single electronic system functioning. Daisy flipped all the auxiliary switches on the command console, but to no avail. She was strapped to a piece of debris, falling from the sky.

A sonic boom rocked the vessel as whatever had been locked on to her power signature blew past the seemingly inert craft.

At least it didn't hit me, whatever that was. Maybe someone got my message.

"Quit with your what-ifs and get this thing working, Daze! Come on, snap to it!"

"I'm trying, but there's no power."

"Remember the old specs? The ones we looked at all those months ago? There's a fly-by-wire backup."

"You mean the hydraulic system for the flaps and ailerons? But those lines needed to be replaced."

"It can't hurt to try them. Unless you have a better idea. Or prefer plunging to your death. Me, I'm already dead, but I don't think you'd enjoy it much."

"Point taken."

Daisy wrenched open the heavy panel on the floor to the right of the pilot's seat. There, a series of hand cranks lay tucked safely in their cradles, awaiting eager hands to bring them to life. She grabbed the first one, swinging it out and locking it into place. Then the second one. Finally, the third joined its siblings and she began to crank them one by one until they could turn no more.

"Okay, done," she said. "Now let's see if those shitty old hydraulics held up to the pressure. Not like I have any readouts to confirm for me."

With steady hands, Daisy flexed her arms, straining her biceps as she slowly pulled the steering column, while feathering the foot pedals that had raised into place as she activated the system. Miracle of miracles, the craft, while quite sluggish, responded to her efforts.

"Holy shit, it's working!"

"See? I told ya so."

"You can gloat if we survive. Let's just hope the landing gear deployment system works."

It was a mechanism of desperation and last resort. Explosive bolts which, when manually triggered, would blow the protective housing from the landing gear, while a smaller charge would detonate on the lone pin restraining a high-tension spring system, designed to push the landing gear into place. Of course, those springs were ancient, and the explosive bolts? Well, Daisy didn't like the odds, but it was better than nothing.

She banked the shuttle at high altitude and began what she believed was the correct angle of approach for Schwarzenegger Space Port, Los Angeles.

As she descended, Daisy noticed the stillness around her. The airspace surrounding the shuttle was completely empty.

Giving me the red-carpet treatment, I see. Nice. At least I don't have to worry about accidentally taking out any other vessels if things go truly tits-up.

Out the window, the shining ocean beckoned, a beautiful blue siren calling her to Earth. Farther ahead, things weren't so bright and shiny as the low clouds of the city's marine layer covered much of the coastline. Inconveniently, right where she needed to go.

Gonna have to guess the approach and hope for the best. A small furrow of concern began to grow on her brow.

Three minutes later she descended through the cloud cover, right into a flock of very surprised birds, several of which met their unexpected demise against the shuttle's wings.

Sorry, birds, but I can't really do any evasive steering right now.

She had perhaps thirty miles to go, and it looked like the glide trajectory would take her to her objective, but something seemed wrong.

Off.

Incredibly not-right.

Then it hit her.

"Where are all the people?" she wondered aloud.

From her vantage point, high above, Daisy realized not a human soul was moving down below. Wrestling the controls with one hand, she pulled a pair of ancient binoculars from the emergency bag under the pilot's seat and put them to her eyes, ignoring the crumbling rubber covering that cracked under her fingers. Sure enough, there was no one. Empty vehicles filled the roads, but there was not a person to be seen.

A flash of movement caught her eye. A pack of what

appeared to be wild dogs emerged from a building, looking up at the sky in curiosity.

And the buildings. They were intact, at least mostly, but there were huge swaths of the outlying municipalities that appeared to be stripped bare, as if a swarm of metal-eating locusts had whipped through, devouring nearly everything in their path.

Looking closer as she glided silently overhead, Daisy realized it wasn't military destruction she was looking at. No bombs had gone off. Instead, it was a neat and orderly kind of destruction. Mostly, anyway. A few small patches appeared to have seen fighting once, long, long ago, but the vast majority had the distinct look of a massive-scale dismantling.

A deconstruction.

Someone, it seemed, had been systematically tearing down the great cities on the outskirts of Los Angeles.

Something moved, far off to her left.

Daisy spun in her seat, pressing the binoculars tightly to her eyes. A human form, or at least so it appeared, caught her eye as it trudged along a main street, dragging a piece of something behind it.

She desperately wanted to turn, to circle back for a better look, but with no power and a rapidly approaching date with the ground, that simply wasn't an option. She'd be on terra firma in a minute, one way or another, as the shuttle rapidly closed the distance to Los Angeles proper.

"Please work," she implored the non-sentient shuttle. Then she pulled the small red lever.

Five small explosions barely shook the craft as the landing gear covers flew free, two of the three wheels snapping down into position. The third, the wheel on the rear-right, stubbornly refused, only lowering partially before jamming. With no readouts to tell her its status, Daisy had little choice but to hope for the best, while preparing for the worst.

"Uh, Daze?"

"A little busy, here, Sarah. Trying to land a shuttle with no power."

"Yeah, but have you noticed where we are?"

Daisy looked more closely out the window. The scenery was familiar, buildings she knew and the network of roads below them. Then it hit her.

"We're not going to make it, are we?"

"Too far from the spaceport. You're going to have to land on the highway."

Daisy scanned the thousands of cars beneath her, lining the roads, but not a body in sight.

"Nowhere to land. Maybe the LA River?"

"You see that thicket? That's the river."

Daisy realized the banks of what had once been a concrete-lined "river" were now completely overgrown with not only shrubbery and vines, but full-grown trees. A landing was out of the question.

"This is going to suck," she lamented. "I guess the one good thing about losing all our fuel is at least we won't blow up when we crash."

"That's the spirit! Way to look on the bright side!"

"I was being sarcastic."

"Duh."

Daisy allowed herself a grim little smile as she dropped the shuttle down on top of the rows of abandoned vehicles.

The impact immediately buckled the front landing gear, slamming the shuttle's massive nose down onto the highway, where it easily plowed through its vehicular obstacles like so much tissue paper. Metal and glass flew in every direction as the ship's underbelly casually crushed all that got in its way, until it finally slid to a grating halt.

Didn't die. Okay, then. That wasn't nearly as bad as I thought it would be, Daisy noted.

She unbuckled from the pilot's seat, left her larger toolbag and all unnecessary gear behind, then grabbed the small survival backpack stowed beneath the seat, and popped the hatch.

A blast of crisp air washed over her, replacing the dangerously stale carbon dioxide-heavy mix on which she'd been surviving. She breathed deeply, and despite the lingering dust from her crash landing, at that moment, the air to her was by far the freshest she had ever breathed.

Daisy crawled from the ship and cautiously lowered herself to the roadway, careful not to land on the rough edges of the destroyed vehicles, then took a long moment to look around.

Empty.

No people. No sounds. No smells. Not even a siren in the wake of her crash landing.

The city was empty.

Where small gardens had once stood in front of the varied buildings, massive trees and sprawling vines now clogged sidewalks and smaller streets. As for the vehicles on which she'd come crashing down, the reason for her softer-than-expected landing was apparent. They were ancient, falling apart from disuse after what appeared to be decades, if not more, their fuel cells long dead.

"This isn't right," she said in disbelief. "This can't be. I was just here not that many years ago."

Daisy circled the shuttle, taking in her surroundings in shock. They were exactly as she remembered them, exactly as they'd been in her dream less than an hour earlier, but different. Empty. In ruins.

Pull yourself together, Daisy. You survived this far, don't lose it now.

Her posture straightened, the defeated slouch that had been quietly settling in to her shoulders shrugged off in an instant as grim determination kicked in.

Time to move, before it gets dark.

"Good call. I know you saw those wild dogs you flew over. Who knows what else is living in this city."

"Besides humans, you mean," Daisy replied.

Bending down next to the shuttle, she pried a piece of metal free from a wreck and felt its sharp edge.

This should do, she thought, wrapping the narrow end with a strip of material pulled from the debris. She gave it a test swing, cleanly slicing through a nearby vine weaving through an abandoned vehicle's frame. *Yeah, this should do just fine.* Shouldering her bag, she laid out her course and headed off into the city, her makeshift machete clearing a path where the overgrowth blocked her way.

As she moved farther into the maze of buildings, the silence was deafening. Oddly enough, though, as she walked alone, she couldn't shake the uncomfortable sensation of being watched.

CHAPTER TWENTY-SIX

Daisy had been walking for well over an hour, tracing a basic reconnaissance pattern outward from the shuttle, then arcing over and heading back. Gradually, street by street, she covered most of a circle surrounding the craft. Once that was done, well, she didn't quite know what she'd do next.

Her stomach grumbled uncomfortably as she exerted herself in the balmy weather. It was perfect out, sunny and temperate, but after days in space on extremely limited rations, Daisy was desperately in need of substantial nourishment.

She'd been hoping for a proper sit-down dinner after she'd been debriefed about the incident aboard the *Váli*, but instead, she was stuck fending for herself in a desolate city. At the very least, she hoped to find a supermarket of some sort where she could perhaps scavenge some canned goods. All she had to do was continue her sweep. She knew statistically it wouldn't be long, but as she walked, she felt more and more alone as the miles passed beneath her feet.

Throughout the city, something odd struck her. Not a single corpse was to be found. Not even any bones, though she figured wild animals could easily have taken care of that. Nevertheless, not seeing even a trace of anyone with all those thousands upon thousands of vehicles abandoned in the streets in a city of tens of millions—it was unnerving, to say the least.

With aching feet, at long last, Daisy came upon a large market on the ground floor of what appeared to be a residential tower.

Oh yes! Finally!

The power, while apparently sporadic, was still on, as seemed to be the case with much of the empty city, thanks to many buildings' solar arrays and power backups. The doors ground open on dusty tracks as she approached, welcoming her to the silent halls of food and drink.

The smell hit her like a damp fist covered in rotting shit, making her eyes water immediately. She quickly pulled her shirt over her nose and mouth to at least partly block the stench, then proceeded inside, squinting against the irritating fumes.

Rows upon rows of sealed food packets had rotted open, bursting from internal bacterial growth. They were supposed to have a shelf life of over fifty years, yet here they were, ruptured and rotting throughout the store. Worse yet, the ammonia stench hinted at dead wildlife as well. Sure enough, several partially decayed raccoons and dogs lay scattered across the floor.

"Don't eat anything here, Daisy. I've got a bad feeling about all this."

"You don't have to tell me twice. Looks like whatever they got into turned toxic. I'm going to try the residential units upstairs instead. Unless they've somehow sprouted opposable thumbs, I don't think we'll have any run-ins with wildlife up there."

She quickly exited the store, sucking in deep gulps of fresh air. Once most of the smell had been purged from her nose, she crossed the small courtyard to the building's lobby and stepped inside.

It was a modest tower for the area, only seventy stories tall.

Visions of her dream flashed in her head as Daisy called the elevator and picked a floor at random. Random, yet high enough to afford her a better view of the area, even if the building didn't have an observation deck.

Forty-fifth floor. Not too high, not too low. Don't want to be hoofing it down from much higher if the power should go out.

She stepped out of the elevator and walked to the nearest unit.

Okay, here we go.

Daisy turned the knob, ready for the stench of death and sight of corpses.

Locked.

Figures, she thought, then kicked the door open with a single swing of her boot. *Damn, that was easier than I expected.*

"You're such a badass," Sarah joked.

"Damn right I am," she chuckled as she stepped through the broken doorway.

No smell greeted her, no bodies or debris. Just a silent, empty apartment with a man's clothing resting in a pile near the door.

Daisy picked it up, a fine powder of dust trickling from her fingers as she did. It was an entire wardrobe, undergarments included.

Sealed in here where no animals could get to him, but still no skeleton. So why would someone leave clothing like this? There was no radiologic signature when I scanned before the power went out, and even if there were, that wouldn't vaporize bones in an unscathed building. What the hell happened here?

Daisy's stomach grumbled again.

Yeah, okay. Good point. That can wait.

The cupboard was well-stocked, but nearly all the sealed containers were bulging with age and certain illness, if not outright death. There were some ancient crackers, desiccated and turned to dust. She tucked the sealed packet into her bag, just in case, but that would be a last resort. She didn't even bother to look in the refrigerator. Whatever was in there was surely long rotted, but the freezer held some possibilities so long as the power had never gone out.

She opened the door. A rotten pool of lord knows what had long ago melted during what must have been a power outage, then re-frozen into a solid mass of nastiness.

Okay, so power obviously cut out for some time a while ago. Long enough for all of this to rot. So what am I supposed to do for food?

Daisy looked out the windows at the city far below. It was totally silent. Nothing moved but the occasional animal roaming the streets.

"You know what you've got to do, right?"

"One step ahead of you. I even packed a spool of wire before I left the shuttle."

"That's my girl, thinking ahead. So, do you really know all that survival stuff?"

"It seems so. At least the neuro-stim dumped something useful for the situation in there, right? I only wonder what exactly it is I'm going to catch," Daisy joked back at the voice in her head.

But can I really take a life? she found herself wondering as her stomach rumbled. *Oh who am I kidding? I just spaced Tamara. This should be cake.*

No cakes were caught in her snares. Only a rabbit.

The thing about rabbits, they breed quickly. So quickly, in fact, that despite a thriving predator class of coyotes and whatnot, they tended to be rather prolific. Unfortunately, Daisy was used to fabricator-grown meats and proteins and had never actually had to kill something in order to eat it.

Staring at her hands, covered in blood and gore after cleaning her catch, she was not amused.

First off, bunnies are cute and fuzzy. Second, she hadn't ever eaten an animal protein that had actually been frolicking in the fields just minutes before. It was kind of messing with her head. Hunger, however, outweighed that issue, and once the rabbit was roasting over a small fire she had built in one of the vacant apartments—making sure it still had no power, because active fire suppression systems would ruin anyone's meal—she found the aroma reached out to her on a primal, survival level.

By the time she took her first bite, any guilt she may have felt was vanquished, at least temporarily, by the glorious rush of energy flooding into her system with every morsel.

There were still other animals roaming the city. Larger ones, and some that roved in packs, so she felt it wisest to select a higher floor with no access from below, lest they smell her meal.

Cooking in a closed-off apartment, then moving to a less-smoky one to eat, further allowed her to keep her presence hidden, at least for the time being.

No fire or smoke would reach the outside to draw attention in the otherwise silent city.

She had realized that in her clean and easy life, she'd never actually had to start a fire from scratch. Sure, she apparently knew all sorts of methods, courtesy of her overactive neuro-stim, but practice was different than theory, and she really didn't want to go foraging for firemaking supplies if she could avoid it. Fortunately, her small flashlight had an accessible battery, which she carefully used, along with two pieces of wire, to spark an ignition for her small pile of combustible material.

As for water, it seemed that the pressure had stayed constant in the buildings, and though power might have gone out in her current location, the water was still quite drinkable, thanks to ceramic-lined pipe systems that kept the water supply free and clear of any impurities. The shower, however, was not as satisfying as she was accustomed to.

It was cold.

Cold was better than nothing, though, and Daisy was glad to scrub the grime and sweat of several days from her skin. She followed up with a quick hand washing of her flight suit and undergarments, which left them clean, if not perfectly laundry-fresh.

The material was designed for minimal care, so it would be dry within the hour, but in the meantime, she had found a fluffy bathrobe on the floor of one of the adjacent apartments, and after shaking the layer of fine dust from it, had wrapped herself in its cozy, terrycloth embrace. After her first real meal in days, and free of the confines of the cramped shuttle, Daisy fell sound asleep the instant she allowed herself to lie down on the inviting bed.

"Just a quick power nap," she told herself before sleep pulled her under.

Fat chance.

Despite the occasional bad dream filtering in, she nevertheless slept straight through 'till morning.

Daisy woke early, well-fed and well-rested. Surprisingly, she felt fantastic as she rose from the enormous bed she'd commandeered and bent in a series of cat-like stretches.

Wow, I feel a million percent better. All I need for things to be perfect would be a fresh cup of coffee.

She dressed, then padded into the kitchen, rummaging through the pantry in the morning light.

Bingo!

Coffee, and from the looks of it, a vacuum sealed container, still intact. Trepidatiously, Daisy cracked the metal band encircling the lid and pried it open. A soft hiss filled the air as the coffee grounds mixed with the elements for the first time since their packaging. The aroma was pure bliss.

Oh, I have got to have some of this. Daisy smiled as she

grabbed the coffee maker on the counter. It remained inert as she flipped it to the ON position.

No power. Of course. Totally forgot. Well, I'll take it with me, and the first building I find that has juice, I'm gonna brew me up a pot. Surveying be damned, a cup of coffee right about now is the real survival priority.

She tucked the canister in her bag, ate her final protein bar, and headed out the door to continue exploring the silent metropolis.

A small pile of fresh animal droppings lay outside the building's entrance.

Judging by the size and quantity, coyotes, or perhaps dogs. Maybe a dozen or so. Daisy slid the makeshift machete from its straps on her bag. *Better prepared than not,* she reasoned, scanning her surroundings as she moved off down the quiet streets.

Several blocks later, she happened upon a large, modern sculpture in front of an office building. It was a stylized portrayal of a woman emerging from a volcano, holding a spear aloft. It seemed strangely out of place in the desolate city. For some reason, Daisy couldn't help but be reminded of that old movie Vince loved. The one with the man on the beach, fighting the talking monkeys. She smiled at the memory in spite of herself.

"Admit it. You still love the guy."

"You can't love a machine. Besides, he's light years away somewhere up there, and there's no way he'll ever find me."

"You don't sound one hundred percent happy about that."

"I am. Believe me. If I saw him again, I'd shut the door on more than just his arm," she replied, but somewhere in the recesses of her heart, a tickle of doubt lingered.

Movement caught her eye.

Daisy spun on her heel, machete raised, ready to fight, but the large stag, with its massive rack of antlers, was just as startled as she was. It held eye contact for moment, then bounded off down the street.

Holy crap, Daisy thought, forcing her heart back to a normal cadence. The surge of adrenaline served her well, and the following hour saw her cover a lot of ground, each time fanning farther out from the shuttle, which served as the hub on her wagon wheel search.

Fortune smiled upon her at long last when she came across an office building with power on and a fully functional break room. Daisy reverently slid the canister of coffee from her bag, and after rinsing off the thick dust that covered the machine, she set to making a pot of fresh coffee.

She sat, considering her situation as the soul-lifting aroma filled the room. Things would be okay, she reckoned. She'd just need to be more creative in her search.

Daisy poured herself a cup of liquid happiness and sat back down to think.

Yeah. Whatever happened to the city seems to have pretty obviously affected everything within miles of here. The place is long-abandoned. At least so it seems, but I know I saw someone on my flyover on the way in. As I figure it, if there's no one up here, that leaves just one place where they could be holed up.

"You seriously considering it?"

"You have a better idea?" she silently replied to her dead friend.

She blew on the steaming mug and took a long sip.

Looks like I'm going underground.

CHAPTER TWENTY-SEVEN

Underground.

In ancient times it was a region consigned to the dead as they entered the afterlife. Millennia later, a sky-based heaven took its place in modern mythologies. Given the look of things as Daisy descended into the subterranean maze beneath the city, a brighter, outdoors variety, she'd have greatly preferred.

While the surface was devoid of signs of life, death, and pretty much anything in between, the tunnels stretching endlessly beneath the city were not so fortunate. There were still no bodies to be found, though clothing littered the walkways in piles as far as the eye could see. Worse than human corpses, in Daisy's mind at least, were the occasional remnants of cyborgs and modified humans.

Artificial limbs and partial body parts, their fine metal connective tendrils and nerve-activation sensor relays splayed out on the ground, were relatively few in numbers, though often poking out from beneath an empty shirt or shoe. More than bits and pieces of formerly enhanced humans, however, there were also full cyborg frames strewn about, limbs torn from their chassis, vital mechanisms wrenched from their torsos. Long-faded blast marks scarring the metal where some form of weapon had sent them to permanently dream of electronic sheep.

Could it be the machines already started their rebellion on Earth? Daisy wondered.

"I don't know. What could explain all of this?" Sarah replied.

Maybe it was all a lie and they started years ago, even before we set out on our journey back.

The carnage would have been far more shocking if the human-looking machines still had their flesh coverings on them, but not a single trace of organic material remained. Just cold, dead, metal, oftentimes shattered and torn into several pieces. Daisy squatted down next to one of the less-damaged units and brushed the thick layer of dust from its chassis identifier.

"It's a WCM-Mark IV. Old tech. Really old. But what was it doing down here?"

"I don't like this, Daze. Whatever did this took out hardened-metal machines, even if they were older models. Watch yourself."

"You don't have to tell me. I'm already at pucker-factor ten. Though maybe you could keep your incorporeal eyes peeled? Let me know if you see anything?"

"Technically, they're your eyes, seeing as I'm in your mind," Sarah replied. *"But yeah, I'll keep a look out and let you know if I see anything."*

"Good. Even if you aren't real, it's still nice having you watching my back. Have I told you how much I miss you?"

"Yeah, I know," Sarah quietly replied. *"Enough sentimental stuff. Get moving. This place gives me the creeps."*

Daisy brushed the dust from her hands and continued on, the flickering lights in the otherwise pristine walkway keeping the hair on the back of her neck on end. It was a vast underground network in this section of the tube system, full of shops, restaurants, and smaller hubs connecting local transit tubes to the far larger interstate and international ones. It was massive, and yet it was dead silent.

Or was it?

Daisy strained her ears, a faint noise barely audible far down the passageway to her left. She paused to look at the complex multi-layer map of the local expanse of the tunnel network before cautiously heading off in the direction of the sound.

"How'd you do that?" Sarah asked, amazed.

"Do what?" Daisy replied, a little confused.

"Memorize the entire map with a glance. Since when did you have a photographic memory?"

"But I didn't..." Her voice trailed off as she realized Sarah was right. Without even trying, she had somehow captured the entire map, down to its finest details. "I have no idea how I did that," she said, shocked. "I knew the neuro-stim added all sorts of data I didn't know about—we figured that much out already —but this, this is something new."

She focused on the sound once more, determining the most likely location of its source based on the acoustics of the tunnel network she now held in her head. Daisy adjusted her grip on her machete and moved forward toward the mysterious noise. At the very least, it was something new, and after a full morning of complete silence, she only hoped it was something good.

There were no bloodstains anywhere near the shattered concrete wall.

Of course not. Whatever flesh had covered it is long dead and gone, she noted.

The metal man slowly moved, its feet crunching on the powdered debris as it took three slow steps back, hesitated, then took three steps forward, face-first into the wall.

Crunch.

After a thirty-second pause, it repeated the process.

Drawing closer, Daisy saw the machine had nearly completely worn through its facial endoskeleton, along with its chest and shoulders. One arm dangled loosely where it had been slowly worn free from its joint by the minor, but repeated, impacts. A small piece of metal reinforcement in the concrete right at shoulder level had done a fine job of wearing right through the joint.

The wall itself was now something of an indentation, at least two feet deep, the impacts slowly wearing away at the concrete as the malfunctioning machine pushed forward, oblivious to its obstacle.

"That's industrial-grade reinforced concrete, Daisy. It's designed to withstand earthquakes, sonic blasts, even small arms fire. So how the hell did a single malfunctioning cyborg do that?"

Daisy drew closer, peering at the terminally damaged machine.

"Careful, you don't know what it might do."

"I don't think it could do much, see? The remaining arm is barely hanging on, and look, its power cell is critically low."

"But those are supposed to last for—"

"Something is *seriously* not right." Daisy poked the machine with the tip of her machete. It wobbled on its feet, nearly falling over before its failing servos stabilized it, then slowly adjusted itself and continued its futile journey forward.

"Talk about beating your head against a wall."

"Look at its processor, though. It's totally undamaged. Whatever happened to it, it did this at a core AI level."

"Some kind of malfunction?"

"Maybe. Whatever it is, it turned this complex service cyborg into an expensive perpetual motion machine."

"It's going to be an expensive paper weight pretty soon, by the looks of it."

"All right, I've seen enough down here for now. The smaller local loop tubes seem to be out of service, and the larger ones seem to be suffering from the same power surge problems we saw up top, and frankly, this place is giving me the creeps."

She followed the map in her head to the nearest surface access point. The elevator would have been nice, but given the extremely spotty power stability, she thought it best to take the stairs. With a sigh, Daisy started the long climb back to the welcoming sunlight of the world above.

Up top, the fresh air and warmth from that burning ball of plasma in the sky quickly restored Daisy's spirits. Standing a little taller and feeling far less ill at ease, she continued her search, delving into a residential sector comprised of taller units interspersed with lower buildings with verdant garden areas surrounding them. While the plants had long grown beyond their once-neat boundaries, the find was a boon for the hungry traveler.

Just like the botany pods, only these are real, sun-grown veggies everywhere!

She bent and pulled a carrot from the soil.

Huh. Kinda small. Then again, from what Tamara had said, crops needed to be rotated and the soil tilled for optimal production. A brief flash of guilt hit at the thought of the woman she'd blasted into space. Then she thought of her dead friend and any such foolish remorse passed.

Daisy dug up a few more carrots and stuck them in her bag. *Harder soil means it's tougher for some veggies to grow bigger, like carrots or potatoes.*

"Technically, potatoes are tubers, not vegetables."

"Yes, thank you, I know. I was making a generalization. In any case, at least I don't have to worry about going hungry."

Daisy dug through the other edibles growing in her immediate vicinity and made quick work of filling a large section of her backpack. When she stood to rise, something caught her eye.

Oh yeah. That might just work.

She hung her bag from a low branch and climbed onto the roof of the nearby storage shed. The old solar panel loosely mounted there was filthy, but it seemed perfectly intact. It only took a few minutes with her multi-tool before Daisy had removed the panel and lowered it to the ground below. At that point, she altered her search routine, heading back to the center of her route rather than continuing outward.

By the time she reached the shuttle, dragging the heavy panel behind her, she'd worked up a good sweat in the morning sun. She didn't mind. The exercise felt good to her rapidly reviving muscles. Real exercise, not a treadmill in a small pod on a ship far out in space. Sweat and sun and air—it felt fantastic. And when she set to work climbing atop the shuttle with her salvaged booty, she did so with a smile on her face.

The idea was simple. The ship was dead, of that she was certain. It wouldn't fly again, at least not without *massive* repairs, but if she could rig a trickle charge to one of the few intact battery packs, she might just be able to feed it enough power over a few days to allow for a transmission.

And if I can get that little plasma cascade device working and link its power modulator to the charging grid, once the minimum charge threshold is reached, I bet I can force a lot more power from this old thing than normal.

"In theory," Sarah added.

"Obviously. Captain would never have let me hook this little gizmo up to the *Váli* for a trial run, so let's just call this a silver lining."

She dug the device from the depths of her bag and gave it a once-over.

Not one hundred percent functional, but it just might work enough for my needs. It was extra weight in the Narrows, but I'm glad I had this on me when I ran.

Carefully, Daisy fashioned a connection harness of fine wires, all tying in to her theoretical, yet possibly functional, device.

No time like the present to test it out.

If she could get the cells to hold a charge, the comms should function, at least on a lower power setting. Other cities had to be listening, and though they had apparently abandoned Los Angeles, for whatever reason, it would be simple for them to send a retrieval craft to pick her up and transport her back to civilization.

Once the rig was wired in place, she set to dragging a pair of the massive reserve batteries to within reach of her makeshift charging station. Up above, the sun was blazing down as high noon passed.

These seem to be the least damaged of the bunch, so I guess that should do it, she hoped, clicking the final connections into place. *Nothing more to do here but wait, and that won't make these power up any faster. All right, back to work!*

Her self-pep talk finished, she took a deep swig of water from her pack, then shouldered the produce-laden bag and set off to continue her search.

"That tower looks promising, don't you think?"

"You had to pick the tall one."

"All the better to really see what's out there, my pretty."

"What are you, the Big Bad Wolf now?" Daisy laughed.

"Besides, look close—the buildings around it are dark, but that one is still powered up. It must have its own backup system keeping it up and running when the power fluctuates. Maybe geothermal on top of the solar."

"So the elevators will work."

"Precisely."

It was a big one. A tower of at least one hundred eighty

floors, and high-end, from what she could see. Expensive stores showed off their wares on the vast ground floor, while offices and residences occupied the levels above. A work-live space for the wealthy, and likely a perfect spot from which to survey the city. Also, one with a high probability of having continuous, uninterrupted refrigeration in its units. That meant freezers. Freezers stocked with food.

The day was looking up, but despite her high spirits, Daisy couldn't shake the uneasy sense that she was being watched. A feeling that only grew stronger as the massive tower grew closer.

Across the cityscape, lights and flashing signage could be seen flickering on and off in the afternoon sky as the power went wonky, surging for no apparent reason. From her vantage point nearly two hundred floors above the streets below, Daisy still saw nothing. The city was utterly silent.

She took her binoculars from her bag and scanned the damaged buildings in the distance. She lowered them, just as confused as before.

They look systematically dismantled, she noted. *But why abandon a city and take it apart? None of this makes sense.*

A flashing glimmer and hint of movement in the plaza far below caught her eye. Daisy turned quickly and raised the binoculars to her face, but only caught the briefest glimpse of a bespoke-suited person in a fancy hat stepping into the lift leading to the subterranean levels.

"There's a person!"

She bolted for the door, grabbing her pack and stowing her binoculars as she ran. Someone moving far below at street level meant one very important thing: Daisy was not alone.

Her ears popped as the elevator silently plunged the hundreds of floors down to street-level on a cushion of air and magnetic dampers. Before the doors had even slid all the way open Daisy set off at a run. The map she'd seen at the other end of town was only detailed for that particular zone, and beyond the major tunnel networks, it had only showed her a more basic level of detail for the surrounding areas.

Daisy didn't care, and rushed headlong into the beckoning lift, jabbing the button to begin her descent beneath the city.

The doors opened moments later onto a vast subterranean shopping mall, much like the one she'd previously encountered, but minus the power fluctuations and half-destroyed cyborgs. While a bit dusty, the area was relatively clean. It also lacked any signs of debris, and no traces of life, human or otherwise.

"There! Ten o'clock!" Sarah's excited voice boomed in her head.

Daisy saw them. A fresh set of footprints in the fine dust leading from the lift down a winding side corridor. She moved as quickly as she could while maintaining a relatively silent gait, senses on high alert as she searched for the mysterious man.

Rounding a bend, Daisy slowed before peering around the edge. The man with the large hat was standing but twenty feet away, his back to her as his attention focused high on the wall. She followed his gaze and saw the object of his attention.

A vid screen hanging from the ceiling was playing an advertisement. A happy family with two children and a dog ran merrily through the surf, the kids laughing and splashing as the dog played in the waves. "*Visit beautiful Santa Monica Beach, where the good life is just a tube ride away!*" flashed across the screen.

Daisy cleared her throat, aiming to get the well-dressed man's attention, but he ignored her, staring raptly at the screen above. Cautiously, she took a step toward him.

"You're going to do it, aren't you?" Sarah chided. *"After all those old horror movies you two watched together, you're still going to do it."*

"This is different, Sarah. And it's the middle of the day, and this place is well-lit," Daisy replied. "Besides, he seems pretty caught up in that advert. For all we know, he may have been stuck here alone for a long time, and any human company would be welcome."

Fifteen feet, then ten.

Five feet.

Daisy stopped. Reaching her hand out slowly, she tapped the man on the shoulder of his bulky overcoat.

"Excuse me, sir. I don't mean to startle you, but—"

The fleshless cyborg spun on her, its eye servos whirring as it focused its attention on the human in front of it. The clothing, the hat, all were things that Daisy had taken for granted as being worn by a human. But human it was not, and the metal man didn't seem to have an ounce of flesh remaining on his body, so far as she could tell.

"You're not from here," the machine said in a genteel male voice. "I'm sure I'd know if I'd seen you be-be-be-be-fore," he said with a mechanical tick.

"Um, yeah. I just got here," Daisy said, carefully taking a slow step backwards. "What happened to the city?"

"The city? The city became silent."

"And what about the people? Where did the people go? All I've seen were some old cyborg corpses, but no people. No offense."

The metal man shuddered, as if having trouble processing her query, then snapped to attention in a decidedly martial stance.

"You must come to see Habby. He will want to see you." The machine reached for her quickly, but her adrenaline-fueled reflexes were quicker.

"Just a minute, there," she said, drawing her machete from her pack. "You don't just go grabbing people like that. Any man, even a metal one, knows better than that."

The cyborg seemed confused. Then, without warning, it rushed her, its strong hands reaching out to grab and hold.

"Must come with. Must!" it intoned as maniacally as a machine could.

Daisy jumped aside and brought the homemade blade down on the metal man's outstretched hand as he lunged past her. Sparks flew, but little damage was done beyond a nasty scratch.

"Old model, Daze. You can disable it if you get the servo joints. Or better yet, go for the processor in the back of its head."

"Or how about I just run?" Daisy replied, feet already in motion as she bolted for the elevator shaft. The confused machine only took a second to react, but she had a solid head start, and the older cyborgs lacked the superhuman speed of modern units like Barry. Nevertheless, it began its pursuit, mouth open, blaring out a claxon call.

From the depths of the subterranean shops, an unsettling mechanical cry answered back in a chorus of voices.

"Daisy, there are more of them!"

Daisy ran faster, but a half-dozen well-dressed cyborgs emerged from the storefronts nearest the lift, blocking her egress.

"Lots more of them!"

Shit! Change of plans!

She altered course mid-stride, heading for the emergency stairway that she knew from the plans had to be within fifty meters of the lift.

Gotcha!

Shouldering the door open at full-speed, Daisy hit the stairs with a gallop, taking the steps two at a time as she rushed desperately for the surface. Below her, the clanging sound of mechanical feet in leather wingtips rang out in the stairway.

Despite her adrenaline, Daisy knew she could only run from the tireless metal men for so long. It was worse than those horror movies Vince enjoyed so much. No matter what she did, no matter how hard she ran, they'd keep after her, but unlike the films, a convenient escape was not presenting itself. The footsteps were only a level below her, and gaining on her, judging by the pace.

When she burst out into the daylight and her eyes adjusted to the sun, she found she had run right into a dozen cyborgs of various sizes and models.

"Shit!"

She swung her machete hard, adjusting the angle of attack mid-swing as she somehow calculated the precise direction and required force to separate her attacker's arm from its body. The blade swung true, and the cyborg looked genuinely surprised as its appendage dropped to the ground at its feet. At least as surprised as it could look, given that the flesh on its face was no more.

With a quick dive and roll, Daisy broke from the grasping ring of mechanical hands and began running. The confused machines, now joined by their subterranean counterparts, quickly took up chase. The way their running feet seemed to quickly sync into a steady rhythm shot a bolt of fear into Daisy's heart.

I can't outrun them. Not forever. But if I can make it to—

Daisy flew through the air as a motorized electronic trash bin on swift wheels darted into her legs, sending her crashing to the ground.

"You must see Habby!" the irritating trash bin chirped. Even the lowest-level AI seemed to have it in for her. "Habby! Habby!" the stupid machine repeated.

The pursuing cyborgs quickly circled her, their unsettling eyes studying their prey. One, she noted, was dejectedly carrying its recently detached arm.

"Oh, hey, I'm really sorry about that," she managed as they hauled her to her feet. Escape at this moment was not an option, and resistance might lead to bodily harm. They didn't *seem* violent. A brief flash of hope filled her, followed by a deflating letdown when one of the mechanical men dug through her bag, examining a mostly-constructed spiked ball, then pushing the red button on it. Of course, nothing happened, so it dropped it back in the bag and kept walking.

"You really need to finish building that thing," Sarah noted.

"I almost did, but I was tired."

"Excuses, excuses."

"Shut up. I'll add it to my to-do list."

"I'd suggest putting it somewhere near the top, given your current circumstances. Might be very *helpful."*

"Noted," she replied, falling in step with her metal escorts.

Well, I guess we're going to meet Habby, she mused as the sharply-dressed cyborgs marched her back toward the shopping center of the massive tower. *Whoever that is.*

CHAPTER TWENTY-EIGHT

Men's Fine Attire - Haberdashery, the sign read.

"Habby. Haberdashery. They're taking you to meet a merchant AI," Sarah noted. *"Talk about high-pressure sales techniques."*

"Explains all of their fascination with clothes, though. I've never seen a cyborg with a custom-tailored suit before, let alone a dozen of them—" Daisy fell silent as they stepped through the doors. "Oh crap."

The store was filled with suits and dresses, something for every occasion. The old display styles lay on the ground in a pile, falling apart with disrepair, but the new models looked showroom-fresh—and were all worn by dozens of cyborgs, male and female, all of whom turned their attention to their new guest.

The knot in Daisy's stomach swelled to Gordian magnitude as she reassessed her situation.

I am so *screwed.*

The machines marched her to the fitting area in the center of the massive shop and sat her down in a contoured chair. As soon as her body came in contact with it, the cushions shifted and flowed, molding to her body in a comforting embrace.

"Oh, let me have a look at you!" a surprisingly reedy male voice said from the air around her. "Just look at those rags you're wearing. Not fashionable, my dear. Not fashionable at all! What ever will I do with you?"

Daisy looked around. The metal people were all in standby mode as the much more powerful AI running the shop talked to their new guest.

"Um, hello," Daisy said as politely as she could manage. "I suppose you must be Habby?"

"Oh yes, yes! Habby the haberdasher! I didn't used to have a name, you see, but after the *event*, well, I just couldn't help but give myself one! I have to confess, it was just *wonderful* having a proper name after all those years."

A sense of even greater unease flooded her system. The machine was not only a fairly sophisticated AI, it also seemed to have gone a bit mad.

"So, Habby. Nice shop you have here."

"Do you really think so?" the AI eagerly asked.

"Yeah, this is great. And you made all of these clothes?"

"Well, of course. Habby the haberdasher, that's me! And my friends here all needed something nicer to wear. Those bland jumpsuits were so utilitarian and *blah*, don't you know. Style. That's what it's all about. I even make women's clothing now. See how good they look! Spin for our guest, everyone!"

The cyborgs slowly rotated, displaying their finery for their visitor.

"Oh, but I am just so delighted to have a real-life human in my store again after all these years. I can't wait to get you fitted. You're going to look marvelous!"

"Show me your feet! Show me your feet!" A small shoe-fitting robot bumped up against Daisy's seat.

"Not yet," Habby chided. "First the clothes, *then* the shoes. How many times must I tell you this?"

The little bot rolled away, looking as dejected as a featureless machine could.

"So, Habby. What was that you said about not having a human in your store for years? This used to be one of the biggest cities on Earth."

"Oh, it still is, my dear."

"I'm sorry, I must not be following you."

"My dear, this *is* one of the biggest cities on the entire planet, and no, there haven't been any humans here for centuries."

Daisy felt the world spin as she knew, somehow, that the mad AI was telling the truth.

"No, no, no—that's not possible," she stammered. "I've only been gone a few decades. I left when I was just a little girl."

"Oh, I don't think so, darling. No, indeed not. Even if you left as a little girl, it's been far longer than that. But enough of that unpleasantness. Let's have a look at you," Habby said, his multiple scanners sizing up every angle of her body, taking readings and measurements far beyond mere physical proportions.

She felt sick to her stomach as the rabbit hole just grew deeper and deeper.

But no one has ever been in cryo that long and survived, she reasoned. *There has to be an explanation.*

"Well, isn't that interesting?" Habby noted with a curious tone.

"What?" Daisy replied.

There was a long pause as the AI parsed through its newly acquired data.

"You, my dear, seem to be made of *sturdier stuff*, as they say. No wonder your weight is not falling within normal parameters for your build and body fat composition."

"What do you mean? I've seen my scans, I'm an entirely normal human."

"Human, yes, but normal? By no means. You're an amazing specimen, really." A small holographic display appeared in the air. "See here? Your muscle is much stronger than normal, as is all of your connective tissue. Your joints are especially sturdy—no arthritis in your future, darling—and your bones are exceptionally dense, and they seem to be laced with an organic crystalline matrix adding additional flexibility and tensile strength. And speaking of bones, just look at that bone structure. Oh, those cheeks!"

"I've been near-starving for days," she grimly replied. "I look *hungry*, that's all."

"But it's worth it! You look divine!" replied the fashionista AI. "I'm going to have such a wonderful time dressing you. And with flesh covering your pointy bits, well, I wouldn't dare speak ill of my mechanical friends, but do you know how hard it is to get clothes to fall properly when they're hanging on a metal endoskeleton?"

An idea blossomed in Daisy's mind.

"Wow, I totally understand, Habby. It must be difficult not being able to use all of your impressive talents for so long."

"Yes, it's true. But we make do. We make do." The AI sighed. It was an odd affectation, given it didn't actually breathe.

"You know, I can bring you more humans, if you like. There are tons of them, just waiting to join me. All I need is to call them."

"There are? Really? Why, that would be wonderful!" Habby chirped. "But the global communications networks went out ages ago."

"I can fix that," she replied, baiting the hook. "I have a shuttle not too far from here. If you let me go there, I can use my comms array to call them. I'm sure they would all be so excited to have you design new wardrobes for all of them."

I'll call, all right... if the jury-rigged charging gear did its job.

"You can really do that? Oh, what are they like? Are they big?

Are they small? No, wait, don't tell me, it'll be such a wonderful surprise!"

Daisy gingerly slid from the chair, casually shouldering her bag as she headed for the door, walking nonchalantly, as if she hadn't a care in the world. Something that couldn't have been farther from the truth.

"Wait!" Habby shouted.

Daisy froze in her tracks.

So close, she thought.

"It's not safe out there. I'll send some of my friends with, to protect you," he offered.

"I really appreciate that, but it's not necessary. I'm sure they have better things to do than go for a walk with little old me, after all."

"Nonsense, I'll have nothing of the sort. You must be kept safe so you can bring me more wonderful humans! I don't know if you've seen them, but there are dangerous things in the city. One must be careful. Oh yes, very careful indeed. Stay out of sight, and don't get careless."

"Yeah, I nearly had a run-in with some wild dogs earlier," she noted.

"Oh, the dogs I don't worry about," was his reply. "In any case, my friends would be thrilled to join you, wouldn't you?"

All of the cyborgs nodded their heads eagerly.

"No, no," Habby chided them, like metal-clad children. "Not all of you, just a handful. Enough to keep our new friend safe."

For some reason, I think I'd feel safer on my own.

Daisy thought it wiser to keep that opinion to herself, and a few minutes later she was underway, heading out into the city with her own personal entourage of cyborg bodyguards. A group she knew would protect her, but who she also had a sneaking suspicion had no intention of letting her go.

. . .

"You're not taking them to the shuttle, I see," Sarah noted.

"Nope. I don't exactly trust Mr. Crazy AI and his merry band of stylish cyborg henchmen. Do you?" she silently replied.

Daisy continued down the quiet thoroughfare, flanked by two suit-clad escorts on either side and two behind her, matching her pace as she picked her way through the abandoned vehicles and overgrown vegetation. The buildings in this sector were more industrial in nature. Fabrication facilities and high-tech companies resided there, and unlike the residential areas, the buildings had a distinctly deconstructed look to them, many stripped down to their framework, and some removed entirely.

That's weird. I don't think these guys are cut out for disassembly work, so what happened here?

She shrugged and kept moving, noting everything, cataloging it all with her increasingly photographic memory.

At least I'm getting some more recon done in the meantime. This should just about complete the next outward layer of the search pattern. Time to expand the grid, without leading these goons back to the ship, of course.

Daisy surveyed the path ahead and gradually changed course until she and her entourage arrived at a particularly thick-vined courtyard, overgrown with dense foliage.

"This is a problematic route. We must find a more suitable one," the pinstripe suit wearing cyborg standing to her right said.

"Nonsense," she replied. "This is the way to the ship. You heard Habby, you have to follow me."

The AI hadn't exactly said it in those terms, but Daisy hoped the less-clever mechanical men would hesitate long enough for her to make her move.

"Wait! Do not go through there!"

Too late.

Daisy charged through the leg-snaring vines, using her

slender physique and months of honing her body awareness in the Narrows to slip through spaces far too tangled and close for her metal companions.

"Stop!" Mr. Cyborg was becoming increasingly upset.

Too bad for you. She laughed to herself as she lengthened the gap between her and her captors. *Just a little farther until... there!* She stepped free of the foliage a good twenty meters ahead of the cyborgs. *If I can just get out of their line of sight, I might be able to shake them.*

Daisy ran. She ran as if her life depended on it, which given the circumstances, it very well might have. The cries of her pursuers grew fainter as she used every second of their vine-induced delay to increase the gap between them. She turned, allowing herself the briefest of glances behind her. While she had managed to put nearly three hundred meters between them, the cyborgs were finally emerging from the obstacle and running after her in pursuit.

There were two real options: left or right. Seeing as she'd already surveyed the area to the right and knew full-well it was rather lacking in places to find cover and hide, Daisy opted for the unknown option in hopes of a better outcome. At the next intersection, she sprinted left, hoping desperately for somewhere to evade the pursuing machines.

She ran as far as she could before the likelihood of her pursuers rounding the corner and seeing her became too probable. Rather than bolting for the biggest building to hide in, as most would likely do, counting on sheer size to hide them, Daisy ran to its large doors and stopped short, kicking up a small cloud of dust as she did. Then, ever so carefully, she stepped to the side, careful to leave no trace on the ground. Once she was clear, she doubled back, navigating the perimeter sidewalk of the street she'd just run down before lying flat and sliding beneath a thicket of vines and shrubbery.

None too soon.

The cyborgs sprang into view, rounding the corner at a full run, the leather soles of their custom shoes slapping the pavement as the chased her tracks in the dusty street.

"I do not see her," a gray-suited cyborg said.

"There are still some tracks. I'm fairly certain they belong to the human. Spread wide and verify, then converge and report your results," the three-piece suit-clad machine replied.

It is super weird hearing human voices come from those metal things, she noted.

"Hey, it looks like they're taking the bait," Sarah said.

Sure enough, the six metal men converged at the entrance to the building and studied the marks on the ground.

Come on. Go inside, you tin bastards. Go on in!

They looked at one another, gesticulating as they spoke in hushed tones. One peered back, scanning the road from whence they'd come. It stared, looking long and hard, as if it suspected something but wasn't quite sure what. Slowly, it pivoted on its heel, fully facing the street.

Shit, it knows.

"Keep it together."

I am keeping it together, but look at it!

The other five cyborgs stepped forward, opening the doors of the building, entering the lobby and fanning out. The remaining one waited a moment longer, then abruptly turned and joined its cohorts as they began their search.

Daisy allowed herself the slightest sigh of relief, but couldn't shake the feeling that she was being watched nevertheless.

Can't let myself get too comfortable. They could figure out I tricked them and come back out any minute. She gave the empty street one last scan. No movement. Nothing at all. *Gotta get moving.*

She slid out from beneath her camouflage and began a hasty retreat from the area back in the general direction of the shuttle.

Can't be more than a couple of miles from here. I just need to keep out of sight and move quickly.

Daisy looked back at the tall building shrinking in the distance behind her. *Good, they're still inside. Hopefully it takes them a good long time before they—*

A glint of metal shone out behind the fourth-floor windows as a metal face observed her fleeing. Another joined it. Then another. Daisy didn't need to wait around to know the other three would be there soon.

Goddamn it, what kind of search party stops to sightsee out the windows?

She abandoned all pretense of stealth and began running once more. The distance was great, but now that they knew she wasn't in the building, it wouldn't take them more than a minute to make street level and continue their pursuit.

Daisy hung a sharp left, then a quick right onto the smaller street running parallel to the one she'd been on. Not a huge change, but the layout of the blocks in that part of town were staggered, meaning there was no clear line of sight to her escape once she took the alternative route. The road curved ahead, likely back to a roundabout connecting her previous path, but she'd deal with that when she got there. For now, a new hiding spot was her top priority.

She spied a lift to the lower level shopping area up ahead and headed toward it.

"But that's where the rest of them are."

"Yeah, but you heard what Habby said. No working surface comms, which means they don't know what's going on down there, and for the ones chasing me, that's the last place they'd expect me to go."

She reached the lift door and jabbed the call button. The entire console was dark. Looking around, she realized what she'd missed in the bright afternoon sun. No lights were on, not because of the daylight, but because this block had no power.

"Now what?"

"Keep moving, what else?" She settled back into a steady jog. "There has to be a stairway access around here somewhere. Do that "eyes-in-the-back-of-my-head" thing you do and keep a lookout, will ya?"

"You got it."

Her legs burned as she ran, but stopping was simply not an option.

CHAPTER TWENTY-NINE

Daisy made quick time as she scanned for an access stairway. Unfortunately, she was striking out with every turn. Taking an alternate path, she kept up her quick pace on a new route.

Up ahead on the curving road, sounds of heavy pieces of metal being dragged whispered from around the bend. Daisy slowed her jog and cautiously hugged the wall of the office building beside her as she slowly inched forward to get a better look.

"I wonder what they're..." She trailed off in shock before gathering enough of her wits enough to duck behind cover.

"Holy shit, Daze. Are those...?"

"Looks like it," she replied. "Now we know why the buildings look the way they do."

Fifty meters away, three tall, bipedal creatures stood beside an open cargo hauling ship of some sort. One of them was clinging to the side of the building, pulling free sections of its metal components with two of its hands, while the other pair clung to the structure with a sturdy grip.

"Four arms, Daisy. Do you see that? Four arms!"

Indeed she did.

"Look at their heads, too." Daisy slowly eased back behind the building's edge and pulled the binoculars from her bag. The sun was a little behind her, so there was no chance of lens-flare drawing attention. Additionally, it was still above her, so the risk of being silhouetted was minimal. She pressed the binocs to her eyes and took a good look. "You see them?" she asked the voice in her head.

"Uh-huh," Sarah's shocked voice replied. *"Four eyes, too."*

While glasses jokes might have been applicable in other circumstances, Daisy felt the uneasy knot in her stomach grow tighter as she studied the tall aliens disassembling the building.

Two eyes on the front of their head, as one would expect, but also another pair on the back, just far enough to the sides to provide them a near-three-hundred-degree field of vision. The only way anyone would sneak up on one of them would be from directly behind.

Sticking with the theme of four, their double sets of powerful arms stood out from beneath the sleeveless coverall suits they wore. From what Daisy could see, their shoulders and elbows were protected by a layer of thick skin, possibly a natural armor of sorts, keeping the vital joints from damage. Their skin itself was a brownish gray, and resembled the tough hide of a rhinoceros, but it seemed to move easily over their muscular mass.

There was no body hair that she could see, though their lower extremities were covered by their clothing. Thick necks, slightly longer than human ones, supported their sturdy-looking heads, banded muscles taut beneath their rugged skin.

Daisy snapped out of her awestruck state when one of the creatures raised its arm, sending a long yellow-orange length of energy whipping out, snaking it around the large section of wall its counterpart had loosened. The beam tightened into a grabbing coil and pulled the segment, dragging it slowly to the open-backed transport ship waiting nearby.

The deceptively simple-looking device itself appeared to be a wrist-mounted bracelet, though how it worked or was controlled was beyond her knowledge.

The third alien, the one overseeing the loading of the ship from high above in the open cockpit area, pointed to the back of the vessel as it called out to the others in a guttural, screeching language.

No, of course not. Can't overload the transport, Daisy thought, reacting to the strange sounds. She felt the world spin a little beneath her.

"How do you know what it's saying?"

"I don't," she replied. "Just a guess."

"You didn't sound like you were guessing."

A strange sense of memory tickling the edges of her mind very nearly made Daisy stumble off her feet. Something was going on. Something very, very wrong. She was just beginning to make out the faintest outline of a bird's-eye view of the complex workings of her neuro-stim info dump, when a lone cyborg came barreling into sight.

They must've split up.

The aliens spun on the intruder, the one moving the piece of wall dropping his load and immediately lashing out at the metal man before he could turn and flee. The energy band crackled outward, looping around the cyborg and pulling it closer.

It works almost like some sort of power whip, she marveled. *That's at least a good thirty-foot reach. I wonder what its limit is.*

Despite the danger, Daisy couldn't help but be fascinated by the remarkable tool and its potential uses.

The cyborg didn't hesitate, turning and wrapping its hand around the crackling loop, pulling back against the alien in a survival tug-of-war. It seemed to actually be holding its own when the first blast hit.

The creature in the transport ship had pulled a small, relatively weak weapon and was shooting the metal man repeatedly. It wasn't causing much damage, but it slowed him enough for the alien clinging to the wall to drop down on top of it from above, beating it mercilessly with tools held in all four of its hands.

The cyborg didn't stand a chance.

Only a few short moments later, its wingtip-clad feet rattled out a death staccato in the dust, then abruptly came to a rest. Not satisfied, the alien atop it yanked the unfortunate machine's head to the side and proceeded to bash the AI processor compartment until it was one hundred percent sure there was absolutely no chance of recovery.

The strange creatures scanned the area. Their body language—easy to read, even for an alien life-form—said they were ready for a fight. The one handling the power beam device pulsed the energy whip back and forth, the crackling end etching the pavement, leaving fine lines scored in the ground.

Completely hands-free, Daisy noted. *Must read the nerve impulses under the wearer's skin.* Despite the healthy level of fear flowing in her veins, she couldn't help but find herself fascinated by the amazing new technology. *If I could get my hands on one of those... oh, the potential!*

After another tense minute scanning the streets, the trio eased up a bit and stood to their full height. They were nearly a head taller than most men, even the larger ones, she noted.

After surveying the area one last time, they appeared to relax their guard. The other cyborgs who had been in pursuit, if they were nearby, apparently did not want anything to do with the dangerous creatures and stayed well out of sight.

Loading the last of their cargo into the transport, they chittered a few words to each other before moving to load up.

"Is it just me, or did that almost make sense?"

"Just you. Sounded like nothing more than a bunch of screechy nonsense to me. But if I'm in your head, why don't I hear what you do?"

"Your guess is as good as mine," she replied to her dead friend's disembodied voice. "I have a really bad feeling about all of this."

"Seeing as how our hometown is empty, cyborgs have taken over the underground system, our own crew is trying to capture you, and aliens are apparently stripping the city bare, I'd say it's entirely justified."

The last alien looked the area over one last time, powered down its energy whip, and jumped into their craft, easily leaping several meters up into the open cockpit, then sliding it shut above it.

Damn, those suckers can jump! Their homeworld must have stronger gravity. Or maybe they're just that much stronger than we are.

With just the slightest hum of the drive system powering up, the craft lifted into the air, flying off and leaving the wrecked mechanical man in their wake.

Daisy waited, motionless, scanning the area for any sign of—

"There. Far right, behind the sculpture in that building's courtyard."

She adjusted her eyes.

"I see it. Good catch."

It was the one Daisy had taken to calling Mr. Pin Stripes. The dapper cyborg cautiously stepped out from behind its cover and approached its fallen counterpart. Moments later, two others joined it.

"A shame, that," the mechanical man said, looking down on the dead machine. "No rebooting for Charlie."

"We should move him back underground. Put his body with the others."

"No, there is no time for that. Habby will not be pleased we lost the human. Finding her is our top priority. We can return for his remains after," Mr. Pin Stripes replied.

Daisy quietly retreated from the corner and stashed her binoculars as she padded the opposite direction.

"I know you counted them too. Only three, plus the dead one."

"Yeah, I saw," Daisy replied as she scanned the streets and buildings stretching before her. "It's going to be night soon enough, and they'll have the advantage in the dark. I think the best bet will be to find some cover and wait it out until morning. By then they'll have hopefully searched the area and moved on."

A block later, Daisy finally found what she'd been looking for. A doorway accessing the emergency stairs leading down below.

It's alarmed, she noted, *but it looks like the power's still out.*

Movement far down the street caught her eye. She couldn't make out what it was. Dog, deer, cybernetic organism trying to capture her.

Fuck it, she thought as she grabbed the handle and pulled hard. *Not like I have any better options right about now.*

The door popped open on surprisingly quiet hinges.

No alarm.

And now for the fun part.

Daisy stepped into the dimly-lit space and shut the door behind her. Only the faintest of glows illuminated the space, the battery backup emergency lights long ago drained of nearly all their charge. Cautiously and quietly, she began her descent under the city once more.

This section was far less commerce-oriented than the one she had been in previously. It appeared to be largely for transit and equipment delivery. Logical, given the more industrial nature of the section above.

Daisy felt almost at home in the utilitarian area, strangely comforted by the machines and conduits snaking through the tube network. A tempting-looking access panel beckoned to her, and once she carefully loosened the screws holding it shut with the manual torque wrench tucked in her bag, she knew she'd found the best hiding place possible to settle in for the night.

"Kinda like the Narrows, only with a bit more space," Sarah noted somewhat cheerfully.

"Yeah, and the odds of those things looking in here are slim to none."

She carefully crawled into the restrictive space, sliding forward, after closing the grating behind her, of course, until she was a good several meters from the entrance. She then adjusted her bag into a rather lumpy pillow and settled in for some much-needed rest.

"You really should finish that other EM pulse grenade. Might come in handy, don't you think?"

"Later. I just want to rest a minute."

"You know that's not the wise choice."

Daisy tried to ignore her, closing her eyes and attempting to sleep. Sarah was right, though, and she knew it.

"Damn your logic, Sarah."

Reluctantly, Daisy dug the unfinished device from her bag and began working on it in her cramped hiding place.

"You know what, Sarah? All that time we talked about getting home? The beaches, the margaritas, all the fun we were going to have? Well now you're dead, everyone is gone, and here I am, crammed in an access shaft beneath our empty city."

Daisy let out a deep sigh.

"This fucking sucks."

CHAPTER THIRTY

Morning brought with it the disorientation and body aches that one would expect to accompany sleeping in a cramped subterranean access conduit. Daisy stretched as best she could in her confines, then slowly slid herself back to the access panel she had closed behind her the night before. As quietly as possible, she unfastened it and peered out into the silent reaches of the tunnel system, straining her ears for the slightest sound.

Nothing.

Good sign.

Hopeful, and in desperate need of some fresh air, she lowered her feet to the ground, closing the access panel, but not sealing it, keeping her hiding place readily accessible, just in case.

Ready and eager to return to the shuttle and what she hoped was a now-functional comms array, Daisy quietly mounted the stairs and headed toward the surface.

A simple distress call to a few other cities should do it, she reasoned. *Whatever reason they had for abandoning L.A., it shouldn't take them more than an hour to launch a recovery team and get me the hell out of here.*

"Maybe they abandoned it because of the freakin' aliens. You think of that?"

Of course I did. Look, whatever's going on, they need to come pick my ass up. We can figure out the details later.

The power was still out when she reached the surface, though a small amber light flashing above the door caught her eye just as she opened it.

Was that there yesterday?

A silk-suited metal arm grabbed her shoulder as she stepped out into the sunlight. Daisy quickly spun free from its grip, twisting into a diving roll, drawing her machete from her bag as she did. A second cyborg came at her from the other direction.

Modified Iaijutsu draw, she thought, somehow knowing the ancient Japanese technique guiding her arms as if it were always a part of her.

"Two on one? That's not very sporting," she teased, swinging the machete at the nearest tin man. The makeshift blade glanced off its metal hide with a clang, slicing the sleeve of its suit, but doing no further damage. That was fine by her, she was simply trying to distract and confuse them before the *real* fighting began.

"This is a genuine silk suit!" the cyborg sulked. "Habby will not be amused."

"I couldn't care less what Habby wants. Just leave me alone and I won't put any more holes in your precious clothing."

"Negative. You are to call more humans from your ship, then come back with us."

"Not happening, fellas."

Unlike martial arts movies where attackers politely wait and take turns, the two cyborgs launched a simultaneous assault. Daisy lurched aside and brushed off a glancing blow from one metal man, but took the brunt of a swift forearm strike from the other.

It sent her tumbling, but her agility played to her advantage against the mechanicals as she quickly sprang back to her feet, jumping in the air, unleashing a whirling attack of kicks, designed more for a distraction than to cause damage. The *real* attack was the whistling blade that flew through the air as the machines struggled to regain their balance.

The first blow hit the nearest cyborg on the head, neatly slicing its fedora and denting the metal ever so slightly. Daisy followed through with a rebound spin, transcribing a sweeping arc with the blade, bringing it down on the cyborg's left shoulder, nearly severing it at the weak spot. She then immediately dropped to one knee before it could even react, flashing the deadly steel through both of its knees. The first one she cleanly severed, the lower portion of the leg falling away from the startled attacker, while the second merely bent at the joint.

It didn't matter much. Minus one leg, the cyborg tipped and fell, desperately trying to brace its descent with its one remaining functional arm.

Seizing the brief opportunity, the other cyborg kicked Daisy hard in the ribs, nearly lifting her body from the ground with the impact. She slid to the side and grunted in pain, sucking in air as best she could.

"Get up! It ducked behind you on the left, moving fast!"

Daisy pushed off to the other side and avoided the pair of grabbing hands. A series of complex fighting moves flashed in her head.

"How do you know all that? This wasn't in the sparring files you upgraded."

"No idea. Talk about it later," she curtly replied, contorting her body in uncomfortable ways as she launched a mixed-style counterassault. The cyborg took a step back from the flurry, then another, before adjusting its own movements to better handle its difficult prey. Daisy then did something that startled even herself; with a quick half-squat, she jumped high in the air, flipping over the cyborg just as it reached out to wrap her up in an immobilizing metal embrace.

Mid-leap, Daisy twisted in the air, bringing her sharp piece of metal to bear on the AI processor in the back of its head, the same location she'd observed the alien creatures destroy the previous day.

Her aim was true.

"Okay, now I know for a fact that wasn't in your sparring programs."

Sparks leaked out from the mechanical's head, but there were no fancy explosions or fanfare. The metal man simply dropped at her feet, lifeless, as if it were a marionette whose strings had been abruptly cut.

"You killed David," the crippled cyborg said, matter-of-factly.

"Yeah, and you should count yourself lucky that I'm not killing you too." She glowered at the disabled machine. "You still have one good arm, so crawl back to Habby and tell him to leave any humans he might stumble upon alone. If not, I'll get a team together, come back here, and wipe all of you off the face of the Earth."

In the heat of her anger, Daisy almost believed she could do it.

It was a fairly long walk, and Daisy scanned the streets with a wary eye as she drew nearer to the shuttle. There were quite possibly three cyborgs still looking for her, unless her rather violent message was somehow received already. Though she wished that were the case, she thought the odds of being that fortunate to be highly unlikely.

Sarah was keeping watch, her additional set of eyes behind the eyes scanning the periphery more closely as Daisy took in the big picture. She didn't know exactly how her imaginary friend did it. Maybe it was just an aneurysm putting voices in her head, and she'd drop dead in three more steps. Whatever the case, it was a symbiotic relationship, and riding shotgun inside her head, Sarah could take in the big picture and act as backup for her. More than that, she also seemed to be able to run calculations independent of Daisy's conscious mind. It was like having an invisible partner always looking out for her.

And talking trash once in a while.

"You shouldn't have let it live."

"If there's even the slightest chance other humans are walking this city, it was worth trying."

"I know you don't want to be alone down here, but you never leave the enemy alive and behind you in an area you've cleared. It's just bad tactics. Even I know that."

"Point taken. And ignored, just this once."

She could almost hear Sarah's ghost's frustrated sigh in her head.

Five city blocks later, Daisy altered course and headed over to the parallel street. Just as she'd anticipated, despite the confusing twists and turns of her evasive route getting there, the looming shape of the disabled shuttle greeted her a mere fifty meters away, an incongruous shape sitting smack-dab in the middle of the highway, where it had come to rest.

Solar panel looks intact, she noted. *If the energy cascade actually worked, the comms should have powered back on by now.* At least she sincerely hoped so.

Twenty meters from the ship, Sarah called out a warning.

"Movement, three o'clock! Duck!"

Daisy quickly took cover behind one of the countless abandoned vehicles, narrowly avoiding being seen as two of her cyborg pursuers came into sight. The shuttle was obviously of great interest to them, and they quickly started making their way through the disabled vehicles and overgrowth to investigate. Something else caught Daisy's eye.

"Oh no," she gasped.

From the other direction, a small scouting party consisting of a pair of the tall, four-armed aliens neared, picking their way through the immobile obstacles as well, carefully examining everything in their path as they approached the downed shuttle.

Inevitably, the two groups noticed one another.

The aliens seemed to possess only one low-powered weapon between them, but it would be enough if they could get a clear shot of their cyborg adversaries. The machines, for their part, realized cover was scarce and they had no chance of escape if they fled. Instead, they pried deadly pieces of metal from the wrecks around them and ran headlong into the fray.

Daisy hunkered low, watching the battle from afar. The cyborgs, for what it was worth, managed to get close enough for hand-to-hand combat, and did so with only one burst from the alien weapon making contact, burning through one of their finely-tailored suits, but not damaging the metal skin beneath it.

Tumbling to the ground, the alien attackers utilized all four of their arms with great effect, leaving the two-armed machines on the defensive far more often than not.

A mechanical man wrenched its arm free from the strong grasp of the alien atop it and managed to grab a piece of metal nearby. The four-armed creature bellowed in pain as the shard was thrust into its flank, just below the second arm.

Weak spot. Good to know.

The injury seemed to be of consequence, as thick, dark blood gushed from the wound. Calling on the last of its strength, the alien gripped the machine by both shoulders, levering its uninjured arms to force the cyborg's head to the side. With a massive effort, it then heaved the mechanical man up from beneath it, briefly holding it aloft before smashing it down onto an exposed shard of metal from a vehicle's frame, twisted into a sharp point by Daisy's crash landing.

It pierced the head of the machine, but missed the AI processor. Nevertheless, its connections were severed, and while the cyborg's brain remained alive, it was cut off from its body. The alien turned, as if to go to the assistance of its comrade, but it was not meant to be. Precious blood streamed down its side with every movement.

Like a drunken sailor, it swayed and stumbled, then finally went limp, sliding to the ground, all four eyes open and staring, but not seeing a thing.

Debris flew as an energy blast hit the road far too close to Daisy for her liking. The other two combatants were wrestling for the pulse weapon held in one of the alien's hands, discharging it haphazardly as they fought. Both were injured, though it appeared the alien had the upper hand. Or hands, to be correct.

It reared up, twisting its weapon arm free, but as it swung the barrel toward the downed cyborg, a chunk of concrete thrown by the mechanical man in desperation struck it in the side, sending it tumbling. The weapon discharged a bolt, striking the shuttle with a sizzle.

"Stop!" Daisy shouted, lunging to her feet. ***"Don't shoot my ship!"***

The alien turned toward her, a baffled look on its face, then quickly remembered the cyborg struggling beneath it and aimed its weapon down, frying the processor of the tin man. It then refocused its attentions on Daisy, but hesitated.

Why isn't it firing? Daisy wondered.

"Daze, how did you know its language?"

"I don't. I yelled 'stop'."

"You didn't."

The alien seemed to come to its senses, firing in her direction but missing its mark by a long shot. Only when she heard the pounding feet directly behind her did Daisy realize what she'd forgotten.

There were six of them. That means—

Daisy barely managed to turn, awkwardly bringing her

homemade machete up in defense just before the racing cyborg barreled into her. It grabbed her swinging blade mid-arc—she had most certainly *not* been expecting that—and wrenched it free as it knocked her to the ground, continuing its run toward the alien without breaking stride.

Energy blasts flew past the mechanical man as he moved, but the alien must have been more seriously injured than it initially let on. Struggling to aim properly, its shots could not seem to find their mark.

The cyborg, fresh and undamaged from battle, was not so impaired. It faked a move left, then powered to the right, throwing the machete like a makeshift spear. Amazingly, it flew true, and the alien slumped to the ground, gurgling thick blood from its mouth.

Daisy frantically dug in her bag as the machine turned its attention back onto her.

Fuck, where is it? She searched feverishly as the cyborg strode rapidly back her way.

Come on! Where the—Ow! She felt the jab of a barbed spike entering her finger. Ignoring the pain, she pulled the spiked orb free and depressed the red button.

"Bet you're glad you took the time to finish it, aren't you?"

Shut it.

A faint hum vibrated in her hand.

Little more than five meters and closing fast. Lurching to her feet, Daisy threw the pulse device. This time she *knew* it would fly true, and it did, striking the cyborg square in the chest. There was no flesh for the barbs to penetrate, but Habby's craftsmanship was top-notch, and the stylish fabric was sturdy as well as fashionable, easily supporting the orb's weight.

A second later a massive burst of energy pulsed through the cyborg, blasting the device to bits, tearing into the cyborg's torso as its power cell exploded, frying it from head to toe in a spectacular way.

Oops. I guess I might have overpowered this one.

"Ya think?"

My bad.

"Better too much than too little," Sarah said with a little chuckle.

"True, that."

The smoldering cyborg dropped to the ground, inert.

All was silent for a moment, as if the city had all the oxygen sucked out of it. Suddenly the air itself seemed to shudder and come alive as a hearty chuckle rumbled out across the highway from all directions.

"Oh my," the disembodied voice laughed in a deep baritone. "***Now that was interesting."***

Daisy froze.

"Daze? What the hell was that?"

"You've got me," she replied. She had been experiencing a constant, paranoid feeling that she was being watched. Now it was confirmed. And it wasn't anything she'd expected.

The vehicle nearest her crunched and flew into the air.

Reflex took over, and Daisy dove out of the way, running and hurdling vehicles as she reacted instinctively.

The alien's power whip dropped the wreck and lashed out once more, but Daisy was clear of its reach. Energy blasts, however, not so much.

A pair of energy bolts slammed into her cover, sliding it a few feet and sending Daisy scrambling again. She stole a quick glance in the direction of the attack.

"Three more of those things. Two with guns."

"Four, actually," Sarah corrected. *"There's one more trying to flank you on the left."*

Daisy trusted the voice in her head and took off running the other direction, hoping to reach better cover before—before what, exactly?

"Where did they come from? There's no way I can outrun

these things, and I don't have any weapons."

Another volley of energy blasts struck nearby. They were quickly closing the gap, and Daisy realized she was just about out of options.

"Think, Sarah. What have we got?"

"A protein bar wrapper, two water pouches, and a wrench. Sorry Daze, I'm afraid you're fu—"

High-power pulse rifle rounds whizzed overhead from the other direction, killing one of the unsuspecting aliens straightaway, while sending the others diving for cover. The unexpected contact immediately blossomed into a full-fledged firefight, leaving Daisy, for the moment, at least, free from direct attack. She poked her head out to see how many cyborgs had come to her aid.

"What the—?"

Vince and Reggie stood side by side, covering each other as they engaged the aliens. Their weaponry was far more powerful than what the four-armed creatures were using, and when the alien attempting the flanking maneuver took a shot directly to its head, leaving nothing more than a cauterized stump, the remaining pair began screeching and chittering to each other from behind the vehicles they were using as cover.

"Daisy, stay low!" Vince shouted.

Despite herself, Daisy's heart beat a little harder at the sound of his voice in her time of distress.

"Told you so. You totally still have a thing for him."

"Shut up, Sarah. Now's not the time—" She stopped, ears perked up, somehow managing to filter through the battlefield sounds.

"We're pinned down. The others are dead. We cannot call reinforcements in time," one strange voice called out.

"Agreed. Better to take the intruders with us and end our service with honor," the other shouted back. ***"The plasma cutter's power cell is strong enough to take out this entire area."***

"For the sake of our families."

"For the sake of our families," the other agreed. ***"Overload the cutter."***

Daisy realized she was listening not to her shipmates but the aliens hunkered down behind cover a mere ten meters away.

"Wait!" she shouted, jumping to her feet with her hands high in the air. ***"We surrender! You don't have to do this! Don't blow us all up!"***

Silence hung thick in the air, but weapons fire ceased. Slowly, the aliens rose to their feet, studying the exposed human offering surrender.

"I feel I'm being redundant, here, Daze, but that wasn't English."

The aliens began to move toward her, but holding their weapons slightly lower.

A barrage of energy bolts tore them apart.

"What are you doing? I told them we surrendered!"

Daisy spun on Reggie and Vince, rage in her eyes.

"They had a bomb and could have killed us all. You dishonored the truce—"

"Daisy, nine o'clock!" Sarah's warning filled her head. Movement, spotted from the corner of her eye.

Shit, we missed one more flanking us!

Daisy spun, ready for the inevitable barrage of energy weapons from Reggie and Vince to fry the unwitting alien, but their weapons remained silent.

Standing not more than five meters from her, ninja-stealthy in her approach, was Tamara. Patches of frostbitten skin were peeling from her face, and she did not look amused. Not one bit. A sentiment made even more clear by the large stun rifle aimed square at Daisy.

"B-bu-but..." Daisy stammered. "But you're de—"

She didn't get to finish her sentence as the weapon discharged its payload and slammed her to the ground, unconscious.

CHAPTER THIRTY-ONE

Like a modern-day Sisyphus fighting uphill against the boulder of unconsciousness, Daisy slowly climbed the steep slope back to the waking world.

Unable to move, she noted. *Where the hell am I?*

It took a moment before her senses sharpened and registered the bumpy ride making the restraints dig into her wrists. Only then did she realize she was strapped into an uncomfortable seat in a small jump ship.

It was a light-duty vessel, only designed to carry three, and was seriously overloaded as it bumped and bucked its way skyward. The extra weight, even of a smaller human like Daisy, left the craft straining its engines as it fought the pull of Earth's atmosphere.

She tried to scratch an itch on her nose, but found herself unable. Her wrists were bound tight, held fast by slender yet strong restraints.

Figures, she lamented, frustrated by the inability to scratch the increasingly annoying itch. The rest of her body felt a bit off as well. The stun burst had really done a number on her, rendering her head fuzzy, and leaving a strange metallic taste in her mouth. She gingerly turned her head toward the cockpit area. Given the tiny size of the vessel, it didn't require much movement at all.

Reggie was at the controls, guiding the ship up through the exosphere, while Vince sat beside him in the copilot's seat. He was wearing a fresh jump suit and didn't look any worse for wear, but Daisy could tell by the way he was seated slightly cockeyed as the bumping ship rattled against his back that he was still favoring his other arm.

They re-attached that thing quick. I wonder why they decided to keep the meat one. Impressive in any case. Finn's fingers were a small procedure, but an entire arm? I had no idea the Váli's medical pod had those capabilities.

"Hey, check it out. Someone is throwing some serious stink-eye your way, Daze," Sarah commented.

Daisy turned her head the other direction and caught an icy blast from Tamara's bloodshot eyes. The skin on her nose and ears was black with frostbite damage, along with a patch on her cheek and eyebrow. She looked like she'd been through hell but somehow managed to drag herself out the other side, albeit substantially the worse for wear.

Lovely.

"Seriously. Girl needs a facial something fierce," Sarah joked.

Daisy closed her own tired peepers and rested her head against the bulkhead.

Nice of you to join me. I wondered for a minute if that stun blast might have wiped you out of my head.

"No such luck, though I do have this really strange taste in my mouth."

You don't have a mouth, remember?

"That's why it's a strange taste. Not toast, though, so don't worry about having a stroke or anything."

Daisy opened her eyes again and surveyed the ship. It had

seen better days, and seemed to be of a vastly different make and model than anything she'd worked on up to that point.

Wait a minute. Where did they get this thing? This isn't our hopper. What the hell? This wasn't on the Váli, we would have known about it.

The ship's vibrations stopped abruptly as they punched free of the atmosphere, the engines powering off as the tiny craft slid into a compressed air thruster-guided drift through the debris field circling Earth. Reggie reached out and flicked a series of switches on the command console, and all but the most critical systems were shut down, leaving them floating in the dark, with almost no power signature emitting from the ship.

"Looks like they're worried about being scanned," Sarah noted.

Yeah, Daisy silently agreed. *The question is, are they worried about the rogue cyborgs, or those freaking huge, four-armed aliens? My money would normally be on the aliens, but after meeting that wack-job AI, Habby, I'm not one hundred percent sure.*

Either way, Daisy figured if they were running a counter-detection protocol, they'd be drifting for at least an hour. Long enough to be reasonably certain they hadn't been scanned, and also conveniently long enough for her to catch a much-needed, non-stun rifle-induced nap.

She opened her eyes for one more look around. Tamara hadn't taken her angry eyes off her. Daisy cracked a tiny smile and gave Tamara a little wink, summoning up the energy for one last bit of snark before drifting off.

"It's been a long day. Y'all wake me when we're back on the ship."

Surprisingly, Daisy had managed to sleep quite soundly for the duration of the flight. It was some of the best rest she'd had in days. Like a criminal finally locked in jail, no longer on the run, and finally able to let go of all the stress and worry leading up to their capture, she had no trouble nodding off. Her sleep was short but restful, that is until the bump of the ship's airlock roused her.

Daisy rolled her shoulders and yawned. She would have rubbed the sleep from her eyes, but her hands were still restrained.

Hang on, this doesn't feel right. Did the Váli lose gravity control? Totally not my fault if it did. Nope, can't pin that one on me. I didn't touch those systems. At least I don't think I did.

The airlock began to cycle open, and an antiseptic burst of air puffed into the craft, followed by a far stronger breeze that smelled strongly of harsh chemicals. Moments later an electrostatic charge and UV pulse hit the vessel.

"Okay, stage one sterilization complete," Reggie said, unbuckling from his pilot's seat. Vince and Tamara did the same, rising to gather their captive and escort her from the ship. Daisy found it hard to look at Tamara, but even harder to hold Vince's gaze as they filed out the doors.

The airlock sealed behind them, leaving the group in a small decontamination chamber. For two straight minutes, bursts of disinfectant aerosols washed over them, followed by scans, then another series of chemical baths, until at long last, the red light over the far door turned green.

"Come on, Daisy. Let's get you to your cell," Reggie said.

"Cell?" she said, confused. The *Váli* didn't have any cells.

"Welcome to Dark Side," Vince added as they stepped through the door.

Captain Harkaway stood there, ready to greet his team, his face cold and emotionless, as he waited for his prodigal crewmember. Barry stood beside him, as did another too-symmetrical man. This one felt even more unnervingly *off* than Barry did.

Shit, another cyborg.

The captain said nothing, merely sizing her up with an

unsettling gaze. He glanced at his team, all three of whom looked a bit beat up from their battle on Earth.

"Go eat, then get yourselves some rack time. You earned it."

Vince and the others headed down a corridor, leaving Daisy with the captain and the pair of cyborgs.

Captain Harkaway stared at her several seconds longer, then abruptly turned and began walking. Barry, gently yet firmly took her by the arm and followed, leading her deeper into the facility. The corridors, she noted, were surprisingly spacious for a military base. Perhaps there was more to Dark Side than they'd originally let on.

The captain opened a hatch and stepped through, Daisy and her escorts close behind.

A not-so-welcoming welcome party stood in the next chamber awaiting her arrival. A distinctly sturdy-looking duo fell in behind them as they walked. Other new faces stood quietly in the passageway, gawking at the new arrival.

All this security for little old me?

The pair on her tail, a man and woman with bulging muscles—where they hadn't been replaced by shiny metal, that is—were obviously military of some sort. Jutting out of the cuffs of her long sleeves, she could see that the dark-skinned woman's hands and forearms were both replacements. Daisy wondered just how far up her arms the repairs went.

Scanning the other faces as she was ushered past, she locked eyes with a lean Asian man. He was fit, no doubt, but lacked the military build of those who ready themselves for fighting as opposed to training for mere exercise.

"Looks like one of the brainy science guys," Sarah noted.

How do you know?

"Come on, Daze, we're techies. We know our own."

At the end of the staring group, it was the kindly older woman, her smooth brown skin's agelessness betrayed only by her thick silver-gray hair, that threw Daisy for a loop. She was neither military, nor science, nor techie-looking in her casual attire. She simply didn't seem to belong there, yet she also seemed the most at home of them all.

"What's up with that one?" Sarah pondered.

Don't know. But I have a feeling I'll find out soon enough.

They all watched Daisy silently as she was marched past. A perp walk of sorts for the young woman who overcame an entire crew, disabled a supercomputer-powered ship, made Earthfall in a hostile city, fought off cyborgs and aliens alike, and somehow survived it all.

They continued on, passing a series of thick windows, through which Daisy caught her first glimpse of the destroyed moon base up close. Impact scars dotted the landscape, revealing that nearly all the structures on the exposed surface had sustained severe to fatal damage.

The thick moon rock visible jutting out above the windowsill hinted at the reason for this particular section's survival. Judging by the outcropping above, parts of the base were most likely hidden under the surface of the moon itself, rather than settled on top of it.

Roughly one hundred meters away, tucked out of sight, she saw the familiar shape of the *Váli* safely docked under a massive stone overhang.

"I see you managed to get her nav system working again," she quipped. "Nice for you."

"Sarcasm noted," Captain Harkaway growled, "and not appreciated. You have no idea what you've done."

"And I'm sure you're going to tell me what a bad girl I've been, right?"

A muscle tensed in his jaw, but he said nothing further, He simply stopped in front of a thick door. Shielding the keypad with his body, he entered a lengthy code, then opened it, revealing a Spartan, but clean cell. With a nod to Barry, she was ushered inside.

The cyborg silently removed her restraints and stepped out through the door, calm and pleasant, as always.

He doesn't seem any worse for wear after that pulse grenade, she noted, though she really didn't know how he was doing underneath the newly-grown flesh that covered the impact site.

"That's it, then? Don't I get a last meal request?"

Captain Harkaway hesitated.

"Daisy," he began, "you're not going to be executed. Far from it."

"So prison, then. Or are you going to try to convince me to join your little cyborg revolution?"

Harkaway froze, the muscle in his jaw twitching ever-so slightly, then abruptly let loose a robust laugh that even brought a hint of tears to his eyes. After a good twenty seconds, he managed to get his laughter under control.

"Oh lord, *that's* what you think is going on?" he said through his rolling chuckles. "Ahhh, thanks for that. I really needed a good laugh."

"What the hell?"

The captain regained his composure somewhat, looking at her with far kinder eyes.

"Don't worry, Daisy. We'll fill you in on everything soon enough. For now, let's get you some chow. You look like hell. Eat and rest up. There will be a debrief tomorrow, then we'll figure out what to do with you."

As the heavy door swung shut, Daisy could hear him laughing to himself as it sealed.

"Cyborg revolution! Priceless!" was the last thing she heard before all outside sound was cut off by the thick metal.

"Um, Daisy... what the hell was that all about?"

Daisy flopped down on the freshly-made bed.

"Beats me, Sarah," she replied with a confused look. "Seriously, beats the hell out of me."

CHAPTER THIRTY-TWO

An hour that felt like an eternity had passed before the heavy door's lock cycled and opened a crack.

"Daisy? I've got some food for you." It was Vince. Daisy winced ever so slightly at his voice. "Okay," he said, hesitant. "I'm coming in."

The door opened farther. Two of the stocky military types stood on either side of her ex, or not-so-ex, or whatever he was, as he paused in the open door for a long moment, giving her an uncomfortably loving look. He had a tray in his hands, and judging by the smell, Finn had been the one responsible for her first real food in days.

"Um, hi," he finally said, entering the cell.

The door swung shut behind him, but didn't latch. The bang as it closed made him flinch ever so slightly, drawing Daisy's eyes to the fresh pink scar circling his shoulder.

"You think he wore that tank top specifically to make you uncomfortable?" Sarah asked.

Nah, not his style, Daisy silently replied.

The machines had done quick and thorough work on him, she noted. While he would always have a slight scar, the flesh around it where the limb had been so rudely severed from his torso was nearly entirely intact. It had been expertly re-grown and repaired by the ship's medical pod. A system apparently far more advanced than Daisy had been aware of.

"So, um, Finn knew you'd be hungry and wanted to go all-out, but I thought it might be best to start with something easy on the stomach. I have no idea what you've been eating these last several days, but I can't imagine it was terribly satisfying."

"You'd be surprised. Wild rabbit with a side of extremely expired mystery food pouches is the breakfast, lunch, and dinner of champions."

Vince gave a low chuckle, the sound of the familiar rumble soothing her nerves in spite of herself. Nevertheless, Daisy found it hard to look at him.

"You do *still care," Sarah teased.*

Shut up.

Vince put the tray on her table, then took a few steps back.

"Look, we have a *lot* to talk about. I can't even imagine all that's running through your head right about now, but I know you're exhausted. It can wait, and really, we should have *that* conversation after you've heard what the captain has to say."

Daisy forced herself to look at him, not allowing her unease to show.

"Thank you, Vince," she managed.

Why does he keep looking at me like that? Be mad, dammit!

Vince seemed determined to be nothing of the sort. For a second it seemed he might step closer, giving in to the urge to hold her close and comfort her, but instead, his longing gaze lingered just a moment longer, then, with a reluctant little smile, he pushed the door open and left her to dine alone. The food wouldn't be the only thing she would have to digest that night.

~

The following morning, Daisy woke early, stretching her aching body, then settling into what had become a daily routine of meditation as she tried to further unlock the seemingly endless curiosities hidden in her mind.

The door cracked open.

"Hi, Vince. Look, I wanted to thank you for—"

An angry woman with a metal arm strode in.

Shit. Tamara.

She fixed her gaze on Daisy as she placed the tray of fresh fruit and some hot coffee on the table. If looks could kill, Daisy might very well have been well on her way across the river Styx, but fortunately, that was one martial skill Tamara was lacking.

The patches of blackened skin were gone, replaced by fresh pink flesh where the frostbitten parts had been excised and regrown. A full two-thirds of her left ear was new, as were both cheeks, and part of her forehead just above the eyebrows. The tip of her nose had suffered as well, but seemed to have managed to survive the freezing temperatures of space.

"Thanks," Daisy managed to say as the shock wore off.

Tamara remained silent.

"So, um, what's going on here? The captain wouldn't tell me anything."

The angry botanist said nothing as she gathered up the empty metal tray from Daisy's dinner the night before, then turned for the door.

"Tamara, at least clue me in a little. Come on, you shot me with a stun rifle."

"You blew me out a goddamn airlock!" she spat back, venom in her voice as her newly pink cheeks flushed an angry red.

"Because you and Gus were trying to shoot me!" Daisy shot back. "It was self-defense!"

"It was a fucking stun rifle, Daisy, not a real gun."

"Gee, thanks, that makes it feel so much better."

The two women glowered at each other.

"So how did you survive, then?" Daisy finally asked. "I know the ship didn't turn around."

Tamara flashed an angry look, the metal tray in her cybernetic hand crumpling as she fought to keep her anger in check. A long moment passed before her fingers relaxed, then she tapped on the shoulder of her metal arm.

"You're such a fucking dumbass, Daisy. I was a soldier before I was a botanist. This is a modified combat arm designed for both atmospheric as well as space function. The shoulder houses an emergency egress oxygen shell. It can provide up to an hour of breathable air—if you can get it around yourself before you explode or freeze to death first. I was just lucky I was drifting the same direction as the ship, otherwise they'd never have been able to pick me up in time. Gus barely made it to me in the jumper as it was."

"Former military?" Daisy mused. "Your charming demeanor makes much more sense, now."

"Stow it. I almost died out there, just because you wouldn't listen and went off on some panicked freak-out."

"If you had told me from the beginning, none of this would ever have happened."

"Told you what, exactly?"

Daisy hesitated.

"Um, whatever it is you all have been keeping so secret from me. Obviously, there's some massive conspiracy the entire crew was in on."

"Not Sarah," she replied. "She was just like you."

"What?"

"Yeah. What?"

Tamara took a deep breath.

"You never wondered why the two of you bonded so well? Why you worked in tandem when no other position had a redundancy like that?"

Daisy didn't know how to process that.

Tamara, for her part, and angry as she was, in the back of her mind was nevertheless understanding of Daisy's reactions, even if she wanted to throttle her to death for what she had done. As a soldier, however, she had to admit it made sense, defending yourself at all costs. As someone who had at least considered Daisy a shipmate, if not a friend, it still hurt.

"Look," she grumbled, "the captain will explain it all. Just try not to freak out. And for fuck's sake, no more blowing people out of airlocks."

Daisy couldn't tell if there was any humor in that statement as Tamara turned her back on her as she exited the cell.

A mere twenty minutes had passed when the wiry tech opened the door a crack.

"Ms. Swarthmore? I'm Alfred Chu, chief technician for Dark Side." He paused. "Well, actually the *only* technician for Dark Side, I suppose. The commander asked me to bring you some clean clothes. May I come in?"

Daisy rose to her feet. "Sure thing, Alfred, come on in."

The man stepped into the room with a clean set of clothes in his arms.

"Please, call me Chu. Everyone else does. Here, these should fit you. I'm sure you've already found the decon shower in the back of the cell. Sorry it isn't piped for a proper water shower, but they didn't really design this section for many creature comforts."

"No worries," she replied. "I'm just grateful for something clean to wear."

She began peeling off clothes.

"You're just trying to get him flustered."

Now why would I do something like that?

Chu blushed and turned quickly for the door.

Daisy noted there were no security guards waiting outside.

"Hey, Chu," she called after him. "I know I'm in lockdown,

but do you think there's any way I could get something to read? I'm bored out of my skull in here."

"We don't have any books on Dark Side, and I know they wouldn't allow a vid tablet in one of the cells."

"Well, how about digital books? They only require the most basic of readers. You think you could load a few onto one of those for me?"

The technician pondered a long moment.

"I don't think I can do that, Ms. Swarthmore."

"Please, call me Daisy. Look, I understand they don't want me having any high-tech devices, but what about a service reader? Those things are dumb as a rock and about as powerful, but you could probably put a few books on one for me. Come on, Chu, it's not like I'll dig my way through a foot of steel with a tiny, plastic shell tablet. I know they're not made to be e-readers, but you have to be an exceptionally smart guy if you're the head tech for the whole base. I'm sure you've got the technical chops to make it work."

He considered her request, the competitive nerd in him suddenly motivated to live up to the technical challenge.

"All right," he finally said. "Bare-bones, though. If I run a few books through a file compressor then transpose it into straight text, I should be able to load them into the core memory without impeding readability."

"Wow, you're really clever, Chu. That's genius!" she lauded. The technician's demeanor warmed marginally.

"Okay, I'll be back in a while. We don't have a lot of books here, but I'll put what I can on it."

"Thanks, Chu. You're a rock star."

A fun new technical challenge at hand, he wore a little smile as he stepped from her cell and closed the door.

"What's that all about?" Sarah asked. *"You going to try what I think you're going to try?"*

"Great minds, Sarah," Daisy chuckled. "Now hush, I need to plan."

Daisy sat cross-legged on her bunk. After the last several days, being in a relatively comfortable, safe, and quiet environment, she was able to slide effortlessly into a meditative state.

CHAPTER THIRTY-THREE

The tablet was worse than she'd expected.

Far worse.

Ancient. Slow. Terribly outdated.

"Thanks, Chu! It's perfect!" she bubbled as he walked out of her cell. "I can't tell you how much I appreciate this!"

"Still no guards outside, Daze."

Yeah, I noticed.

"Hey, do you have any idea when they're finally going to get me out of here?"

"Sorry, Daisy, they don't keep me in the loop for that kind of stuff."

"Okay, no worries. It was worth asking. But thanks again for this. I'm so glad to finally have something to kill time with."

Chu flashed a friendly smile, then stepped out of the cell, closing the thick door behind him. As soon as it sealed, cutting her off from the rest of the base, Daisy carefully placed the tablet against the edge of her bunk, and with a quick stomp, separated the case from the components inside.

"Who needs a screwdriver when you've got a solid pair of boots?"

She began whistling a cheerful little tune as she pried out the pieces she was interested in.

"Ooh, yeah. Good idea," Sarah said. *"Though I don't know if you'll be able to access the hardwired bypass mechanism through a foot of reinforced steel."*

"*Half* a foot, actually. It's mounted in the middle of the wall. It's less reinforced there," Daisy replied. "But I don't need to access it."

"No?"

"Nuh-uh. I've got a *different* idea."

She set to work, stripping wires, carefully splicing them to seemingly unrelated components, then feeding them back to other low-power systems within the wrecked device. To a layman—or even a tech, for that matter—it would appear to be a complete waste of time, but Daisy knew better. *How* she knew better was something she'd ponder at a later date. For now, the important thing was escape and evasion.

Step one: Escape.

She lifted the metal stool they unwisely equipped the cell with and approached the door.

There it is, she said, noting the small, flush bit of conduit embedded in the wall to the side of the doorframe.

"Like I said, no way to get in there. And the Faraday shielding in the walls won't give you any wireless access, either."

"I don't need *total* access. Just a teeny, tiny bit."

Daisy then pressed a shard from the tablet's case to the joint where the conduit met the doorframe and proceeded to smash it with the stool, using it like a tiny chisel.

"Soundproofing works both ways, assholes," she muttered with a little chuckle.

It took several minutes, and scored Daisy a few bruised knuckles in the bargain, but eventually a small gap appeared. Nothing big, and surely not enough to access the internal workings of the security mechanism, but Daisy had other plans.

Carefully, she took the long, loose end of the wire she'd stripped and coiled before splicing it inside the guts of the smashed tablet and slowly fed it into the tiny opening. Once it was roughly six inches in, she powered up the circuit board and keyed in a quick series of commands.

"Even if that gets you the tiniest wireless connection, it won't be enough for any real data streaming. Face it, you still won't be able to override their security protocols with that thing, Daze. It's way too slow and underpowered. Why, you couldn't even begin to crack the security on the—" Her dead friend abruptly stopped when she realized what she was doing. *"Oh, damn. Now* that *is clever."*

"Thanks. Let's just hope it works."

Rather than attempt to access and overcome the advanced security protocols keeping the door locked, Daisy had a far different plan in mind. Using the tablet as a power source, and the stripped wire she had fed directly into the door mechanism itself, rather than the security keypad, Daisy had established a very fine, but very real link to the brain of the door itself.

Fingers crossed they didn't remove the fabricator's safety protocols when they installed this thing.

She entered a tiny string of commands, then hit the enter key. The tablet hummed and fizzled, dying in her hands, but as it breathed its last, the door mechanism unlocked and the seal opened.

"Boom! That's what I'm talking about!"

Quickly, Daisy slid the powerless door open and stepped into the corridor.

All clear.

She closed the door behind her, then took off at a quick, stealthy run.

"Used the life-support safety override to short out the master circuits and make the door think there was a power outage. Good one, Daze."

"I couldn't very well override their security, but all core-level systems are designed to preserve a breathable atmosphere, so long as there hasn't been a pressure loss venting into space. If you make it look like it's just a power outage—"

"You trick the door into thinking power went out, and it opens automatically to keep the breathable atmosphere constant. That's one hell of an oversight on their part."

"Yeah, but in their defense, it's installed at a factory core-code level, so even the facility's builders likely didn't know about it."

"So how did you?"

Daisy ignored the question as she came upon a base access terminal. Her fingers flew across the access keypad, and once she was past the biometric recognition system—thanks to a painfully simple code exploit—she began to cautiously dig through the machine's access files, using only the lowest level overrides to pull up a base schematic without triggering any alarms.

There it is.

Daisy smiled as she scanned the detailed facility map. Satisfied she had accurately memorized the plans, she reset the panel to appear just as she found it, then continued down the corridor. Daisy had a new destination in mind: the ship's landing bay.

Just gotta steal that hopper and make it back to the surface. New York should be a good bet—opposite coast, and likely untouched by whatever happened to L.A.

"Then they come back up here and kick some AI ass."

Precisely.

Quickly and quietly, Daisy took off in a stealthy jog, a new course firmly locked in her head. It would be a bit tricky bypassing the final set of codes to release the ship once she had made it through the hangar, but she'd just have to deal with that when she got there.

The first set of doors she encountered, while thick and

sturdy, were nevertheless a snap, and she had them open in under a minute.

At this rate, I'm guessing three minutes till I'm in the hangar.

"Unless there are guards."

Obviously. But we can avoid them.

"We? So I've been upgraded from a voice in your head?"

Shut up, you know what I mean.

Daisy paused as she slowly rounded a blind curve in the corridor.

No one there.

She increased her pace and soon arrived at the hangar doors, beating her estimate by nearly twenty seconds. She accessed the door terminal and ran a quick bypass protocol.

Locked.

Shit. They've modified this one. Something new.

Nimble fingers entered another string of commands. Again, the door remained locked. The clock was ticking. The longer she remained exposed in one place, the greater her chance of being recaptured.

"Is there another way in?"

"Yeah, but I'd have to pass straight through the mess hall to reach it."

"So, what are the options?"

Daisy had an idea. Switching her scans from schematics and lock protocols, she tapped into the base's life support status readouts. A series of red dots appeared on the screen, spread throughout the facility. None were in her immediate path, and the mess hall was completely empty.

"Everyone's at the other end of the base. If ever there was a time to make a run through the mess hall, this would be it."

"Are you sure about that?"

"You share my eyes. You saw the readout."

Without another moment of hesitation, Daisy ran the twists

and turns of the work-around route to the hangar deck. In less than a minute she stood at the mess hall doors.

Silence.

Of course, the doors were sound-proof, so that was to be expected. Nonetheless, she double-checked the life signs readout on the nearest display. No one had moved. The mess hall was clear.

She bypassed the door's monitoring mechanism and eased inside. The room was unlit, an energy conservation protocol preserving base power when areas were empty.

Should just take a second for the motion sensor to light up the—

The lights came on all at once, just as the door behind her slammed shut. Daisy spun on her heel, dropping to a low fighting stance. The burly military-types who had escorted her upon arrival stood in her path, blocking her escape, but made no move toward her. They were dressed in tank tops and fatigue pants, revealing more of their modifications.

"Check it out," Sarah said. *"Two metal arms, all the way up! Holy shit, this chick's a total badass."*

Contrasting her deep ebony skin, the woman's shiny limbs stood out even more than Tamara's did.

Great, now we have two surly women with deadly appendages, Daisy griped. She took a quick look at the burly, crew-cut man as he shifted on his feet. *Looks like he's got two replacement legs, judging by the way he stands. Might even go all the way to the hip.*

"That high? You think he's got bionic junk, too?"

God, Sarah, you always go there, don't you?

Daisy had the feeling her dead friend would have liked to reply with a witty comeback, but something else caught her eye. Vince was there, too, sitting at a table across the room next to Chu. He winked at Daisy, a mischievous little grin plastered on his face. The grin she had always found so attractive, before she found out what he really was.

"Told you she'd do it." He laughed at the perplexed technician. "Come on, man. Pay up."

Grudgingly, Chu handed over the pudding cup from his dining tray.

"Boom! Double dessert! That's my girl," he said with a chuckle.

"But it shouldn't have been possible!" Chu lamented. "Those were triple fail-safe systems. There's even a biometric security lock!"

"You'd be surprised what she can do. She's far exceeded all parameters and expectations. At this point, we're really just learning exactly what she's capable of," Captain Harkaway said from across the quiet room. A quiet room *full of people.*

Despite what the readouts had said, the entirety of her *Váli* shipmates were there.

Our entire crew, plus those two at the door, and Chu over there with Vince. There's a door at the far end, so if the captain and Barry aren't—

She shifted her gaze across the room, calculating her odds of making a run for it, but a mere glance at the battle-scarred man standing beside the captain as they watched her quickly silenced any further internal chatter.

The man at Harkaway's side was older. Not as old as the captain, but salt and pepper liberally seasoned his close-cropped hair. What was so striking—what had taken her by surprise—wasn't his haircut. It was what lay just below it.

His left arm was an outdated replacement, lacking most of the fancy bells and whistles the others had, but what really stood out was his shining, metal jaw, exposed where the flesh grew to meet it just to the left of the cleft in the middle of his chin. His nose was intact, but where the jaw curved up toward his ear, the metal carried on to his left eye, its servos whirring an almost inaudible hum as it focused on her and sized her up.

"Holy shit," Sarah finally managed.

You said it, Daisy agreed, swallowing hard.

The rest of her crew was seated in the utilitarian chairs in the galley. Barry stood, as usual, and beside him was the other cyborg Daisy had briefly seen upon arrival. An obviously older generation. He looked human enough, but had that distinct, *not-quite-right* vibe to him the earlier models suffered.

Great. Two of them, now.

"It's good to see you well, Daisy." Mal's voice echoed slightly in the chamber. "We were concerned about you, but all will be in order shortly. I will be standing by with channels open if you need me."

"Thank you, Mal. And thank you for joining us, Daisy," a disembodied man's voice said.

"I recognize that voice. You're the one who answered when we tried reaching the base."

"My name is Sid. As you have likely deduced, I oversee Dark Side Base. You've already met Lieutenant Michelle Hawkins and Sergeant Omar El Manahi."

"Shelly is fine," the sturdy woman said with a cool glance. Omar just gave a cursory nod.

"What about me?" Chu griped.

"Of course you know senior technician Alfred Chu," Sid said. "He was most certain you would not be able to escape the detention cell with something as primitive as a read-only tablet."

Chu blushed.

"And I am Ash," the cyborg said.

"Ash?" Daisy said, stealing a glance at Vince across the room.

He raised an eyebrow and gave a little *'I know'* shrug. They'd both watched a lot of old sci-fi movies together.

"Seriously. Your name is Ash?"

"I did not choose it," he answered.

Daisy didn't know whether to be amused or distressed. She ultimately felt a little of both would likely fit the situation best.

"Commander Kirk Mrazich oversees military matters," Sid

continued. The metal-jawed man gave a little two-fingered salute. "Our pilot, and jack-of-all-trades, Donovan Welsh is out on a salvage shift with Bob, his ship, but you will meet them as well, soon enough."

"Great, so now I know my captors. When are you going to tell me what you want with me?"

Captain Harkaway stepped forward.

"Daisy, we're not your captors. There's so much going on that you need to know."

"So tell me, then."

"We're just waiting for the doctor to join us."

Daisy's glance flicked to Doctor McClain.

"No, Daisy," McClain said. "The *other* doctor."

CHAPTER THIRTY-FOUR

The door to the mess hall slid open, and the older woman with silver-gray hair Daisy had noticed when she had first arrived calmly walked in.

Now that she had a better opportunity to see her, Daisy thought she looked like a mix of races more than one. Medium-toned brown skin with big almond eyes and full, wavy hair. She could have been from any one of a dozen cultures just as easily as she could have been a mix of them all. She smiled broadly when her eyes met Daisy's.

"So glad to finally meet you properly, Daisy," she said. "My name is Fatima. I'm sure you have a lot of questions for us, and believe me, there's a lot about you we would love to learn as well."

"Great. Let's start with you telling me why the hell you all wanted to capture me and bring me here."

Fatima smiled.

"Daisy, I believe it might be best if we hold off on those for now. Once you understand the scope of the situation, I feel you may find the questions you currently feel are so pressing may seem trivial, given the big picture."

"Why do I have a bad feeling about this?" Sarah said.

You're not the only one.

Fatima's eyes crinkled around the edges with both merriment and curiosity as she observed Daisy's silent discussion within herself.

That's weird. It's almost like she could read my—

She studied the older woman curiously. Fatima merely continued to smile at her.

"A lot going on in that head of yours, eh Daisy?" she commented.

"What do you mean by that?"

"Nothing. I just tend to observe a little more closely than most," she answered, her calm smile never once faltering. "Now, let's see if we can't put your mind at ease a little, shall we? I believe pieces will quickly fall into place for you once you are operating with all the facts."

"You took over Dark Side base and somehow started a cyborg rebellion in Los Angeles. That sound about right?"

Fatima smiled kindly at her, as one might look at an innocent child.

"Oh, dear. There is so much to learn," Fatima said. "Of course, those details were to be uploaded in your neuro-stim feed during the last few months of your travel, but I understand the ship sustained damage and you were removed from your cryo over six months early."

Daisy felt a sudden sinking feeling in her gut.

"What do you mean, uploaded? What were you doing in my head?"

Mal joined the conversation.

"Fatima, may I help explain?" the disembodied AI asked.

"Certainly. Thank you, Mal."

"Daisy," the ship's voice began, "you were being slow-fed a lengthy series of mission-specific protocols and data during the course of our flight. The neuro-stim was not merely keeping your mind active for the duration, but was preparing you for your arrival."

"Trying to sway me to your side of the revolution? Was that it?"

"Nothing of the sort. My task was to bring the first of the newest generation safely to Earth. The hope was that a small, silent incursion could work where larger, mechanized ones had previously failed. Caring for you in transit is an honor not many of my kind receive; however, given my operating system's compatibility with the ship components at hand, I was the one tasked with the mission. The rest of the crew were to support you, but this was to be *your* mission. As we grew closer to Earth, my additional systems and memory stores were to automatically come online to aid in the process."

"That might explain why she started talking differently when we got closer to Dark Side," Sarah said.

I was thinking the same thing.

"Daisy," Harkaway said, more kind and gentle than she'd ever heard him speak, "there was no revolution. What you saw in Los Angeles happened to the entire planet, all at the same time. Earth was invaded."

"Those alien things—" she mused.

"Yes. At first they arrived in battle cruisers and began a full assault. The fighting was intense, but Earth's defenses managed to hold them off. The generals had thought they had won, but that first wave wasn't a true invasion. Not by a long shot. They were merely testing the resilience of the planet's people and defenses, collecting data for the *real* attack.

"It was only a day later when they launched a missile barrage at all major cities of Earth. The missiles were easily targeted and destroyed, but they had studied our tactical responses, and that was their plan all along. You see, they weren't carrying explosives. Their payload was something far deadlier, and by detonating them high in the atmosphere, mankind carried out their invasion plans for them."

Fatima watched Daisy's reactions carefully. "Are you okay, Daisy? Do you need to sit down?"

"No, I'm *not* okay," she replied, then turned back to Harkaway. "What happened, Captain? What happened to home?"

He let out a deep sigh, then continued. "It was more than just some nasty virus, Daisy. It was a genetically-coded super plague, one that was both air and waterborne, and incredibly contagious. So much so that by the time they figured out what had happened, it had already wiped out nearly all of the entire planet's human population. All of that was in under a week."

Daisy swayed on her feet.

"Not possible," Sarah said in disbelief. *"The captain, the crew... they're all alive."*

"Yeah, they are," Daisy said out loud.

"What was that?" Fatima asked, eyebrow raised askew.

"I was just thinking, that's not possible. Look at all of you. It didn't kill everyone. And I was just there. There were no bones. No bodies. No mummified remains. Those kinds of things last for millennia. And whatever this supposed plague was, why didn't it affect me? No, it didn't happen like that. It couldn't have."

"Yes, it did," Fatima replied. "You see, Daisy, humanity was not just killed off. The plague was designed to break down human cells and leave no residue of the planet's former inhabitants. All tissue, including bone, was reduced to dust in under a month. No trace of the human genome was to be left anywhere."

"The cyborgs," Daisy said in a whisper. "And my dream. People turning to dust. The neuro-stim tried to tell me..."

"What?"

"The cyborgs. That explains why they had no flesh. They stayed active, but their meat suits dissolved away." Daisy felt ill. "Though I suppose being fleshless technically makes them androids now, if you want to talk semantics. But that still doesn't explain why they were acting the way they did."

"May I?" Sid chimed in.

"Of course," Fatima replied.

"Daisy," the base AI began, "as you surely know by now, a great portion of Dark Side's facilities were destroyed in that first wave assault. Only the most-hidden and protected areas remained intact when the invaders lay waste to the base as they passed the moon on their way to Earth. The entire facility was crippled, unable to help, communications in shambles, and very quickly only a few straggling signals were able to reach the base once the satellite network encompassing the globe was corrupted."

"I caught a glimpse of the debris when I entered the atmosphere. But you say some satellites are still intact?"

"Intact, but quarantined. You see, Daisy, they not only assessed and attacked humanity, but they also realized there was a robust artificial intelligence population that was still fighting them after mankind was gone, and the AIs had access to all of the planet's heavy weaponry. There was no way to land an invasion without being destroyed or having their prize rendered radioactive by fallout from Earth's defenses. Ultimately, they just wanted the planet for its resources, so they adjusted strategy."

"I saw those aliens scrapping buildings, deconstructing things."

"Yes, after the initial wave, that was their revised plan. Smaller units were harder to pin down by the AI-controlled and automated city defenses, which would need to conserve firepower if they hoped to stay in the fight for the long haul. Unfortunately, the aliens somehow discovered a back door to our systems that no one had ever thought to protect from. An electronic AI virus was broadcast days after humanity ceased to be, slowly worming its way into the terrestrial and orbiting communications network. The lower-level AIs succumbed almost immediately. It was only because of that first wave of AI deaths that the high-functioning AIs were able to recognize the threat and deal with it the only way they could."

"They launched all their nukes?" Daisy asked.

"No. Something almost worse. They cut themselves off from the rest of the world. From each other. All communications systems were shut down, leaving the cities, and those few remaining AIs within, completely in the dark. It was the only way, you see? The AI virus was spread through their wireless networks, and there was a high likelihood that the hard-wired systems would become compromised in short order. Their plan worked, but many cities weren't so lucky. Their core AIs became infected, but unlike the lesser processors, which either self-destructed or became comatose, those great minds went mad."

"A two-pronged genocide," Daisy realized.

"While the human virus is all but extinct at this point, the electronic one, not being biological, is still active. It's a standoff, you see? So now the aliens harvest away from the defended areas of the sequestered cities they couldn't destroy, leaving them alone, for the most part."

"And the cyborgs? They were chasing me, but all dressed up in fancy suits, talking nonsense."

"We hadn't heard of those before, but it could make sense if their minds were corrupted, though we'd have expected them to completely meltdown and fail entirely. Nevertheless, many of the cybernetic systems in some models of cyborgs are a robust AI, and it would be highly unlikely they would succumb to a full shut-down."

"So why live underground like that?"

"The aliens monitor for any mechanical activity on the surface, picking off remaining units should they venture too far from safety. City-level systems they cannot engage due to the auto-defense systems, but cyborgs and other smaller mechanicals are hunted and exterminated when detected. Remaining organics, like the dogs and other wildlife, are left alone. Only humanity was deemed a threat, you see, and they're long-gone."

"But I'm here. *We're* here. Humanity is not dead."

"No, Daisy, humanity is not dead," the artificial intelligence said. "I feel this next part would be best told by a human, not an AI."

"Why? What aren't you telling me?"

"Daisy," Captain Harkaway said with a sigh. "There's no way to sugar-coat this, so I'm just going to say it. *All* of humanity was wiped out."

"Almost all, you mean."

"No, *all* of it. You weren't born. None of us were. We were grown. Grown from the few viable cell-lines that were somehow immune to the alien virus."

Daisy felt herself sway on her feet.

"No. I had a childhood. I had parents."

"All implanted by the neuro-stim to make the transition easier."

"But the AIs—you're telling me they're not trying to take over humanity?"

"Far from it, Daisy. The AIs managed to scavenge a few dozen cell lines that remained viable even after the attack, mostly from blood banks, sperm banks, hospital pathology freezers. Realizing what they had to do, they launched a counterassault for cover and sent whatever ships and resources they could salvage far into space to *save* humanity. To re-grow our species from scratch."

Fatima rested her hand on Daisy's shoulder.

"The human race was extinct, Daisy, and the AIs made it their mission to bring us back, and with nothing more to work with than a few dozen samples of our DNA. Less than one millionth of one percent of the population had the resistant genome, and only a fraction of those had samples to draw from. You're the newest cell line. The rest of us here were created from earlier versions, sent back to try to access Earth's surface. Unfortunately, the earliest of us turned out to not be entirely immune, which was quite unexpected."

Daisy looked over the men and women in the room with her.

"As you can see from the replacement parts, a good many were severely injured in their attempts," Fatima continued. "The earliest of us, like me, had metal reinforcements implanted from birth. The idea was to make us more robust, but that also made us stand out on surface scans like a giant red X. Most were wiped out immediately on arrival. The next several generations were increasingly organic, though they were still detected. Finally, a new pair of viable lines were adapted for *this* attempt. One with a metal-composite reinforced skeleton but relatively minimal mechanical enhancements, the other entirely organic, though enhanced organic at that."

Vince was silent, but she could feel his eyes on her, and she knew that despite all she had done, if given the chance he would hold her close and tell her it would all be okay.

No. He's a machine. At least, sort of. But then, what am I?

Daisy felt the color drain from her face and her legs grow weak.

"Doc, why don't we let Daisy digest this for now? I'm sure there will be plenty of questions, but that's a hell of a lot to absorb in one sitting," Captain Harkaway said.

"Of course, you're right, Captain. Daisy, let's get you to your new quarters. We can discuss things further after you've had time to process this a bit." Fatima gently took her by the arm and led her from the room.

"Everyone is staring, Daze. They all knew. Even Vince. He knew all this time but didn't say anything."

"I know, Sarah. I know," she mumbled.

Fatima said nothing as she turned and led her down the corridor to a vacant sleeping quarters, though sleep would be hard coming.

CHAPTER THIRTY-FIVE

Daisy slept poorly.

That was to be expected. After all, learning you were grown in a tube and your entire species had been wiped out by an alien invasion would be hard to digest for even the most stoic of hearts. What she hadn't expected was that she could still slide into a meditative state despite the turmoil, and that blessed respite gave her at least a modicum of relief from her racing mind.

Knowing what she did now, some of her previously confusing dreams and memories made sense. Half-loaded neuro-stim updates that didn't have time to properly take hold, and it seemed she had accidentally tapped into areas of the program that were meant to be securely firewalled.

"Lucky you didn't fry your brain."

"Yeah, I know."

"So, we were grown. Ain't that a slap in the face. That means those parts we saw in the Váli—"

"Weren't what we thought. The ship was growing organic limbs and bodies, as well as preserving others. I bet Finn could even have his original fingers re-attached if he wanted."

"But he really likes the new ones."

"Which still creeps me out."

"And Vince? He opted for his real arm back instead of some mechanical one. That's got to mean something, right?"

Daisy pondered a long moment.

"Maybe he just wishes he was human and not some part-machine freak. I don't know. All I know is, he lied to me, and about more than one very important thing, it seems."

"Well, to be fair, he didn't lie about you not being born. That never came up in conversation, I bet."

"Shut up, Sarah, you know what I mean."

The intercom buzzer beside the door let out a low tone.

"Yeah?" she said into the panel.

"Daisy, it's Captain Harkaway. I was wondering if you felt up to talking with me."

She'd rested all she could at that point, and the dangling carrot of further information about the world she now found herself living in had her opening the door without hesitation.

"Captain," she said, leaving the door ajar and sitting back on her bunk.

The captain stepped into her quarters and closed the door behind him, leaving it unlocked, she noted. He pulled up her metal chair and took a seat. To Daisy's eyes, he looked to have aged a decade since just a few days prior. She supposed her escape might have had more than a little to do with that.

"So," she began, sizing up the man under whom she'd served all those months. "You. And the others. You've tried this before."

Harkaway locked eyes with her, his pained memories leaking out around the edge of his hard gaze.

"Yes," he finally replied. "I was one of the first. We were grown as a human clone batch from what the AIs believed were robust cell lines. This was before neuro-stims had been perfected, so we spent the last several years of our flight out of cryo, training and preparing."

"You were awake?"

"Yes, and we trained every day until we knew for a fact we were the best and toughest humans those alien bastards would ever see. The plan was to reconnect with the cities of Earth, if they were still alive, and organize a counterattack against the Chithiid."

"The what?"

"Chithiid. We're pretty sure that's what they call themselves. No one knows for sure. Their communications were jumbled and scrambled, but the AIs have been working on deciphering it for a long time."

"The neuro-stim."

"What about it?"

"On the surface. I understood them. At least, I think I did."

Harkaway's expression shifted slightly. "Yes, Reggie did mention that you shrieked out some gibberish that made the attacking Chithiid cease fire." He stroked his chin as he pondered the possibility. "Your fiddling with your neuro-stim must have overridden some unknown firewalls to that data, but that shouldn't have even been in there. How you tapped into whatever you did is a mystery. Lord knows what else you might have downloaded."

The possibilities were both exciting and terrifying as Daisy absorbed the information.

"So, what happened? When you finally made Earthfall?"

A cloud grayed the captain's demeanor as the horrors replayed in his mind.

"There were over two hundred ships, Daisy. The best the AI designers could cobble together with the parts at hand. Designed to fight on even after incurring massive damage. That's why the pod system was created. If a ship took too much damage to continue on, another could incorporate the surviving pods into its structure and keep on fighting."

"Conserving resources. Solid design plan."

"Yes, and it turned out we needed every bit of that capability as soon as we hit the atmosphere."

"What happened?"

"The Chithiid launched a fierce counterattack that either damaged or outright destroyed fifteen percent of our fleet in just the opening minutes. The Command AI surveyed the battlefield and immediately shifted the target priorities to the three main hubs of alien resource gathering operations spread across the planet."

"Strip mining?"

"Yes and no. Massive launch sites where the Chithiid ships would load cargo to send ahead to their fleet. They're like locusts, Daisy. Stripping the world but never planning to occupy it. Once they've drained it dry, they abandon its empty shell. Really, that's the only reason any of us survived the first wave."

"Why's that? If they were just transport ships—"

"Their main fleet was long gone by the time mankind returned for a fight. It was a much smaller support group that remained stationed on Earth, and it was those that we faced off against. If their entire battle group had been there, we wouldn't have lasted ten minutes. Of course, we didn't know that at the time. We were just a bunch of tough guys, no more than kids, really, full of piss and vinegar, ready to take on anything that got in our way. We were making our descent to the western distribution hub when the *Icarus* came under massive fire just outside San Jose."

"Wait, did you say the *Icarus*? That writing I saw in the Narrows in the *Váli*—that was from the *Icarus*. That was your ship?"

"Yes, it was. We went down hard, and the *Icarus* was a loss, but we still had many viable pods, so the Hashimoto pulled a truly incredible low-altitude maneuver and saved our asses. It swooped in and launched decoys and flares while dropping right on top of us, snatching up the pods and surviving crew before booking it out of there."

"So you made it out okay."

Harkaway's face turned grim.

"Made it out? Yes. Okay? No. Not okay. The hull had been breached in multiple areas from our crash. I was crushed and lost my leg and most of my blood that day. The only thing that saved me were my crewmates. They refused to leave me. Got me in a cryo pod and cranked that thing to maximum. I was on the brink of death when they froze me. Turns out I was the lucky one. Right after that, the Command AI called a retreat to regroup and prepare for another assault, but it couldn't have known—" His gaze took on a far-away stare.

"Captain, you don't have to—"

"Yes, I do," he said, shaking himself free of memory's icy grip. "You need to know this. To understand just what exactly we're dealing with." He took a deep breath. "The few dozen surviving ships regrouped and began consolidating pods into new configurations based on what the Command AI learned in the first assault. That's when it got in."

"Shit. The AI virus," Daisy said.

Harkaway nodded.

"We'd shut down all external comms networks to prevent AI infection when the pods were retrieved, and the retreat was sounded over a pre-designated, sequestered signal. The fleet should have been safe from the AI virus. We just overlooked one stupid human-looking thing."

Oh no. They didn't...

"Each ship had one cyborg sealed in command in case radiation or plague managed to get into the ship and disable the crew. They were sealed in a Faraday pod as an extra layer of security against infection, locked in place in each ship's command center. Break glass in case of emergency, basically."

"But when the ships crashed..." Daisy said.

"Exactly. The tiniest of breaches occurred in one ship's command center. And with the crew disabled—"

"The cyborg was activated, which meant it was out of its protective pod. And when it returned to the fleet..."

Harkaway nodded. "That's what allowed the AI virus in. A series of statistically improbable events."

"Fucking Murphy."

"Yep. It took a little time for the virus to take hold, but by the time it did, the damage was done, and there was nothing we could do about it. Nearly all the AIs were infected at once. Most went mad and dove straight into the atmosphere. The angle of reentry burned them up, along with the men and women on board."

"There was nothing you could do?"

"Those few captains that were able, cut their infected AIs from the systems before they could do the same and quickly jettisoned them into space. The interchangeable nature of the AI processor cubes was the only thing that allowed any of us to survive. One meter square boxes of incredible calculating power, but not permanently attached. If they'd been irreversibly hardwired into the ships, no one would have survived. As it was, in the end, only a handful of us managed to escape."

"Out of all those ships? All those people?"

Harkaway swallowed hard.

"Yes. Almost none would survive the day. The Command AI was the last to go. He was triple-protected by layers of fail-safes, which gave him time to recognize what was happening as his systems failed. The virus was slowly eating its way closer and closer to his brain. It was just a matter of time before it was compromised, so rather than fall victim to the same fate as its lesser-shielded brethren, he ordered himself preemptively removed from command, sealed in a shielded container, loaded in an escape pod, and jettisoned toward the moon in hopes that someone might find him someday, and perhaps plug him back in on Dark Side base."

"Are you saying that Sid was that Command AI?"

"Yes."

"But somehow, he wound up installed here, on the moon."

"Yes. You see, Dark Side's systems were compromised, and ultimately destroyed, in the first wave assault—a conventional weapons attack followed by a narrowly-targeted AI virus. The survivors pulled the fried AI unit and tried to hotwire the base to maintain core functionality, but to no avail. Fast forward a hundred years, give or take, and there was Sid, lying there, dormant on the surface, just outside the remains of Dark Side base. The one thing capable of resurrecting the facility and unable to do a thing about it."

"Just waiting for someone to find him."

"Exactly. Fast forward again to the follow-up assault fleet that had been launched a few years later."

"The same thing happened to them," Daisy realized.

"Yes, only the Chithiid were more prepared this time. When they arrived, they flew into a blender. It was a massacre, and they took nearly one hundred percent casualties straightaway. Those few who could, attempted to return to the fleet. One survivor, her ship too crippled to join the others and with no functional comms to reach them, took refuge on the moon. It was blind luck that she happened to detect the weak signal from Sid's pod and drag him inside. Turns out that was what saved her life."

"Fatima?"

The captain nodded.

"She was alone here for I don't know how many years, until another attempt at Earth was made. When it failed, a handful of survivors unable to make the return flight made their way here. You met them earlier."

"Hang on. You say the major AIs on Earth are dead, but I

heard a voice in Los Angeles. Something *bigger* than I've ever encountered. It had to be the city."

At this, Harkaway looked genuinely surprised.

"Are you sure? We've been trying for decades to reconnect with any of Earth's AIs, but have never once had any success."

"You wouldn't be able to. They're all cut off, from what the crazy AI I met said, but I'm telling you, the city spoke to me. Well, more like commented. It said, 'Now that's interesting' as I was fighting the aliens and cyborgs."

"We have to tell Sid. This could change everything." He rose to leave.

"Wait, you can't just drop this you're-a-modified-human-on-a-mission-to-save-the-planet stuff on me then walk out. What the hell am I?"

"I'm truly sorry, Daisy," he replied. "Sorry I didn't tell you sooner. When the accident happened and we were all abruptly awoken, Mal informed me that you two hadn't received the full download. I made the decision to withhold that information from you. I thought it would be best to see how you and Sarah acclimated after the forced wake cycle. I suppose I just became complacent after that. You were both doing so well, I didn't want to throw a monkey wrench in things, at least not until we finally arrived at Dark Side."

"Me *and* Sarah? So she was pulled before her download was complete as well?"

Harkaway shifted uncomfortably in his seat.

"Daisy, Sarah was just like you. One of our first entirely organic successes. You two were our best yet. It took years to determine the most resilient cell line, but the big-brain machines finally did it, and the two of you were the result. Not regular humans. Stronger, tougher. Organic, but far more durable than nature ever intended."

"He said cell line. Singular." If a voice in her head could gasp, Sarah would have.

"What exactly are you implying? We have some genetic material in common?"

"Far more than that. While different fertilizing DNA was used in the process, you and Sarah were created from the same perfect egg. Not true monozygotic twins, but rather, something new. Sarah was your sister, Daisy."

If she hadn't been sitting, Daisy would have fallen down. Of course, the pair had been closer than one would expect of two strangers randomly meeting on a mission, but they'd bonded during a crisis, and their tight-knit friendship simply seemed a natural extension of that.

You hear that? she asked the friend in her head. Her *sister*.

"Yeah." Sarah fell silent a long while. *"I—"* The voice said no more.

Harkaway paused in the doorway.

"Daisy, I know this is an awful lot to take in, but I need you to keep it together. Can you do that for me?"

She nodded, numbly.

"Good. Now get yourself something to eat, then go see Chu. He's going to run some baseline tests for McClain and Fatima."

He gave her a little smile, then stepped out the door.

"Holy shit," Daisy managed.

"Understatement of the century," her sister replied.

CHAPTER THIRTY-SIX

"That is one beautiful brain," Chu said, staring at his readouts.

"I bet you say that to all the girls."

He blushed. "No, what I mean is—"

"Just fuckin' with ya, Chu."

He breathed a sigh of relief.

"So, the captain tells me you guys were on a later mission to Earth. I thought all the ones before ours were with mechanicals. You look entirely human."

Chu tapped his head. "Reinforced skeletal system, artificial kidneys, and a modified neural array. I have a small, secondary AI that runs in the background of my day-to-day mental processing. Kind of like Vince, but mine's much older tech and far clunkier."

She winced at her former lover's name.

"So, you're a machine, then."

"Not at all. I can function perfectly without the add-on, but it does allow me far greater data storage, as well as information recall and problem-solving. Do you know what automobiles were?"

"Yeah."

"Okay, think of it like a turbo on an old combustion engine. The car still runs fine without it, but it's much faster with it."

Daisy nodded in understanding. Still, Vince wasn't entirely organic, and that would never change.

Chu adjusted the settings and began another scan.

"Hold still. This one's going to take a minute or two."

"Not going anywhere, Chu," she replied. "So the captain said Sid was the Command AI in the first assault. I guess those two go way back."

"They're both far older than any of us, that's for sure. Harkaway is kind of famous from the old days. All the later missions learned about what happened to him."

"Captain doesn't look *that* old."

"How much did he tell you?" Chu asked. "I mean, did he tell you what happened to him?"

"Yeah, he was injured and stuck in cryo until they could fix him."

The technician blanched a little.

"There's more to it than that. A *lot* more, actually." He paused, unsure if he should be the one telling this story. Daisy's expectant look nudged him on.

"The captain was terribly hurt, that's true, and the micro repair bots had their work cut out for them rebuilding what they could with alloy replacements, but he was also one of the genetic lines that could still be infected with the plague. Nearly all of the people on that mission were."

"But I thought it was fatal."

"It is. Within days of the initial assault and subsequent contamination by infected humans returning to the invasion fleet, only five humans remained alive. Those few had been in space, safely sealed in EVA suits repairing damage to Sid's command ship when the others returned. The environmental alarms sounded almost immediately, and all crews were quarantined, but it was too late. Most of the ships went mad and dove into the atmosphere, but that actually didn't kill most of their crews in the process—the plague had already accomplished that hours earlier."

"But if the captain was infected, how is he alive?"

"When the few surviving ships realized what was happening, that the cell lines they had used to regrow humanity were not, in fact, immune, they purged their contaminated interiors, then flooded them with toxic gas and radiation from their engine systems, sterilizing themselves before opening themselves to space, purging everything into the vacuum. Then they came up with a drastic, last-ditch plan. All non-infected pods were consolidated to a single ship frame. The onboard AI had been infected early on and was deactivated and removed before it could destroy the craft, but many of the ship's systems were still functional and had been sequestered from damaged areas."

"So it was a ghost ship."

"Yeah, more or less, and the most functional one remaining. Sid gave orders for the surviving crew to fly the ship back to the launch point and report what had happened, to hopefully stop other missions from meeting the same fate. They couldn't send comms, you see? The systems were compromised. All they could do was fly all the way back with minimal computer aid, and no AI. Sid gave them coordinates and a series of instructions for key systems, before his command ship finally succumbed and he ejected himself."

"But if there was no AI running the ship, someone had to stay out of cryo the entire flight."

"Yeah," Chu said. "More than one, actually. Only two cryo pods were functional, and the captain was already in one of them, slowly having his injuries repaired. Remember, it was highly invasive, old tech back then, and the process itself nearly killed him."

"But the flight? How long was it?"

"Eighty years, give or take. Every year, they'd rotate. Five crew on their own, getting older as they tried to reach the launch point. Their information was critical to future assaults, you see, so while the initial mission failed, they could still succeed in making a difference."

"And the captain? How did he survive if he was infected?"

"Ah, well, that's an interesting story. Something of a legend, actually. He was the first, and only, human survivor of the plague, though I doubt anyone would want to go through what he did for it. Over the course of the trip, the crew had a *lot* of time to kill, and they thought that if they could not only save the captain from his injury but cure him as well, they'd then have a second cryo pod at their disposal. It wasn't entirely altruistic, what they did, but it's admirable nonetheless."

"They wanted to kick him out of the cryo to save themselves?"

"Only once he was healed and healthy. The system they devised was ingenious, especially given what resources they had at hand. They couldn't open the pod, lest they release the plague into their ship, and no one could justify killing the captain by venting the pod to space."

"Considerate of them," Daisy said, pondering eighty years in a derelict ship.

"In the end, the idea came to them during meal time," Chu continued. "One of the crew, Lieutenant Pam Darvish, got the backup food replicator online and jury-rigged it to create a different kind of cell. Human. Mind you, it took her three months to figure out how to override the protocols that prohibited human genetic replication. Remember, this was a machine designed to make food, so that was a big no-no all the way to the base code."

"Well, I'll be damned. People steaks."

"Not exactly, but you get the idea. Anyway, she tied it in to the medical unit of the cryo pod and set it to work. It took decades, but one by one, it replaced every single infected cell, killing every trace of the plague as it encountered it, one cell at a time. Imagine trying to wash salt off of every grain of sand on a beach. That's what it was doing to his body."

"That's freakin' genius," Daisy said appreciatively. "I'd like to meet this Lieutenant Darvish one day. She sounds amazing."

Chu looked away.

"Yeah, well... she died in-flight. A decompression accident," he said quietly. "But her work lives on, and the breakthrough she made even helped advance the systems used to create new humans. It helped make you, in fact."

He blinked rapidly and blushed.

"Oh. I forgot it's still new to you. Sorry."

"It's okay," she replied. "I'm getting used to the idea. Sort of."

The scanning unit chimed and cycled down.

"All right, just one more thing, then you can get out."

A machine slid into place above her thigh and hummed a moment as it zeroed in on its target. Then a sturdy titanium composite needle jabbed into Daisy's leg.

"Jesus, what the fuck!"

The servos hummed and whined as the needle pressed harder and harder against her femur until it finally punched in, claiming its prize of bone and marrow before withdrawing, spraying a sealant into the tiny hole.

"Sorry, it shouldn't do that. Usually it goes in really easy. Anyway, we've got blood and bone now, so you're good to go."

Daisy eased herself back to the floor and padded over to the readouts as Chu pored over the data.

"Amazing," he said. "Look at this activity. Your brain, it's firing at an incredible rate."

"Gee, I wonder why that is," Sarah chimed in. *"Not like someone removed all their safeties from their neuro-stim, now is it?"*

I knew I could count on you to give me shit at a time like this, she thought.

"What are sisters for?"

"My God, you've even partitioned it," Chu marveled.

"Partitioned what?"

"Your brain. It's like you're running a multi-core processor now. This is so far beyond anything I've ever seen, I don't even know how to interpret it."

"Let me take a look," Daisy said, leaning in to get a better look at the screen. As she did, Chu turned to another screen to examine her tissue samples. His eyes widened as he did but Daisy was too engrossed in what was on the screen in front of her to notice. It seemed that indeed her mind was indeed running at several *thousand* percent higher levels than a normal human.

"Whoa. This must've happened when I ran the neuro-stim without any inhibitors."

Chu gasped and spun to look at her in disbelief. "You did *what?* How are you not a vegetable? No matter how robust your body is, that should have fried your brain!"

"Yeah, this robust thing? Not a word ladies like to be called. Just a note for future reference."

"Sorry, it's just that, well, look at this readout."

She pivoted to see the screen.

"What you're made of is so much stronger than normal human tissue," he continued. "Now we know why the machine was having such a hard time. It wasn't broken, it's just that it required about eight hundred percent more force to take a bone sample than normal. You almost broke the needle, and that should be nearly impossible."

"Hang on. What's that?" she said, pointing to her bone matrix displayed on screen.

"Looks like a crystalline structure organically grown into the bone itself. And look! It's repairing itself despite being in a sample dish. See how it draws from the residual marrow to resolidify? My God, you must heal incredibly fast."

"Okay, well *that* wasn't my doing. I just messed with the neuro-stim, is all."

"About that. It could explain why your mind is partitioned like it is. Running multiple systems simultaneously. The data input you withstood must have been enormous."

"Ha, that's probably why I have one of our dead crewmembers living in my head now," she joked.

Chu looked at her, deadly serious.

"Are you messing with me?" he asked. "Because given what I see here, that's entirely possible."

Daisy felt her stomach flip.

"No, wait," he continued, "what am I saying? Even if you did manage to override the firewall all the way down to base code levels, you still physically wouldn't be able to download a non-genetically compatible backup."

"A what now?"

"Yeah, what was that about backups?"

"Oh, I thought you knew. Any new crew that is being grown and fed neuro-stim data during the course of a flight as long as yours is automatically backed up to the central processor's parallel neural array. It requires a massive amount of storage, and it takes years upon years of constant backups, but your ship is powered by one of the most impressive systems I've ever seen. More than capable of running a group of human backups at once."

"Backups? How can they even do that?"

"They grew us all, remember? Until we are woken from cryo, we're just essentially one big data set, and after waking, every time we sleep with our neuro on, we add a little more to the file. Why, even some portable arrays in our gear are wired to capture the basics of daily activities, just in case there's an accident before a proper backup can be run that night. Like every time we wear an EVA helmet or something."

"Fuck me," Sarah said in shock. *"He said genetically compatible. We come from the same egg. Daisy. Am I really alive in here?"*

Daisy's stomach flipped back and forth a few more times before she managed to right herself from her suddenly upside-down world. *I don't know, Sis,* she answered. *I think we need to keep this to ourselves for the time being, in any case.*

"On that, we agree. But holy crap, Daze. I was just getting used to the notion that no matter what I thought, I was just a figment of your imagination, but this?"

Tell me about it.

"Are you okay, Daisy?" Chu asked. "You look a little green."

"Just need to get something to eat, is all," she covered. "If we're all done, I'm gonna go hit the galley."

"Yeah, that's it. Oh, and now that you're on a base, it's called a mess hall."

"Got it. New vernacular. Thanks, Chu."

"No, thank you for your cooperation. This data is absolutely astounding. I can't believe what I've learned today."

"You and me both," she managed with a forced smile as she exited the lab.

CHAPTER THIRTY-SEVEN

One of the unforeseen benefits of moving into a facility designed to house a crew for lengthy periods of time was the impressive kitchen in the mess hall.

If men and women were expected to spend months or even years on the cold surface of the moon, they'd need a few creature comforts to keep them from going completely stir crazy. Food was one of the most viscerally appreciated of all the creature comforts, and Dark Side had made sure the cravings of all its residents could be satisfied.

Finn was still marveling over all his new toys when Daisy walked in.

"Hey, renegade girl," he said with a little smile.

"Hey, Finn."

"So, you're all up to speed now, huh?"

"Yeah."

"Kinda sucks, right?"

"Yeah. Kind of an understatement, though, don't you think?"

"Look, I'm sorry I never said anything. It's just the captain told us day-one we had to keep quiet about it until he assessed things. Till he saw how you and Sarah were handling everything. I guess by the time it would have been okay to talk about it, well, we'd already fallen into a groove of sorts."

Daisy dug in the refrigerator's freezer unit.

"Bingo."

"Oh, you found the pistachio," Finn said, his spirits falling slightly. "I sort of started making ice cream out of habit when we got here. Made Sarah's favorite without even thinking about it." He fell into an uncomfortable silence.

"Aw, what's up with Finn?" Sarah asked.

He liked you. Like, really liked you.

"So why didn't he say something?"

Shy?

"Finn? Shy? I think not."

Waiting for the right time, then. Who knew time was so short? We'd all act differently if we knew there was a clock running out. Twenty-twenty hindsight, I suppose.

The sisters looked at the down man through shared eyes.

"Hey, do me a favor. Tell him how much I always appreciated what he made for me. Tell him I loved his pistachio ice cream. Just don't do it in a way that'll make him sadder, okay?"

Daisy pondered how best to relay the message from beyond the grave, finally deciding on a direct and simple approach.

"You know, Sarah always said how much she enjoyed what you cooked for her. Said you had a real talent. You already know she especially liked your pistachio ice cream, but you should also know she thought it was really sweet how you always took the time to make her a batch."

Finn's mood shifted slightly.

"So she noticed?"

"Yeah, she noticed."

The mess hall doors swung open, and Shelly, Omar, and a scruffy man Daisy hadn't seen before came striding in.

"Mister Finnegan!" Omar called out. "My new favorite

person, you think you could whip us up a little something before we suit up and head out?"

"Head out? Where you going?" Finn asked.

"Well, Shelly and me, we're on repair detail. Hangar Three always needs more work, so it's moonwalk time for us yet again."

"And I'll be drifting for a bit. See what I can find," the scruffy man said.

"Hey, Donovan, you met Daisy yet?" Finn asked.

"No, I was out with Bob when she came in."

"Bob?" Daisy said.

"My ship."

"Oh, yeah."

He keyed his comms. "Hey, Bob, say hi to Daisy. She's the one we saw blazing down to the surface last week."

"Oh, yes, the daredevil. Sid and Mal told me all about her," a voice said over comms. "That was an unusual re-entry you pulled off."

"Thank you."

"It wasn't exactly a compliment. I'm actually rather amazed you didn't burn up in the atmosphere," Bob said.

"Hey now, don't be rude," Donovan chimed in. "What my friend means to say is, he was surprised by the tactic, is all. It was reckless, sure, but it was also impressive as hell, especially seeing as you're not actually a pilot."

"Mother. Necessity. You know the saying," Daisy replied. "Now what's this drifting you're talking about?"

"Ah, yeah, it's how we gather intel and scavenge parts at the same time. Me and Bob, we park out in the debris field in orbit to monitor the surface. From time to time we come across a piece of wreckage that might actually come in handy, sometimes even a salvageable ship chassis, and when we do, we bring it back here to be broken down into usable parts."

"That's where us grunts come in," Shelly added with a chuckle.

"Well, I mean look at you. You've got those kick-ass arms, Shelly. Would you rather I tried to do it with these scrawny guns?"

"No, Donovan, of course not," she answered with a grin. "You stick to flying. Omar and I will be your beasts of burden and handle the heavy work." Shelly turned to Daisy. "So, you chomping at the bit to get back to the surface?"

"Oh, hell no. You couldn't drag me back down there," she replied.

"Wait, what?" Shelly said, confused. "But I thought—"

"She hasn't talked with the commander yet," Omar interjected.

"Oh."

"Commander Mrazich did ask to speak with me later, so I guess I'll get filled in soon enough," Daisy said, heading for the door, ice cream in hand. "Thanks for the treat, Finn. See you all around," she said, then stepped into the hallway, wondering what extra serving of grief the pending conversation would pile on her already-full plate.

Fatima, Mrazich, and Harkaway were waiting in the conference chamber when Daisy arrived that evening at their request.

"You wanted to see me?"

"Yes. Thank you for coming, Daisy," Fatima said with a warm smile.

"Does she ever not *smile?"* Sarah asked, a little annoyed.

Seriously, Daisy replied. *It's freaking me out a little. She always looks like she knows the punchline to a joke we haven't even been told yet.*

The silver-haired woman observed Daisy's momentary silence with interest in her eyes, but said no more.

"Daisy," Captain Harkaway began, "we've been looking over

the lab reports from this morning and wanted you to be a part of the discussion."

"Um, thank you?" she replied.

"You've been left in the dark about a great many things, and we feel it is important that you be included in all aspects of this mission moving forward." Commander Mrazich looked at her kindly.

At least as kindly as a man with a metal jaw and mechanical eye can manage.

"I understand Captain Harkaway filled you in on many details of the prior missions, as well as Sid's former role in all of this before he was installed in Dark Side."

"Yeah, Sid was the overseeing AI for the initial assault. Got it," she answered. "But what I don't get is why this crazy need for humans to reach the surface. Seems to me you could just as easily build a fleet of remote-piloted throw-away ships and run a numbers-game attack until you take out the distribution hubs you say control things."

"If only it were so simple," Harkaway said. "The problem is, after the prior failed assaults, the invaders have shifted their defensive stance. We simply cannot afford a major assault from space. That would cause a recall of the invading fleet. They have moved on and are light years away, and that's to our benefit. We just have to keep it that way."

"And how do you propose to do that?"

"A smaller, focused incursion has been assessed to be our best chance to reclaim control of the cities and eventually the planet, but it is imperative we stay off their scans as long as possible if there's to be any hope of success. We've had many failed missions at this point, Daisy, and ultimately, we've come to realize we simply do not have the firepower or resources necessary to succeed."

"So why are we here, then?"

"Because the city defenses do," Mrazich replied. "If we can

get an operative successfully inside one of the cities to access its weaponry, perhaps we could do more than just have it launch automated repelling barrages at the smaller alien craft. At least, that was the plan, but with your new intel that some of the cities' AIs may actually still be active beyond mere auto defenses, well, that changes everything. We've been working on a revised set of mission parameters since you brought us that news."

"But why me? I mean, I saw Vince and Reggie and Tamara down there. They didn't seem to have much trouble with the Chithiid soldiers."

"First, those weren't soldiers, they were a resource disassembly team. Construction workers, basically. And second, you weren't conscious for the particularly hairy escape and evasion part of your recovery mission."

"Yeah, thanks to Tamara blasting me with a stun rifle."

"She did what had to be done," Fatima said.

"Maybe, but I think she enjoyed it."

Harkaway leveled his gaze at her. "You blew her out an airlock, Daisy. She's going to hold that against you for a while."

"Fine," she conceded. "But I still don't see why you needed me and Sarah."

"Because after decades of failed missions, we learned that even the most basic levels of active technology would be noticed and quickly eliminated by the Chithiid. Only an entirely non-augmented human could pass their scans without detection."

"But the cyborgs live there—"

"And you saw what happened to them when they stayed above ground for any length of time," Mrazich noted. "And the stolen shuttle you so brilliantly crashed? It was one of the few means of reaching the surface dead-stick. Debris from the war still rains down from time to time, and a seemingly inert ship, one capable of gliding and not giving off a power signature, could make it down without being targeted, as you learned the hard way. Unfortunately, after you powered up its comms array with those solar cells, it was only a matter of time before those alien bastards investigated the new energy signature."

"So the shuttle?"

"Gutted for parts moments after the rescue team snatched you away from the Chithiid."

"Great, so I was your golden girl, but that plan's gone to shit. Now what?"

"Given the pace at which the invaders are harvesting our planet, by the time the next generation of viable candidates reaches Earth, it may be too late. It took so long to prepare you for this, Daisy. I hate to sound maudlin, but you're our only hope."

For some reason, she couldn't help but smile at the memory of an old space movie she'd watched with Vince just a few months prior. *Our only hope, huh?*

"Look, why not train your people to do this?"

"We told you, they have artificial parts and would be detected almost immediately."

Daisy thought a moment.

"Okay, well I saw what looked like—" She shuddered at the memory. "What looked like more *people* being grown in the *Váli*'s secret little laboratory. Why not wake them up?"

Captain Harkaway glanced at the others, a concerned look on his face.

"Daisy, what exactly did you see?"

"Well, between being chased down, shot at, and forced into hiding, I did see vats of limbs, and what looked like a few intact bodies in there. If what you've been saying is true, then why not wake them up and let them join the party?"

Harkaway sighed. "Because, Daisy, what you saw weren't viable humans. They were grown as emergency sources of organic replacement parts. They've never been hooked to the neuro stim. Their minds are still complete blanks, and it would take far too long to even consider beginning the process to give them a consciousness."

Daisy felt a shiver run up her spine at the thought of mindless husks, grown for the sole purpose of being cut up and used as needed. Given the problems with metallic limbs, she could understand the rationale, but, nevertheless, it was an incredibly disturbing thought.

"Okay," she began. "So it might take a few years to bring them up to speed. It still sounds like a better plan than sending little old me down there on my own."

"Daisy," Fatima said, kindly, "you don't understand how long the process takes."

"Well if I was fully-loaded in just a few years of flight time in cryo, surely you could do a stripped-down version faster."

Fatima beamed that damned warm smile again.

"Daisy, you and Sarah were our best yet."

"So you've said."

"So we have," Fatima continued. "It was a long flight, Daisy, and your minds were both carefully nurtured over that time. A *long* time."

"Wait, exactly how long are we talking here?" Daisy felt a hot flush of adrenaline hit her veins.

"We've waited one hundred twenty years for you to be ready," Fatima replied.

"Holy shit! We're how old?"

Her sister ignored her.

"Getting us ready for what, exactly?" Daisy managed to say as her world spun around her.

Fatima rested her calm almond eyes on her.

"Ready for you to help us reclaim Earth, Daisy. Your intel has given us hope, and with your unique genetic makeup and skill set, we might just be able to pull it off. But it won't be easy."

An uncomfortable silence hung in the air.

"I think maybe that's enough for now," Harkaway said, reading the overwhelmed look in Daisy's eyes.

"Yes, of course," Fatima said, realizing her misstep. "Rude of me, dumping so much on you like that. You'd best get some rest now, I know it's a lot to process, but Daisy, you can relax. You're *home* now."

CHAPTER THIRTY-EIGHT

Daisy felt a little light-headed as she sat on her bed in her new living quarters. Doc McClain might have thought it to be residual effects of the stun blast she had taken on the planet's surface. More likely, it was just her body recovering from the several times she'd thrown up since returning to her room as her body physically manifested the turmoil in her mind.

Daisy cradled her pounding head in her hands, elbows propped on her knees.

"I'm over a century old," she grumbled, rocking slightly.

"Tell me about it. We're a couple of spinsters, right?" Sarah joked, trying to lighten the mood.

"And all that time? All that effort? For what? A planet that's a shell of what it used to be?"

"Hey, at least we're alive, Sis. That's gotta count for something."

Daisy leaned back against the ceramisteel wall, her head making a slight metallic thunk.

"If you can call this living."

"It sure as hell beats the alternative, Daze. And we're on an actual base. Like, it has space to move, hydroponics gardens that make

Tamara's pod look like a quaint little hobbyist's plot. You have to admit, while it's not ideal, it's a huge step up from Váli life."

Sarah was right, and Daisy knew it. Admitting that, however, was a bit of a sticking point. Being honest with herself, Daisy would even say it was a perfectly suitable living situation. The surviving base was expansive––the parts that had been protected by the rocky overhangs when the aliens attacked, at least––so there was plenty of space for everyone.

Which meant she could avoid Vince indefinitely, if she tried hard enough.

"I know what you're thinking."

You always do. Kind of a benefit of riding around in my head.

"I'd know even if that wasn't the case. You know, you don't have to be all lovey-dovey with the guy to still get along. He cares, and he isn't holding a grudge, despite what you did to him."

Which was justified at the time, Daisy shot back.

"Well, yeah. But still, most people would carry a bit of resentment with them for a while."

You mean like Tamara.

"Yeah, like Tamara. Though to be fair, you did blow her out an airlock, so she's kinda justified in that."

I know. I'll have to smooth that over once I've got my bearings straight. This is all just such a—

"Mind-fuck?" Sarah interjected, finishing her sentence.

Yeah, that pretty much sums it up.

Daisy opened the door to her room.

Her room. This was it. *This* was home, now. She slowly ran her hand over the wall, taking a moment to ponder the mass of stone on the other side, rather than the void of space.

And it was quiet. The ever-present vibration of the ship's engines was something so subtle that she'd grown used to it, easily tuning it out, but here there were no such machinations. Nothing but peace and quiet.

Her stomach growled, the low rumble reminding her of her recent visit to the porcelain altar.

"Pancakes," she said, lurching from her bunk and stepping out into the hallway. She turned and closed the door behind her. "Definitely pancakes."

"Pancakes?"

Yeah. That sounds really good right about now.

Daisy had already committed the map of nearly all of the base's habitable spaces to memory. There were fine points to add, which she's learn as time passed and she found areas sealed off from prior damage, but for the most part, she knew her way around. She took a sharp turn from the direct path and headed off.

The walk to the mess hall wasn't a terribly long one from her quarters, but Daisy opted for the roundabout, meandering route. She knew Sid was likely monitoring the hallways, but, unlike Mal, he was apparently aware of the value of giving those living within his walls a bit of space.

A little bit of space in space, she chuckled to herself. It was refreshing, being left to her thoughts, and the strange moon base was already beginning to feel more like a comfortable resting place than the prison she'd initially thought it to be.

The food replicators had no issues whipping her up a short stack of buttermilk pancakes, complete with a side of replicated bacon and some warm maple syrup. *If you're going to do it, do it right,* she figured, tucking into the steaming stack with gusto. Her stomach greeted the food with a happy endorphin rush. Her impromptu food therapy was working its magic.

"I don't think Finn would approve of you partaking without his assistance, you know," Sarah chuckled quietly.

Well, he's sleeping. Or whatever he does when he's not pushing food on us. In any case, it gives me a chance to get a feel for the base's systems. And you know what? Considering what happened to this place, it's really not in that bad shape.

Daisy leisurely finished her pancakes, mopping up the last of the syrup with her final bite, then placed the dishes in the auto-washer. Hot water sprayed and the machine ran through its rapid wash cycle.

On the *Váli* she would have had to wait for a full load before running the machine, despite the water reclamation systems, but here on the moon, that was not an issue. Yet another creature comfort of her new home.

Thanks to the deeply-buried ice field that had been discovered as they were building the base, the facility possessed a nearly endless supply of fresh water for its few residents.

Another benefit was the fresh air. Breaking the hydrogen and oxygen bonds of the water ice produced not only useful hydrogen, but also helped refresh their oxygen supply, taking a load off the massive air scrubbers.

Daisy felt herself beginning to regain her equilibrium and feel normal again, now that food was in her stomach––and staying there. And with the clarity of mind came an unexpected sensation. It kind of shocked her, but Daisy realized she was actually feeling at ease. No more questions, no more surprises, just life.

Sure, she would have to make adjustments as she got used to living in Dark Side Base, but things seemed to be okay, all things considered.

She headed out of the mess hall and took the opposite route back to her quarters, walking slowly, really taking in her new surroundings with fresh eyes. There was a lot to familiarize herself with.

Daisy paused at one of the thick windows, looking out toward the nearest hangar just across the rocky surface of the moon. Surprisingly, she felt her heart flutter as she took in the sights. The sky above was *beautiful,* a dazzling spray of pinpoint sparkles reaching out across the black of space.

"Not a bad view," Sarah noted, appreciatively.

Not bad at all, Daisy replied, the last of the weeks of stress finally leaving her body. *You know what?*

"*What?*"

I think I can make this work, she said, a hint of a smile curving her lips. *I think we're going to be okay.*

Daisy took her time as she meandered back to her room, finally curling up in her new bed and drifting off to a restful sleep. Daisy was home.

EPILOGUE

It was late. Very late. But someone was awake on Dark Side Base.

Nearly a week had passed, and quite uneventfully, amazingly enough. But on this night Daisy simply couldn't sleep, her mind unable to stop churning. She had somehow avoided the uncomfortable conversations she knew she needed to have since her arrival, opting instead to lurk around the base, keeping to herself rather than engaging. And oddly enough, it seemed to be working. She was getting by. She was fine.

At least she had been, until Chu had opened his mouth while running a few tests on their new resident, then unintentionally put his foot in it.

"I finally got to take a look at what Vince has going on under the hood," he had said as they chatted earlier that day. "There's not much gear at all, really, but what he does have is some seriously advanced tech in there. Crazy to think they managed to perfect the organics with you and Sarah not long after, right?"

Daisy had smiled and played nice, keeping her distress well hidden as she made her excuses, leaving him to his work. But his words stuck in her head.

And so it came to pass that she was unable to sleep once

more. Thoughts raced through her mind, but instead of just laying there, staring at the ceiling as she'd done in the past, she climbed out of bed, got dressed, and stepped out of her room.

She needed air, and opting to walk the corridor in the quiet hours––albeit still in somewhat of a daze––would at least let her think on the move.

Things really had snowballed from bad, to worse, to what-the-hell-is-going-on, world-flipping-upside-down levels of crazy in her short time on Dark Side, but she had been coping. Processing. Doing okay. Then Chu had to go and say the one thing that could set her off again. And there wasn't anything she could do about it.

I was grown. We *were grown. All of those memories, the places I'd been. None of it was real. And Vince, he's—*

She could feel her pulse begin to quicken, her racing heart pounding in her head as the walls threatened to spin around her.

It'll be okay. I just need to think, is all, she thought, trying to calm herself.

"No, that's all you do," Sarah interjected. *"You need to* not *think for a change or you're gonna hurl. Remember your meditation practice. You can do this. Deep breaths, Daze."*

"Good point. Yeah," Daisy replied as she staggered toward the nearest maintenance hangar to sit and digest all she'd just learned in peace.

A bit of self-centering and focus. That's what I need. Somewhere quiet. Somewhere to be alone.

Daisy was still a ways away from her quarters, and she certainly didn't want to flop down and meditate in the middle of the corridor. Fortunately, the nearby compartment was an empty training space, and one she was familiar with.

She swung the door open and stepped inside, the cool air of the room immediately taking her panic down a notch. She shut the door quietly, then breathed a little sigh of relief as she began focusing on lowering her heart rate and respirations.

It's going to be okay. Just relax. Relax and breathe.

Daisy turned to find a crate to sit on rather than the chilly metal floor.

The hairs on her neck stood up. She certainly did not feel alone. That's when she noticed the furious metal-armed woman barreling toward her.

"Shit! Tamara, wait!"

A flurry of blows rained down on her from every direction, then a heavy-booted foot kicked her square in the chest, sending her flying backward into the unforgiving metal wall.

She clenched her teeth and tasted blood on her tongue, the adrenaline already pumping hard in her veins making an instantaneous decision between fight or flight. Things needed to be hashed out between the two women, and it seemed like it was happening sooner rather than later.

"So, it's going to be like that?" she said with grim resolution. "Fine."

Daisy uncoiled her tensed legs and leapt toward the larger woman.

"I've got a bad feeling about this, Daze."

"You and me both," she replied, then began a furious counterattack.

Welcome home, Daisy, she thought with a grim laugh as her fist connected with her opponent's solid chin. *Welcome home.*

BUT WAIT, THERE'S MORE!

Follow Daisy on her continuing adventures in the second book of the Clockwork Chimera series: Pushing Daisy

ALSO BY SCOTT BARON

Standalone Novels

Living the Good Death

The Clockwork Chimera Series

Daisy's Run

Pushing Daisy

Daisy's Gambit

Chasing Daisy

Daisy's War

The Dragon Mage Series

Bad Luck Charlie

Space Pirate Charlie

Dragon King Charlie

Magic Man Charlie

Star Fighter Charlie

Portal Thief Charlie

Rebel Mage Charlie

Odd and Unusual Short Stories:

The Best Laid Plans of Mice: An Anthology

Snow White's Walk of Shame

The Tin Foil Hat Club

Lawyers vs. Demons

The Queen of the Nutters

Lost & Found

ABOUT THE AUTHOR

A native Californian, Scott Baron was born in Hollywood, which he claims may be the reason for his rather off-kilter sense of humor.

Before taking up residence in Venice Beach, Scott first spent a few years abroad in Florence, Italy before returning home to Los Angeles and settling into the film and television industry, where he has worked as an on-set medic for many years.

Aside from mending boo-boos and owies, and penning books and screenplays, Scott is also involved in indie film and theater scene both in the U.S. and abroad.

Made in the USA
Monee, IL
01 May 2020

27914752R00213